THE ANNOTATED
CHRISTMAS
CAROL

Charles Dickens by Daniel Maclise, 1839. *Courtesy The Library of Congress*

THE ANNOTATED CHRISTMAS CAROL

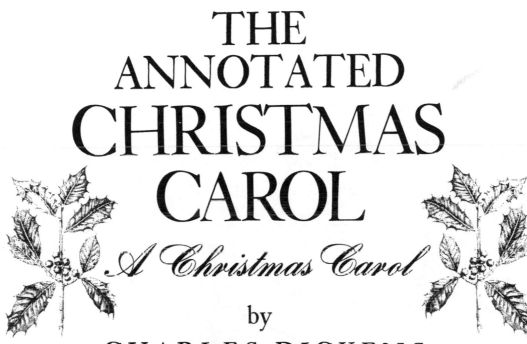

A Christmas Carol

by

CHARLES DICKENS

Illustrated by John Leech

WITH AN INTRODUCTION, NOTES,
AND BIBLIOGRAPHY BY

MICHAEL PATRICK HEARN

 AVON
PUBLISHERS OF BARD, CAMELOT AND DISCUS BOOKS

Annotations and introduction text composed in Janson Linotype by The Monotype Composition Company Incorporated, Baltimore, Maryland.

Color separation photography by Rex Color Separations Incorporated, Miami, Florida.

Book Design by: *Shari de Miskey*.

AVON BOOKS
A division of
The Hearst Corporation
959 Eighth Avenue
New York, New York 10019
Copyright © 1976 by Michael Patrick Hearn
Published by arrangement with Clarkson N. Potter, Inc.
Library of Congress Catalog Card Number: 76-21345
ISBN: 0-380-01722-9

First Avon Printing, September, 1977

AVON TRADEMARK REG. U.S. PAT. OFF. AND IN
OTHER COUNTRIES, MARCA REGISTRADA, HECHO EN
U.S.A.

Printed in the U.S.A.

For my father

In researching this study of *A Christmas Carol*, I have relied primarily on the following institutions: The Beinecke Rare Book and Manuscript Library, Yale University; The British Library; The Houghton Library, Harvard University; The Library of Congress, and The New York Public Library. I am also grateful to Oxford University Press for permission to quote from *The Pilgrim Edition of the Letters of Charles Dickens*, edited by Madeline House and Graham Storey, and to John Podeschi, bibliographer of the Richard Gimbel–Charles Dickens collection in The Beinecke Rare Book and Manuscript Library, for his early encouragement and help.

M.P.H.

CONTENTS

INTRODUCTION

The front cover of *A Christmas Carol*, 1843 (exact size)

INTRODUCTION

A Christmas Carol remains the most popular work of England's most popular novelist, and it has had something of a life of its own beyond its author's reputation. Should all of Charles Dickens' marvelous creations, from Mr. Pickwick to Edwin Drood, be suddenly threatened with extinction, the story of Mr. Scrooge would certainly survive. It has become a part of Christmas folklore. All misers are Ebenezer Scrooge, all plum puddings the same as that devoured by the Cratchits. Besides having written a thoroughly entertaining narrative, Dickens possessed the special ability of defining better than anyone before or since the spirit of the holiday season. In what he called "the Carol philosophy," he went beyond merely venerating Christmas for "its sacred name and origin" to acknowledging its basic humanism: "a good time: a kind, forgiving, charitable, pleasant time: the only time I know of, in the long calendar of the year, when men and women seem by one consent to open their shut-up hearts freely, and to think of other people below them as if they really were fellow-passengers to the grave, and not another race of creatures bound on other journeys." By the time of his death, Dickens had already secured so sure a place in the mythology of the holiday that a story circulated about a little costermonger's girl in Drury Lane who, on hearing of his funeral, asked, "Dickens dead? Then will Father Christmas die too?"

Few modern readers realize that *A Christmas Carol* was written during a decline of the old Christmas traditions. Dickens has even been credited with almost single-handedly reviving the holiday customs. By the early nineteenth century, there seemed little left of the old celebrations that had begun in A.D. 601 when Pope Gregory instructed his missionary St. Austin of Canterbury, in converting the Anglo-Saxons, to make the local winter feast a Christian festival.[1]   The result of this conversion was a strange conglomeration of pagan customs adapted to Christian purposes. These traditions originated from the celebrations of the Roman Saturnalia, Yule (the Saxon feast for the return of the

Charles Dickens. *The Illustrated London News*, April 8, 1843. *Courtesy The Library of Congress*

1 Because the early church fathers feared it came too close to the Roman festival of Saturnalia (a seven-day feast celebrating the New Year), December 25 had to wait until the second century to be proclaimed a holy day. Not until the fourth century was the birth of Christ celebrated as a public feast.

2 For example, holly, used in pagan divination, became a Christian symbol: three red berries and three green leaves on a common stalk represented the Holy Trinity. The Druids venerated mistletoe, in the belief that this parasitic evergreen possessed mystical and medicinal qualities. And the early Christians decorated the altars of converted local temples with this remarkable greenery—as Dickens noted in *A Child's History of England* (1852–1854)—"the same plant we hang up in houses at Christmas Time now—when its white berries grew upon the Oak." "In fighting for Christmas," G. K. Chesterton in *Charles Dickens* (London: Methuen & Co., 1906, p. 161) explained, Dickens "was fighting for that trinity of eating, drinking and praying which to moderns appears irreverent, for the holy day which is really a holiday."

3 In *The Lawfulness and Right Manner of Christmas Shewn in a Familiar Conference between a Churchman and a Dissenter* (1710), the Puritan argued that the celebration of Christmas was condemned in the Scriptures and that its coming at the same time as the Saturnalia gave proof that the local superstitions venerated in Christian homes were rituals in praise of the Roman corn goddess Ceres. The response to such accusations was that the customs were symbolically Christian, as was decorating with holly, ivy, and other greenery to "remind us that Our Blessed Saviour was *God* and *Man*, and that he should *Spring up like a tender plant*, be always *Green and Flourishing, and live for Evermore.*" (A similar sentiment as a motto attached to a portrait of a benefactor from Queen Elizabeth's day is the central theme of *The Haunted Man* [1848]: "Lord, Keep my Memory Green.")

4 The result of such persecution received expression in the chapbook *Christmas Lamentation* (1635):

> Christmas is my name: farre have I gone . . .
>   Without regard;
> Houses where musicke was wont for to ring,
> Nothing but bats and howlets doe sing. . . .
> House where pleasure once did abound,
> Nought but a dogge and a shepheard is found
>   Welladay!
> Place where Christmas revels did keep,
> Is now become habitations for sheepe. . . .

Sun, in honor of the god Thor), and the Druid holiday.**2** Apparently the Medieval Church saw no conflict between the Christian and pagan intentions; as Chaucer noted, the Roman god Janus was welcome wherever Christian men sang "Nowel." Under the Anglo-Norman kings, the holiday festivals grew to twelve days of celebration, from Christmas Eve until Epiphany. As early as 1170, at the command of Henry the Second, the court welcomed the season with plays, masques, and other spectacles; and the clergy promoted religious instruction and entertainment through miracle plays. During the Middle Ages, many legendary feasts and pageants were sponsored by the English nobility; among these Christmas extravagances was the order of Henry III in the thirteenth century to slaughter six hundred oxen for one holiday banquet. These festivities did not lessen under the auspices of the Church of England; Henry VIII was not merely a promoter of the Christmas pageants but a performer as well. The court continued to support playwrights and poets in honoring the season; Ben Jonson wrote a celebrated *Masque of Christmas* (1616), and Robert Herrick composed several carols and other verse venerating these holidays.

Everything changed under Cromwell. He attacked the old customs as pagan superstition, condemned in the Scriptures; it was blasphemous to celebrate the birth of Christ in the Roman tradition of the Saturnalia.**3** The Puritans showed no patience with such simple customs as mince pies which were seen now as "an abomination, idolatry, superstition and Popish observance." The first blow to the old festivities came with an ordinance of 1642 on the suppression of the performance of plays. On June 3, 1647, Parliament ordained that the feast of the Nativity of Christ could not be celebrated with the other holy days. The final condemnation came on December 24, 1652, which proclaimed that "no observance shall be had of the five and twentieth day of December, commonly called Christmas day; nor any solemnity used or exercised in churches upon that day in respect thereof."

The defeat of the Royalists by the Puritans was accepted also as a conquest of the old holidays. The author of *The Arraignment, Conviction, and Imprisoning, of Christmas* (1645) found old Father Christmas "much wasted, so that he hath looked very thin, and ill of late." He was now an outcast, because his season had formerly been "a time observable for the common People to bring in large offerings to the Pope holinesse, to maintain the Cardinalls, Priests, and Fryers."**4** The suppression of Christmas became proof of the degeneracy of the time; good fellowship declined, and the wealthy neglected the old Christmas spirit of charity.

The Restoration of the English monarchy failed to completely revive the splendor of Christmas Past. Many people looked back nostalgically to the glories of the season; Needham's *History of the Rebellion* (1661) seemed to express the general attitude:

> Gone are those golden days of yore,
>> When Christmass was a high day:
> Whose sports we now shall see no more;
>> 'Tis turn'd into Good Friday.

Many of the old traditions, however, were still preserved in the countryside. "The spirit of hospitality has not quite forsaken us," observed the author of *Round about our Coal-Fire, or Christmas Entertainments* (1740); "Several of the gentry are gone down to their respective seats in the country, in order to keep their *Christmas* in the old way, and entertain their tenants and trades folks as their ancestors used to do, and I wish them a merry *Christmas* accordingly." But by the end of the eighteenth century many of the old trappings and entertainments had completely vanished. Such items as plum porridge and peacock pie from the old bills of fare were now unknown. The court harbored little interest in celebrating the season in the old way. The masques, pageants, banquets and other festivities were no longer on the same scale as before the Revolution; even the New Year's Ode given by the Poet Laureate was forgotten.

The Industrial Revolution further discouraged the simple pleasures of the season; employees now were not given time off to celebrate Christmas Day. "If a little more success had crowned the Puritan movement of the seventeenth century, or the Utilitarian movement of the nineteenth century," G. K. Chesterton observed in his introduction to *A Christmas Carol* (1924 edition), the old holiday traditions would "have become merely details of the neglected past, a part of history or even archeology.... Perhaps the very word carol would sound like the word villanelle."

Fortunately, a few brave voices were raised in praise of the holiday. Charles Lamb in a brief essay, "A Few Words on Christmas" described some of the games and other delights of his holidays past; he defined Christmas as "the happiest time of the year. It is the season of mirth and cold weather. It is a time ... when mistletoe, and red-berried laurel, and soups, and sliding, and school-boys, prevail; when the country is illuminated by fires and bright faces; and the town is radiant with laughing children." A handful of scholars and historians

5 Dickens perhaps knew this book well: the old gentleman depicted by Seymour "Enjoying Christmas" with a copy of Hervey's book in his hand shows a striking resemblance to that other old gentleman Mr. Pickwick, first drawn by Seymour only a few months later in the first monthly part of *The Posthumous Papers of the Pickwick Club*, April 1836.

6 Many of the English Christmas customs originated in the country, but by the sixteenth century, when the nobles spent more time in the cities, the local celebrations lost much of their character. A revival of 1589, begun by the country gentlemen of Norfolk and Suffolk, attempted to save the old traditions with a new emphasis on brotherhood between the poor and the more fortunate. The anonymous author of the chapbook *Round about our Coal-Fire, or Christmas Entertainments* (1740) affectionately recounted the former holiday celebrations in the countryside: "the rooms were embower'd with holly, ivy, cypress, bays, laurel, and missleto, and a bouncing *Christmas* log in the chimney glowing like the cheeks of a country milk-maid.... This great festival in former times kept with us so much freedom and openness of heart, that every one in the country where a Gentleman resided, possessed at least a day of pleasure in the *Christmas* holydays."

7 Another American, Clement C. Moore, added to popular Christmas mythology the common conception of Santa Claus, the holiday patriarch derived in part from Father Christmas and the legendary St. Nicholas. His "An Account of a Visit from St. Nicholas" (1822) is now as much a part of the holiday season as Dickens' *A Christmas Carol*. By the end of the nineteenth century, largely through the cartoons of Thomas Nast, this American Ghost of Christmas Presents became as well known to English children as their own Father Christmas; but as of 1843, when Dickens wrote his story, Moore's poem was not widely known outside the United States. See also "Santa Was an American" by Martin Gardner, *The New York Times Book Review*, December 7, 1975, pp. 8–12.

8 "There is no living writer, and there are very few among the dead, whose approbation I should feel so proud to earn," Dickens wrote Irving on April 21, 1841 (see *Letters of Charles Dickens*, National Edition, 1908). "And with everything you have written, upon my shelves, and in my thoughts, and in my heart of hearts, I may honestly and truly say so.... I should like to travel with you, astride the last of the coaches, down to Bracebridge Hall." Although the two authors got along famously during Dickens' American tour of 1842, Irving was offended by Dickens' attitude toward the United States in *American Notes* and *Martin Chuzzlewit* and so he did not cultivate Dickens' admiration. See "Washington Irving and Charles Dickens" by W. C. Desmond Pacey, *American Literature*, January 1945, pp. 332–39.

shared Lamb's respect for the old Christmas pleasures. Among the most important early studies was Thomas K. Hervey's *The Book of Christmas* (1835); it was notable not only for its in-depth history and evaluation of the English Christmas but also for its jolly etchings by Robert Seymour, the first illustrator of *The Pickwick Papers* (1836).**5** Other scholars tried to preserve the old songs still sung in the country.**6** The earliest significant collection was Davies Gilbert's *Ancient Christmas Carols* (1822), but the most ambitious anthology was that by William Sandys, published in 1832. Sandys, an expert on Cornish customs and one of Dickens' correspondents, found the preserving of the old songs not an easy task. "In many parts of the kingdom, especially in the northern and western parts," he explained in his introduction, "the festival is still kept up with spirit among the middling and lower classes, though its influence is on the wane even with them; the genius of the present age requires work and no play, and since the commencement of this century a great change may be traced. The modern instructors of mankind do not think it necessary to provide popular amusements, considering mental improvement the one thing needful."

However it was an American who best portrayed how the English Christmas still might be preserved. In his description of an old-fashioned Christmas celebrated at Bracebridge Hall, Yorkshire, in *The Sketch Book of Geoffrey Crayon* (1819), Washington Irving**7** recognized that the old traditions now "resemble those picturesque morsels of Gothic architecture, which we see crumbling in various parts of the country, partly dilapidated by the waste of ages, and partly lost in the additions and alterations of later days." During this holiday when its "tone of solemn and sacred feeling ... blends with our conviviality, and lifts the spirit to a state of hallowed and elevated enjoyment," the Squire of Bracebridge Hall entertained his guests with dances, songs, blindman's buff, an amateur masque, and other amusements in the same good fellowship characterized by the country gentlemen of centuries past.

One of Irving's most avid admirers was Charles Dickens, who expressed a particular affection for the doings at Bracebridge Hall.**8** In his first Christmas work, the short essay "A Christmas Dinner" in *Sketches by Boz* (1836), Dickens shared Irving's sentiment that this day was "the season for gathering together of family connexions." This sketch described an urban Christmas family-party, celebrated "in a strain of rational goodwill and cheerfulness, doing more to awaken the sympathies of every member of the party in behalf of his neighbour, and to perpetuate their good feeling during the ensuing year, than half the homilies that have ever been written, by half the Divines that have ever lived."

This early piece was just preparation for the "good-humoured Christmas chapter" of *The Pickwick Papers*. Here, in fiction, Dickens captured all the sentiments and customs honored by Irving in his holiday essays. The "old-fashioned" drive down to Dingley Dell was as spirited as that to Bracebridge Hall, and when Pickwick and his fellow club members arrived at the ancient country estate, Old Wardle occupied their stay with such songs, dances, mistletoe, blindman's buff, and other sports that would have delighted old Squire Bracebridge himself. Although the story takes place in the immediate past, the Christmas at Dingley Dell recalls an earlier period, a preindustrial England, full of amusements which "are not quite so religiously kept up, in these degenerate times." These festivities were pervaded by the feeling that "in all his bluff and hearty honesty; it was the season of hospitality, merriment, and open-heartedness; the old year was preparing, like an ancient philosopher, to call his friends around him, and amidst the sound of feasting and revelry to pass gently and calmly away."

Inspiration for another Christmas story did not come to Dickens until, like Marley's Ghost to Ebenezer Scrooge, seven years later. One could hardly have predicted that so good spirited a work as *A Christmas Carol* might have been written by the end of 1843. It had been a terrible year for Dickens, full of disappointments and seemingly insurmountable pressures. For the first time since his phenomenal success with *The Pickwick Papers*, Dickens faced the possibility of a decline in popularity and income. His new novel *Martin Chuzzlewit* was coolly received. Although selling prodigiously in England, *American Notes* (1842) concerning his tour of the New World offended readers across the Atlantic, and the monthly parts of the new novel showed a marked decrease in sales. His family pressed him for money, and his own extravagance in keeping a large house on Devonshire Terrace depleted his earnings. He also had to face the responsibility of his wife's being pregnant with their fifth child. He was desperate to regain the public's faith in his writing. In a clumsy attempt to stimulate the novel's sales, he sent his hero to the United States. Trying to capitalize on the interest in *American Notes*, he continued his vitriolic criticism of American democracy in action. The result was disastrous. The English showed little interest, and the Americans were further irritated; "Martin has

"Christmas Eve at Mr. Wardle's" by Phiz, *The Pickwick Papers*, 1836. *Courtesy The Library of Congress*

No. 1, Devonshire Terrace, London, by Daniel Maclise. *Courtesy The Library of Congress*

9 "Firstly and mainly," Dickens explained in a letter of February 1, 1843, "because I am fully engaged in doing my best for similar objects by different means. And secondly, because this question involves the whole subject of the condition of the mass of the people in this country. And I greatly fear that until Governments are honest, and Parliaments pure, and Great men less considered, and small men more so, it is almost a Cruelty to limit, even the dreadful hours and ways of Labor which at this time prevails. Want is so general, distress so great, and Poverty so rampant—it is, in a word, so hard for the Million to live by any means—that I scarcely know how we can step between them, and one weekly farthing." (*The Pilgrim Edition of the Letters of Charles Dickens, Volume Three, 1842–1843*, edited by Madeline House, Graham Storey, Kathleen Tillotson, and Noel C. Peyrouten, associate editor, Oxford: Clarendon Press, 1974, pp. 435–36.)

made them all stark raving mad across the water," he wrote John Forster, his friend and biographer.

Chapman and Hall, his publishers, too were distressed at the poor return on the new novel, and they awkwardly suggested that their most important author's monthly salary be reduced from £200 to £150. Dickens was furious, and by late June he seriously contemplated leaving the firm to join forces with their printers Bradbury and Evans. "A printer is better than a bookseller," he wrote Forster, June 28, "and it is quite as much the interest of one (if not more) to join me." Forster, acting as Dickens' literary advisor, knew of Bradbury and Evans' proposal to Dickens, but he tried to discourage the novelist from changing publishers at this delicate time. Dickens was momentarily appeased; but he admitted, "I am so irritated, so rubbed in the tenderest part of my eyelids with bay-salt . . . that a wrong kind of fire is burning in my head, and I don't think I *can* write."

The composition of the novel, what he called his "Chuzzlewit agonies," was indeed becoming difficult. He considered other projects that might relieve him of his present troubles. He hoped to go to the continent, perhaps to Italy, where it not only was cheaper to live than in London, but also might provide him material for a series of travel sketches. Another story to recapture the public lost by *Martin Chuzzlewit* seemed more immediate. Even if he was unsure of the public taste, he was sure of his abilities. "I feel my power now, more than I ever did," he wrote Forster on November 2. "I have a greater confidence in myself than I ever had. That I *know*, if I have health, I could sustain my place in the minds of thinking men, though fifty writers started up to-morrow. But how many readers do *not* think!"

Among the possibilities intended to "sustain my place in the minds of thinking men" were several pamphlets. Dickens had recently become preoccupied with the child labor question. The first report of the Commission for Inquiring into the Employment and Condition of Children in Mines and Manufactories (1842) so incensed Dickens that he went to Cornwall in the fall of that year to see the appalling conditions for himself. One of the four Infant Labour Commissioners, Dr. Thomas Southwood Smith, kept Dickens informed of the progress of the second report (1843) to encourage the famous novelist to write about the commission's findings. At first Dickens was reluctant to "take up the subject,"**9** but when the actual report was published, Dickens was "so perfectly stricken down by the blue book" that he decided to write a cheap pamphlet to

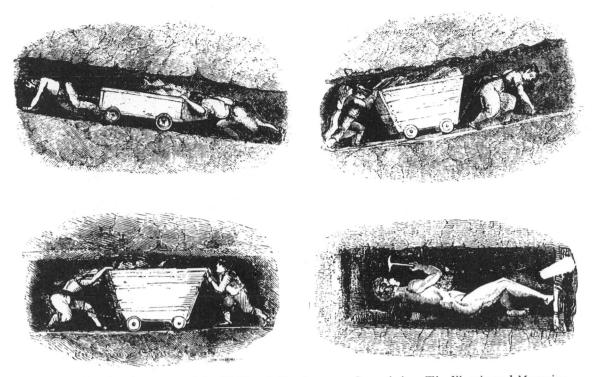

Illustrations for the report of the Children's Employment Commission, *The Illuminated Magazine,*
Vol. 1, 1843. *Courtesy General Research and Humanities Division, The New York Public Library,
Astor, Lenox and Tilden Foundations*

be called "An Appeal to the People of England, on behalf of the Poor Man's Child."[10]

Dickens, however, was delayed in writing this appeal and was soon involved in other projects. Miss Burdett Coutts, a wealthy friend and philanthropist (to whom he dedicated *Martin Chuzzlewit*), asked Dickens' council in regard to a request to give financial support to the Ragged Schools of Field Lane, Holborn. His response was to visit these free institutions for the poor, located in a dismal part of London. "The school is held in three most wretched rooms on the first floor of a rotten house," he wrote in his "sledge-hammer account of the Ragged Schools" to Miss Coutts on September 16. "One room is devoted to the girls: two to the boys. The former are much the better looking —I cannot say better dressed, for there is such thing as dress among the seventy pupils."[11] Dickens recognized the great difficulty in giving these wretches even the simplest of religious instruction. "To gain their attention in any way," he continued, "is a difficulty, quite gigantic. To impress them, even with the idea of a God, when their own condition is so desolate, becomes a monstrous task. To find anything within them ... to which it is possible to appeal, is at first, like a search for the philosopher's stone." Dickens heartily encouraged Miss Coutts to assist these institutions, but he added, "My heart so sinks within me when I go into these scenes, that I almost lose the hope of ever seeing them changed. Whether this effort will succeed, it is quite impossible to say."

10 According to a letter to Southwood Smith, March 6, 1843 (*Letters*, Clarendon Press, vol. 3, pp. 459–60). Dickens was evidently moved by the blue book's descriptions of parish orphans and other children of the destitute, employed generally at seven years, some as young as three, who were brutalized, ill-fed, and ill-clothed, during their fifteen- to eighteen-hour workday; they were promised skilled training and other education but received little, and their meager wages went directly into their parents' pockets.

11 *Letters*, Clarendon Press, vol. 3, pp. 562–64.

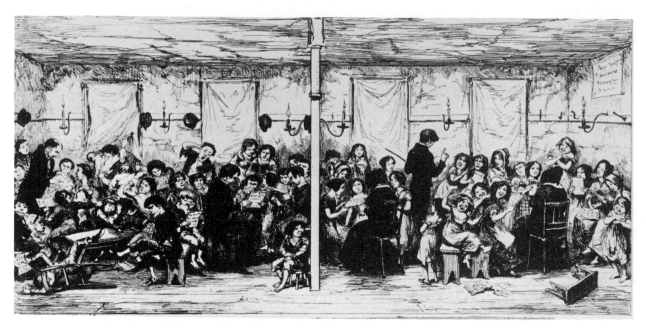

"The Ragged School" by George Cruikshank, *Our Own Time*, 1846. *Courtesy The Prints Division, The New York Public Library, Astor, Lenox and Tilden Foundations*

12 In a letter to Macvey Napier, September 16, 1843 (*Letters*, Clarendon Press, vol. 3, p. 565).

Dickens, however, was determined to help the education of the poor in his own way. He approached the editor of *The Edinburgh Review* with the idea of an article about "certain voluntary places of instruction, called 'The Ragged Schools' ... and of the schools in Jails—and of the ignorance presented in such places, which would make a very striking paper—especially if they were put in strong comparison with the effort making, by subscription, to maintain exclusive Church Instruction. I could shew these people in such a state so miserable and so neglected, that their very nature rebels against the simplest religion—and that to convey to them the faintest outlines of any system of distinction between Right and Wrong, is in itself a Giant's task, before which Mysteries and Squabbles for Forms, *must* give way."**12** Expressing a warning that Dickens not unnecessarily attack the church, the editor accepted the proposal, but a confusion over the deadline prevented the article from being written.

By the end of the year, Dickens found an opportunity in a public forum to express his opinions on the conditions of the poor. The Atheneum, a charitable institution for the Manchester working class, invited the novelist to speak at a fund-raising soirée of October 5. This invitation gave him the opportunity to visit his sister Fanny and her family who lived in the city, so he accepted. Sharing the platform with Disraeli and others, Dickens spoke passionately on the education of the poor. He praised the Atheneum for recognizing through its lectures and other opportunities for bodily and intellectual exercise that even "with the clanking of stupendous engines and the whirl of machinery, the immortal mechanism of God's own hand, the mind, is not forgotten in the din and uproar." **13**   He had little patience with those who still held to the old axiom "A little learning is a dangerous thing": "Why, a little hanging was considered a very dangerous thing, according to the same authorities, that because a little hanging was dangerous, we had a great deal of it; and because a little learning was dangerous, we were to have none at all." To instruct such people as to which was "the most prolific parent of ignorance," " 'a little learning' and a vast amount of ignorance," Dickens offered to take them "i..to certain jails and nightly refuges . . . where my own heart dies within me when I see thousands of immortal creatures condemned, without alternative or choice, to tread, not what our great poet calls 'the primrose path to the everlasting bonfire,' but one of jagged flints and stones, laid down by brutal ignorance, and held together by years of this most wicked axiom." He found hope in such institutions as the Atheneum where the working man who as yet not able to keep "the wolf of hunger from his door" might still "once have chased the dragon of ignorance from his hearth."

The speaker was touched by the audience's enthusiastic applause, and something about "the bright eyes and beaming faces" before him inspired a desire to try to capture the warmer feelings of the people at large. He recognized who his audience was; from the literary point of view, he realized that such institutions as the Atheneum were "of great importance, deeming that the more intelligent and reflective society in the mass becomes, and the more readers there are, the more distinctly writers of all kinds will be able to throw themselves upon the truthful feeling of the people, and the more honoured and the more useful literature must be."

During the remainder of his three-day visit to Manchester, Dickens was obliged to keep several appointments and had to hurry about the streets. One evening while on such a journey, his mind still burning with thoughts of Ignorance and Want and the necessity of throwing himself "upon the truthful feeling of the people," Dickens conceived the story of *A Christmas Carol*. On his return home, this inspiration so possessed him that over the book's writing he "wept and laughed and wept again, and excited himself in a most extraordinary manner in the composition; and thinking whereof he walked about the black streets of London, fifteen and twenty miles many a night when all sober folks had gone to bed."

In the book's composition Dickens relied heavily on his earlier writing. The rudimentary plot came from

13 In his speech delivered at the first annual *soirée* of the Atheneum, Manchester, October 5, 1843 (see *The Speeches of Charles Dickens*, edited by K. J. Fielding, Oxford: Clarendon Press, 1960, pp. 44–52).

/Title/

A christmas Carol
In Prose;
Being a Short Story, of christmas.
By charles Dickens

The Illustrations by John Leech

chapman and Hall 186 Strand
MDCCC XL III.

My own, and only MS of the Book
Charles Dickens

Stave I.

Marley's Ghost.

Marley was dead: to begin with. There is no doubt whatever, about that. The register of his burial was signed by the clergyman, the clerk, the undertaker, and the chief mourner. Scrooge signed it; and Scrooge's name was good upon 'Change, for anything he chose to put his hand to. Old Marley was as dead as a door-nail.

Mind! I don't mean to say that I know, of my own knowledge, what there is particularly dead about a door-nail. I might have been inclined, myself, to regard a coffin-nail as the deadest piece of ironmongery in the trade. But the wisdom of our ancestors is in the simile; and my unhallowed hands shall not disturb it, or the country's done for. You will therefore permit me to repeat, emphatically, that Marley was as dead as a door-nail.

Scrooge knew he was dead? Of course he did. How could it be otherwise? Scrooge and he were partners for I don't know how many years. Scrooge was his sole executor, his sole administrator, his sole assign, his sole residuary legatee, his sole friend and sole mourner. And even Scrooge was not so dreadfully cut up by the sad event, but that he was an excellent man of business on the very day of the funeral, and solemnized it with an undoubted bargain.

The mention of Marley's funeral brings me back to the point I started from. There is no doubt that Marley was dead. This must be distinctly understood, or nothing wonderful can come of the story I am going to relate. If we were not perfectly convinced that Hamlet's Father died before the play began, there would be nothing more remarkable in his taking a stroll at night, in an easterly wind, upon his own ramparts, than there would be in any other middle-aged gentleman rashly turning out after dark in a breezy spot—say Saint Paul's Churchyard for instance—literally to astonish his son's weak mind.

Scrooge never painted out old Marley's name. There it

14 In an address given at a banquet in Dickens' honor, Boston, February 1, 1842 (see *Speeches*, Clarendon Press, p. 19).

Steel etching by Phiz, "The Goblin and the Sexton," *The Pickwick Papers*, 1836. *Courtesy The Library of Congress*

the Christmas tale related at the famous party at Dingley Dell. In "The Goblins Who Stole A Sexton," the prototype for Scrooge may be found in the ill-tempered gravedigger Gabriel Grub. On Christmas Eve, this man, who can think of nothing better to do than to drink from a bottle of Hollands and dig a grave, is confronted by a band of goblins in an old churchyard. They spirit the sexton away to their enchanted cavern to view panoramas of Christmas life. In their den, old Gabriel sees both the rich and the poor and how they and he should celebrate the holiday. Through this supernatural medium, Gabriel Grub, like Ebenezer Scrooge, is converted to a new, reformed life.

The scenes and sentiments of the new story in part came too from the previous writing on Christmas. *A Christmas Carol* shares the attitude of the "good-humoured Christmas chapter" of *The Pickwick Papers*: "Happy, happy Christmas, that can win us back to the delusions of our childish days; that can recall to the old man the pleasures of his youth; that can transport the sailor and the traveler, thousands of miles away, back to his own fireside and quiet home!" The Fezziwig Ball sports the active good-fellowship of the old Christmas hosted by Old Wardle; the holiday party of Scrooge's nephew exudes the same spirited domesticity of the earlier family party in *Sketches by Boz*.

What distinguishes *A Christmas Carol* from the earlier holiday pieces is the conscious recognition that this festive season "is a time, of all others, when Want is keenly felt, and Abundance rejoices." In writing *A Christmas Carol*, Dickens retained his purpose as a writer, what he had adhered to in his previous works, "an earnest and true desire to contribute ... to the common stock of healthful cheerfulness and enjoyment." **14** But in the new book, he added a new approach in its composition; as he wrote in a letter of April 3, 1844:

I have great faith in the Poor; to the best of my ability I always endeavor to present them in a favourable light to the rich; and I shall never cease, I hope, until I die, to advocate their being made as happy and as wise as the circumstances of their condition in its utmost improvement, will admit of their becoming. I mention this to assure you of two things. Firstly, that I try to deserve their attention. And secondly that any such mark of their approval and confidence as you relate to me, are most acceptable to my feelings, and go at once to my heart.

Through this growing social consciousness, Dickens found the proper form in which to make his "Appeal to the People of England, on behalf of the Poor Man's Child." He no longer had to follow his initial scheme for the "appeal"; there may have been an inkling of his intentions, when he wrote to Dr. Smith on March 10, that by the end of the year "you will certainly feel that a Sledge hammer[15] has come down with twenty times the force—twenty thousand times the force—I could exert by following out my first idea. Even so recently as when I wrote to you the other day, I had not contemplated the means I shall now, please God, use. But they have been suggested to me, and I have girded myself for their seizure—as you shall see in due time."

The form and purpose having been chosen, Dickens proceeded to draw heavily on his own experience to flesh out the narrative. He depended greatly on his own childhood. The boy Scrooge, left in the schoolhouse, delights in the same books beloved by the boy Dickens. The warmth and exuberance of the Cratchits' humble but hardly insignificant Christmas dinner recalls Dickens' own celebrations when a child in Camden Town. The pathos of the death of Tiny Tim, too, came from those early years; the boy Charles knew the tragedy of child mortality due to the deaths of both a brother and sister in infancy. "It is from the life, and I was there," he wrote of an episode in *Dombey and Son* with an assurance also applicable to *A Christmas Carol*; "I remember it all as well, and certainly understood it as well, as I do now. We should be devilish sharp in what we do to children."

These experiences were further expanded into the metaphor of the demon children Want and Ignorance. In defending the boy and girl, the Ghost of Christmas Present speaks out for all the children "wretched, abject, frightful, hideous, miserable," who labored in the factories and the Cornish mines and who attended the Ragged Schools. Through these children Dickens could act as prophet to warn the public at large of the consequences of its great indifference. In composing his story, Dickens was surely visited by all three ghosts of past, present, and future.

With all the elements clearly falling into place, Dickens frantically worked to complete the story. He locked himself up in his house, and while struggling through the next two installments of the "Chuzzlewit agonies," he feverishly worked on the manuscript. All other projects (such as the article on the Ragged Schools) had to be postponed, because "I plunged headlong into a little scheme . . .; set an artist at work upon it; and put it wholly out of my own power to touch the Edinburgh subject until after Christmas is turned. For carrying out the notion I speak of, and

[15] John Forster in his biography of Dickens identified this "sledgehammer" as a reference to *The Chimes* (1844), a conclusion shared by Walter Dexter in his notes to the Nonesuch Press edition of the Letters, 1938; but it seems more likely that Dickens, already planning it, was referring to what would become *A Christmas Carol*.

16 In a letter to Macvey Napier, October 24, 1843 (*Letters*, Nonesuch Press, vol. 1, p. 543).

17 In a letter of November 25, 1843 (*Letters*, Clarendon Press, vol. 3, p. 602).

being punctual with Chuzzlewit, will occupy every moment of my working time, up to the Christmas Holidays."**16** He worked all hours of the day and late into the night. He broke appointments, such as that with his solicitor Thomas Mitton, because his "note found me in the full passion of a roaring Christmas scene!"**17** He could not receive all his friends when they came to visit him. "At the time when you called, and for many weeks afterwards," he explained to Edward Bulwer-Lytton, the novelist, "I was so closely occupied with my little Carol (the idea which had just occurred to me), that I never left home before the owls went out, and led quite a solitary life." So closely did he work on the story that within six weeks (by the second week in November) he presented the completed manuscript to the printers. "To keep the Chuzzlewit going, and to do this little book, the Carol, in the odd times between the parts of it," he wrote his American friend C. C. Felton, "was, as you may suppose, pretty tight work. But when it was done I broke out like a madman."

At the completion of the manuscript, the Christmas fervor still burned within him, and when the holidays did arrive, he celebrated them with an exuberance that his friends (including Forster, William Thackeray, and Thomas Carlyle) had not witnessed before. "Such dinings, such dancings, such conjurings, such blindman's-buffings, such theatre-goings, such kissings-out-of-old-years and kissings-in of new ones, never took part in these parts before," he wrote Felton. "And if you could have seen me at a children's party at Macready's the other night, going down a country dance with Mrs. M., you would have thought I was a country gentleman of independant property, residing on a tip-top farm, with the wind blowing straight in my face every day." These giddy activities seemed totally justified, because from all immediate indications, *A Christmas Carol* would be an unquestioned success, both artistically and financially.

Apparently Chapman and Hall at first expressed limited enthusiasm in publishing the Christmas book. They proposed instead issuing either a cheap edition of the already published work or a new magazine edited by Dickens. The author rejected both suggestions: he thought the cheap edition premature and that it might do damage to himself and the titles in print; and he feared the magazine might appear to the public that he was "writing tooth and nail for bread, headlong, after the close of a book taking so much out of one as Chuzzlewit." He had still not fully recovered from his run-in with the publishers, but through Forster's negotiations, Chapman and Hall agreed to bring out *A Christmas Carol* on commission terms. Under this proposal made by Dickens himself, the author was charged the full cost of production and would thus receive the entire profits of the sale; the publishers retained only a fixed commission on the total number of copies sold. Dickens rationalized that under these terms he would receive the largest possible earning. He likely now saw Chapman and Hall as little better than his printers, but his experience with the financial facts of publishing was obviously limited and perhaps ill-advised.

For his "little Carol," Dickens devised an elaborate scheme of production. He had to pay all these costs, but he also insisted that the price be low (five shillings) to encourage as many buyers as possible and thus larger sales. Dickens personally went over every aspect of the book's makeup. He approved the russet binding (blind-stamped with the title in gold), the color endpapers, the gilt edges, and the title page printed in green and red. With Forster he discussed the cover design and advertising, and as late as December he had the title page "materially altered" to blue and red as these leaves "always look bad at first."[18] At this time the green endpapers (printed with an ink that easily rubbed off the page) were changed to yellow. Despite his having an eye on the financial, Dickens did not skimp on the artistic. Dickens produced an elaborate volume that far excelled any other work sold then for a mere five shillings.

To illustrate the story, Dickens chose the *Punch* cartoonist, John Leech (1817–1864). Author and artist had first become acquainted as early as 1836 when, at the suicide of Robert Seymour, Leech desired to succeed him as illustrator of *The Pickwick Papers*. At George Cruikshank's introduction, the young artist went to speak with Dickens and presented him with a drawing "Tom Smart and the Chair," illustrating an episode from the book. Dickens was cordial when he wrote Leech, "I have to acknowledge the receipt of your design for the last Pickwick, which I think extremely well-conceived, and executed," but he was reluctant to commit himself as his publishers had already employed another artist, Hablot Knight ("Phiz") Browne, "a gentleman of very great ability, with whose designs I am exceedingly well satisfied, and from whom I feel it neither my wish, nor interest, to part."[19] Leech pursued the possibility of securing another commission from Chapman and Hall, but Dickens evidently wanted to get rid of the artist, because when he wrote of the interview to his publishers, he showed less enthusiasm[20]: "He left the Inclosed

18 In a letter to Thomas Mitton, December 6, 1843 (*Letters*, Nonesuch Press, vol. 1, p. 549).

19 Unless otherwise noted, all quotations from Dickens' correspondence with Leech are taken from "Letters to John Leech," *The Dickensian*, Winter Number 1937–1938, pp. 3–13.

20 "The chair's not bad," he wrote Chapman and Hall in August 1836, "but his notion of the Bedroom is rather more derived, I should be disposed to think from his own fourth pair back, than my description of the old rambling house" (see "The Agreement to Write *Pickwick*," *The Dickensian*, Winter 1936–1937, pp. 7–8).

"Tom Smart and the Chair" by John Leech, un-published drawing for *The Pickwick Papers*, 1836. *Courtesy The Library of Congress*

John Leech. *Courtesy General Research and Humanities Division, The New York Public Library, Astor, Lenox and Tilden Foundations*

21 A caricature of the actor J. P. Harley as "The Strange Gentleman," now in the Walter Dexter collection, the British Library (reproduced in *The Dickensian*, Spring Number 1938, p. 109). "I enclose Mr. Leech's sketch," Dickens wrote Harley; "you can tell me what you think of it when I see you to-morrow morning. *I* think he has not got the face well, or the hat. The general character is very good" (quoted in "The Letters of John Leech," *The Dickensian*, Spring Number 1938, p. 6).

Sketch from Tom Smart, here yesterday—as a specimen I suppose. As he threatened to call to-day, I have left out a note for him, saying that I supposed he wanted you to see it, and I have sent it on accordingly." No commission was forthcoming from Chapman and Hall, but about a year later Leech sent another drawing**21** which was likewise lukewarmly received by Dickens.

Within three years, Leech established himself as one of the leading cartoonists in this age of comic artists. Among the first contributors to *Punch*, Leech soon dominated the humor weekly with his satires on modern manners. In autumn of 1842 when the monthly parts of *Martin Chuzzlewit* were announced for publication, Leech with more restraint than before again approached Dickens as a collaborator. Certainly the novelist could no longer ignore Leech's reputation. "I have never forgotten the having seen you some years ago," he energetically wrote the artist, November 5, 1842, "or ceased to watch your progress with much interest and satisfaction. I congratulate you heartily on your success; and myself on having had an eye upon the means by which you have obtained it." Dickens now seriously considered Leech as his collaborator, if not on *Martin Chuzzlewit*, then on another project which never materialized. "In the meantime let me say with perfect sincerity, that I shall hope, in any case, to improve your acquaintance, and not to lose sight of you anymore." By November 7, Dickens asked the artist to dine with him, and this invitation became the source of their long and hearty friendship.

Not until the third week in October 1843 did Dickens finally have something for Leech to illustrate. As "Phiz" was occupied with illustrating the monthly parts of *Martin Chuzzlewit*, Dickens had to employ another artist to decorate *A Christmas Carol*. Although Leech got the commission, Dickens devised the elaborate, costly scheme for the illustration of the book: full-page, hand-colored steel engravings and textual woodcuts. As he had with every other part of the book's design, Dickens carefully went over each illustration with Leech. For the woodcuts, Leech seems to have first prepared pen-and-ink sketches for Dickens' approval, and then final pencil and wash drawings for the engraver. These textual illustrations were cut by W. J. Linton,**22** but evidently Leech etched the steel engravings himself.**23** For these plates, the artist first made wash drawings and then, to guide the colorers, finished watercolors. As the pencil sketches were transferred to the wood blocks, alterations were made from the original art to the finished illustrations; similarly, changes occurred between the watercolors and the completed hand-colored plates. Small differences in details may be spotted in comparisons between nearly every preliminary drawing and the finished illustration. For example, in the color sketch of "Scrooge's third visitor" (now in the Pierpont Morgan Library), the ghost's robe is red; likely at Dickens' request, it became green in the final plate in agreement with the text. Leech was a nervous, easily offended artist, and Dickens likely took pains to please and appease him. Leech was disappointed with the final hand-coloring. "This was a primitive process," explained Edgar Browne, Phiz's son. "Leech of course set the pattern, the copyist would spread out a number of prints all around a large table, having a number of saucers ready prepared with appropriate tints, blue for skies . . . then all the coats, and so on, till every object was separately coloured, and the work was done. The effect was cer-

22 William James Linton (1812–1897) was one of the most skilled of Victorian wood engravers. Generally based on drawings by other artists, Linton's engravings often graced *The Illustrated London News* and other publications. He encouraged younger artists, the most successful being Walter Crane; and he wrote the verses that accompanied Crane's art for *The Baby's Aesop* (1887). In 1866, Linton emigrated to the United States where he established the Appledore Press in Hamden, Connecticut; and in 1891, he received an honorary degree from Yale University. Apparently Linton cared little for the great English novelist. "Warm-hearted and sentimental, but not unselfish," Linton wrote in his memoirs *Threescore and Ten Years, 1820–1890* (New York: Charles Scribner's Sons, 1894, p. 161), Dickens "was not the gentleman. There was no grace of manner, no soul of nobility in him."

23 The design of *A Christmas Carol* followed the same scheme of an earlier Leech book *The Wassail Bowl* (1842): a small volume bound in russet cloth with a Christmas motif stamped in gold on the cover and illustrated with both inserted steel engravings and textual woodcuts. Dickens likely knew this publication (a collection of comic sketches by his friend Mark Lemon), which may have influenced his decision to employ Leech to decorate his Christmas story.

Preliminary pen-and-ink sketch for "The Christmas Bowl" by John Leech. *Courtesy The Beinecke Rare Book and Manuscript Library, Yale University*

24 In *Phiz and Dickens as they appeared to Edgar Browne* (London: James Nisbet & Co., Ltd., 1913, p. 21).

25 Quoted in "The Letters of John Leech," *The Dickensian*, Spring Number 1938, p. 101, but mistakenly said to be 1847, instead of 1843.

26 Leech did receive serious critical appreciation. In his lecture "The Fireside: John Leech and John Tenniel" (included in *The Art of England*, 1883), John Ruskin praised "the kind and vivid genius of John Leech, capable in its brightness of finding pretty jest in everything, but capable in its tenderness also of rejoicing in the beauty of everything, softened and illumined with its loving wit the entire scope of English social scene." "In all his designs, whatever Mr. Leech desires to do, he does," Dickens wrote in a review of the artist's *The Rising Generation* (*The Examiner*, December 30, 1848). "His drawing seems to us charming; and the expression indicated, though by the simplest means, is exactly the natural expression, and is recognized as such immediately.... Into the tone as well as in the execution of what he does, he has brought a certain elegance which is altogether new, without involving any compromise of what is true. Popular art in England has not had so rich an acquisition." The popularity of Leech's work in *Punch* made his sketches immediately recognizable by his monogram, a doctor's leech (a glass bottle containing a bloodsucking leech used to rid a patient of poisons in the system).

27 Tenniel paid homage to his predecessor on *Punch* by drawing a parody of Leech's famous drawing of "Scrooge's Third Visitor" with Gladstone as the miser, published December 30, 1893.

tainly gay, but generally too crude to be pleasant."**24** "I do not doubt, in my own mind," Dickens tried to console Leech, December 14, "that you unconsciously exaggerate the evil done by the colourers. You can't think how much better they will look in a neat book, than you suppose. But I have sent a Strong Dispatch to C and H, and will report to you when I hear from them. I quite agree with you, that it is a point of great importance."**25** Leech had no reason to worry; these hand-colored plates remain as fresh and charming as when they were first produced.

Dickens was satisfied with Leech's work on the book. For each of the subsequent Christmas Books, Leech contributed illustrations. Although *A Christmas Carol* was the only Dickens book he illustrated entirely on his own, Leech was the only illustrator to be represented in each volume of the holiday series. He never illustrated a Dickens novel. The last drawing that he made for a Dickens text was a woodcut, the frontispiece to the cheap edition of the *Christmas Books* (1852), the first collected edition of the five stories. This design, a new version of the frontispiece to the 1843 edition, is in some respects superior to the earlier steel engraving "Mr. Fezziwig's Ball." By the time of the later edition, Leech's style had matured, and as he was not a skilled etcher with the genius of a Cruikshank, his drawings gained in strength by being transferred to wood. This woodcut is one of his finest designs.

Leech was a pivotal figure in the history of caricature.**26** His work fell somewhere between the grotesque energy of Cruikshank and the more solid, natural drawing of John Tenniel,**27** who succeeded Leech at *Punch*. As his career developed, he relied on questions of manners (anticipating George DuMaurier's *Punch* cartoons) and on sporting subjects in the

"The Spirit of Christmas Present" by John Tenniel, *Punch*, December 30, 1893. *Courtesy General Research and Humanities Library, The New York Public Library, Astor, Lenox and Tilden Foundations*

spirit of Rowlandson and Gilchrist (carried on by Randolph Caldecott after Leech). A prolific artist, Leech produced his most enduring designs for *A Christmas Carol*. Despite the odd omission of a drawing of Bob Cratchit with Tiny Tim on his shoulder (a subject that nearly every illustrator of the book since Leech has depicted**28**), the set of eight drawings beautifully complement the settings and sentiments of Dickens' text. The novelist reserved only praise for this "great popular artist of the time, whose humour was so delicate, so nice, and so discriminating, and whose pencil like his observation was so graceful and so informed with the sense of beauty that it was mere disparagement to call his works 'caricatures.' "**29** Whether it be in the Fezziwig Ball or in the depictions of Marley and the other ghosts, every other illustrator of the story has had to pay his respects to Leech's original conceptions in some way. When "The Library Edition of Dickens' Works" appeared in 1859, the half title page of the *Christmas Books* contained a small engraving of Scrooge and Marley drawn by Phiz, but it is Leech who will always be the illustrator popularly linked with the Dickens Christmas. Other artists (Daniel Maclise, Edwin Landseer, Richard Doyle, Tenniel, and others) all contributed one or more drawings to the subsequent volumes, but it was Leech's spirit that dominated the series.

With the illustrations cut and colored and the manuscript at the printers, the completed volume took only a few weeks to be produced, and came out just a few days before Christmas. The first presentation copies arrived around December 17, and Dickens' immediate feelings toward the book were encouraging. The few friends fortunate enough to receive advance copies shared his enthusiasm. "I am extremely glad you *feel* the Carol," he wrote Mitton, December 6. "For I knew I meant a good thing. And when I see the effect of a little *whole* as that, on those for whom I care, I have a strong sense of the immense effect I could produce with an entire book."**30** Carlyle was among those to receive the precious early copies, and he was so strongly moved that, according to Thackeray, this "Scotch philosopher who nationally does not keep Christmas Day, on reading the book, sent out for a turkey, and asked two friends to dine—this is a fact."**31**

Dickens did not have long to wait for the public's verdict. From the date of publication, the sales were tremendous; on one day, Christmas Day, six thousand copies were sold, and by December 27, Dickens could proudly announce that "as the orders were coming in fast from town and country, it would soon be necessary

28 From the first "newly illustrated" edition (that by the American Sol Eytinge, Jr., in 1868), *A Christmas Carol* has been fortunate in its illustrators. Fred Barnard, Charles E. Brock, Charles Dana Gibson, Fritz Kredel, Arthur Rackham, Philip Reed, Ronald Searle, Everett Shinn, and Jessie Wilcox Smith are among the many artists who have pictured Dickens' celebrated characters.

29 In a speech given at the second anniversary dinner of the Newsvendor's Benevolent Institution, held at Albion Tavern, January 27, 1852 (*Speeches*, Clarendon Press, p. 136).

30 A letter of December 6, 1843 (*Letters*, Clarendon Press, vol. 3, p. 605).

31 Carlyle was not noted for his Christmas cheer. As he wrote in his journal, December 28, 1857, "All mortals are tumbling about in a state of drunken saturnalia, delirium, or quasi-delirium, according to their several sorts; a very strange method of thanking God for sending them a Redeemer; a not singularly worth 'redeeming,' too, you would say." He and Mrs. Carlyle did join in some festivities with the Dickenses, and he and his wife were among those who celebrated the holiday with the novelist when "he broke out like a madman" on completing *A Christmas Carol*. Dickens gave an early copy of the story to the great philosopher who then presented it to a friend with the inscription, "Read with satisfaction; presented with satisfaction, and many Christmas wishes." Mrs. Carlyle noted the effect Dickens' book had on her husband when she wrote her sister Jeanie Welsh, December 23, 1843, that "the vision of *Scrooge*—had so worked on Carlyle's nervous organization that he has been seized with a perfect *convulsion* of hospitality, and has actually insisted on *improvising two* dinner parties with only a day between" (*Jane Welsh Carlyle: Letters to Her Family. 1839–1863*, London: J. Murray, 1924, p. 169). Dickens clearly had hoped to please Carlyle; his economic writing clearly influenced passages in the Christmas story. Kathleen Tillotson in "The Middle Years from the *Carol* to *Copperfield*" (*Dickens Memorial Lectures 1970*) has suggested that the novelist may have recalled both the title and structure of Carlyle's *Past and Present* (1843) in composing *A Christmas Carol*. Years later, Carlyle was rather harsh in his appraisal of Dickens' intentions. "His theory of life was entirely wrong," Carlyle was quoted by Sir Charles Gavan Duffy in *Conversations with Carlyle* (New York: Charles Scribner's Sons, 1892, p. 75). "He thought men ought to be buttered up, and the world made soft and accommodating for them, and all sorts of fellows have turkey for their Christmas dinner."

Not everyone was pleased with the story. The poet Samuel Rogers, to whom Dickens sent a copy of *A Christmas Carol*, found it dull and the colloquialisms in the style offensive (P. W. Clayden's *Rogers and His Contemporaries*, vol. 2, 1889, pp. 239–40).

32 In a letter to Thomas Mitton (*Letters*, Nonesuch Press, vol. 1, p. 550).

33 In a letter to Mrs. Thackeray, March 11, 1844 (*The Letters and Private Papers of William Makepeace Thackeray*, collected and edited by Gordon N. Ray, Cambridge, Massachusetts: Harvard University Press, 1945, vol. 2, p. 165). Thackeray was so delighted with Dickens' "Christmas Books" that he wrote his own series, the most celebrated volume being *The Rose and the Ring* (1847).

Dickens was similarly touched by a notice of praise for his story by another friend. "Blessings on your kind heart, my dear Dickens," wrote Lord Francis Jeffrey, founder and editor of *The Edinburgh Review*, "and may it always be as light and full as it is kind, and a fountain of kindness to all within reach of its beatings! We are all charmed with your 'Carol'; chiefly I think for the genuine goodness which breathes all through it, and is the true inspiring angel by which its genius has been awakened.... Well, you should be happy yourself, for you may be sure you have done more good, and not only fastened more kindly feelings, but prompted more positive acts of beneficence, by this little publication, than can be traced to all the pulpits and confessionals...since Christmas 1842." Dickens was evidently deeply touched by Lord Jeffrey's support of his work; he named his third son (born 1844) after the editor, and dedicated *The Cricket on the Hearth* (1845), the third Christmas Book, to his friend.

Sheet music cover, *The Christmas Carol Quadrilles*, 1844. *Courtesy The Music Division, The Library of Congress*

to reprint."**32** By January 3, 1844, he wrote Forster that "two thousand of the three printed for second and third editions are already taken by the trade." Dickens described its prodigious success to Felton: "And by every post all manner of strangers write all manner of letters to him about their homes and hearths, and how this same Carol is read aloud there, and kept on a little shelf by itself. Indeed, it is the greatest, as I am told, that this ruffian and rascal has ever achieved."

The reviewers too took the little book to their hearts. Tom Hood of *Hood's Magazine* (January 1844) lauded the appearance of "that famous *Gobbling Story*, with its opulence of good cheer, and all the Gargantuan festivity of hospitable tide": "A happy inspiration of the heart that warms every page. It is impossible to read, without a glowing bosom and burning cheeks, between love and shame for our kind...." Dickens was touched by such notices and typically thanked those who sang praises for his "Carol." "I cannot thank you enough for the beautiful manner and the true spirit of friendship in which you have noticed my 'Carol,'" he wrote Laman Blanchard, a friend and reviewer. "But I *must* thank you because you have filled my heart up to the brim, and it is running over. You meant to give me great pleasure, dear fellow, and you have done it. The tone of your elegant and fervent praise has touched me in the tenderest place.... I have derived inexpressible gratification from what I know was a labour of love on your part. And I can never forget it." Another review, Thackeray's piece in *Fraser's Magazine* (February 1844) pleased Dickens too: "Boz writes that my notice of him has touched him to the quick, encouraged him, and done him good."**33** Dickens obviously realized that the highest praise was that expressed by one novelist for another. "The last two people I heard speak of [*A Christmas Carol*] were women," Thackeray wrote; "neither knew the other, or the author, and both said, by way of criticism, 'God bless him!'... There is not a reader in England but that...he will say of Charles Dickens, as the woman just now, 'God bless him!' What a feeling is this for a writer to be able to inspire, and what a reward to reap!"

With the "prodigious success" of the new story came the usual nuisances Dickens had learned to expect with each publication of his work since the early days of *The Pickwick Papers*. Composers without remuneration to the author capitalized on Dickens' book by publishing quadrilles and songs dedicated to his conceptions. More annoying to the novelist were the unauthorized dramatizations of his work without any financial arrangement paid to the story's creator. At least two separate and distinct productions opened in early February 1844, and their dramatists took odd liberties with the original text. One of these plays was *A Christmas Carol; or The Miser's Warning!*, a drama in two acts by C. Z. Barnett, first performed at the Royal Surrey Theatre, and published in 1852. This production's many alterations were not improvements on the original: for example, Scrooge's nephew received a coy surname "Frank Freeheart," and a new character "Dark Sam" was introduced for the single purpose of picking Bob Cratchit's pocket, so that the clerk may be befriended by Scrooge's nephew with a sovereign. Dickens attended a performance of another adaptation, that by actor-playwright Edward Stirling, first performed at the Adelphi Theatre. The novelist was unimpressed: "Better than usual, and Wright seems to enjoy Bob Cratchit, but *heart-breaking* to me. Oh Heaven! if any forecast of *this* was ever in my mind! Yet O. Smith was drearily better than I expected. It is a great comfort to have that kind of meat underdone; and his face is quite perfect." Dickens reluctantly had learned to tolerate these infringements on his art and rights; these

Drawing by Mr. Findlay, *A Christmas Carol; or The Miser's Warning*, a drama by C. Z. Barnett, February 5, 1844. *Courtesy The British Library Board*

A Christmas Carol, a drama by Edward Stirling, *The Illustrated London News*, February 17, 1844. *Courtesy General Research and Humanities Library, The New York Public Library, Astor, Lenox and Tilden Foundations*

34 A Christmas dare not pass without ushering in several new dramatizations of *A Christmas Carol*. It is impossible to estimate how many adaptations of the story have been performed by schools, church groups, and the legitimate stage since the book's publication. The movie industry early saw the entertainment possibilities in the Dickens classic. The first motion picture version, an Essanay silent picture, was released in 1908; but perhaps the most successful screen adaptation was that film starring Alastair Sim as Scrooge, produced in 1954. With less care, it was adapted as a musical sporting Albert Finney as the miser, singing an undistinguished score by Leslie Bricusse; the libretto took alarming and inexplicable liberties with the story, as in changing its date from 1843 to 1860. During the Great Depression, Franklin Delano Roosevelt and Lionel Barrymore each read the book over the radio; similarly Alec Guinness (who took the role of Marley's Ghost in the musical film) portrayed Scrooge on the radio in the 1950s. Recently Lawrence Olivier recorded his reading of *A Christmas Carol*; Paul Scofield and Ralph Richardson have also performed the story, for Caedmon Records. Television has produced many dramatizations, including a 1955 CBS musical with libretto by Maxwell Anderson. The networks have been particularly imaginative in animated cartoon versions: in the 1950s, Walt Disney produced an unorthodox film of Scrooge as a mouse miser, and UPI's *Mr. Magoo's Christmas Carol* has often been revived on television. The finest cartoon version was that made in 1969 by Richard Williams, who beautifully animated the original Leech drawings with Sim recreating his role as Scrooge. This sensitive and accurate interpretation of the Dickens classic in both word and picture well deserved the Academy Award for the best animated feature of 1970.

plays at the least helped to publicize the individual works.**34**

Another consequence of the book's popularity was the publication of foreign editions. Notable among these was the German edition of the English text published by Bernhard Tauchnitz of Leipzig. On a visit to London the previous summer, Tauchnitz had secured the rights to authorized continental editions of the works of English authors, Dickens among them; advance proofs were provided to his company, and he advertised that his "edition sanctioned by the author" would be published simultaneously with the London edition. For this volume (set from the uncorrected first printing and illustrated with a redrawn plate of Leech's "Marley's Ghost" as frontispiece), Dickens was reportedly liberally paid. The first foreign translation appeared only a few months after publication, as *Les Apparitions de Noël*, in *Révue Britannique* (May to June 1844). Since this early French translation, the story of Scrooge has appeared in one form or another in nearly every tongue.

Not all foreign editions were sanctioned by the author. The earliest American versions likely appeared without Dickens' knowledge. In 1844, Carey and Hart of Philadelphia issued a reasonable reproduction of the Chapman and Hall edition; this (like the Tauchnitz edition) was set from the uncorrected first printing, and the hand-colored illustrations were crude redrawings of

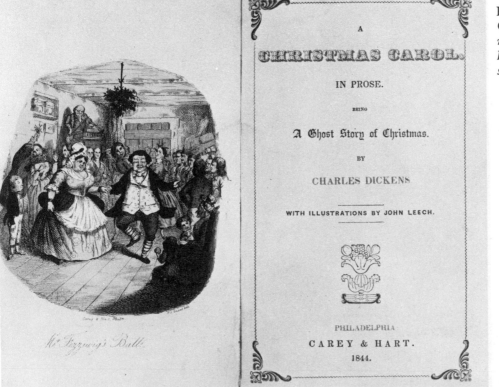

A

CHRISTMAS CAROL.

IN PROSE.

BEING

A Ghost Story of Christmas.

BY

CHARLES DICKENS.

WITH ILLUSTRATIONS BY JOHN LEECH.

PHILADELPHIA
CAREY & HART.
1844.

Mr. Fezziwig's Ball.

Frontispiece and title page of the Carey and Hart edition of *A Christmas Carol*, 1844. *Courtesy The Beinecke Rare Book and Manuscript Library, Yale University*

the Leech plates. The Carey and Hart volume was far more attractive than another pirated edition, that of Harper and Brothers.**35** This cheap pamphlet, bound in blue wrappers and printed in double columns, sold for six cents; it was hastily produced and lacked any illustration. Despite Dickens' impassioned plea for international copyright protection during his American tour the previous year, he failed to prevent the unauthorized publication of his work abroad.

However, he was determined to stop this piracy at home. In the past his only recourse was public protest, but he was now prepared to bring legal action against these flagrant infringements on his rights. What sparked this attack was the publication on January 6, 1844, in the sixteenth number of *Parley's Illuminated Library*,**36** of "A Christmas Ghost Story reoriginated from the original by Charles Dickens Esquire and analytically condensed for this work." Dickens was already well aware of this publication's unscrupulous dealings,**37** but it was not until January 8, 1844, that he found the means to attack these pirates.

Through his solicitor Mitton, Dickens filed an affidavit to obtain an injunction to stop publication of

35 E. L. Carey and A. Hart had long been competitors with Harper & Brothers (particularly over the American rights to Edward Bulwer-Lytton's novels). It was customary for an American publisher to secure rights to a foreign book either by receiving the first copy of the publication or by "announcing" it in the trade first.

E. L. Carey was the brother of Henry Carey of Lea & Blanchard (formerly Carey & Lea), the only American publisher who paid Dickens any remuneration for American editions of his books. In late 1836, Carey had pirated *The Pickwick Papers*, and when it proved so successful, he sent some payment to "Mr. Saml. Dickens." Although the moneys were not much, Dickens was so delighted with the gesture that he authorized Carey's American editions of his books; but in December 1842, he dissolved his negotiations with Lea & Blanchard, not because he was displeased with them, but on principle because he was furious with the current copyright laws. See *Messrs. Carey & Lea of Philadelphia, A Study in the History of the Book-trade* by David Kaser (Philadelphia: University of Pennsylvania Press, 1957).

36 Not to be confused with the original "Peter Parley," the American author Samuel Griswold Goodrich (1793–1860). Dickens had met him in the United States and found him "a scoundrel and a Liar; and if he would present himself at my door, he would, as he very well knows, be summarily pitched into the street" (a letter to Thomas Hood, October 13, 1842, The British Library). Dickens felt Goodrich had betrayed him on the copyright question; they had spoken cordially while in Washington on the importance of a strong international copyright law (the *Peter Parley* books were widely pirated overseas), but when he returned to Boston, Goodrich presided over a meeting where he argued that the law need not be changed. Dickens was determined to "ever proclaim said Parley to be a Scoundrel." Perhaps some of this animosity toward the real Peter Parley was transferred to the hated pirates of *Parley's Illuminated Library*.

37 In December 1842, Dickens learned of *Parley's* plagiarism of *The Old Curiosity Shop, Barnaby Rudge,* and *American Notes* in its cheap pages. "The fellow who publishes these Piracies hasn't a penny in the World," Dickens wrote T. N. Talfourd, December 30; "but I shall be glad to know, at your convenience, whether the Law gives us any means of stopping him short" (*Letters*, Clarendon Press, vol. 3, pp. 410–11). Apparently the reply was negative, and Dickens did not begin legal proceedings at this time.

First page of the *Carol* piracy in *Parley's Illuminated Library, The Dickensian,* Winter 1937–38. *Courtesy General Research and Humanities Division, The New York Public Library, Astor, Lenox and Tilden Foundations*

38 In a letter to Mitton, January 7, 1844 (*Letters*, Nonesuch Press, vol. 1, p. 559).

39 In a letter to Clarkson Stanfield, January 9, 1844 (*Letters*, Nonesuch, vol. 1, p. 559).

40 See also *Charles Dickens in Chancery....* by Edward Tyrrell Jaques (London, New York: Longmans, Green and Co., 1914); and "At the Dickens House: Legal Documents Relating to the Piracy of *A Christmas Carol*" by S. J. Rust, *The Dickensian*, Winter Number 1937–1938, pp. 41–44.

this journal. As he was directly involved in the publication of *A Christmas Carol* (and he needed to sell as many books as possible to ease his debts), he could no longer tolerate this competition with his original work. "I have not the least doubt that if these Vagabonds can be stopped, they must be," he wrote Mitton. "So let us go to work in such terrible earnest that everything tumble down before it.... Let us be *sledge-hammer* in this, or I shall be beset by hundreds of the same crew, when I come out with a long story."**38** Mitton proceeded to register the book's copyright in Dickens' name and followed the author's further instructions.

Dickens was furious with what *Parley's Illuminated Library* had done to his book. "The story is practically the same," he explained to Mitton; "with the exception of the name Fezziwig, which is printed *Fuzziwig.* That the incidents are the same, and follow in the same order. That very frequently indeed ... the language is the same. That where it is not, it is weakened, degraded; made tame, vile, ignorant, and mawkish." Dickens' evaluation can easily be supported by quoting the pedestrian opening of the pirated version:

Everybody, as the phrase goes, knew the firm of "Scrooge and Marley;" for, though Marley had "long been dead" at the period we have chosen for the commencement of our story, the name of the deceased partner still maintained its place above the warehouse door; somewhat faded, to be sure, but there it was....

The incidents are indeed the same, but the style has none of the flavor, none of the wit, of Dickens' original. Dickens was fully justified in filing affidavits "against a gang of Robbers who have been pirating the Carol; and against whom the most energetic vengeance of the inimitable B is solemnly (and carefully) denounced."**39** As "A Christmas Ghost Story reoriginated," Dickens's book had been "made to appear a wretched, meagre, miserable thing; and is still hawked about with my title and my name—with my characters, my incidents, and whole design."

When Dickens (through his counsel) filed a petition for the cessation of publication, the defendants Lee and Haddock moved to dissolve the injunction. They argued that when, in 1841, Lee and the writer Henry Hewitt "analysed, abridged, re-originated, and published the plaintiff's well known and then recently published works, *The Old Curiosity Shop* and *Barnaby Rudge* ... the plaintiff had never interfered with those publications."**40** They further explained that Hewitt, working from critical notes by Lee, "made very considerable improvements, and in some instances large original additions" as in supplying for the "song about a lost child travelling in the snow" an original carol of sixty lines. The defendants concluded that in their "colorable imitation of the Plaintiff's said work," the "numerous incongruities involving . . . the unhinging of the whole story have been tastefully remedied in the said Henry Hewitt's work." Four additional affidavits were filed[41] including one from Hewitt claiming that "besides the defects or wants of harmony pointed out by . . . Lee this deponent detected so many others as to induce him in numerous instances to abandon the plot of the plaintiff's tale and to substitute what this deponent verily believes to be more artistical style of expression and of incident."

But the Vice-Chancellor, Sir J. Knight Bruce, would have none of this nonsense. As Dickens reported to Forster, Bruce demanded that Lee and Haddock's counsel "produce a passage which was not an expanded or contracted idea from my book. And at every successive passage he cried, 'That is Mr. Dickens' case. Find another!' He said that there was not a shadow of doubt upon the matter. That there was no authority which would bear a construction in their favour; the piracy going beyond all previous instances." Dickens was jubilant at the court's findings, and he announced to Forster, "The Pirates are beaten flat. They are bruised, bloody, battered, smashed, squelched, and utterly undone."

Dickens, however, spoke too soon. He plunged into no less than six chancery suits and demanded £1,000 in damages from the publishers and their plagiarists; he even considered publishing the petitions in a number of *Martin Chuzzlewit* to acquaint the public with the injustice afforded him by the pirates. The defendants were far from being "utterly undone"; they were not yet out of legal tricks. Lee and Haddock declared bankruptcy, and Dickens was forced to take action against the assignees. Dickens was being pressured on all sides; one defendant went so far as to send an associate to intimidate Dickens at his home by threatening to publish a damaging advertisement in addition to further legal action. Dickens remained firm. The booksellers who had hawked the periodical finally gave in, but the publishers persisted in their legal entanglements. Dickens realized by January 29 (in a letter to Blanchard) that "through the villainy of the law, which after declaring me robbed, obliges me to bring action against men for whom it demands no security for the expenses to which I shall be put"; he would be forced to pay £300 in legal fees. "Never mind. I declare war

41 Among these documents was one filed by Edward Leman Blanchard, a playwright and novelist, who should not be confused with Dickens' friend S. Laman Blanchard. "When I went down to my Solicitor's today," Dickens wrote Laman Blanchard on January 29, 1844, "the first thing said was 'Who do you think has made an affidavit?' 'God knows, Bunn?' 'Your friend, Mr. Blanchard.' 'D——d nonsense.' 'O, but he has, and there aren't two Laman Blanchards, for I went down to Sarjeant Talfourd's directly, and his clerk says there's only one, and it's your friend!!!! But you can't see the cream of the thing without seeing the affidavit itself. Oh my stars!" (*Letters*, Nonesuch Press, vol. 1, p. 565).

42 In a letter to T. N. Talfourd, May 5, 1844 (*Letters*, Nonesuch Press, vol. 1, p. 598).

43 In a letter, February 12, 1844 (*Letters*, Nonesuch Press, vol. 1, p. 567).

against the Black Flag; and down it shall come, if strong and constant hauling will do it."

By May, the actions had not been settled, and Dickens had to withdraw his suits with the hope he would be charged only the costs for bringing them before the court. As the pirates had no assets, Dickens was legally responsible for the court costs. "I have dropped —dropped!—the action and the chancery suit against the bankrupt Pirates," he wrote a friend on May 5. "We have had communication with the assignees, and find their case quite desperate. . . . By Lee and Haddock (the vagabonds) I do lose of course, all my expenses, costs and charges in those suits."**42** His total losses were estimated to be £700, a sum he could ill afford. Despite his desperate attempts to protect his legal rights, Dickens failed to save his "little carol" and subsequent work from the encroachments of plagiarism. A few years later, when he was again beset by pirates, Dickens bitterly opposed bringing the culprits to trial. "I shall not easily forget," he wrote Forster in August 1846, "the expense, and anxiety, and horrible injustice of the Carol case, wherein, in asserting the plainest right on earth, I was really treated as if I were the robber instead of the robbed."

At the height of the chancery suit action, Dickens was struck with yet another financial setback. When the threat of the court costs had become apparent, Dickens desperately looked to the *Christmas Carol* accounts from Chapman and Hall. He had expected the earnings to clear him of the past year's debts and the legal expenses. "Prepare yourself for a shock!" he wrote Mitton. "I was never so knocked over in my life, as when I opened this Carol account on Saturday night; and though I had got over it by yesterday and could look the thing good humoredly in the face, I have slept badly as Macbeth ever since—which is, thank God, almost a miracle with me."**43** Although he "had set my heart and soul upon a Thousand clear," the profit on the first six thousand copies was a paltry £230; after all the production costs had been accounted for, Dickens was left with enough money to pay only a fraction of his many debts. He did not dare predict much of a gain on the next four thousand. "Such a night as I have passed!" he wrote Forster on February 10. "I really believed I should never get up again, until I had passed through all the horrors of a fever. I found the Carol accounts awaiting me, and they were the cause of it." Dickens quickly noticed the irony of the situation: "What a wonderful thing it is, that such a great success should occasion me such intolerable anxiety and disappointment!" The weight of his debts was so heavy that "all the energy and determination I can possibly exert will be required to clear me before I go abroad." He was determined to reduce his expenses, because "if I do not, I shall be ruined past all mortal hope of redemption." Dickens perhaps exaggerated his dilemma, because, by March, with the half year accounts being encouraging, he was far from the ruin he had predicted.

The blame of the book's disastrous profits must be given to Dickens himself. The author had demanded an expensive, luxurious product, but he had intentionally set the low selling price. The gilt edges, elaborate binding, eight woodcuts and steel engravings, and the enormously expensive hand-coloring all cut deeply into the profits. Perhaps Chapman and Hall were in part to blame; they might have advised the innocent author on the realities of publishing costs.

Dickens decided that the culprits responsible for the poor showing of *A Christmas Carol* were Chapman and Hall. His opinion had changed little; he was furious, even before the accounts arrived, because they had not promoted the book as he had expected. "Can you believe that with the exception of Blackwood's," he reported to Mitton on December 4, "*the Carol is not advertised in One of the Magazines!* Bradbury . . . says that nothing but a tremendous push can possibly atone for such fatal negligence. Consequently, I have written . . . and said—Do this—Do that—Do the other—keep away from me—and be damned."[44] This irritation likely influenced his belief that Chapman and Hall were cheating him on the book's production costs. "I have not the least doubt," he complained to Mitton, "that they have run the expenses up anyhow purposely to bring me back and disgust me with the charges. If you add up the different charges for the plates, you will find that they cost me more than I get." His bitterness was evident in his comment that what he had finally earned on the popular Christmas book was little more than he had received on an earlier work, "a poor thing of little worth published without my name." Seeing "the shadow of war" before him, Dickens wrote Chapman and Hall a curt business letter.

His only alternative was to change publishers. He thought Bradbury and Evans would prove far more profitable. His entire earning on the sales of *A Christmas Carol*, from January through December 1844, was a modest £726, for the first seven thousand copies. The printers now offered him £2,800 down on assignment of a fourth share in everything he might write during the next eight years, and they would pay Chapman and Hall the remainder of Dickens' debt.[45]

44 *Letters*, Clarendon Press, vol. 3, pp. 604–5.

45 After a dispute with Bradbury and Evans in 1858, Dickens returned to Chapman and Hall, who remained his publishers until his death in 1870.

"The Tetterbys" by John Leech, *The Haunted Man*, 1848

Ironically, the sentiments of good-fellowship and mercy, the tone of *A Christmas Carol*, did not touch its purveyor in his dealings with either his publishers or the pirates of the story. Although the book had been his most popular work in several years (he now referred to himself as "the author of A Christmas Carol in prose and other works"), Dickens suffered more anxiety and disappointment upon publication of the Christmas book than from any previous work.

In spite of all these troubles, Dickens did not overlook the necessity to follow *A Christmas Carol* with a sequel for the next holiday season. Dickens reported to Forster that the new story would be "a great blow for the poor"; it would be powerful, "but I want to be tender too and cheerful; as like the Carol in that respect as may be, and as unlike it as much as a thing can be. The duration of the action will resemble it a little, but I trust to the novelty of the machinery to carry that off; and if my design be anything at all, it has a grip upon the very throat of the public." This second Christmas book, *The Chimes*, set the pattern for the subsequent volumes; it was a companion to *A Christmas Carol* but in a less expensive format. Dickens was ecstatic over the new story: "I believe I have written a tremendous book, and knocked the Carol out of the field. It will make a great uproar, I have no doubt." *The Chimes*, as did the other three sequels, did sell better than *A Christmas Carol*; but none ever succeeded in knocking the first out of the field. They are little read today, among the most neglected of Dickens' work; they lack the magic of the first Christmas book. With the exception of *The Battle of Life* (an uncharacteristic, brief, sentimental romance of sacrifice), each of the Christmas series retains the basic structure of *A Christmas Carol*: the resolution of a human problem through the intervention of a supernatural force, acting on the protagonist's psychology generally through the agent of memory. Each volume is dependent on Dickens' "Carol philosophy—cheerful views, sharp anatomization of humbug, jolly good temper . . . and a vein of glowing, hearty, generous, mirthful, beaming references in everything to Home, and Fireside." Dickens just reclothed the same story in a new holiday dress. The later stories are forced, dependent on a formula; by the time of *The Haunted Man* (1848), Dickens felt obligated to write still another holiday story, because he hated "to leave a gap at Christmas firesides which I ought to fill." He obviously realized his ideas were now hackneyed; *The Haunted Man* was the last of the Christmas Books. Even the characters were repeating themselves: the Tetterbies are crude imitations of the Cratchits, and the chemist Redlaw has a similar history but less distinctive character than Scrooge. As Chesterton observed in *Charles Dickens* (1906), "All the good figures that followed Scrooge when he came growling out of the fog fade into the fog again." Not without their curiosities, these later books fail to sustain a unique, unified tone as in the tale of Scrooge's conversion; they are dependent more on intentions than on inspiration, and what they lack in spirit, they also lack in expression. The other Christmas stories in the many holiday numbers of Dickens' periodicals, *Household Words* and *All The Year Round,* are even less successful than the worst of the Christmas Books; these later stories written in collaboration with other authors did not follow Dickens' but another's plan, so they are even free of the original Carol philosophy. More characteristic of the earlier tone are Dickens' several holiday essays, "A Christmas Tree," "What Christmas Is as We Grow Older," "A December Vision," and others; these intimate articles were direct expressions of Dickens' Christmas thoughts and experiences and restore in part the Carol philosophy so lacking in the subsequent Christmas fictions.

A legacy of the enormous popularity of Dickens' Christmas Books was the establishment of a unique branch of English letters: the holiday book. Most were ephemeral pieces, now long forgotten, which had little in common with Dickens' originals except for a likely imitation in design and illustration. Dickens' artists were often called on to illustrate these books (for example, Cruikshank contributed to the undistinguished *The Snow Storm* by Mrs. Gore, 1845) and the growing number of Christmas supplements to such periodicals as *The London Illustrated News.* Perhaps the most enduring of these seasonal works is Thackeray's *The Rose and the Ring* (1855), a comic fairy tale directly inspired by Dickens' Christmas Books; it still retains a following uniquely its own. Hans Christian Andersen's *Christmas Greetings to My English Friends* (1847), another special example of this genre, was a collection of seven fairy tales dedicated to Dickens.**46** Andersen's use of Christmas is often as touching as Dickens': "The Little Fir Tree" and "The Snow Queen" deserve their status as holiday classics, and the story of the Little Match Girl displays a pathos comparable to that of Tiny Tim. Oscar Wilde, in part a direct descendant of both Dickens and Andersen, wrote an unusual holiday fairy tale, "The Young King" (first published in the December issue of *The Ladies' Magazine* and later as a part of *The House of Pomegranates,* 1891). This latter fantasy appears to be Wilde's unique adaptation of *A Christmas Carol* to embody his own aesthetic principles and theory of Christian martyrdom: in the

46 "A Thousand Thanks, my dear Andersen," Dickens wrote in January 1848, "for your kind and dearly-prized remembrance of me in your Christmas book. I am very proud of it, and feel deeply honoured by it, and cannot tell you how much I esteem so generous a mark of recollection from a man of such genius as yours." See *Hans Andersen and Charles Dickens, A Friendship and Its Dissolution* by Elias Bredsdorff (Copenhagen: Rosenkilde and Bogger, 1956, p. 30).

"Even in death—God bless us every one." *Christmas Eve With the Spirits...,* 1870. *Courtesy The Library of Congress*

47 The author elusively explained his reasons for anonymity as being "for any Author who, having written and published many works with his name attached, wishing to test whether his writing deteriorates or improves, published one anonymously, and consequently without any *prestige* attaching to his name" and "for any Author publishing his first work and wishing it to be fairly tested by its own merits alone." Evidently the second is the true reason. He seems to have had two other purposes in mind: to suggest to the reader that this *Christmas Eve* may be by Dickens, and to protect himself from any legal action from the author's estate.

48 The holiday book also made its way across the Atlantic. Frank Stockton early wrote fine Christmas stories, and Bret Harte composed an amusing parody of Dickens' *The Haunted Man.* More current popular examples of this genre include O. Henry's "The Gift of the Magi" (1911), Valentine Davies' *Miracle on Thirty-Fourth Street* (1947), and Dr. Seuss' *How the Grinch Stole Christmas* (1957) with its whimsical cousin of Ebenezer Scrooge. Perhaps the finest of American holiday stories is Truman Capote's touching *A Christmas Memory* (1957).

conversion of the vain, sensuous young Prince through the medium of three dreams lies the same machinery as that of the miser Scrooge and the agents of the three ghosts. Other holiday books of the nineteenth century blatantly plagiarized Dickens' ideas; *Christmas Eve With the Spirits ... With Some Further Tidings of the Lives of Scrooge and Tiny Tim* (1870) purported to tell the remainder of Scrooge's story from his conversion to his death.**47**   The twentieth century has produced one Christmas story comparable to the best of Dickens; Dylan Thomas' *Child's Christmas in Wales* (1954) is unsurpassed by any other seasonal work, and it shares much of the flavor of Stephen Dedalus' boyhood Christmas described by James Joyce in *Portrait of the Artist as a Young Man* (1916). Each of these numerous Christmas stories, each written by artists who differ in style, owes something of its spirit to Dickens; what is known of these Christmases past was in part defined by the Dickens philosophy.**48**

A Christmas Carol (both a single volume and collected as one of the *Christmas Books,* 1852) continued to sell so well that by 1892 the author's son could announce in his introduction to the Macmillan collected edition that it "shares with *Pickwick* and *David Copperfield* the distinction of being the most universally popular of all the books of Charles Dickens." This sustained interest in the old Christmas story was in part supported by Dickens himself in his public readings; *A Christmas Carol* was the first of his books to be read publicly, and it remained the most frequently read adaptation of his works in all his public tours. Since that statement of Charles Dickens the Younger, the first Christmas book has gone beyond the popularity of even *Pickwick* and *David Copperfield*.

Although the public taste for the story has remained consistent, the critical response has been mixed. "Who can listen to objections regarding such a book as this?" Thackeray wrote in his review. "It seems to me to be a national benefit, and to every man or woman who reads it, a personal kindness." Obviously many others have found things to object to in the story. It has been seen as "saturated with exaggerated Christmas fervour" and "larded with soggy and indigestible lumps of sickly sentiment"; "neither in conception nor characterization" can this book be placed "in the same class as the greater novels."[49] By the latter part of the nineteenth century, Dickens had fallen out of favor with most critics, and he could not seriously be considered an artist. "He knew nothing of the nobler power of superstition," complained John Ruskin, "was essentially a stage manager, and used everything for effect on the pit... it is Dickens' delight in grotesque and rich exaggerations which has made him, I think, nearly useless in the present day. I do not believe he has made *any* one more good-natured."[50] Dickens, however, remained beloved by the poets. Swinburne found the story "delightful" and argued that, if Dickens had never written any lengthier work, he "would still be great among the immortal writers of his age by grace of his matchless excellences as a writer of short stories," particularly the earliest Christmas Books.[51] The young Robert Louis Stevenson, too, was profoundly affected by these stories; as he wrote a friend, "they are too much perhaps. I have only read two of them yet, and feel so good after them and would do anything, yes and shall do anything, to make it a little better for people.... I want to go out and comfort some one; I shall never listen to the nonsense they tell one about not giving money—I *shall* give money; not that I haven't done so always, but I shall do it with a high hand now."[52] Despite such praises for the little books, it became conventional not merely to underrate Dickens' powers as an artist but also to deride his popularity. "In literature as in dress," André Maurois explained in his appreciation of Dickens, "there are fashions. Certain books are deemed beautiful or graceless, certain authors admirable or damnable, not because the reader experiences pleasant or unpleasant emotions, but because he ought to experience them."[53]

During the twentieth century the fashion has slowly

Charles Dickens reading, *The Illustrated London News*, March 19, 1870. Courtesy The Library of Congress

49 Norman Berrow, "Some Candid Opinions on *A Christmas Carol*," *The Dickensian*, Winter 1937–1938, p. 21; and Nicholas Bentley, "Dickens and His Illustrators," *Charles Dickens 1812–1870, A Centenary Volume*, edited by E. W. F. Tomlin (London: Weidenfeld and Nicolson, 1969, p. 219). Bentley evidently agrees with George Gissing who, in *Charles Dickens; A Critical Study* (1903), wrote that he could not find in *A Christmas Carol* "anything to be seriously compared with the finer features of his novels."

50 In two letters to Charles Eliot Norton, June 19 and July 8, 1870 (*The Works of John Ruskin*, edited by E. T. Cook and Alexander Wedderburn [London: George Allen; New York: Longmans, Green & Co., 1909], vol. 37, pp. 7, 10).

51 In "Charles Dickens," *A Pilgrimage of Pleasure* (Boston: Richard D. Badger and the Gorham Press, 1913), pp. 104–5.

52 In a letter to Mrs. Sitwell, September 1874 (*The Letters of Robert Louis Stevenson*, edited by Sidney Colvin [New York: Charles Scribner's Sons, 1911], vol. 1, p. 178).
   Elliott L. Gilbert, in "The Ceremony of Innocence: Charles Dickens' *A Christmas Carol*" (*PMLA*, January 1975, p. 29), argued that Stevenson, in his short story "Markheim," "reproduces... the basic philosophical structure of Dickens' tale."

53 *Dickens*, André Maurois, translated by Hamish Miles (London: John Lane, 1934), p. 107.

54 Michael Steig, "Dickens' Excremental Vision," *Victorian Studies* (March 1970), pp. 339–54.

"Scrooge" by Charles Dana Gibson, *People of Dickens*, 1899. *Courtesy The New York Public Library, Astor, Lenox and Tilden Foundations*

turned in favor of Dickens, and by the centenary of his death in 1970, he was universally recognized as one of the great literary figures of the Victorian Age. Disgust with *A Christmas Carol* has persisted in some literary circles. Many agree with Richard Aldington's evaluation in *Four English Portraits* (1948): one must be a "ruthless" Dickensian to deny that the death of Tiny Tim is "an unwarrantable hitting below the sentimental belt, . . . that the conversion of Ebenezer Scrooge is as full of cant as it is of improbability." While some critics persist in overlooking the Christmas stories, others have published a few eccentric studies based upon current literary trends. For example, it has been argued that Dickens á la Jonathan Swift had an "excremental vision," apparent in *A Christmas Carol;* thus descriptions of the London fog and even Bob Cratchit's "stool" are given unconscious symbolic significance which unfortunately discloses more about the critic's obsessions than those of the author.**54** Similarly, Elliot L. Gilbert in his essay "The Ceremony of Innocence: Charles Dickens' *A Christmas Carol*" (PMLA, January 1975) unconvincingly argued "the Scrooge problem," that the miser's conversion is immediate and lacks psychological depth, with support from the opinions of several eminent scholars; but this approach is actually a study of Dickens' critics, not of Dickens. Sadly, such indulgences in scholarly taste waste much fine intellectual energy in the pursuit of confining a classic piece of writing to a narrow literary trend or to support a current critical prejudice.

Of far more significance are the few modern voices that have praised *A Christmas Carol*, not as a minor work in the Dickens canon but as a crucial milestone in the development of the artist as a mature writer. Chesterton early recognized the importance of this book in Dickens' total output. "The mystery of Christmas is in a manner identical with the mystery of Dickens," he explained in *Appreciations and Criticisms of the Works of Charles Dickens* (1911). "If ever we adequately explain the one we may adequately explain the other." Likewise, Edmund Wilson in his pivotal study "Dickens: The Two Scrooges" of *The Wound and the Bow* (1941) took as metaphor for Dickens' entire career the story of the miser's conversion. "If we try, after rereading the whole of Dickens, to forget the detail of this immense mass of people and scenes, and to isolate the two or three essential impressions which dominate the rest and in a way give the general tone," Maurois suggested in his fine study, "I feel for my own part that I should be left first and foremost with certain scenes from the Christmas books." Edgar

Johnson, author of the finest critical biography of Charles Dickens, credited *A Christmas Carol* with being "indeed the very core of Dickens' vision of what the relations between men should be, a warm and glowing celebration of sympathy and love."[55]

In considering the persistent criticisms of *A Christmas Carol*, the reader may learn how truly significant a work of art the book is. A major complaint has been —as in the words of Nicholas Bentley—"Scrooge is hardly more than a symbol of avarice"; the miser is merely a puppet manipulated by the author to the point of his unconvincing conversion. This simplistic platitude cannot be supported by a reading of the text of *A Christmas Carol*. To understand Scrooge, one must also comprehend the nature of Dickens' characters in general. Chesterton tried to defend Dickens by arguing that all his figures are caricatures, and then proceeded to prove that there is an art in exaggeration; perhaps George Orwell was more perceptive in his analysis of Dickens' creations. He recognized that the novelist "did not think of himself as a caricaturist, and was constantly setting in action characters who ought to be static."[56] "The monstrosities he created," Orwell continued, "are still remembered as monstrosities, in spite of getting mixed up in would-be probable melodramas. Their first impact is so vivid that nothing that comes afterwards effaces it."

Ebenezer Scrooge is a fine example of Orwell's argument. When first met, the miser is portrayed in such broad strokes that he could easily be the ogre of any family, not just the Cratchits. Dickens' method is caricature: "a squeezing, wrenching, grasping, scraping, clutching, covetous old sinner!" He exudes a dreary atmosphere of "his own low temperature always about him," as prevalent as the London fog or as engulfing as "the infernal atmosphere" of Marley's Ghost. In his words as in his actions, Scrooge lives up to his physical description. He is cold to his clerk's comfort and feels no sympathy for his nephew. When asked to give to charity, he replies in the cant of the utilitarian economic theoreticians of the time: "Are there no prisons? Are there no workhouses? If they would rather die, they had better do it, and decrease the surplus population." At first glance, Dickens has created a man without qualities. So strong and convincing is this introduction that the name "Scrooge" has entered the language as descriptive of the most hardhearted of misers.

Yet Scrooge is not so simple a character as first presented. One quality of his personality which anticipates the possibility of his redemption is his sense of

55 Edgar Johnson, "Dickens: The Dark Pilgrimage," *Charles Dickens 1812–1870*, p. 50.

56 "Charles Dickens" (1939), *Critical Essays* (London: Secker and Warburg, 1946), pp. 7–56.

humor. This characteristic was made more evident in Dickens' public readings. Charles Kent in *Dickens As A Reader* (1872) noted that Scrooge's "Good morning!" aimed at his nephew was "delivered with irresistibly ludicrous iteration." The callous attack on Christmas with its wild threat of boiling in Christmas puddings and driving stakes of holly through hearts also suggests the miser's "keen sense of humour," and "one almost feels as if he were laughing in his sleeve from the very commencement." The tone is sarcasm, as when Scrooge tells his nephew, "You're quite a powerful speaker, I wonder you don't go into Parliament."

This strange suggestion of humor is further developed in the interview with Marley's Ghost. During this discussion, one is jarred by Scrooge's flippancy and lack of fearful respect. His jokes are made with some reluctance, but his attitude still conflicts with the reader's initial presentation of the "old screw." Here perhaps Dickens' attitude as the author should be considered. He portrays Scrooge at the start exactly as the businessman wishes to be seen by the world. As he has no friends, no confidants, and "nobody ever stopped him in the street," his character is determined by how he acts in his office and how he treats the few people he will have business with. The "squeezing, wrenching, grasping, clutching, covetous old sinner" is the public Scrooge.

It is, however, when Marley's Ghost appears that the reader gets a glimpse of the private Scrooge. Dickens as the omnipotent author can portray the intimate Scrooge, in his dressing gown, behind his apartment door, in a state none of his associates have had the opportunity to observe. Even the initial materialization of the spirit does not disrupt Scrooge's privacy; he views the spirit as an hallucination, of his own creation, not of imagination through fancy but instead through the cold facts of indigestion; the specter is no more than a bit of beef, a blot of mustard, a crumb of cheese, a fragment of an underdone potato, to the pragmatic Scrooge. His joke that there is more of gravy than the grave about this spirit is but a private jest of the hidden Scrooge.

Dickens is not satisfied to leave the impression that this is a contradictory characteristic of the miser's personality. He demands sympathy for this man. When the spirit screams and Scrooge falls to his knees, the miser's actions that follow are as shocking as the apparition's. One could hardly predict from the Scrooge of Dickens' initial description that anything could affect this man, as "hard and sharp as flint, from which

Pen and watercolor drawing of Marley's Ghost by Ronald Searle, *A Christmas Carol*, 1961. *Courtesy Perpetua Books*

no steel had ever struck out generous fire." His indifference to the wretched state of the poor would
seem to prove that nothing could affect his own purposes. Yet in the interview with Marley's Ghost, Dickens has stripped Scrooge of all his defenses. Through
his terror, the horrible old man earns the reader's sympathies. During the conversation, he displays humility
and desires comfort from the spirit; he is not unlike
other men. He expresses a touch of tenderness toward
his old partner: he inquires why the specter is chained
and admits they had always been good friends. The
Scrooge here presented is psychologically more complex than in his introduction. Clearly this man may
receive salvation.

Orwell complained that "Dickens' characters have
no mental life. They say perfectly the thing that they
have to say, but they cannot be conceived as anything
else. They never learn, they never speculate." Obviously Orwell has forgotten the story of the miser's redemption. Ebenezer Scrooge's example may be unique
in Dickens' work: the story's motivation is the re-
generation of a single lost soul; it is basically a one-
character narrative told through the mind of the protagonist. Dickens carefully unfolds the secret workings
of this man's mind and heart. The possibility of retribution is first evident in the journey with the Ghost
of Christmas Past. When taken back to his boyhood
home, the old man cries out in joy and a tear of happiness falls down his cheek. When the ghost confronts
him with the reality of this sentiment, Scrooge shrugs
it off as a pimple. This crustiness soon passes; on viewing the Norfolk coach filled with laughing boys on
their way home for the holidays, Dickens asks, "Why
did his cold eye glisten, and his heart leap as they went
past! Why was he filled with gladness when he heard
them give each other Merry Christmas!" How could
these feelings be aroused in the same man who said, "If
I could work my will, every idiot who goes about with
'Merry Christmas,' on his lips, should be boiled with
his own pudding, and buried with a stake of holly
through his heart"?

Through the visitations of the three spirits, Dickens
reveals further the repressed feelings of this once seemingly unredeemable soul. At first these gentler sentiments appear to be selfish; he cries as he pities his
former self, a boy left alone in a dismal schoolhouse
during the holidays. The touching memories of his
childhood affect him emotionally because he once experienced them, but they also teach him a lesson. He
shows that he is not without sympathy for his fellowman; he atones for the three sins committed earlier in

Pen and wash drawing of the Ghost of Christmas
Past by Ronald Searle, *A Christmas Carol*, 1961.
Courtesy Perpetua Books

the day. On seeing himself, a lonely forgotten boy, he reflects on his abuse to a young caroler. At the introduction of his beloved sister Fanny when a little girl, Scrooge remembers her son, his nephew Fred, and seems "uneasy in his mind," likely regretting his harsh words to the young man. And finally, during the wild gaiety of the Fezziwig Ball, he takes a moment to consider his own cruel treatment of his poor clerk, and he expresses a glint of remorse for his callousness. His deep concern for others is given further development when, at the Cratchits' poor house with the Ghost of Christmas Present, Scrooge shows true concern for a child's fate:

"Spirit," said Scrooge, with an interest he had never felt before, "tell me if Tiny Tim will live."

"I see a vacant seat," replied the Ghost, "in the poor chimney corner, and a crutch without an owner, carefully preserved. If these shadows remain unaltered by the Future, the child will die."

"No, no," said Scrooge. "Oh no, kind Spirit! say he will be spared."

These sentiments of painful remorse are prevalent in the scenes he is shown. He weeps on seeing himself as a child; on hearing a tune known to his sister and sung by his niece, "he softened more and more and thought that if he could have listened to it often, years ago, he might have cultivated the kindness of life for his own happiness with his own hands, without resorting to the sexton's spade that buried Jacob Marley." He pitifully realizes the lost possibilities of his avaricious life when he sees the daughter of his former sweetheart Belle: "and when he thought that such another creature, quite as graceful and as full of promise, might have called him father, and been a springtime in the haggard winter of his life, his sight grew very dim indeed." In the sad scene where he breaks off his engagement, the girl gives him the key to his salvation, "in a changed nature, in an altered spirit, in another atmosphere of life, another Hope as its great end." The process of his change of mind is affected by that of his heart; the emotional instructs the intellectual. In these journeys with the spirits, the other atmosphere is revived in him. In the lifting of his cold, hard character like the passing of the dismal fog to the glorious golden sunshine of Christmas day, it is evident that Scrooge was not totally free of the Christmas spirit; it just lay dormant within him. So little was needed to revive it: the old man is so caught up in the gaiety of forfeits at his nephew's party that "wholly forgetting in the interest he had in what was going on, that his voice made no

"She left him, and they parted" by Arthur Rackham, *A Christmas Carol*, 1915

sound in their ears, he sometimes came out with a guess quite loud, and very often guessed right, too." So carried away with the festivities of the Fezziwig Ball, Scrooge seems to be "speaking unconsciously like his former, not his latter self." Chesterton's supposition that Scrooge was all along secretly dispersing Christmas turkeys to the poor is pure fancy, but certainly the old man had also retained within him like the flame of memory never completely "bonneted" the possibility of resurrecting his old Christmas spirit.

His choice to isolate himself from all the joys and nuisances of daily life has allowed him to forget the sentiments that were once part of his character; the process of his return to his former self is long and carefully constructed. In the pictures of the Cratchit household, Scrooge finds the example for his later life and the medium for his salvation. When he poignantly asks that the Ghost of Christmas Yet to Come show him "some tenderness connected with a death," he is spirited to the Cratchits' first Christmas following the recent death of Tiny Tim. Scrooge at this point is ready to alter his life; he will accept whatever the spirit shows him. That his conversion is an active process is evident in that, when he is taken to his office, he sees no figure of himself: "It gave him little surprise, however, for he had been revolving in his mind a change of life, and thought and hoped he saw his new-born resolutions carried out in this." Despite this seemingly encouraging sign, he is confronted with his true legacy: death. His only mark on the world is a cold, gray stone in a forgotten graveyard. Confronted with this vision of no apparent means to absolve himself, Scrooge promises to alter the future, not only his own welfare but that of his fellowmen. This change of life is not so sudden (as Chesterton said) "as the conversion of a man at a Salvation Army"; the process as presented in Dickens' narrative is precise and subtle, playing on the man's deeper repressed feelings aroused from a recollection of his former self, an education through the example of his clerk and nephew, and a warning of what his fate will be should he follow the same path in life. Scrooge must admit with the chemist Redlaw of *The Haunted Man* the necessity of every life, even that of an old bachelor miser:

In the material world, as I have long taught, nothing can be spared; no step or atom in the wondrous structure could be lost, without a blank being made in the great universe. I know, now, that it is the same with good and evil, happiness and sorrow, in the memories of men.

"'How are you?' said one..." by Arthur Rackham, *A Christmas Carol*, 1915

"Bob Cratchit and Tiny Tim on Christmas Day"
by Jessie Willcox Smith, *Dickens's Children*, 1912.
Courtesy Charles Scribner's Sons

Scrooge must agree with Jacob Marley, "Mankind was my business!" Clearly, of the two demon children protected by the Ghost of Christmas Present, the one Scrooge in his own life must beware of is the boy Ignorance.

As determined by the slow steps in the miser's alteration, Scrooge's failure as a human being began in his suppressing the sentiments of his childhood. "If we can only preserve ourselves from growing up," Dickens explained in "When we stopped growing" (*Household Words*, January 1, 1853, p. 363), "we shall never grow old and the young may love us to the last. Not to be too wise, not to be too stately, not to be too rough with innocent fancies, or to treat them with too much lightness —which is as bad—are points to be remembered that may do us all good in our years to come." Dickens actively kept these thoughts in his life as well as in his writing. In composing Scrooge's life, Dickens relied on his own: the boy Scrooge is the boy Dickens, the Cratchits of Camden Town were the Dickenses of Bayham Street. "Here was a child who had suffered," explained Maurois, "who was to keep all through his life that sympathy with the poor which cannot easily be attained by those who have not lived the life of the poor. . . . From now on he would have a war to wage against the hard of heart who exploit children, against the hypocrites who style themselves religious and yet lack charity, against bullying schoolmasters, against prisons and poverty and insolence, and he would wage it victoriously." Unlike the miserly Scrooge, Dickens kept his childhood active within himself. "No one, at any rate no English writer," wrote Orwell, "has written better about childhood than Dickens. In spite of the fact that children are now comparatively sanely treated, no novelist has shown the same power of entering into the child's point of view." Dickens displayed this rare ability in recording Scrooge's childhood and both the joyous and pitiful scenes in the Cratchit home. The first indication of retribution comes in the return to Scrooge's childhood. Through his avarice he has denied his natural feelings of wonder and joy in favor of indifference to the troubled world, but on his recollection of times past, his reactions are unashamed and instinctual, for the ghost has touched him deeply. On spotting the old, familiar country road, the old man cries out "with fervour"; on recognizing Ali Baba, he proclaims the name "in ecstasy." These recollections of course are not all pleasant, because nostalgia demands a touch of pain in the joy.

For Dickens it is not enough to merely recollect what it was like to be a child; one must also be like a child. What distinguishes Scrooge from his clerk is that Bob Cratchit has not forgotten how to be childish. Despite the hard facts of poverty, Cratchit never suspects it below his dignity to go down a slide with a group of boys or to play blindman's buff. Similarly, the miser's nephew, although neglected by his uncle, too retains the spirit of a child within him as he fills his Christmas with children's games. In his journey, Scrooge awakens to this characteristic of both his clerk and nephew. The metaphor that Dickens most frequently employs to describe Scrooge at his most joyous and uninhibited is that of a child. When the Ghost of Christmas Present motions them to leave Fred's party, Scrooge begs "like a boy to be allowed to stay until the guests depart." In his conversion, Scrooge admits to being "as merry as a schoolboy." This childish spirit even infects the narrator himself, as in his reference to Belle's children "What would I not have given to be one of them! . . . I should have liked, I do confess, to have had the lightest license of a child, and yet been man enough to know its value."

It is through a child that Scrooge will earn his inevitable salvation. Although he has neglected his nephew and in releasing Belle he has no children of his own, Scrooge has another chance to redeem himself through being "a second father" to Tiny Tim. Marley's Ghost laments, "Were there no poor homes to which [that Blessed Star] would have conducted *me!*" This warning is exemplified by another spirit, similarly fettered with the symbols of his avarice, "who cried piteously at being unable to assist a wretched woman and an infant." Scrooge's second visitor, both man and child, arouses in Scrooge through glimpses of childhood past regret for his abuse of another child, the caroler he threatened with a ruler. In Scrooge lies the prototype of David Copperfield; this child "deserted by his schoolmates" is the same figure of "singular abilities, quick, eager, delicate, and soon hurt, bodily and mentally," the boy Charles Dickens abused by his parents' indifference and bullied by an unjust educational system. This boy is a character often portrayed in Dickens' work: the child surprisingly unchildlike in his observations.

Here lies a paradox in Dickens' conception of childhood and what constitutes the childlike spirit. What is most sympathetic about the adults, Scrooge, Bob Cratchit, and Fred, becomes apparent when they act childish; what is most remarkable about the children is their maturity. Pip of *Great Expectations* is surprisingly observant for his tender years: "Within myself, I had sustained from my time when I could speak that my sister

"He had been Tiny Tim's blood-horse all the way from church" by Arthur Rackham, *A Christmas Carol,* 1915

... was unjust to me." Paul Dombey is even more extreme; he was "never so distressed as by the company of children. . . . 'Go away, if you please,' he would say to any child who came to bear him company. 'Thank you, but I don't want to.'" This ambivalence toward other children is shared by Judy Smallweed of *Bleak House* (1853) who "never owned a doll, never heard of Cinderella, never played at any game. She once or twice fell into children's company when she was about ten years old, but the children couldn't get on with Judy, and Judy couldn't get on with them. She seemed like an animal of another species, and there was instinctive repugnance on both sides." She is but one branch on the great family tree of adult children. "There has only been one child in the Smallweed family for several generations," Dickens described Judy's lineage. "Little old men and women there have been, but no child, until Mr. Smallweed's grandmother, now living, became weak in her intellect, and fell (for the first time) into a childish state."

Among these mature children must be included Tiny Tim. He is remarkably reflective, with an almost supernatural power of observation, that baffles even his loving father:

Somehow he gets thoughtful sitting by himself so much, and thinks the strangest things you ever heard. He told me . . . that he hoped the people saw him in the church, because he was a cripple, and it might be pleasant to them to remember upon Christmas Day, who made lame beggers walk, and blind men see.

This wretched crippled boy possesses the wisdom that Scrooge so sorely lacks. During the joyous merrymaking of the Cratchit home, this child takes time to sing "a song about a lost child in the snow." It is this character who adds the more perceptive and original corollary to his father's greeting: "God bless us every one!" This child of "singular abilities, quick, eager, delicate" even in death possesses a "childish essence from God." If "these shadows remain unaltered," the fate of child creatures like Tiny Tim and Paul Dombey is the grave. The other individuals robbed of their childhoods like Scrooge and Tom Gradgrind of *Hard Times* become social monsters. Because the old man sees his folly, Tiny Tim does not die. Scrooge realizes that although the losses of his own life may not be recovered, perhaps this boy may not have to run a similar course under that other idol Gain. In *The Haunted Man*, Dickens presented a horrifying vision of the consequences due to neglect of the child:

All within this desolate creature is barren wilderness. All within the man bereft . . . is the same barren wilderness. . . . From every seed of evil in this boy, a field of ruin is grown that shall be gathered in, and garnered up, and sown again in many places in the world, until regions are overspread with wickedness enough to raise the waters of another Deluge. Open and unpunished murder in a city's streets would be less guilty in its daily toleration, than one such spectacle as this. . . . He is the growth of man's indifference; you are the growth of man's presumption. The beneficent design of Heaven is, in each case, overthrown, and from the two poles of the immaterial world you come together.

The warning Scrooge views in the demon children Want and Ignorance; he is shown the terrible seeds of human indifference. By his concern for Tiny Tim, Scrooge may act as an example as to how each person might prevent the approaching plague.

Dickens' view of the child goes beyond his personal obsession derived from his own experience and beyond the immediate beneficence toward a single child to an accusation of the society as a whole as to its terrible responsibility. *A Christmas Carol* may be seen, as in the words of Edgar Johnson, as "a serio-comic parable of social redemption: the miserly Scrooge is the embodiment of the pursuit of material gain and indifference to human welfare represented by both the businessmen and the nineteenth century economists, and his conversion is a symbol of that change of heart in society on which Dickens had set his own heart."[57] Scrooge is the archetypical "economic man," the utilitarian who exists only for the accumulation of money; he prays to that other idol Gain, for he is a disciple of what Carlyle called the cult of Mammonism. Scrooge's life like Marley's is weighed down by "cashboxes, keys, padlocks, ledgers, deeds, and heavy purses wrought in steel." His profession demands precision, exactness, and has no place for human sentiment that might unbalance the laws of mathematics and economics; appropriately, he threatens the young caroler with a ruler.

In his callous opinions, Scrooge reiterates the economic cant of the political theorists of his day. The poor are poor because they have made themselves so, and Scrooge cannot be bothered to provide the means "to make idle people merry." The only refuges Scrooge is willing to provide for them are the prisons and the workhouses. His debt to society has been paid through compulsory taxation; there is no need for him to provide charity at Christmas or any other day of the year. He loses nothing in these transactions, because the

[57] Johnson, "Dickens: The Dark Pilgrimage," p. 50.

Color woodcut of Marley's Ghost by Philip Reed,
A Christmas Carol in Prose, 1940. *Courtesy Philip Reed*

Treadmill and Poor Law were instituted to protect men such as him from being cheated by their creditors. Whatever might be the correct solution to the dilemma, Scrooge does not care whether the poor live or die as long as they do not disrupt his utilitarian ends.

Scrooge does not merely express the ideas of popular political cant, but also his character is motivated by its hardhearted facts. He views all sentiment as humbug; any emotion that might hinder business is nonsense. At the burial of his partner, he honors it not with bereavement but with the making of an undoubted bargain. He completely lacks a sense of the fanciful; any flight of the imagination must have some basis in fact, in indigestion or a cold in the head. He comprehends nothing beyond his "factious purposes." Not even his senses can be trusted when they present something so extraordinary as his dead partner's ghost. He may see the apparition, but, because it does not conform to his narrow, utilitarian worldview, it is mere "humbug."

This economic man is confronted by another utilitarian, his partner Marley. The ghost tries to warn his friend of the false path he followed in life and what road he should have taken: "The common welfare was my business; charity, mercy, forbearance, and benevolence, were, all, my business." To have saved him from ceaseless wanderings after death, all that would have been needed was for him to improve the condition of one poor family. The true defender of the destitute is the Ghost of Christmas Present. This vision of Father Christmas is the only purely active spirit in the story. The Ghost of Christmas Past has the ability to present only "shadows of the things that have been"; it does not judge, it cannot alter what has been. The Ghost of Christmas Yet To Come lacks any power for reflection; this grim reaper cannot be diverted from its inevitable course. Only the Ghost of Christmas Present has the ability to comment on the events and to offer alternatives to Scrooge's miserable life.

This ghost early establishes its position. It explains that the light of its torch falls most of all upon a poor dinner "because it needs it most." It demonstrates no patience with the narrow Puritanism that would deny the common man his simple pleasures in the name of God. The most spirited Christmas scenes are those of the less fortunate. The working classes running to the bakeries for a hot holiday meal are as festive as "the Lord Mayor, in the stronghold of the mighty Mansion House." The ghost finds its way to the hovel of a Cornish miner and his family and on to a ship in a storm at sea. The most memorable holiday scenes in all

English literature are those in the humble house of Bob Cratchit and the lower-middle-class parlor of Scrooge's nephew Fred. Despite their poverty, each can sing some ancient carol whose cheer transcends their common misery.

There may be tenderness in these pictures of poverty, but the ghost shows no mercy toward Scrooge. At the height of the holiday season, following a children's Twelfth Night party, Scrooge is bluntly confronted with two children who know nothing of twelfth-cake and conjuring. The Ghost of Christmas Present in a voice like Thomas Carlyle's discloses the monster girl and boy, Want and Ignorance, protected in the folds of his robe. These two miserable creatures embody Dickens' most powerful indictment of the utilitarian mind. Without the spirit of Christmas to comfort them, the narrow Puritanism and Mammonism would release these wretched beings upon the world. They foreshadow the Ghost of Christmas Yet To Come whose work they will do should Man in the present not shelter them. Society has a responsibility to find a new solution to prevent the crime and misery apparent only as children at the moment. When Scrooge demands if the two have any refuge, the ghost cruelly replies in Scrooge's own words the evil economic cant, "Are there no prisons? Are there no workhouses?" Notice how easily Dickens makes the transition from the two demon children to the fearful Ghost of Christmas Yet To Come; in the third spirit lies the Doom which must be erased from the child's brow. Dickens argues that not only is the creation of a poor class the result of the whim of the wealthy but also the possibility of protection and advancement for a better life also restricted by the interests of the rich.

What Dickens offers as a solution to the social condition is a change of heart. The Christmas spirit that harbors these children is their only refuge; only if it dwells within other men can the Doom be removed from their young brows. As Orwell observed, "It seems that in every attack Dickens makes upon society he is always pointing to a change in spirit rather than a change of structure." Dickens does not give specific alternatives. He does not disclose how Scrooge was a second father to Tiny Tim. The author consciously avoids such specifics, as when Scrooge, in telling the portly gentleman his offer, discreetly whispers into the gentleman's ear. Dickens gives no ready-made plan to be followed.

As a political tract, *A Christmas Carol* fails dismally. "From one angle the *Christmas Carol* appears as propaganda in favour of pathetic resignation," argued T. A.

Color woodcut of Bob Cratchit and Tiny Tim by Philip Reed, *A Christmas Carol in Prose*, 1940. *Courtesy Philip Reed*

58 As Scrooge in speaking of Fezziwig defines the relationship between employer and employed: "He has the power to render us happy or unhappy; to make our service light or burdensome; a pleasure or a toil. Say that his power lies in words and looks; in things so slight and insignificant that it is impossible to add and count 'em up: what then? The happiness he gives, is quite as great as if it cost a fortune."

Jackson in *Charles Dickens: The Progress of A Radical* (1938). "Bob Cratchit . . . has little enough to be thankful for, and yet is presented as still finding excuses for his wretched old screw of an employer. . . . For Bob Cratchit a miserly boss was, in a time of economic depression such as prevailed in 1843, just one more of those ills which, since it could not be cured, must be endured." The change in consciousness must come from the employer, not the employee; Bob Cratchit never demands what Carlyle thought every working man deserved, "a fair day's wages for a fair day's work." Dickens sees nothing in the clerk's character to be criticized; as expressed in his speech before the Manchester Atheneum, the relationship between employer and employed, like that of squire and servant at Dingley Dell, is one of mutual trust and benevolence.**58** It is Scrooge, not Bob Cratchit, who must change. Dickens defined his purpose as "in a whimsical kind of masque which the good humour of the season justified, to awaken some loving and forebearing thoughts, never out of season in a Christian land." Dickens' means toward economic reform is to change the individual who is the cause of the injust system, not the system itself; it is psychological, not political. Evidently Dickens saw no need to change the structure of society before there were better people to live in it. Most social critics prefer the argument that a change in the system will ultimately improve human nature. Dickens' purposes perhaps explain in part why his story is still frowned upon by the utilitarian world. Dickens' argument appeals more to the poet than to the political scientist.

In considering the social intent of this "carol in prose," one must recognize how unreligious a Christmas story it is. Lang found it merely "Christianity illuminated by the flames of punch." Dickens' religious convictions did not correspond to the Established Church. He did not accept its dogmas and had little interest in questions of miracles. When he refers in *A Christmas Carol* to Biblical characters, they appear on tiles in an old fireplace; they seem to have more in common with children's storybooks than with the Holy Scriptures. Dickens' Christmas story surprisingly lacks any major church scene; although the spirits take the miser to many holiday gatherings, never once do they visit a place of worship. "His Christmas," explained Ruskin, "meant mistletoe and pudding—neither resurrection from the dead, nor rising of new stars, nor teaching of wise men, nor shepherds." Dickens' story is free of clerical preaching; *A Christmas Carol* is a domestic sermon. When referring to current pious dogma, Dickens attacks rather than supports its tenets; he judges it according to how it affects the common man, and if it is wanting in charity, he voices his opposition. He does not tolerate callous Puritanism: "There are some upon this earth of yours who lay claim to know us, and who do their deeds of passion, pride, ill-will, hatred and bigotry, and selfishness in our name; who are strangers to us and all our kith and kin, as if they had never lived." He had no need for "mysteries and squabbles for forms" when the people these principles should be confronting remain "in a state so miserable and so neglected, that their very nature rebels against the simplest religion." Through *A Christmas Carol* Dickens offered a popular religion that he hoped would touch all men. As Thackeray understood, this "charity sermon" is free of theological discussion and full of simple holiday pleasures and feelings: "I believe it occasioned immense hospitality throughout England; was the means of lighting up hundreds of kind fires at Christmas time; caused a wonderful outpouring of Christmas good-feeling; of Christmas punch-brewing; an awful slaughter of Christmas turkeys, and roasting and basting of Christmas beef."**59** Dickens' "charity-sermon" was to be preached, not in the pulpit at Westminster, but by the hearth of the common man.

Dickens did not ignore the Christmas story in his book. His carol refers many times to the Biblical accounts, but what Dickens emphasizes are the good works of Christ. His sympathies were at one time linked to the Unitarian Church and its creed, "Believe in the supremacy of God the Father, and in the humanity and divine mission of Jesus of Nazareth." It has been suggested that the theme of *A Christmas Carol* parallels an axiom of the popular contemporary theologian Thomas Arnold, "the salvation of man's soul is effected by the change in his heart and life wrought by Christ's spirit."**60** This humanity of Christ was what Dickens tried to teach his own children in his introduction to *The Life of Our Lord* (1849): "No one ever lived, who was so good, so kind, so gentle, and so sorry for all people who did wrong, or were in any way ill or miserable, as He was." He stressed the poverty of Christ and that he chose his disciples from among the poor: "Heaven was made for them as well as for the rich, and God makes no difference between those who wear good clothes and those who go barefoot and in rags. The most miserable, the most ugly, deformed, wretched creatures that live, will be bright Angels in Heaven if they are good here on earth." And it is through an active Christ, his good works and example, that Dickens derived his

59 In a lecture "Charity and Humour" (1853) (quoted in *Dickens: The Critical Heritage*, edited by Philip Collins [London: Routledge and Kegan Paul, 1971], p. 354).

60 According to N. C. Peyrouton, "The Life of Our Lord," *The Dickensian*, Spring Number, May 1963, p. 106.

religion; as Tiny Tim observed, one must reflect during this season of merrymaking on "He who made lame beggers walk and blind men see."

Central to Dickens' interpretation of Christ's teachings is His attitude toward children. When Scrooge visits the Cratchit home at the death of Tiny Tim, he hears a line from the Gospels: "And He took a child, and set him in the midst of them." Christ's tenderness toward a little child is the religious teaching that Scrooge must follow. Marley's Ghost laments, "Why did I walk through crowds of fellow-beings with my eyes turned down, and never raise them to that blessed Star which led the Wise Men to a poor abode?" Like the Wise Men, Scrooge is led by a Christmas vision to the home of a poor child, Tiny Tim, whom through Christ's example the miser might save him from his sad fate. Christmas as a time for children has a scriptural basis: "it is good to be children sometimes, and never better at Christmas, when its mighty Founder was a child himself." Through the divine grace of this Christmas spirit, Scrooge discovers his particular salvation in coming to the aid of this Christchildlike boy. Truly, as Dickens suggests, "Spirit of Tiny Tim, thy childish essence was from God!"

All these intentions, personal, social, religious, are well meaning, yet they would be sought in other sources if *A Christmas Carol* did not succeed as a work of literature. Chesterton argued that "the historical and moral importance is really even greater than the literary importance," but this conclusion does not explain why this story in particular should survive all the other well-intentioned pamphlets of the last century. *A Christmas Carol* is a work of art and must be considered as such to place it firmly in its proper perspective within Dickens' work.

Despite the ghost machinery (and the author's jest "in this Ghostly little book, to raise the Ghost of an idea"), the story's form cannot strictly be labeled "a ghost story." "For all his moral Christmas ghosts, and his interest in the ghostly," wrote Andrew Lang in his introduction to the *Christmas Books* (1897), "Dickens never...wrote a good ghost story *au naturel*. He brought in the fantastically grotesque: he had not the success in this province, because he had not the seriousness, of De Foe, of Scott, and Bulwer-Lytton." *A Christmas Carol* is closer to being a fable, and such a form demands a strict structure. As Edgar Johnson observed, the story is a seriocomic parable of social redemption. Marley's Ghost is the symbol of divine grace, and the three Christmas Spirits are the working of that grace through the agencies of memory, example, and fear."**61** Weaknesses have crept into the design. For example, if the Ghost of Christmas Past is the agent of memory, the scene in Belle's home seven years ago does not seem justified; unless he were in the habit of being a Peeping Tom, Scrooge never experienced this recollection. In tone as in detail, this scene seems to be more characteristic of the journey with the Ghost of Christmas Present. It seems to repeat the sentiment of the previous scene, the breakup of the engagement; Dickens in his public readings wisely deleted the arbitrary episode. The scene is rarely included in other adaptations of the text.**62**

As Lang explained, Dickens created "a ghost with a purpose." His structure remains complex and clear. Chesterton found the story as "everywhere irregular. . . . It has the same kind of artistic unity that belongs to a dream. . . . The incidents change wildly: the story scarcely changes at all. *The Christmas Carol* is a kind of philanthropic dream, an enjoyable nightmare, in which the scenes shift bewilderingly and seem as miscellaneous as the pictures in a scrapbook, but in which there is one, constant state of the soul, a state of rowdy benediction and a hunger for human faces." Chesterton, however, failed to look beneath the surface of event; although a dream, the story does not ramble from its intent or its plan. Nearly every one of these "bewildering scenes" has a specific purpose in the direction of Dickens' parable. Although the technique of shifting scenes is sprawling, the line of argument moves as steadily as the unfaltering Ghost of Christmas Yet To Come. Nearly every act and attitude of Scrooge in the opening pages of the book is revived later in the narrative. Through the revelations of his past life, he regrets his past cruelties, to the boy singing a carol, to his nephew, and to his clerk. The Ghost of Christmas Present plays devil's advocate when he confronts Scrooge with his own callous political theories. Through the Ghost of Christmas Yet To Come, Scrooge sees the consequences of these acts: each scene is a step closer to his ultimate end, forgotten and unloved in death.

The story develops carefully as in many fables and fairy tales. Dickens characteristically borrows the opening from the traditional folktale, "Once upon a time. . . ."**63** From the fairy tale, he also adopted the supernatural medium; Marley's Ghost acts in his visitation to Scrooge in the same tradition as the fairy godmother in the French *contes de fées* and the animal guides in the German *Hausmärchen*. Like the folk protagonist, Scrooge is presented with three stages of development toward his fairy tale reward. And Dick-

61 In "The Christmas Carol and the Economic Man," *American Scholar* (Winter 1951–52, p. 98).

62 Often when a work of literature becomes popular fable, the common versions eliminate those elements from the original text which appear to conflict with the author's seeming purpose. For example, translations of Charles Perrault's "La Belle au bois dormant" ("The Sleeping Beauty in the Wood") generally omit the distasteful, anticlimactic scene of the evil mother-in-law eating the royal children. The author has his own intentions, but they may also conflict with the narrative power within the story itself.

63 "No one was more intensely fond than Dickens of old nursery tales," wrote Forster in his biography, "and he had a secret delight in feeling that he was here only giving them a higher form. The social and manly virtues he desired to teach, were to him not less the charm of the ghost, goblin, and the fairy fancies of his childhood; however rudely set forth in those earlier days. What now were to be conquered were the more formidable dragons and giants that had their places at our own hearths. . . ."
Earle Davis, in *The Flint and the Flame: the Artistry of Charles Dickens* (Columbia, Missouri: University of Missouri Press, 1963, pp. 148–49), suggested that Dickens, in his first short fiction, was influenced by the chapbooks (the cheap, popular literature of his childhood) and that Dickens "in writing the first Christmas Books was to provide a higher form for the old chapbook manner. He appropriated the fairy tale atmosphere and intended to preach a moral."

64 Quoted in *Dickens Criticism: Past, Present and Future Directions*, a symposium with George H. Ford and others (Cambridge, Massachusetts: A Charles Dickens Reference Center Publication, 1962, pp. 10–11).

ens' story too ends "happily ever after" with a line as effective and memorable as that traditional phrase: "And so as Tiny Tim observed, God Bless Us Every One!"

The world of fairy tales is evident in the style. Dickens infuses his descriptions with an animism as prevalent as that in the work of Grimm and Andersen. Inanimate objects possess the same touch of the grotesque as the living characters. His style can no longer be called naturalism; as Edgar Johnson explained, "the elements of the fairy tale are superimposed on the everyday world, and the deep symbolic truths of myth gleam through the surface."**64** The clock in the bell tower strikes the hours "as if its teeth were chattering in its frozen head," and Scrooge's house plays hide-and-seek with the other buildings; Spanish onions wink and French plums blush in the marketplace, and the fog and frost are transformed into "the Genius of the Weather." As Orwell commented, "His imagination overwhelms everything, like a kind of weed." Dickens' effect is ironic: the London personified is so animated with life in all its details that the utilitarian protagonist who "had as little of what is called fancy about him as any man in the City of London" does not realize the strange forces about him until he spies the face of his dead partner in his door knocker.

In these descriptive passages Dickens' style is at its liveliest. Thackeray objected somewhat to the liberal use of free verse in the text; Dickens' prose does depend heavily on poetic elements, on alliteration, assonance, apostrophe, simile, internal rhyme. Dickens knew what he was doing in his Christmas Books: he warned Forster in regard to *The Battle of Life*, "If going over the proofs you find the tendency to blank verse (I *cannot* help it, when I am very much in earnest) too strong, knock out a word's brains here and there." And Dickens was never more in earnest than in *A Christmas Carol*. The reader easily comes across passages which could easily be scanned as verse, such as

Beat on the handle with the handle of his knife,
And feebly cried Hurrah

and

Beware them both, and all of their degree,
But most of all beware this boy, for on his brow I see.

Obviously the author cannot help himself. His presence is so often felt in the style that truly Dickens himself is constantly "standing in the spirit at your elbow." He is so caught up in his descriptions that those of the markets piled high with seasonal delights are often just great lists of marvelous objects. In these paragraphs about the London streets and those of Scrooge's boyhood home, the senses are all stimulated; individual passages are restricted to odors or tastes or sounds or sights. "Every thing is piled up and up, detail on detail, embroidery on embroidery," wrote Orwell. "It is futile to object that this kind of thing is rococo—one might as well make the same objection to a wedding-cake. Either you like it or you do not like it." These descriptions are often overwhelming, like the season itself; Christmas is a time of excess, too much eating and too much drinking. Not everyone reacts the same to these passages; they may either delight the reader with their festive Christmas cheer or sicken him. Flaubert employed a similar device in the wedding scene of *Madame Bovary*, but the French novelist was always in control of his material, never carried away like Dickens. Similarly not everyone reacts the same way to Dickens' humor; puns and jests and other jokes abound and in the oddest places and from the most unexpected characters. Dickens knew there are many kinds of laughter, as different as Fred's hearty humor and the unsettling outbursts of Mrs. Dilber and her cronies.

The spirit of Dickens' style is at its most characteristic in the great scenes of Christmas pleasure, the festivities of Fezziwig, Bob Cratchit, and the nephew Fred. "As you read any of the passages where Dickens is at his happiest," observed Maurois, "there are certain words which perpetually occur: there is *brisk*, there is *jolly*, there are all the adjectives expressive of openheartedness, cheerfulness, sympathy, zeal." Their spirit is infectious; these must have been the passages that he said possessed him. Here Dickens is often his most intimate, author to reader. He frequently uses the personal pronouns "you" and "I" in trying to establish a rapport with his audience. This tone is sustained throughout the narrative so that the story moves with a rapidity and immediacy lacking in his lengthier, more labored novels.

No matter how emotionally involved the author is with his material, Dickens never steers clear of his intended purposes. Often when the action is at its most giddying and exuberant, Dickens jars the reader with a scene or statement of abject poverty. *A Christmas Carol* is a story of contrasts. The Ghost of Christmas Past, intent on his mission to teach Scrooge a lesson, takes the miser without warning from the joyous Fezziwig Ball to the pitiful interview with his sweet-

65 Dickens presented "My own, and only MS of the Book" (bound in red morocco, stamped in gold) to his solicitor Thomas Mitton, who had been so helpful in the suits against the piracy of *A Christmas Carol*. Five years after Dickens' death, Mitton sold it to a London bookseller, Francis Harvey, reportedly for £50. It was quickly purchased by an autograph collector, Henry George Churchill, who in turn, in 1882, sold it to the firm of Robson and Kerslake for £200. Stuart M. Samuel, a Dickens collector, bought it from them for £300; and it was from Samuel that J. Pierpont Morgan secured the manuscript. There is no record of what Morgan paid for the priceless volume. Before it left England (perhaps for the last time), the manuscript was published in facsimile in 1890 by Eliot Stock in London and Brentano's in New York. In 1967, the Pierpont Morgan Library published their own edition which is currently available in paperback from Dover Publications, Inc.

heart. Likewise the Ghost of Christmas Present alarmingly buffets the old man from the bustling London streets to the misery of a Cornish miner's hut to a storm at sea and back again to the cozy but active domesticity of Fred's Christmas party; the gale at sea bluntly transforms into the boistrous laughter of the nephew. Stave Four sustains its atmosphere of scattered gloom and mystery, but here again contrast is crucial. Dickens juxtaposes the terrifying picture of the miser's forgotten corpse with "some tenderness connected with a death" in the Cratchit house, now dressed in mourning. Some critics have objected to the author's manipulation of the reader, but they cannot criticize him for carelessness in the writing. Nothing is arbitrary in these frantic shifts in time and place. The story is tightly constructed and painstakingly executed.

Dickens wrote the story in a few weeks during an impassioned inspiration, but a glance at the original manuscript (now in the Pierpont Morgan Library**65**) demonstrates with what great care Dickens constructed the story. Unlike the previous novels, *A Christmas Carol* did not appear in monthly installments, but was composed as a sustained, complete work from its inception. The critic John Butt in his study *Pope, Dickens, and Others* (1969) recognized the significance of this new approach to composition by Dickens; *A Christmas Carol* was "the first time [Dickens] had attempted to direct his fertile imagination within the limits of a carefully constructed and premeditated plot." It is a transitional work between the early novels and his mature work. Butt continued, "This is the first occasion of Dickens discovering a plot sufficient to carry his message, a plot, that is to say, the whole of which bears upon his message and does not overlap." It is the first example in Dickens' work to fuse together his purpose of "healthful cheerfulness and enjoyment" and his "great Faith in the Poor." As Butt explained, Dickens had, through *A Christmas Carol*, "at last begun to keep a steadier eye on his purpose and design of his work which was to characterize his novels from *Dombey and Son* onwards." This, the first Christmas book, defined not only the holiday itself, but also the nature of Dickens' subsequent work.

A Christmas Carol was always one of Dickens' personal favorites. He recognized its importance in respect to his entire output. He seems never to have been completely satisfied with the writing. From the early galleys until the final authorized version published the year of his death, Dickens was constantly revising the text. His many changes between the manuscript and the first edition demonstrate his struggle to choose the right word or phrase. Many alterations are minor punctuation and spelling corrections (he had particular difficulty including the "u" in "parlour," "honour," and "flavour") and a toning down of his exclamations ("Good God" becomes "Good Heaven," "Lord bless me" merely "Bless me"), but often he greatly improved a passage (for example, the awkward "why do spirits come on earth, and only to me" in the manuscript to the more polished "why do spirits walk the earth, and why do they come to me" in the final text). For the first collected, cheap edition of the *Christmas Books* and in the final Charles Dickens Edition of 1870, Dickens slightly altered spellings and punctuation. His most drastic remolding of the text was prepared for his public reading tours; during the many years he traveled both in England and America, he constantly reworked his prompt copy (now in the Berg Collection of the New York Public Library**66**). In 1867 he gave permission to his American publishers to issue his public reading version to be distributed in the halls where he spoke.

The present edition includes the first, uncorrected printing of *A Christmas Carol in Prose* (1843).**67** Significant textual differences in the many states of the story are indicated in the notes in the margins. The other annotations deal with the literary, autobiographical, and other concerns suggested by the familiar text.

Over one hundred years have passed since the first edition of *A Christmas Carol*, and there is no indication that the story's popularity will ever wane. Many people still react to its philosophy with "Bah! Humbug!" The economic man today works his way but with a different vengeance. The current utilitarian does not view the season as "a poor excuse for picking a man's pocket every twenty-fifth of December"; he rejoices in it, because its present commercialism pays homage to that other idol Gain. The old Christmas spirit, apparent in a Salvation Army Santa Claus or a young caroler in the snow, still carries his torch, even if in a feeble way, to combat both Want and Ignorance. The secular sentiments of Christmas still prevail because of Dickens' carol. Despite the machinations of modern industrialization and the other brutalities of a progressive society, Christmas remains "a kind, forgiving, charitable, pleasant time; . . . when men and women seem by one consent to open their shut-up hearts freely." For Dickens to have added even a little to this common good makes his contribution to the world of letters unique and enduring. As Thackeray advised, "God bless him!"

66 A facsimile of this copy was edited by Philip Collins and published by the library in 1971. The published reading version was apparently only issued in the United States; in 1858, Bradbury and Evans issued a "Reading Edition," a cheap paperback reprint of the standard book.

67 A few obvious typographical omissions made by the printers in the first edition but corrected in the second have been silently added in the present reproduction of the first printing.

A
CHRISTMAS
CAROL
IN PROSE (1843)

Mr. Fezziwig's Ball.

A CHRISTMAS CAROL.

IN PROSE.

BEING

A Ghost Story of Christmas.

BY

CHARLES DICKENS.

WITH ILLUSTRATIONS BY JOHN LEECH.

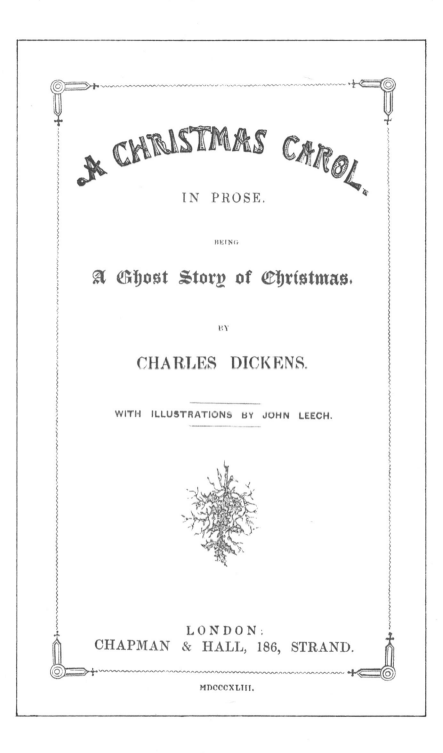

LONDON:
CHAPMAN & HALL, 186, STRAND.

MDCCCXLIII.

PREFACE.

1 *Preface.* For the first collected edition of the *Christmas Books* (1852), Dickens wrote a new introductory note:

I have included my little Christmas Books in this cheap edition, complying with a desire that has been repeatedly expressed to me, and hoping that they may prove generally acceptable in so accessible a form.

The narrow space within which it was necessary to confine these Christmas Stories when they were originally published, rendered their construction a matter of some difficulty, and almost necessitated what is peculiar in their machinery. I never attempted great elaboration of detail in the working out of character within such limits, believing that it could not succeed. My purpose was, in a whimsical kind of masque, which the good humor of the season justified, to awaken some loving and forbearing thoughts, never out of season in a Christian land. I have the happiness of believing that I did not wholly miss it.

Only the second paragraph (slightly revised, "masque" become "mask") was retained for the preface to the authoritative Charles Dickens Edition of 1870.

I HAVE endeavoured in this Ghostly little book, to raise the Ghost of an Idea, which shall not put my readers out of humour with themselves, with each other, with the season, or with me. May it haunt their houses pleasantly, and no one wish to lay it.

Their faithful Friend and Servant.

C. D.

December, 1843.

A CHRISTMAS CAROL.   1

STAVE I.   2

MARLEY'S GHOST.

MARLEY was dead: to begin with. There is no 3
doubt whatever about that. The register of his
burial was signed by the clergyman, the clerk, the
undertaker, and the chief mourner. Scrooge signed 4
it: and Scrooge's name was good upon 'Change, for 5
anything he chose to put his hand to. Old Marley 6
was as dead as a door-nail.

Mind! I don't mean to say that I know, of my
own knowledge, what there is particularly dead
about a door-nail. I might have been inclined,
myself, to regard a coffin-nail as the deadest piece
of ironmongery in the trade. But the wisdom of
our ancestors is in the simile; and my unhallowed

1 *Carol.* A song or ballad of joy celebrating the birth of Christ. Dickens wrote at least one Christmas carol in verse—the one sung in *The Pickwick Papers* (Chapter 28); it was later set to the tune of "Old King Cole" and published in an edition of *The British Book of Song.*

2 *Stave I.* The word *stave* is an archaic form of "staff," a stanza of a poem or a song. Dickens here extends the pretense of his story being "a Christmas carol in prose" by calling its chapters verses. In the two subsequent Christmas books, he revived the conceit by setting off his chapters according to the books' titles: *The Chimes* (1844) is divided like the tolling of a clock into four "quarters," and the divisions of *The Cricket on the Hearth* (1845) are called "chirps."

3 *Marley.* According to *The Dickensian* (September 1938), Dickens took the name of Scrooge's partner from one Dr. Miles Marley, who practiced in Cork Street, Piccadilly. At a St. Patrick's Day party at which both were guests, Dr. Marley, who was aware of the novelist's interest in unusual names, mentioned that he thought his own surname quite remarkable; Dickens reportedly replied, "Your name will be a household word before the year is out."

4 *Scrooge.* Dickens likely derived his miser's name from the colloquial or vulgar word *scrooge:* to crowd or squeeze. This meaning is apparent in the old man's description as "a squeezing, wrenching, grasping, scraping, clutching, covetous old sinner!" There are other variants of the word's spelling: scroodge, scrowde, scrowge, skrouge; as in *The Old Curiosity Shop* (1841, Chapter 39), "Kit hit a man on the head with a handkerchief of apples for 'scrowdging' his parent with unnecessary violence." See Stave 4, Note 18.

5 *Scrooge's name was good upon 'Change.* He was financially sound and his credit would be honored. "'Change" is the Royal Exchange, the financial center of London, which lies between Threadneedle and Cornhill streets; opposite, on the northwest, lies the Bank of England and on the southwest the Mansion House. Over the doorway of the Exchange is the inscription, "The earth is the Lord's and the fullness thereof."

6 *Old Marley was dead as a door-nail.* This common simile is generally credited to William Layland (c. 1332–1400) who included it in his *The Vision of Piers Plowman* (1362) as "ded as a dore-nayle"; but it seems to be of an earlier date. F. H. Ahn in his notes to an 1871 edition of *A Christmas Carol* identified it as appearing in an ancient British ballad "St. George for England":

> But George he did the dragon kill,
> As dead as any door-nail.

Dickens, however, likely knew the simile from Shakespeare, in *Henry IV, Second Part*, Act V, Scene 3, lines 126–27; and in *Henry VI, Second Part*, Act IV, Scene 10, line 43.

That the phrase was used in the story was due to its odd appearance in a dream that Dickens recorded in a letter to C. C. Felton, September 1, 1843, only two months before he began writing *A Christmas Carol:* "Apropos of dreams, is it not a strange thing if writers of fiction never dream of their own creations: recollecting I suppose, even in their dreams, that they have no real existence? *I* never dreamed of any of my own characters and I feel it so impossible.... I had a good piece of absurdity in my head a night or two ago. I dreamed that somebody was dead. I don't know whom, but it's not to the purpose. It was a private gentleman and a particular friend; and I was greatly overcome when the news was broken to me (very delicately) by a gentleman in a cocked hat, top boots, and a sheet. Nothing else. 'Good God,' I said. 'Is he dead!' 'He is as dead Sir,' rejoined the gentleman, 'as a door-nail. But we must all die Mr. Dickens—sooner or later my dear Sir.'..." (*Letters*, Nonesuch Press, Vol. 1, p. 536). This gentleman's attire slightly suggests that of Marley's Ghost: "pig-tail, usual waistcoat, tights, and boots."

7 *assign.* Or assignee, one to whom the property and affairs of the deceased are transferred. Scrooge, being Marley's sole partner and sole friend, inherited the whole of the estate.

8 *residuary legatee.* One to whom the remainder of an estate after the payment of debts and charges is bequeathed.

hands shall not disturb it, or the Country's done for. You will therefore permit me to repeat, emphatically, that Marley was as dead as a door-nail.

Scrooge knew he was dead? Of course he did. How could it be otherwise? Scrooge and he were partners for I don't know how many years. Scrooge was his sole executor, his sole administrator, his **7,8** sole assign, his sole residuary legatee, his sole friend and sole mourner. And even Scrooge was not so dreadfully cut up by the sad event, but that **9** he was an excellent man of business on the very day of the funeral, and solemnised it with an undoubted bargain.

The mention of Marley's funeral brings me back to the point I started from. There is no doubt that Marley was dead. This must be distinctly understood, or nothing wonderful can come of the story I am going to relate. If we were not per- **10** fectly convinced that Hamlet's Father died before the play began, there would be nothing more remarkable in his taking a stroll at night, in an easterly wind, upon his own ramparts, than there would be in any other middle-aged gentleman rashly **11** turning out after dark in a breezy spot—say Saint Paul's Churchyard for instance—literally to astonish **12** his son's weak mind.

Scrooge never painted out Old Marley's name. There it stood, years afterwards, above the warehouse door: Scrooge and Marley. The firm was known as Scrooge and Marley. Sometimes people new to the business called Scrooge Scrooge, and **13** sometimes Marley, but he answered to both names: it was all the same to him.

Oh! But he was a tight-fisted hand at the **14** grindstone, Scrooge! a squeezing, wrenching, grasping, scraping, clutching, covetous old sinner! Hard and sharp as flint, from which no steel had ever struck out generous fire; secret, and self-contained, and solitary as an oyster. The cold within him

9 *an excellent man of business.* The Dickensian (April 1924) reported that Scrooge was a "financier," "something in the nature of a company promoter or a moneylender." Scrooge thus does not provide any actual services or goods; he deals only in the exchange of money.

10 *Hamlet's Father.* To foreshadow the coming of Marley's Ghost, Dickens alludes to perhaps the most celebrated ghost in English literature. The reference here to this spirit is particularly significant, because on its disappearance in the play, the officer Marcellus recounts an ancient Christmas legend:

> It faded on the crowing of a cock.
> Some say that ever 'gainst that season comes
> Wherein our Saviour's birth is celebrated,
> The bird of dawning singeth all night long;
> And then, they say, no spirit can walk abroad. . . .

11 *Saint Paul's Churchyard.* This churchyard is an irregular street encircling St. Paul's Cathedral and burial ground in the heart of the city. "The actual graveyard has long since been closed up," noted Ahn in his 1871 edition. "The narrowness of the way here, and the many small outlets into Paternoster Row, render it a place peculiarly susceptible to draft."

12 *his son's weak mind.* In the original manuscript (now in the Pierpont Morgan Library), Dickens digressed from his narrative to discuss Hamlet's character: "Perhaps you think that Hamlet's intellects were strong. I doubt it. If you could have such a son tomorrow, depend on it, you would find him a poser. He would be a most impracticable fellow to deal with; and however credible he might be to the family, after his decease, he would prove a special incumbrance in his lifetime, trust me."

Dickens wisely deleted this amusing but distracting passage before the manuscript went to the printers.

13 *he answered to both names: it was all the same to him.* Dr. Zelda Teplitz, Clinical Associate Professor of Psychiatry at Georgetown University School of Medicine, in her paper "The Christmas Carol in Relation to Dickens," delivered at the American Psychoanalytic Association, in New York, December 13, 1974, has pointed to several curious correspondences in this double image of Scrooge and Marley. Dr. Teplitz explored this relationship between the living and dead partners as it seemed applicable to Dickens' feelings toward his sister-in-law Georgina Hogarth who had joined the Dickens household in 1842 and her beloved sister Mary who died in 1837. "I trace in many respects a strong resemblance between her mental features and Georgina's," he wrote his mother-in-law, May 8, 1843, "so strong a one, at times, that when she and Kate and I are sitting together, I seem to think that what has happened is a melancholy dream from which I am just awakening. The perfect like of what she was, will never be again, but so much

of her spirit shines out in this sister, that the old time comes back again at some seasons, and I can hardly separate it from the present" (*Letters*, Nonesuch Press, Vol. 1, p. 519). Likewise, Scrooge and Marley are so similar that the ghost of the dead partner returns to the miser "at some seasons" in a vision, Scrooge's melancholy dream.

The double as "the living man, and the animated image of himself dead" is developed further in *The Haunted Man* (1847) in which the chemist Redlaw, like Scrooge, is redeemed by the visitation of a ghost—not that of a dead partner, but rather a replica of himself.

"Redlaw and the Phantom" by John Leech, *The Haunted Man*, 1848

14 *Scrooge!* The miser's character was in part based on that of the old gravedigger Gabriel Grub of "The Story of the Goblins Who Stole a Sexton" in *The Pickwick Papers*: "An ill-conditioned, cross-grained, surly fellow—a morose and lonely man, who consorted with nobody but himself, and an old wicker bottle which fitted into his large deep waist coat pocket—and who eyed each merry face, as it passed by him, with such a deep scowl of malice and ill-humour, as it was difficult to meet, without feeling something the worse for."

That Dickens should have changed his protagonist's occupation from that of gravedigger to miser may have been suggested by an actual carol, "Old Christmas Returned, or Hospitality Revived" which is described in Sandys' collection as "Being a looking-glass for rich Misers, wherein they may see (if they be not blind) how much they are to blame for their penurious house-keeping, and likewise an encouragement to those." The song includes the maxim:

Who feeds the poor, the true reward shall find,
Or helps the old, the feeble, lame, and blind.

15 *frosty rime.* Hoarfrost, or frozen mist; this refers metaphorically to Scrooge's grayness.

16 *the dog-days.* July 3 to August 11, often the hottest days of the year, when the dog star Sirius rises and sets with the sun and thus adds its heat to the weather. Popular belief says that dogs often go mad at this time of the year, called by the Romans "caniculares dies."

17 *didn't know where to have him.* Did not know how to get at him, how to affect him; as in *Henry IV, First Part*, Act III, Scene 3, lines 144–45; "Why, she's neither fish nor flesh; a man knows not how to have her."

18 *"came down."* A pun: to come down as applied to the weather is to fall down freely, but in its slang sense it means to be liberal with money or to make a generous contribution.

19 *evil eye.* The supernatural power to cause great destruction at a glance, a superstition known to almost all peoples from ancient times to the present. The Romans passed laws against it, and many tales of witches blighting crops, causing storms, and even killing with a stare, have been frequently recorded throughout history. The person possessing this power is not necessarily evil; he is more often pitied than condemned for his extraordinary affliction. Dickens, however, attaches a moral significance to Scrooge's stare; as disclosed in Stave 2, "There was an eager, greedy, restless motion in the eye, which showed the passion [Gain] that had taken root, and where the shadow of the growing tree would fall."

20 *"nuts."* This current interjection of distaste meant in its original sense agreeable or gratifying, here used as "good luck."

21 *his counting-house.* Gwen Major in her article "Scrooge's Chambers" (*The Dickensian*, Winter 1932–1933) identified this office as in St. Michael's Alley, not far from the London Exchange.

froze his old features, nipped his pointed nose, shrivelled his cheek, stiffened his gait; made his eyes red, his thin lips blue; and spoke out shrewdly **15** in his grating voice. A frosty rime was on his head, and on his eyebrows, and his wiry chin. He carried his own low temperature always about with **16** him; he iced his office in the dog-days; and didn't thaw it one degree at Christmas.

External heat and cold had little influence on Scrooge. No warmth could warm, nor wintry weather chill him. No wind that blew was bitterer than he, no falling snow was more intent upon its purpose, no pelting rain less open to entreaty. Foul **17** weather didn't know where to have him. The heaviest rain, and snow, and hail, and sleet, could boast of the advantage over him in only one respect. **18** They often "came down" handsomely, and Scrooge never did.

Nobody ever stopped him in the street to say, with gladsome looks, "My dear Scrooge, how are you? when will you come to see me?" No beggars implored him to bestow a trifle, no children asked him what it was o'clock, no man or woman ever once in all his life inquired the way to such and such a place, of Scrooge. Even the blindmen's dogs appeared to know him; and when they saw him coming on, would tug their owners into doorways and up courts; and then would wag their tails as though they said, "no eye at all is better than an **19** evil eye, dark master!"

But what did Scrooge care? It was the very thing he liked. To edge his way along the crowded paths of life, warning all human sympathy to keep its distance, was what the knowing ones call **20** "nuts" to Scrooge.

Once upon a time—of all the good days in the year, on Christmas Eve—old Scrooge sat busy in **21** his counting-house. It was cold, bleak, biting weather: foggy withal: and he could hear the people in the court outside go wheezing up and down, beating their hands upon their breasts, and stamping their feet upon the pavement-stones to warm them. The city clocks had only just gone three, but it was quite dark already: it had not been light all day: and candles were flaring in the windows of the neighbouring offices, like ruddy smears upon the palpable brown air. The fog came pouring in at every chink and keyhole, and was so dense without, that although the court was of the narrowest, the houses opposite were mere phantoms. To see the dingy cloud come drooping down, obscuring everything, one might have thought that Nature lived hard by, and was brewing on a large scale.

The door of Scrooge's counting-house was open that he might keep his eye upon his clerk, who in a dismal little cell beyond, a sort of tank, was copying letters. Scrooge had a very small fire, but the clerk's fire was so very much smaller that it looked like one coal. But he couldn't replenish it, for Scrooge kept the coal-box in his own room; and so surely as the clerk came in with the shovel, the master predicted that it would be necessary for them to part. Wherefore the clerk put on his white comforter, and tried to warm himself at the candle; in which effort, not being a man of a strong imagination, he failed.

"A merry Christmas, uncle! God save you!" **22** cried a cheerful voice. It was the voice of Scrooge's nephew, who came upon him so quickly that this was the first intimation he had of his approach.

"Bah!" said Scrooge, "Humbug!"

He had so heated himself with rapid walking in the fog and frost, this nephew of Scrooge's, that **23** he was all in a glow; his face was ruddy and handsome; his eyes sparkled, and his breath smoked again.

"Christmas a humbug, uncle!" said Scrooge's nephew. "You don't mean that, I am sure."

"I do," said Scrooge. "Merry Christmas!

22 *A merry Christmas, uncle!* Compare the arrival of the nephew Fred with that of his mother Fan in Stave 2; each tries to rescue Scrooge from his daily drudgery.

23 *this nephew of Scrooge's.* Charles Kent in *Charles Dickens as a Reader* (1872) wrote that this introduction to the nephew Fred "was, quite unconsciously but most accurately, in every word of it, a literal description of [Dickens] himself, just as he looked upon any day in the blithest of all seasons, after a brisk walk in the wintry streets or on the snowy high road."

24 *buried with a stake of holly through his heart.*
"It was the custom in medieval times," reported Carol
L. Bernhardt in her notes to the 1922 edition of *A
Christmas Carol*, "to bury a murderer at a cross-roads
with a stake driven through his heart." (The same
procedure was used to dispose of a vampire.) Evidently Scrooge views anyone who would waste his
money on celebrating Christmas to be little better
than a murderer.

what right have you to be merry? what reason
have you to be merry? You're poor enough."

"Come, then," returned the nephew gaily. "What
right have you to be dismal? what reason have
you to be morose? You're rich enough."

Scrooge having no better answer ready on the
spur of the moment, said, "Bah!" again; and
followed it up with "Humbug."

"Don't be cross, uncle," said the nephew.

"What else can I be" returned the uncle,
"when I live in such a world of fools as this?
Merry Christmas! Out upon merry Christmas!
What's Christmas time to you but a time for pay-
ing bills without money; a time for finding yourself
a year older, and not an hour richer; a time for
balancing your books and having every item in 'em
through a round dozen of months presented dead
against you? If I could work my will," said
Scrooge, indignantly, "every idiot who goes about
with ' Merry Christmas,' on his lips, should be boiled

24 with his own pudding, and buried with a stake
of holly through his heart. He should!"

"Uncle!" pleaded the nephew.

"Nephew!" returned the uncle, sternly, "keep
Christmas in your own way, and let me keep it in
mine."

"Keep it!" repeated Scrooge's nephew. "But
you don't keep it."

"Let me leave it alone, then," said Scrooge.
"Much good may it do you! Much good it has
ever done you!"

"There are many things from which I might have
derived good, by which I have not profited, I dare
say," returned the nephew: "Christmas among the
rest. But I am sure I have always thought of Christmas time, when it has come round—apart from the
veneration due to its sacred name and origin, if
anything belonging to it can be apart from that—as
a good time: a kind, forgiving, charitable, pleasant

time : the only time I know of, in the long calendar of the year, when men and women seem by one consent to open their shut-up hearts freely, and to think of people below them as if they really were fellow-passengers to the grave, and not another race **25** of creatures bound on other journeys. And therefore, uncle, though it has never put a scrap of gold or silver in my pocket, I believe that it *has* done me good, and *will* do me good ; and I say, God bless it ! "

The clerk in the tank involuntarily applauded : becoming immediately sensible of the impropriety, he poked the fire, and extinguished the last frail spark for ever.

" Let me hear another sound from *you* " said Scrooge, " and you 'll keep your Christmas by losing your situation. You 're quite a powerful speaker, sir," he added, turning to his nephew. " I wonder you don't go into Parliament."

" Don't be angry, uncle. Come ! Dine with us to-morrow."

Scrooge said that he would see him—yes, indeed **26** he did. He went the whole length of the expression, and said that he would see him in that extremity first.

" But why ?" cried Scrooge's nephew. " Why ?"

" Why did you get married ?" said Scrooge. **27**

" Because I fell in love."

" Because you fell in love !" growled Scrooge, as if that were the only one thing in the world more ridiculous than a merry Christmas. " Good afternoon !"

" Nay, uncle, but you never came to see me before that happened. Why give it as a reason for not coming now ?"

" Good afternoon," said Scrooge.

" I want nothing from you ; I ask nothing of you ; why cannot we be friends ?"

" Good afternoon," said Scrooge.

" I am sorry, with all my heart, to find you so

25 *fellow-passengers.* Changed to "fellow-travellers" in the Ticknor and Fields public reading edition. Edward Guiliano, of the State University of New York at Stony Brook, has brought my attention to the use of this word in *Little Dorrit* (1857), written when Dickens was preparing his first commercial reading tour. The metaphor of man as a blind tourist traveling through life is a major theme of this novel: life as a journey, with every person being a brother or sister of every other person, who should think like Scrooge's nephew that those below him "as if they really were fellow-passengers to the grave, and not another race of creatures on other journeys," each affecting one another's life, on the path to death; "thus even day and night, under the sun and under the stars, climbing the dusty hills and toiling along the weary plains, journeying by land and journeying by sea, coming and going so strangely, to meet and to act and react on one another, move all we restless travelers through the pilgrimage of life."

26 *he would see him—.* He would see him damned first; as in "Plague on't; an I thought he had been valiant, and so cunning in fence, I'd have seen him damn'd ere I'd have challeng'd him" (*Twelfth Night*, Act III, Scene 4, lines 311–13).

27 *"Why did you get married?"* In agreement with contemporary economists, Scrooge did not approve of his nephew's marrying before he had a sufficient income to support a family. To marry for love was sentimental nonsense; as disclosed in Stave 2, Scrooge broke his own engagement to be married because it conflicted with his finances, and obviously he thought his nephew should have followed his example. Dickens, of course, had no sympathy for Scrooge's opinion.

Dickens developed his attitude further in *The Chimes* (1844); Mr. Filer, the economist, complains with regard to such young married couples that there is "no hope to persuade 'em that they have no right or business to be married." The critics of the second Christmas book tended to agree with Mr. Filer; Dickens received considerable criticism for supposedly encouraging the poor to marry.

28   *fifteen shillings a-week.* Fifteen shillings a week was the common wage of clerical workers of the time.

29   *Bedlam.* A corruption of "Bethlehem," referring to the Hospital of St. Mary's of Bethlehem in London, which was founded as a priory in 1247 but became a hospital for the insane as early as 1402. In 1547, after the dissolution of church property by Henry VIII, it was incorporated as a royal foundation as a madhouse. The term was current as early as the late sixteenth century, as in *Henry IV, Second Part,* Act V, Scene 1, Line 131 ("To Bedlam with him! Is the man growne mad?"). The word *bedlam,* or uproar, comes from this common term, synonymous with "madhouse."

30   *seven years.* Originally Dickens had Marley die "ten years ago, this very day," but halfway through the story he decided on the far more effective "seven years, this very night." Traditionally the number seven has supernatural powers. According to Brand's *Popular Antiquities,* the seventh year commonly brings great changes, often great dangers, to a man's life. Note that the name "Scrooge" has seven letters; this number is said to be fatal to men. Coincidentally it was exactly seven years before the publication of *A Christmas Carol* that Dickens wrote his last holiday story, "The Story of the Goblins Who Stole a Sexton." Dr. Teplitz, in her paper (cited in Note 13), points to other curious events in Dickens' life that occurred seven years before and which seem to correspond to the composition of *A Christmas Carol.* Dr. Teplitz has also noted that Dickens refers to the number seven in talking of Marley's death exactly seven times.

31   *At this festive season of the year...it is more than usually desirable that we should make some slight provision for the poor and destitute, who suffer greatly at the present time.* Compare Scrooge's reply to this modest proposal to that given in Thomas Carlyle's *Chartism* (1840): "Do we not pass what Acts of Parliament are needful; as many as thirty-nine for the shooting of partridges alone? Are there not treadmills, gibbets; even hospitals, poor-rates, New-Poor Law? So answers...Aristocracy, astonishment in every feature."

resolute. We have never had any quarrel, to which I have been a party. But I have made the trial in homage to Christmas, and I 'll keep my Christmas humour to the last. So A Merry Christmas, uncle !"

"Good afternoon !" said Scrooge.

"And A Happy New Year !"

"Good afternoon !" said Scrooge.

His nephew left the room without an angry word, notwithstanding. He stopped at the outer door to bestow the greetings of the season on the clerk, who, cold as he was, was warmer than Scrooge; for he returned them cordially.

"There 's another fellow," muttered Scrooge; who **28** overheard him: " my clerk, with fifteen shillings a-week, and a wife and family, talking about a merry **29** Christmas. I 'll retire to Bedlam."

This lunatic, in letting Scrooge's nephew out, had let two other people in. They were portly gentlemen, pleasant to behold, and now stood, with their hats off, in Scrooge's office. They had books and papers in their hands, and bowed to him.

" Scrooge and Marley's, I believe," said one of the gentlemen, referring to his list. " Have I the pleasure of addressing Mr. Scrooge, or Mr. Marley ?"

30 " Mr. Marley has been dead these seven years," Scrooge replied. " He died seven years ago, this very night."

" We have no doubt his liberality is well represented by his surviving partner," said the gentleman, presenting his credentials.

It certainly was; for they had been two kindred spirits. At the ominous word " liberality," Scrooge frowned, and shook his head, and handed the credentials back.

31 " At this festive season of the year, Mr. Scrooge," said the gentleman, taking up a pen, " it is more than usually desirable that we should make some slight provision for the poor and destitute, who suffer greatly at the present time. Many thousands are in want of common necessaries; hundreds of thousands are in want of common comforts, sir."

"Are there no prisons?" asked Scrooge.

"Plenty of prisons," said the gentleman, laying down the pen again.

"And the Union workhouses?" demanded Scrooge. **32** "Are they still in operation?"

"They are. Still," returned the gentleman, " I wish I could say they were not."

"The Treadmill and the Poor Law are in full **33** vigour, then?" said Scrooge.

"Both very busy, sir."

"Oh! I was afraid, from what you said at first, that something had occurred to stop them in their useful course," said Scrooge. " I'm very glad to hear it."

"Under the impression that they scarcely furnish Christian cheer of mind or body to the multitude," returned the gentleman, " a few of us are endeavouring to raise a fund to buy the Poor some meat and drink, and means of warmth. We choose this time, because it is a time, of all others, when Want is keenly felt, and Abundance rejoices. What shall I put you down for?' [']

"Nothing!" Scrooge replied.

"You wish to be anonymous?"

"I wish to be left alone," said Scrooge. " Since you ask me what I wish, gentlemen, that is my answer. I don't make merry myself at Christmas, and I can't afford to make idle people merry. I help to support the establishments I have mentioned: they cost enough: and those who are badly off must go there."

"Many can't go there; and many would rather **34** die."

"If they would rather die," said Scrooge, "they had better do it, and decrease the surplus population. **35** Besides—excuse me—I don't know that."

32 *the Union workhouses.* The Poor Law of 1834 provided that two or more parishes unite to provide a home for the destitute where they might labor in exchange for their room and board. It divided England and Wales into twenty-one districts and empowered in each a commissioner to form "poor law unions" by grouping parishes together for administrative purposes and to build workhouses to contain the poor. The able-bodied were worked in penury, and their dependents were kept in the house where as little as possible was spent on food and shelter. They were characterized by strict discipline; the sexes were segregated and classified, and preliminary inquiries into the private lives of the inmates were generally conducted. It was considered a disgrace to go to such a place. Dickens fiercely attacked these institutions; "I believe there has been in England, since the days of the Stuarts," Dickens wrote in a postscript to *Our Mutual Friend* (1865), "no law so often infamously administered, no law so openly violated, no law so habitually ill-supervised. In the majority of the shameful cases of disease and death from destitution that shock the Public and disgrace the country, the illegality is equal to the inhumanity—and known language could say no more of their lawlessness." Not until 1871 was the law more humanely administered, through the establishment of local Boards of Guardians and Guardians' Committees. Not until the 1940s was the law replaced by modern social welfare.

33 *The Treadmill.* A mill operated by persons walking on steps fastened to the circumference of a great and wide horizontal wheel. This form of criminal punishment was introduced as hard labor in 1817, at Brixton Prison.

34 *many would rather die.* For example, Betty Higden of *Our Mutual Friend*, whose "highest sublunary hope" was "patiently to earn a spare bare living, and quietly to die, untouched by workhouse hands."

35 *the surplus population.* Michael Slater noted in the 1971 Oxford paperback of *A Christmas Carol* the influence of the great fear of overpopulation held by the English since the publication of Thomas Malthus' *Essay on the Principles of Population* (1803). This economist made clear "What the surplus is, Where it is" when he wrote: "A man who is born into a world possessed, if he cannot get subsistence from his parents, on which he has a just demand, and if society do not want his labour, has no claim of *right* of the smallest portion of food, and, in fact, has no business to be where he is. At Nature's mighty feast there is no vacant cover for him. She tells him to be gone...."
Mr. Filer, a student of Malthus, shares this opinion: the poor "have no earthly right or business to be born. And *that* we know they haven't. We reduced it to a mathematical certainty long ago!" Dickens harbored no sympathy for political economists; in *Hard Times* (1854), his most scathing attack on these

" 'Sees-unable weather' " by George Cruikshank, *The Comic Almanac*, 1841. *Courtesy The Library of Congress*

philosophers, he planned to name among the victims, two of the Gradgrind children, after Adam Smith and Malthus.

36 *flaring links.* Torches, made of tow with pitch or tar, from a form of the word *lint*, frayed linen. "In Dickens' day," noted E. Gordon Browne in his 1907 edition of *A Christmas Carol*, "the link-boy was a common sight especially when the fog, or 'London particular,' as it was sometimes called, wrapped the whole city in darkness. There are still to be seen outside the houses in and around Mayfair and Belgravia the torch extinguishers, which were in the shape similar to those attached to candlesticks, and were made of iron."

37 *a church.* Frank S. Johnson in his article "About 'A Christmas Carol' " (*The Dickensian*, Winter 1931–1932) identified this as St. Michael's Church, near the Royal Exchange, London.

" But you might know it," observed the gentleman.

" It's not my business," Scrooge returned. " It's enough for a man to understand his own business, and not to interfere with other people's. Mine occupies me constantly. Good afternoon, gentlemen!"

Seeing clearly that it would be useless to pursue their point, the gentlemen withdrew. Scrooge resumed his labours with an improved opinion of himself, and in a more facetious temper than was usual with him.

Meanwhile the fog and darkness thickened so, that
36 people ran about with flaring links, proffering their services to go before horses in carriages, and conduct
37 them on their way. The ancient tower of a church, whose gruff old bell was always peeping slily down at Scrooge out of a gothic window in the wall, became invisible, and struck the hours and quarters in the clouds, with tremulous vibrations afterwards, as if its teeth were chattering in its frozen head up there. The cold became intense. In the main street, at the corner of the court, some labourers were repairing the gas-pipes, and had lighted a great fire in a

brazier, round which a party of ragged men and boys **38** were gathered: warming their hands and winking their eyes before the blaze in rapture. The water-plug being left in solitude, its overflowings sullenly congealed, and turned to misanthropic ice. The brightness of the shops where holly sprigs and berries crackled in the lamp-heat of the windows, made pale faces ruddy as they passed. Poulterers' and grocers' trades became a splendid joke: a glorious pageant, with which it was next to impossible to believe that such dull principles as bargain and sale had anything to do. The Lord Mayor, in the strong-hold of the mighty Mansion House, gave orders to his **39** fifty cooks and butlers to keep Christmas as a Lord Mayor's household should; and even the little tailor, whom he had fined five shillings on the previous Monday for being drunk and blood-thirsty in the streets, stirred up to-morrow's pudding in his garret, while his lean wife and the baby sallied out to buy the beef.

Foggier yet, and colder! Piercing, searching, bit-ing cold. If the good Saint Dunstan had but nipped **40** the Evil Spirit's nose with a touch of such weather as that, instead of using his familiar weapons, then indeed he would have roared to lusty purpose. The

38 *a brazier.* A large flat pan for holding coals, used as a heater.

39 *Mansion House.* The official residence of the Lord Mayor of London, built in 1739–1753, and giv-ing its name to the immediate neighborhood, the eastern end of Cheapside, in the heart of the city.

40 *Saint Dunstan.* An English monk (924–988) who was also a painter, jeweler, blacksmith, and the patron saint of goldsmiths. He was also skilled in politics; he became the chief advisor of King Eadred, and later King Eadgar, who made Dunstan Archbishop of Can-terbury. In *A Child's History of England* (1852–1854), Dickens acknowledged him to be "the real king, who had the real power. . . . a clever priest, a little mad, and not a little proud and cruel;" and he described the most famous legend about the saint: "[Dunstan] was an ingenious smith, and worked at forge in a little cell and he used to tell the most extraordinary lies about demons and spirits, who, he said, came there to persecute him. For instance, he related that one day when he was at work, the devil looked in at the little window, and tried to tempt him to lead a life of idle pleasure; whereupon, having his pincers in the fire, red-hot, he seized the devil by the nose, and put him in such pain, that his bellowings were heard for miles and miles. Some people are inclined to think this nonsense a part of Dunstan's madness . . . but I think not. I observe that it induced the ignorant people to consider him a holy man, and that it made him very powerful. Which was exactly what he always wanted."

"The Most Approved Method of Pulling a Fel-low's Nose (as practiced by St. Dunstan)" by George Cruikshank, *Vol. 1 of My Sketch Book,* 1834. *Courtesy The Library of Congress*

41 *mumbled.* Bit gently with the mouth mostly closed.

42 *May nothing you dismay!* Dickens has slightly misquoted the opening lines of this famous old carol, preserved by William Sandys in *Christmas Carols, Ancient and Modern* (1833):

> God rest you merry gentlemen,
> Let nothing you dismay.

This carol was probably the most widely sung Christmas song of the time. "In the metropolis a solitary itinerant may be occasionally heard in the streets," wrote Sandys, "croaking out 'God rest you merry gentlemen,' or some other old carol, to an ancient and simple tune."

43 *the ruler.* Scrooge, a man of mathematics and measurements, appropriately threatens the boy with this essential tool of his trade.

44 *the singer fled in terror.* This episode was adapted from a similar attack on a young caroler in "A Story of the Goblins Who Stole a Sexton": "Now, Gabriel . . . was not a little indignant to hear a young urchin roaring out some jolly song about a merry Christmas, in this very sanctuary. . . . As Gabriel walked on, and the voice drew nearer, he found it proceeded from a small boy. . . . So Gabriel waited until the boy came up, and then dodged him into a corner, and rapped him over the head with his lantern five or six times, to teach him to modulate his voice. And as the boy hurried away with his hand to his head, singing quite a different sort of tune, Gabriel Grub chuckled very heartily to himself. . . ."

"London Carol Singers" by Robert Seymour, *The Book of Christmas*, 1836. *Courtesy The Library of Congress*

41 owner of one scant young nose, gnawed and mumbled by the hungry cold as bones are gnawed by dogs, stooped down at Scrooge's keyhole to regale him with a Christmas carol : but at the first sound of—

> " God bless you merry gentleman !
> **42**   May nothing you dismay ! "

43 Scrooge seized the ruler with such energy of action,
44 that the singer fled in terror, leaving the keyhole to the fog and even more congenial frost.

At length the hour of shutting up the counting-house arrived. With an ill-will Scrooge dismounted from his stool, and tacitly admitted the fact to the expectant clerk in the Tank, who instantly snuffed his candle out, and put on his hat.

" You'll want all day to-morrow, I suppose ? " said Scrooge.

" If quite convenient, Sir."

" It's not convenient," said Scrooge, " and it's not fair. If I was to stop half-a-crown for it, you'd **45** think yourself ill used, I'll be bound ? "

The clerk smiled faintly.

" And yet," said Scrooge, " you don't think *me* ill-used, when I pay a day's wages for no work."

The clerk observed that it was only once a year.

" A poor excuse for picking a man's pocket every **46** twenty-fifth of December ! " said Scrooge, buttoning his great-coat to the chin. " But I suppose you must have the whole day. Be here all the earlier next morning ! "

The clerk promised that he would ; and Scrooge walked out with a growl. The office was closed in a twinkling, and the clerk, with the long ends of his white comforter dangling below his waist (for he boasted no great-coat), went down a slide on Corn- **47** hill, at the end of a lane of boys, twenty times, in honour of its being Christmas-eve, and then ran home to Camden Town as hard as he could pelt, to **48** play at blindman's-buff. **49**

Scrooge took his melancholy dinner in his usual **50** melancholy tavern ; and having read all the news-papers, and beguiled the rest of the evening with his banker's-book, went home to bed. He lived in chambers which had once belonged to his deceased **51** partner. They were a gloomy suite of rooms, in a lowering pile of building up a yard, where it had so little business to be, that one could scarcely help fancying it must have run there when it was a young house, playing at hide-and-seek with other houses, and have forgotten the way out again. It was old enough now, and dreary enough, for nobody lived in it but Scrooge, the other rooms being all let out as offices. The yard was so dark that even Scrooge, who knew its every stone, was fain to grope with his hands. The fog and frost so hung about the black old gateway of the house, that it

45 *half-a-crown.* This English coin (once worth five shillings and now out of circulation) was an-ciently stamped with a crown.

46 *every twenty-fifth of December.* Scrooge cannot even say the word *Christmas;* unlike his nephew he does not acknowledge "the veneration due to its sacred name and origin," and it is just another work-ing day to the old miser.

47 *Cornhill.* A well-known thoroughfare in Cheap-side, London; it derived its name from the corn mar-ket once held there.

48 *Camden Town.* Once a suburb, now a part of London, east of Regent Street, known for its small cottages and cheap houses; Dickens lived there as a boy. See Stave 3, Note 30.

49 *blindman's-buff.* A popular parlor game, not ex-clusive to the Christmas season, in which the con-testant is blindfolded and then must catch a guest and guess whom he has caught. The game is of ancient origin and was known to the Greeks; in the Middle Ages, it was called "hoodman blind," because the player was blinded with a hood. Joseph Strutt in *The Sports and Past-Times of the People of England* (1801) defined this old game as "where a player is blinded and buffeted by his comrades until he can catch one of them, which done, the person caught is blinded in his stead." A 1740 chapbook *Round about our Coal-Fire* reported that "it is lawful to set any-thing in the way for Folks to tumble over, whether it is to break Arms, Legs, or Hands." By the nine-teenth century, the blindman had the right to kiss his captive. See also Stave 3, Note 66.

One of the most memorable games of blindman's-buff in English literature is that played by Mr. Pick-wick at the Christmas party at Dingley Dell: ". . . but it was a still more pleasant thing to see Mr. Pickwick, blinded shortly afterwards with a silk handkerchief, falling up against the wall, and scrambling into cor-ners, and going through all the mysteries of blind-man's buff, with the utmost relish for the game, until at last he caught one of the poor relations, and then had to evade the blind-man himself, which he did with a nimbleness and agility that elicited the admira-tion and applause of all beholders."

50 *his usual melancholy tavern.* Gwen Major in her article (cited in Note 21) identified this place as Garraway's Coffee House.

51 *chambers.* In her article on the typography of *A Christmas Carol* (cited in Note 21), Gwen Major convincingly argues that Scrooge's apartments were in a house that once stood at 46 Lime Street, in the Langborn Ward. Her description of this once-fine house follows Dickens': by the nineteenth century, it had become offices for many firms (including three wine merchants), and stood far back and alone up a narrow courtyard, known for its old gates; the building had once been a private residence, and most of the rooms were known for having been left in much the same condition as in the time of Charles I. Ms. Major noted that after the building was demolished in 1875, it was appropriately replaced by a bank.

52 *the Genius of the Weather.* A guardian or attendant spirit, at the time more commonly called "the clerk of the weather."

53 *the City of London.* That part of the old metropolis, about a square mile in extent, which comes within the jurisdiction of the Lord Mayor and the City Corporation. It has its own police force and courts of justice. The Royal Exchange, the Mansion House, Cornhill, and Saint Paul's Cathedral are all in this district of the old City of London.

54 *the corporation, alderman, and livery.* Ahn in the notes to his 1871 edition examined this system: "The corporation of every city or incorporated borough, consists of a mayor, alderman, and common-councilmen. The mayors, who in London, York, and Dublin, have the title of Lord, are chosen annually by the livery out of the court of aldermen, who in their turn are chosen and elected for life by the freemen. Each alderman represents a ward, of which in London there are 26, and 206 common-councilmen. None but freemen (burgesses) can engage in trade in London, and all must belong to some of the guilds or companies, many of the members of which are entitled to wear its distinguished dress or livery—hence livery-men."

55 *not a knocker, but Marley's face.* In the article "The 'Marley' Knocker" by T. W. Tyrell (*The Dickensian,* October 1924), this door knocker was identified as one that hung on the front door of No. 8 Craven Street when it was occupied by one Dr. David Rees in the 1840s. (Was Dr. Rees a colleague of the Dr. Marley mentioned in Note 3?) It was such a striking knocker that if he had seen it, Dickens would not have forgotten it.

Thackeray similarly played with an odd knocker in his Christmas book *The Rose and the Ring* (1855); for being brazen with the Fairy Blackstick, the porter Jenkins Gruffanuff is transformed into a brass door knocker.

The Marley door knocker, *The Dickensian,* October 1924. *Courtesy General Research and Humanities Division, The New York Public Library, Astor, Lenox and Tilden Foundations*

52 seemed as if the Genius of the Weather sat in mournful meditation on the threshold.

Now, it is a fact, that there was nothing at all particular about the knocker on the door, except that it was very large. It is also a fact, that Scrooge had seen it night and morning during his whole residence in that place; also that Scrooge had as little of what is called fancy about him as any man in **53** the City of London, even including—which is a bold **54** word—the corporation, aldermen, and livery. Let it also be borne in mind that Scrooge had not bestowed one thought on Marley, since his last mention of his seven-years' dead partner that afternoon. And then let any man explain to me, if he can, how it happened that Scrooge, having his key in the lock of the door, saw in the knocker, without its undergoing any in- **55** termediate process of change: not a knocker, but Marley's face.

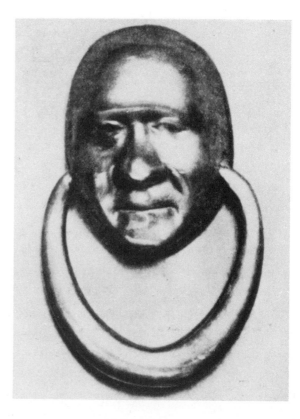

Marley's face. It was not in impenetrable shadow as the other objects in the yard were, but had a dismal light about it, like a bad lobster in a dark cellar. It was not angry or ferocious, but looked at Scrooge as Marley used to look: with ghostly spectacles turned up upon its ghostly forehead. The hair was curiously stirred, as if by breath or hot-air; and though the eyes were wide open, they were perfectly motionless. That, and its livid colour, made it horrible; but its horror seemed to be, in spite of the face and beyond its control, rather than a part of its own expression.

As Scrooge looked fixedly at this phenomenon, it was a knocker again.

To say that he was not startled, or that his blood was not conscious of a terrible sensation to which it had been a stranger from infancy, would be untrue. But he put his hand upon the key he had relinquished, turned it sturdily, walked in, and lighted his candle.

He *did* pause, with a moment's irresolution, before he shut the door; and he *did* look cautiously behind it first, as if he half-expected to be terrified with the sight of Marley's pigtail sticking out into the hall. But there was nothing on the back of the door, except the screws and nuts that held the knocker on; so he said "Pooh, pooh!" and closed it with a bang.

The sound resounded through the house like thunder. Every room above, and every cask in the wine-merchant's cellars below, appeared to have a separate peal of echoes of its own. Scrooge was not a man to be frightened by echoes. He fastened the door, and walked across the hall, and up the stairs: slowly too: trimming his candle as he went.

You may talk vaguely about driving a coach-and- **56** six up a good old flight of stairs, or through a bad young Act of Parliament; but I mean to say you might have got a hearse up that staircase, and taken it broadwise, with the splinter-bar towards the wall, **57**

56 *driving a coach-and-six...through a bad young Act of Parliament.* As Acts of Parliament were often so loosely worded and filled with so many loopholes that an accused person could easily escape prosecution, the Irish agitator Daniel O'Connell boasted that he could drive a coach drawn by six horses through any such legislation.

57 *splinter-bar.* The crossbar in front of a carriage, which supports the springs.

58 *Scrooge's dip*. His tallow candle; it is made by the wick being dipped repeatedly in melted wax.

59 *lumber-room*. A storeroom, sometimes for firewood, but more often for unused household items.

60 *gruel*. Oatmeal or other cereal boiled in lots of water. It is often taken to relax one. This meager fare was common food provided in the prisons and workhouses; it was a staple of Oliver Twist's diet. Small wonder Scrooge should think these institutions adequate for the poor; he lives no more extravagantly than their inmates.

61 *the hob*. An old-fashioned fire grate: a raised stone, or iron shelf, on either side of an open fireplace, where things are placed to keep warm. Hobs were added when the fireplace was converted from wood to coal burning.

62 *built by some Dutch merchant long ago*. The fireplace was likely installed during the emigration of Dutch merchants after the Revolution of 1688–1689, when William the Statholder of the United Netherlands became William of Orange of Great Britain.

63 *Dutch tiles*. "In the house on the Brook at Chatham, where the boy Dickens lived," wrote Johnson in his article (cited in Note 37), "was a fireplace with Dutch tiles illustrating the scriptures, reminding us of the old fireplace over which Scrooge sat with Cains, Abels, Apostles, etc. Some of these tiles are still in existence." The majority of Scrooge's tiles illustrate the Old Testament: Cain and Abel, Gen. 4; Pharaoh's daughter, Exod. 2; the Queen of Sheba, 2 Chron. 9; Abraham, Gen. 11–26; and Belshazzar, Dan. 4 and 5.

and the door towards the balustrades : and done it easy. There was plenty of width for that, and room to spare; which is perhaps the reason why Scrooge thought he saw a locomotive hearse going on before him in the gloom. Half a dozen gas-lamps out of the street wouldn't have lighted the entry too well, so you may suppose that it was pretty dark with **58** Scrooge's dip.

Up Scrooge went, not caring a button for that : darkness is cheap, and Scrooge liked it. But before he shut his heavy door, he walked through his rooms to see that all was right. He had just enough recollection of the face to desire to do that.

59 Sitting room, bed-room, lumber-room. All as they should be. Nobody under the table, nobody under the sofa; a small fire in the grate; spoon and **60** basin ready; and the little saucepan of gruel **61** (Scrooge had a cold in his head) upon the hob. Nobody under the bed; nobody in the closet; nobody in his dressing-gown, which was hanging up in a suspicious attitude against the wall. Lumber-room as usual. Old fire-guard, old shoes, two fish-baskets, washing-stand on three legs, and a poker.

Quite satisfied, he closed his door, and locked himself in; double-locked himself in, which was not his custom. Thus secured against surprise, he took off his cravat; put on his dressing-gown and slippers, and his night-cap; and sat down before the fire to take his gruel.

It was a very low fire indeed; nothing on such a bitter night. He was obliged to sit close to it, and brood over it, before he could extract the least sensation of warmth from such a handful of fuel.
62 The fire-place was an old one, built by some Dutch merchant long ago, and paved all round with quaint
63 Dutch tiles, designed to illustrate the Scriptures. There were Cains and Abels; Pharaoh's daughters, Queens of Sheba, Angelic messengers descending

through the air on clouds like feather-beds, Abrahams, Belshazzars, Apostles putting off to sea in butter-boats, hundreds of figures, to attract his thoughts; and yet that face of Marley, seven years dead, came like the ancient Prophet's rod, and swallowed up the whole. If each smooth tile had been a blank at first, with power to shape some picture on its surface from the disjointed fragments of his thoughts, there would have been a copy of old Marley's head on every one.

"Humbug!" said Scrooge; and walked across the room.

After several turns, he sat down again. As he threw his head back in the chair, his glance happened to rest upon a bell, a disused bell, that hung in the room, and communicated for some purpose now forgotten with a chamber in the highest story of the building. It was with great astonishment, and with a strange, inexplicable dread, that as he looked, he saw this bell begin to swing. It swung so softly in the outset that it scarcely made a sound; but soon it rang out loudly, and so did every bell in the house.

This might have lasted half a minute, or a minute, but it seemed an hour. The bells ceased as they had begun, together. They were succeeded by a clanking noise, deep down below; as if some person were dragging a heavy chain over the casks in the wine-merchant's cellar. Scrooge then remembered to have heard that ghosts in haunted houses were described as dragging chains.

The cellar-door flew open with a booming sound, and then he heard the noise much louder, on the floors below; then coming up the stairs; then coming straight towards his door.

"It's humbug still!" said Scrooge. "I won't believe it."

His colour changed though, when, without a pause, it came on through the heavy door, and

64 *butter-boats.* A serving dish for melted butter; Dickens is comparing the size and shape of these vessels to those of the Apostles' ships on the tiles.

65 *the ancient Prophet's rod.* Exod. 7:1–13, describes how Aaron's staff, transformed into a snake, swallowed up all the other serpents made from the rods of the Pharaoh's magicians.

66 *If each smooth tile had been a blank at first, with the power to shape some picture on its surface from the disjointed fragments of his thoughts.* Scrooge's ability to see shapes and pictures in amorphous surfaces revealing images of his subconscious is the same psychological process exploited in the Rorschach tests, in which an individual is asked to describe pictures he sees in inkblots. This "way to stimulate and arouse the mind to various inventions" is beautifully described by Leonardo Da Vinci in his notebooks: "If you look at any walls spotted with various stains or a mixture of different kinds of stones, if you are about to invent some scene, you will be able to see in it a resemblance to various different landscapes adorned with mountains, rivers, rocks, trees, plains, wide valleys, and various groups of hills. You will also be able to see diverse combats and figures in quick movement, and strange expressions of faces, and outlandish costumes, and an infinite number of things which you can reduce into separate and well conceived forms." (*Leonardo Da Vinci's Note-Books*, edited by Edward McCurdy, New York: The Empire State Book Company, 1923.)

Da Vinci noted that this process not only affected the eyes but also one's ears, "as it does with the sound of bells, in whose clanging you may discover every name and word that you can imagine." In his second Christmas Book *The Chimes* (1844), Dickens similarly employs the clanging of bells to reveal the supernatural medium.

67 *dragging chains.* Andrew Lang in his introduction to the Gadshill Edition of the *Christmas Books* (1897) observed that this "old-fashioned phenomenon of clanking chains derived from classical superstition." Dickens noted in "A Christmas Tree" (*Household Words*, Christmas number, 1850) that the number of ghosts in haunted houses are "reducible to a very few general types and classes; for, ghosts have little originality, and 'walk' in a beaten track"; among their common pursuits is "the rattling of a chain." Not all authorities agree with Dickens' giving Marley's Ghost such a burden. "Dragging chains is not the fashion of English Ghosts," wrote Francis Grose in his *Antiquities of England and Wales* (1782–1787); "chains and black vestments being chiefly the accoutrements of foreign spectres, seen in arbitrary governments; dead or alive, English Spirits are free."

Preliminary pencil and wash drawing by John Leech for "Marley's Ghost." *Courtesy The Houghton Library, Harvard University*

68 *its.* Spirits are believed to be sexless; Dickens refers to each of the Christmas ghosts only as "it."

69 *the dying flame leaped up.* "If, during the time of an Apparition, there is a lighted candle in the room," wrote Grose in his book (cited in Note 67), "it will burn extremely blue: this is so universally acknowledged, that many eminent philosophers have busied themselves in accounting for it, without once doubting the truth of the fact." Dickens possibly knew this superstition from Shakespeare: Brutus observes at the appearance of Caesar's ghost, "How ill this taper burns!" (*Julius Caesar*, Act IV, Scene 3, line 275).

70 *"I know him! Marley's Ghost!"* The illustrator John Leech took this simile literally and amusingly portrayed the flame with a face, crying, "Marley's Ghost!"

71 *Marley had no bowels.* Certain parts of the body were at one time designated the seats of human affections; the bowels were thought to be the center of compassion, as in the First Epistle of St. John 3:17: "But whoso hath this world's goods, and seeth his brother have need, and shutteth up his bowels of compassion from him, how dwelleth the love of God in him?"

Thus Marley, like Scrooge, lacked in life any pity for his fellowman. Dickens may also be reasserting the physical fact that "Marley was dead to begin with"; from Egyptian times, corpses were disemboweled before burial, to retard the body's deterioration.

72 *"for a shade....to a shade."* "For a shade," for a ghost; "to a shade," to a degree.

68 passed into the room before his eyes. Upon its
69 coming in, the dying flame leaped up, as though it
70 cried "I know him! Marley's Ghost!" and fell again.

The same face: the very same. Marley in his pig-tail, usual waistcoat, tights, and boots; the tassels on the latter bristling, like his pigtail, and his coat-skirts, and the hair upon his head. The chain he drew was clasped about his middle. It was long, and wound about him like a tail; and it was made (for Scrooge observed it closely) of cash-boxes, keys, padlocks, ledgers, deeds, and heavy purses wrought in steel. His body was transparent: so that Scrooge, observing him, and looking through his waistcoat, could see the two buttons on his coat behind.

71 Scrooge had often heard it said that Marley had no bowels, but he had never believed it until now.

No, nor did he believe it even now. Though he looked the phantom through and through, and saw it standing before him; though he felt the chilling influence of its death-cold eyes; and marked the very texture of the folded kerchief bound about its head and chin, which wrapper he had not observed before: he was still incredulous, and fought against his senses.

"How now!" said Scrooge, caustic and cold as ever. "What do you want with me?"

"Much!"—Marley's voice, no doubt about it.

"Who are you?"

"Ask me who I *was*."

"Who *were* you then?" said Scrooge, raising his
72 voice. "You're particular—for a shade." He was going to say "*to* a shade," but substituted this, as more appropriate.

"In life I was your partner, Jacob Marley."

"Can you—can you sit down?" asked Scrooge, looking doubtfully at him.

"I can."

"Do it then."

Marley's Ghost.

Half-title vignette by Phiz, *Christmas Books*, "The Library Edition of Dickens' Works," 1859. *Courtesy The British Library Board*

73 *as if he were quite used to it.* The ghost's familiarity with this spot anticipates its statement, "I have sat invisible beside you many and many a day."

74 *"Because . . . a little thing affects them."* As Lang observed in his introduction to the Gadshill Edition, "Scrooge vainly pleads the popular theory of hallucinations," that ghosts and other specters are caused by indigestion. Interpreters of dream psychology, from Aristotle to Sigmund Freud, argued that dreams are the result of natural disorders or other stimuli on the mind. Dickens recognized that the cause of a dream lay in "the fragments of reality I can collect which helped to make it up." Just the suggestion of something during the waking hours may create phantoms; that Marley should appear to Scrooge for the first time since his partner's death seven years before may have arisen merely by the portly gentleman's asking whether he was addressing Mr. Marley or Mr. Scrooge. As Thomas De Quincey (a favorite author of Dickens) explained in *Suspiria De Profundis* (1845), "He whose talk is of oxen will probably dream of oxen." One is often aroused from sleep by some outside sound or other influence that corresponded to something else in a dream; for example, the Ghost of Christmas Yet To Come proves to be no more than Scrooge's bedpost and bed-curtains. The bridging of dream objects and the actual has often been explored in literature; one is reminded that in Alice's dreams a pack of playing cards are really only falling leaves and the Red Queen is merely a kitten after all.

Scrooge asked the question, because he didn't know whether a ghost so transparent might find himself in a condition to take a chair; and felt that in the event of its being impossible, it might involve the necessity of an embarrassing explanation. But the ghost sat down on the opposite side of the fire-**73** place, as if he were quite used to it.

"You don't believe in me," observed the Ghost.

"I don't," said Scrooge.

"What evidence would you have of my reality, beyond that of your senses?"

"I don't know," said Scrooge.

"Why do you doubt your senses?"

74 "Because," said Scrooge, "a little thing affects them. A slight disorder of the stomach makes them cheats. You may be an undigested bit of beef, a blot of mustard, a crumb of cheese, a fragment of an underdone potato. There's more of gravy than of grave about you, whatever you are!"

Scrooge was not much in the habit of cracking jokes, nor did he feel, in his heart, by any means waggish then. The truth is, that he tried to be smart, as a means of distracting his own attention, and keeping down his terror; for the spectre's voice disturbed the very marrow in his bones.

To sit, staring at those fixed, glazed eyes, in silence for a moment, would play, Scrooge felt, the very deuce with him. There was something very awful, too, in the spectre's being provided with an infernal atmosphere of its own. Scrooge could not feel it himself, but this was clearly the case; for though the Ghost sat perfectly motionless, its hair, and skirts, and tassels, were still agitated as by the hot vapour from an oven.

"You see this toothpick?" said Scrooge, returning quickly to the charge, for the reason just assigned; and wishing, though it were only for a second, to divert the vision's stony gaze from himself.

"I do," replied the Ghost.

"You are not looking at it," said Scrooge.

"But I see it," said the Ghost, "notwithstanding."

"Well!" returned Scrooge. "I have but to swallow this, and be for the rest of my days persecuted by a legion of goblins, all of my own creation. Humbug, I tell you—humbug!"

At this, the spirit raised a frightful cry, and shook its chain with such a dismal and appalling noise, that Scrooge held on tight to his chair, to save himself from falling in a swoon. But how much greater was his horror, when the phantom taking **75** off the bandage round its head, as if it were too warm to wear in-doors, its lower jaw dropped down upon its breast!

Scrooge fell upon his knees, and clasped his hands before his face.

"Mercy!" he said. "Dreadful apparition, why do you trouble me?"

"Man of the worldly mind!" replied the Ghost, "do you believe in me or not?"

"I do," said Scrooge. "I must. But why do spirits walk the earth, and why do they come to me?"

"It is required of every man," the Ghost returned, "that the spirit within him should walk abroad among his fellow-men, and travel far and wide; and if that spirit goes not forth in life, it is condemned to do so after death. It is doomed to wander through the world—oh, woe is me!—and witness what it cannot share, but might have shared on earth, and turned to happiness!"

Again the spectre raised a cry, and shook its chain, and wrung its shadowy hands.

"You are fettered," said Scrooge, trembling. "Tell me why?"

"I wear the chain I forged in life," replied the Ghost. "I made it link by link, and yard by yard; I girded it on of my own free will, and of my own free will I wore it. Is its pattern strange to *you?*"

In a letter to Forster, September 30, 1844, Dickens described a recent dream he had had while in Italy. Like Scrooge with his indigestion, Dickens was afflicted with "a return of rheumatism in my back, and knotted round my waist like a girdle of pain." He said that he saw a figure, dressed in a robe. At first he could not tell who the woman was, but soon he was certain it was the spirit of his dead sister-in-law Mary Hogarth. He questioned her of the true religion, and she replied that Catholicism would be the best for him. When he awoke, he contemplated the dream and tried to unravel "the fragments of reality" that had caused the vision. He reasoned that the figure had been suggested by a space on the wall where a religious painting must have once hung; he had speculated what it might be, perhaps a madonna. Before retiring, he had heard the convent bells and had thought of the Catholic services; these random contemplations must have been the source for the spirit's reply. "And yet," he concluded the letter, "for all this, put the case of that wish being fulfilled by any agency in which I had no hand; and I wonder whether I should regard it as a dream, or an actual Vision!" Dickens' doubt is shared by Scrooge, when in Stave 2, he contemplates the spirits, "Was it a dream or not?"

75 *taking off the bandage round its head . . . its lower jaw dropped down upon its breast!* The dead were often bound round the chin and head to keep the mouth closed. Note below, for example, Sir John Everett Millais' sketch of Dickens on his deathbed.

Charles Dickens on his deathbed by John Everett Millais, 1870. *Courtesy The Library of Congress*

76 *It comes from other regions...and is conveyed by other ministers.* From Heaven and the heavenly hosts. Like the spirit Virgil in the fourth canto of Dante's *Inferno,* Marley's Ghost talks in "veiled speech," because Christ is unknown and cannot be named in the infernal world. In the same manner, the ghost in regard to his inability to follow Christ's teachings failed to raise his eyes "to that blessed Star which led the Wise Men to a poor abode."

In other respects, Dickens' description of the ghost's visit may have been influenced by the great Italian poem. As the poet Virgil is the guide to the poet Dante, the miser Marley is the guide to the miser Scrooge; like Scrooge and Marley, Dante and Virgil are "kindred spirits." Both visions theoretically occur over three days: Dante's at Easter, Scrooge's at Christmas. Dickens' view of the Invisible World retains much of the atmosphere of Dante's. Marley would have been in the Fourth Circle, that of the Avaricious; as the condemned in Dante's work must roll great weights, Marley and his fellow specters are burdened with the weight of chains, cashboxes, and other symbols of their former trade. Note also that both authors title their work by technically inappropriate literary forms; Dante calls his poem a comedy, Dickens his story a carol.

77 *I cannot rest, I cannot stay, I cannot linger anywhere.* Dickens in the galleys carefully changed this sentence from "I may not rest, I may not stay, I may not linger"; in the final text, Dickens has removed any possibility of choice for the spirit.

Scrooge trembled more and more.

" Or would you know," pursued the Ghost, " the weight and length of the strong coil you bear yourself? It was full as heavy and as long as this, seven Christmas Eves ago. You have laboured on it, since. It is a ponderous chain !"

Scrooge glanced about him on the floor, in the expectation of finding himself surrounded by some fifty or sixty fathoms of iron cable : but he could see nothing.

" Jacob," he said, imploringly. " Old Jacob Marley, tell me more. Speak comfort to me, Jacob."

76 " I have none to give," the Ghost replied. " It comes from other regions, Ebenezer Scrooge, and is conveyed by other ministers, to other kinds of men. Nor can I tell you what I would. A very little

77 more, is all permitted to me. I cannot rest, I cannot stay, I cannot linger anywhere. My spirit never walked beyond our counting-house—mark me !—in life my spirit never roved beyond the narrow limits of our money-changing hole ; and weary journeys lie before me !"

It was a habit with Scrooge, whenever he became thoughtful, to put his hands in his breeches pockets. Pondering on what the Ghost had said, he did so now, but without lifting up his eyes, or getting off his knees.

" You must have been very slow about it, Jacob," Scrooge observed, in a business-like manner, though with humility and deference.

" Slow !" the Ghost repeated.

" Seven years dead," mused Scrooge. " And travelling all the time ?"

" The whole time," said the Ghost. " No rest, no peace. Incessant torture of remorse."

" You travel fast ?" said Scrooge.

" On the wings of the wind," replied the Ghost.

" You might have got over a great quantity of ground in seven years," said Scrooge.

The Ghost, on hearing this, set up another cry, and clanked its chain so hideously in the dead silence of the night, that the Ward would have been justi- **78** fied in indicting it for a nuisance.

"Oh! captive, bound, and double-ironed," cried **79** the phantom, " not to know, that ages of incessant labour by immortal creatures, for this earth must pass into eternity before the good of which it is susceptible is all developed. Not to know that any Christian spirit working kindly in its little sphere, whatever it may be, will find its mortal life too short for its vast means of usefulness. Not to know that no space of regret can make amends for one life's opportunities misused! Yet such was I! Oh! such was I!"

" But you were always a good man of business, Jacob," faultered Scrooge, who now began to apply this to himself.

" Business!" cried the Ghost, wringing its hands again. " Mankind was my business. The common welfare was my business; charity, mercy, forbearance, and benevolence, were, all, my business. The dealings of my trade were but a drop of water in the comprehensive ocean of my business!"

It held up its chain at arm's length, as if that were the cause of all its unavailing grief, and flung it heavily upon the ground again.

" At this time of the rolling year," the spectre said, " I suffer most. Why did I walk through crowds of fellow-beings with my eyes turned down, and never raise them to that blessed Star which led the Wise Men to a poor abode? Were there no poor homes to which its light would have conducted *me!*"

Scrooge was very much dismayed to hear the spectre going on at this rate, and began to quake exceedingly.

" Hear me!" cried the Ghost. " My time is nearly gone."

" I will," said Scrooge. " But don't be hard upon

78 *the Ward*. An officer or watchman of the ward, one of twenty-six parishes or divisions of London, here likely Langborn Ward. It was in 1829 that the modern metropolitan police force was formed under Sir Robert Peel; policemen are called "bobbies" after Peel.

79 *"Oh! captive, bound, and double-ironed."* Dickens obviously felt uncomfortable with this phrase; in the Berg prompt copy, he changed it to "Man cruel man," and in the Ticknor and Fields public reading edition, to "O blind man, blind man."

me! Don't be flowery, Jacob! Pray!"

"How it is that I appear before you in a shape that you can see, I may not tell. I have sat invisible beside you many and many a day."

It was not an agreeable idea. Scrooge shivered, and wiped the perspiration from his brow.

"That is no light part of my penance," pursued the Ghost. "I am here to-night to warn you, that you have yet a chance and hope of escaping my fate. A chance and hope of my procuring, Ebenezer."

"You were always a good friend to me," said Scrooge. "Thank'ee!"

"You will be haunted," resumed the Ghost, "by Three Spirits."

Scrooge's countenance fell almost as low as the Ghost's had done.

"Is that the chance and hope you mentioned, Jacob?" he demanded, in a faultering voice.

"It is."

"I—I think I'd rather not," said Scrooge.

"Without their visits," said the Ghost, "you cannot hope to shun the path I tread. Expect the first to-morrow, when the bell tolls one."

"Couldn't I take 'em all at once, and have it over, Jacob?" hinted Scrooge.

"Expect the second on the next night at the same hour. The third upon the next night when the last stroke of twelve has ceased to vibrate. Look to see me no more; and look that, for your own sake, you remember what has passed between us!"

When it had said these words, the spectre took its wrapper from the table, and bound it round its head, as before. Scrooge knew this, by the smart sound its teeth made, when the jaws were brought together by the bandage. He ventured to raise his eyes again, and found his supernatural visitor confronting him in an erect attitude, with its chain wound over and about its arm.

The apparition walked backward from him ; and at every step it took, the window raised itself a little, so that when the spectre reached it, it was wide open. It beckoned Scrooge to approach, which he did. When they were within two paces of each other, Marley's Ghost held up its hand, warning him to come no nearer. Scrooge stopped.

Not so much in obedience, as in surprise and fear : for on the raising of the hand, he became sensible of confused noises in the air ; incoherent sounds of lamentation and regret ; wailings inexpressibly sorrowful and self-accusatory. The spectre, after listening for a moment, joined in the mournful dirge ; and floated out upon the bleak, dark night.

Scrooge followed to the window : desperate in his curiosity. He looked out.

The air was filled with phantoms, wandering hither and thither in restless haste, and moaning as they went. Every one of them wore chains like Marley's Ghost ; some few (they might be guilty governments) were linked together ; none were free. Many had been personally known to Scrooge in their lives. He had been quite familiar with one old ghost, in a white waistcoat, with a monstrous iron safe attached to its ancle, who cried piteously at being unable to assist a wretched woman with an infant, whom it saw below, upon a door-step. The misery with them all was, clearly, that they sought to interfere, for good, in human matters, and had lost the power for ever.

Whether these creatures faded into mist, or mist enshrouded them, he could not tell. But they and their spirit voices faded together ; and the night became as it had been when he walked home.

Scrooge closed the window, and examined the door by which the Ghost had entered. It was double-locked, as he had locked it with his own hands, and the bolts were undisturbed. He tried to

80 *dull.* Here, meaning in monotonous tones. Kate Field in *Pen Photographs of Charles Dickens' Readings* (1871) complained that the one failure in Dickens' characterizations in his public reading of *A Christmas Carol* lay in his ghosts being "perhaps too monotonous—a way ghosts have when they return to earth. It is generally believed that ghosts, being 'damp, moist, uncomfortable bodies,' lose their voices beyond redemption and are obliged to pipe through eternity on one key.... Solemnity and monotony are not synonymous terms, yet every theatrical ghost insists that they are, and Dickens is no exception to the rule."

say "Humbug!" but stopped at the first syllable. And being, from the emotion he had undergone, or the fatigues of the day, or his glimpse of the Invisible **80** World, or the dull conversation of the Ghost, or the lateness of the hour, much in need of repose; went straight to bed, without undressing, and fell asleep upon the instant.

Preliminary pencil and wash drawing by John Leech for "The Phantoms." *Courtesy The Houghton Library, Harvard University*

STAVE TWO.

————◆————

THE FIRST OF THE THREE SPIRITS.

When Scrooge awoke, it was so dark, that looking out of bed, he could scarcely distinguish the transparent window from the opaque walls of his chamber. He was endeavouring to pierce the darkness with his ferret eyes, when the chimes of a [1,2] neighbouring church struck the four quarters. So he listened for the hour.

To his great astonishment the heavy bell went on from six to seven, and from seven to eight, and [3] regularly up to twelve; then stopped. Twelve! It was past two when he went to bed. The clock was wrong. An icicle must have got into the works. Twelve!

He touched the spring of his repeater, to correct [4]

[1] *ferret eyes*. The ferret, a member of the weasel family, has sharp, red eyes; in England it is used to drive rabbits and rats from their burrows. Scrooge thus has a penetrating glance.

[2] *a neighboring church*. Gwen Major in her article "Scrooge's Chambers" (cited in Stave 1, Note 21) identified this place as St. Andrew's Undershaft, at the corner of Leadenhall Street and St. Mary Ave.

[3] *six*. Apparently Scrooge generally rose at six in the morning; this was the usual hour of waking for Londoners of the time.

[4] *his repeater*. Repeating watch or clock, invented about 1676, to strike the hour and quarter hour as desired.

5 *"three days after the sight of this First of Ex-change pay to Ebenezer Scrooge or his order."* This quotation is slightly different from that in the orig-inal manuscript: "sixty days [in a state effective] after sight pay to me or my order." The phrase is the tech-nical form in which a bill of exchange is worded; each one, drawn up for a debt or credit without an actual exchange of money, is prepared in three sets as the first, second, and third exchange, so that if one was lost, the others would be available, and once one is accepted the others become worthless. Scrooge is worried, because, if not presented by the date assigned in writing, the bill becomes worthless. Dickens may have changed the payment from sixty to three days to increase the miser's worry. Scrooge has already lost one day according to the clock and has far less time to settle the accounts, so the loss of even one working day would certainly be more distressing.

6 *United States' security.* At the time of the story, the English found it no security at all. During the early 1830s, individual states, without backing from the federal government, borrowed heavily from for-eign capitalists (particularly the English) to finance public works. Due to the financial crisis of 1837, many states repudiated their bonds, and thus weakened American credit abroad.

this most preposterous clock. Its rapid little pulse beat twelve; and stopped.

"Why, it isn't possible," said Scrooge, "that I can have slept through a whole day and far into another night. It isn't possible that anything has happened to the sun, and this is twelve at noon!"

The idea being an alarming one, he scrambled out of bed, and groped his way to the window. He was obliged to rub the frost off with the sleeve of his dressing-gown before he could see anything; and could see very little then. All he could make out was, that it was still very foggy and extremely cold, and that there was no noise of people running to and fro, and making a great stir, as there unquestionably would have been if night had beaten off bright day, and taken possession of the world. This was a

5 great relief, because "three days after sight of this First of Exchange pay to Mr. Ebenezer Scrooge or his order," and so forth, would have become a mere

6 United States' security if there were no days to count by.

Scrooge went to bed again, and thought, and thought, and thought it over and over and over, and could make nothing of it. The more he thought, the more perplexed he was; and the more he endeavoured not to think, the more he thought. Marley's Ghost bothered him exceedingly. Every time he resolved within himself, after mature in-quiry, that it was all a dream, his mind flew back again, like a strong spring released, to its first posi-tion, and presented the same problem to be worked all through, "Was it a dream or not?"

Scrooge lay in this state until the chimes had gone three quarters more, when he remembered, on a sudden, that the Ghost had warned him of a visi-tation when the bell tolled one. He resolved to lie awake until the hour was past; and, considering that he could no more go to sleep than go to Heaven, this was perhaps the wisest resolution in his power.

The quarter was so long, that he was more than once convinced he must have sunk into a doze unconsciously, and missed the clock. At length it broke upon his listening ear.

"Ding, dong!"

"A quarter past," said Scrooge, counting.

"Ding, dong!"

"Half past!" said Scrooge.

"Ding, dong!"

"A quarter to it," said Scrooge.

"Ding, dong!"

"The hour itself," said Scrooge, triumphantly, "and nothing else!"

He spoke before the hour bell sounded, which it now did with a deep, dull, hollow, melancholy ONE. Light flashed up in the room upon the instant, and the curtains of his bed were drawn.

The curtains of his bed were drawn aside, I tell you, by a hand. Not the curtains at his feet, nor the curtains at his back, but those to which his face was addressed. The curtains of his bed were drawn aside; and Scrooge, starting up into a half-recumbent attitude, found himself face to face with the unearthly visitor who drew them: as close to it as I am now to you, and I am standing in the spirit at your elbow.

It was a strange figure—like a child: yet not so **7** like a child as like an old man, viewed through some supernatural medium, which gave him the appearance of having receded from the view, and being diminished to a child's proportions. Its hair, which hung about its neck and down its back, was white as if with age; and yet the face had not a wrinkle in it, and the tenderest bloom was on the skin. The arms were very long and muscular; the hands the same, as if its hold were of uncommon strength. Its legs and feet, most delicately formed, were, like those upper members, bare. It wore a tunic of the purest white; and round its waist was bound a lustrous

7 *It was a strange figure.* The ambiguity of the Spirit's age suggests that it not only is more than two thousand years old but that it remains young and fresh like summer flowers, "for it is good to be children sometimes, and never better than at Christmas, when its mighty Founder was a child himself." This duality is symbolic of memory itself, which is not limited to one's actual age; it encompasses the entire life of a man, from infancy through old age.

The illusion of youth also suggests the *Christkind*, the Germanic Christ Child who, during the Reformation, replaced the more Roman St. Nicholas; this figure, thought to be a girl, was said to be a messenger who came to announce the coming birth of Christ. Supposedly the name *Christkindl* was corrupted with the image of Father Christmas (see Stave 3, Note 12) to form *Kris Kringle*, the prototype for the American Santa Claus. Note that Dickens describes the Ghost of Christmas Past only as "it"; the spirit may be either male or female. In the Alastair Sim film, it was portrayed as an old man; in the Mr. Magoo cartoon, as a child; and in the movie musical *Scrooge*, it was played by Dame Edith Evans. John Leech, perhaps wisely, did not try to picture this spirit, the only one of Scrooge's unearthly visitors not to be illustrated.

The *Christkind* is traditionally portrayed in a white gown and white veil with a wreath of candles about the head. Dickens in his description suggests an actual candle, a precise metaphor for memory. The strange alterations in the spirit's form reflect the constant transmutations of a candle through its drippings and flame due to atmospheric changes. That Scrooge is gazing at an actual candle with "fragments of all the faces" of his past in the spirit's face is proven by the extinguisher it carries under its arm.

belt, the sheen of which was beautiful. It held a branch of fresh green holly in its hand; and, in singular contradiction of that wintry emblem, had its dress trimmed with summer flowers. But the strangest thing about it was, that from the crown of its head there sprung a bright clear jet of light, by which all this was visible; and which was doubtless the occasion of its using, in its duller moments, a great extinguisher for a cap, which it now held under its arm.

Even this, though, when Scrooge looked at it with increasing steadiness, was *not* its strangest quality. For as its belt sparkled and glittered now in one part and now in another, and what was light one instant, at another time was dark, so the figure itself fluctuated in its distinctness: being now a thing with one arm, now with one leg, now with twenty legs, now a pair of legs without a head, now a head without a body: of which dissolving parts, no outline would be visible in the dense gloom wherein they melted away. And in the very wonder of this, it would be itself again; distinct and clear as ever.

"Are you the Spirit, sir, whose coming was foretold to me?" asked Scrooge.

"I am!"

The voice was soft and gentle. Singularly low, as if instead of being so close beside him, it were at a distance.

"Who, and what are you?" Scrooge demanded.

"I am the Ghost of Christmas Past."

"Long past?" inquired Scrooge: observant of its dwarfish stature.

"No. Your past."

Perhaps, Scrooge could not have told anybody why, if anybody could have asked him; but he had a special desire to see the Spirit in his cap; and begged him to be covered.

"What!" exclaimed the Ghost, "would you so soon put out, with worldly hands, the light I give?

Is it not enough that you are one of those whose passions made this cap, and force me through whole trains of years to wear it low upon my brow!"

Scrooge reverently disclaimed all intention to offend, or any knowledge of having wilfully " bon- **8** neted" the Spirit at any period of his life.   He then made bold to inquire what business brought him there.

" Your welfare !" said the Ghost.

Scrooge expressed himself much obliged, but could **9** not help thinking that a night of unbroken rest would have been more conducive to that end.   The Spirit must have heard him thinking, for it said immediately :

" Your reclamation, then.   Take heed !"

It put out its strong hand as it spoke, and clasped him gently by the arm.

" Rise ! and walk with me !"

It would have been in vain for Scrooge to plead that the weather and the hour were not adapted to pedestrian purposes ; that bed was warm, and the thermometer a long way below freezing ; that he was clad but lightly in his slippers, dressing-gown, and nightcap ; and that he had a cold upon him at that time.   The grasp, though gentle as a woman's hand, was not to be resisted.   He rose : but finding that the Spirit made towards the window, clasped its robe in supplication.

" I am a mortal," Scrooge remonstrated, " and liable to fall."

" Bear but a touch of my hand *there*," said the Spirit, laying it upon his heart, " and you shall be upheld in more than this !"

As the words were spoken, they passed through the wall, and stood upon an open country road, with fields on either hand.   The city had entirely vanished.   Not a vestige of it was to be seen. The darkness and the mist had vanished with it, for it was a clear, cold, winter day, with snow upon the ground.

8 *"bonneted."* A pun: to "bonnet" means to knock a person's hat down over his eyes as well as to snuff out a candle with its bonnet, or extinguisher cap.

9 *Scrooge . . . could not help thinking that a night of unbroken rest would have been more conducive to that end.* Scrooge still cannot avoid being facetious; despite the appearance of the ghost for his own spiritual good, he remains the perfect utilitarian.

10 *a thousand odours . . . connected with a thousand thoughts, and hopes, and joys, and cares long long forgotten.* The influence of the senses, in this case the sense of smell, recalls Marcel Proust's work, in summoning up "the remembrance of things past."

11 *a pimple.* It is, of course, a tear.

12 *a little market-town . . . with the bridge, its church, and winding river.* Johnson in "About 'A Christmas Carol'" (cited in Stave 1, Note 36), identified this description as referring to Strood, Rochester, and the river Medway, where Dickens spent part of his childhood. Johnson also noted that Dickens erased the word "castle" from the original manuscript, an apparent reference to Rochester Castle. Dickens again described all these scenes in his unfinished *The Mystery of Edwin Drood* (1870).

"Country Church—Christmas Morning" by Robert Seymour, *The Book of Christmas*, 1836. *Courtesy The Library of Congress*

"Good Heaven!" said Scrooge, clasping his hands together, as he looked about him. "I was bred in this place. I was a boy here!"

The Spirit gazed upon him mildly. Its gentle touch, though it had been light and instantaneous, appeared still present to the old man's sense of feeling. He was conscious of a thousand odours floating in the air, each one connected with a thousand thoughts, and hopes, and joys, and cares long, long, forgotten!

"Your lip is trembling," said the Ghost. "And what is that upon your cheek?"

Scrooge muttered, with an unusual catching in his voice, that it was a pimple; and begged the Ghost to lead him where he would.

"You recollect the way?" inquired the Spirit.

"Remember it!" cried Scrooge with fervour—"I could walk it blindfold."

"Strange to have forgotten it for so many years!" observed the Ghost. "Let us go on."

They walked along the road; Scrooge recognising every gate, and post, and tree; until a little market-town appeared in the distance, with its bridge, its church, and winding river. Some shaggy ponies now were seen trotting towards them with boys upon their

"Coming Home" by Robert Seymour, *The Book of Christmas*, 1836. *Courtesy The Prints Division, The New York Public Library, Astor, Lenox and Tilden Foundations*

backs, who called to other boys in country gigs and carts, driven by farmers. All these boys were in great spirits, and shouted to each other, until the broad fields were so full of merry music, that the crisp air laughed to hear it.

"These are but shadows of the things that have been," said the Ghost. "They have no consciousness of us."

The jocund travellers came on; and as they came, Scrooge knew and named them every one. Why was he rejoiced beyond all bounds to see them! Why did his cold eye glisten, and his heart leap up as they went past! Why was he filled with gladness when he heard them give each other Merry Christmas, as they parted at cross-roads and-bye ways, for their several homes! What was merry Christmas to Scrooge? Out upon merry Christmas! What good had it ever done to him?

"The school is not quite deserted," said the Ghost. "A solitary child, neglected by his friends, is left there still."

Scrooge said he knew it. And he sobbed.

They left the high-road, by a well remembered lane, and soon approached a mansion of dull red **13** brick, with a little weathercock-surmounted cupola,

13 *a mansion of dull red brick.* Compare this description of Scrooge's schoolhouse with another, that in *David Copperfield* (1850, Ch. 5): "Salem house was a square brick building with wings, of a bare and unfurnished appearance....I gazed upon the schoolroom into which he took me, as the most forlorn and desolate place I had ever seen....A long room, with three long rows of desks, and six of forms, and bristling all round with pegs for hats and slates...."

The school described was the Wellington House Academy where Dickens received his brief formal education (a year and a half) before leaving at fifteen. It was also the subject of the article "Our School" included in *Reprinted Pieces* (1868).

14 *plain deal forms*. Long, unpainted, and unvarnished school benches, generally made of pine.

15 *a lonely boy was reading*. This child was the boy Charles Dickens. "He was a very little and very sickly boy," as Forster described him in the biography, "subject to attacks of violent spasm which disabled him from any active exertion. He was never a good little cricket-player. He was never a first-rate hand at marbles....But he had great pleasure in watching the other boys...at these games, reading while they played; and he had always the belief that this early sickness had brought to himself one inestimable advantage, in the circumstances of his weak health having strongly inclined him to reading."

"The whole passage is in the spirit of [Charles] Lamb's 'New Year's Eve,' a favourite essay with Dickens," observed Kathleen Tillotson in "The Middle Years from the *Carol* to *Copperfield*" (*Dickens Memorial Lectures, 1970*); "Elia looks back upon 'that "other me" there, in the background' in tender love and pity, and regret—"From what have I fallen!"—and suggests that 'over the intervention of forty years, a man may have leave to love himself without the intervention of self-love.'"

on the roof, and a bell hanging in it. It was a large house, but one of broken fortunes; for the spacious offices were little used, their walls were damp and mossy, their windows broken, and their gates decayed. Fowls clucked and strutted in the stables; and the coach-houses and sheds were overrun with grass. Nor was it more retentive of its ancient state, within; for entering the dreary hall, and glancing through the open doors of many rooms, they found them poorly furnished, cold, and vast. There was an earthy savour in the air, a chilly bareness in the place, which associated itself somehow with too much getting up by candle-light, and not too much to eat.

They went, the Ghost and Scrooge, across the hall, to a door at the back of the house. It opened before them, and disclosed a long, bare, melancholy **14** room, made barer still by lines of plain deal forms **15** and desks. At one of these a lonely boy was reading near a feeble fire; and Scrooge sat down upon a form, and wept to see his poor forgotten self as he had used to be.

Woodcut by George Cruikshank, *Our Own Time, 1846. Courtesy The Prints Division, The New York Public Library, Astor, Lenox and Tilden Foundations*

Not a latent echo in the house, not a squeak and **16** scuffle from the mice behind the panneling, not a drip from the half-thawed water-spout in the dull yard behind, not a sigh among the leafless boughs of one despondent poplar, not the idle swinging of an empty store-house door, no, not a clicking in the fire, but fell upon the heart of Scrooge with softening influence, and gave a freer passage to his tears.

The Spirit touched him on the arm, and pointed to his younger self, intent upon his reading. Sud- **17** denly a man, in foreign garments: wonderfully real and distinct to look at: stood outside the window, with an axe stuck in his belt, and leading an ass laden with wood by the bridle.

"Why, it's Ali Baba!" Scrooge exclaimed in **18** ecstacy. "It's dear old honest Ali Baba! Yes, yes, I know! One Christmas time, when yonder solitary child was left here all alone, he *did* come, for the first time, just like that. Poor boy! And Valentine," said Scrooge, "and his wild brother, **19** Orson; there they go! And what's his name, who **20** was put down in his drawers, asleep, at the Gate of Damascus; don't you see him! And the Sultan's **21** Groom turned upside-down by the Genii; there he is upon his head! Serve him right. I'm glad of it. What business had *he* to be married to the Princess!"

To hear Scrooge expending all the earnestness of his nature on such subjects, in a most extraordinary voice between laughing and crying; and to see his heightened and excited face; would have been a surprise to his business friends in the city, indeed.

"There's the Parrot!" cried Scrooge. "Green **22** body and yellow tail, with a thing like a lettuce growing out of the top of his head; there he is! Poor Robin Crusoe, he called him, when he came home again after sailing round the island. 'Poor Robin Crusoe, where have you been, Robin Crusoe?' The man thought he was dreaming, but he wasn't.

16 *Not a latent echo in the house . . . but fell upon the heart of Scrooge with softening influence, and gave a freer passage to his tears.* Kathleen Tillotson in her lecture (cited in the previous note) disclosed that of this passage, "The whole impression, and half the details, come from Tennyson's 'Mariana' (first published in *Poems, Chiefly Lyrical*, 1830)."

17 *his younger self, intent upon his reading.* In the autobiographical fragment that became part of *David Copperfield*, Dickens described in detail his introduction to the world of books, similar to that of the boy Scrooge: "My father had left a small collection of books in a little room upstairs, to which I had access . . . and which nobody else in our house ever troubled. From that blessed little room, Roderick Random, Peregrine Pickle, Humphrey Clinker, Tom Jones, the Vicar of Wakefield, Don Quixote, Gil Blas, and Robinson Crusoe, came out, a glorious host, to keep me company. They kept alive my fancy, and my hope of something beyond that place and time,—they, and the Arabian Nights, and the Tales of the Genii, —and did me no harm; for whatever harm was in some of them was not there for me; *I* knew nothing of it." So dear were these books to young Charles that it must have been tragic for the boy to have had to pawn, among the first of his father's belongings, these treasured volumes.

Dickens apparently enjoyed the giving of books at Christmas; in "A Christmas Tree," he reveled in describing "how thick the books begin to hang . . . many of them, and with deliciously smooth covers of bright red or green" that contain the favorite stories of his and Scrooge's childhoods. The effect of these early books on Dickens' writing is inestimable.

The young Scrooge and David Copperfield are among the few fortunate children in Dickens' work to have found the rare pleasure hidden in literature. The sense of the fanciful enlivened by this early reading is completely foreign to the young Smallweeds of *Bleak House*, "complete little men and women" who "bear a likeness to old monkeys with something depressing on their minds." The education given the Smallweed twins "discarded all amusements, discountenanced all story-books, fairy tales, fictions, and fables, and banished all levities whatsoever." Judy "never heard of Cinderella," Bart "knows no more of Jack the Giant Killer, or of Sinbad the Sailor, than he knows of the people in the stars."

18 *Ali Baba.* One of Dickens' favorite stories from one of his favorite books, *The Arabian Nights*. "Oh, now all common things become uncommon and enchanted to me!" So Dickens described the magic of *The Arabian Nights* in "A Christmas Tree." "All lamps are wonderful; all rings are talismans. . . . Yes, on every object that I recognize among those upper branches of my Christmas Tree, I see this fairy light! When I wake . . . on the cold dark winter mornings, the white snow dimly beheld, outside, through the frost on the windowpane, I hear Dinarzade."

Next to Shakespeare and the New Testament, *The Arabian Nights* is the book most frequently alluded to in Dickens' writing; among the tales most often mentioned is "Ali Baba and the Forty Thieves" (notably in the opening of *The Haunted Man* and in the description of schoolmaster M'Choakumchild in *Hard Times*). The influence of the stories was, however, not limited merely to passing references; Dickens borrowed the structure of Scheherazade's presentation of the tales to compose the string of stories in *Master Humphrey's Clock* (1840) and David Copperfield's dormitory sketches, told to his hero Steerforth.

Dr. Elizabeth Sewell, the Joe Rosenthal professor of Humanities at the University of North Carolina, Greensboro, has brought my attention to the childhood reading of another British man of letters, William Wordsworth, described in Book V of his *The Prelude* (1805). His "precious treasure" was a cheap, yellow-canvas-backed abridgement of *The Arabian Nights*, and when he learned that it was only a selection from the tales, he tried unsuccessfully to save up with a friend to buy the complete set of stories.

19 *Valentine . . . and his wild brother, Orson.* The heroes of *The History of Two Valyannte Brethern, Valentyne and Orson* (1495), a popular French romance translated into English about 1565 by Henry Watson. Like *Robinson Crusoe* and *The Arabian Nights*, this book was written for adults, but when popularized in abridged form in numerous chapbooks, *The History of Valentine and Orson* became a favorite story for children.

Valentine and Orson were the twin sons of Bellisant, the sister of King Pepin and wife of the Emperor of Constantinople. At birth the brothers were parted; Orson being carried away by a bear was brought up as a wild man, Valentine as a knight of the French court. It is the story of the brothers' eventual reunion and the restoration of Orson's birthright.

20 *what's his name.* Bedreddin Hassan, a character in *The Arabian Nights*. See Note 21.

21 *the Sultan's Groom.* A character in "Noureddin Ali of Cairo and his Son Bedreddin Hassan" (Nights 20–23 of *The Portable Arabian Nights*, edited by Joseph Campbell, 1952). The hero Bedreddin Hassan on meeting a Genie learns of a woman equal to himself in beauty. She, the daughter of a vizier, is promised to wed a sultan's hunchbacked groom; but at the wedding, Bedreddin is transported to the palace by genii and displaces the ugly husband-to-be, who is made by the spirits to hang upside-down during the wedding night. As the genii must return before dawn, Bedreddin still in his bed clothes journeys back with them; but at daybreak as they are passing over Damascus, he is left at the city gates. After nearly a dozen years, during which time he was employed as a cook, Bedreddin is finally restored to his wife and their son, born in his absence.

In "A Christmas Tree," Dickens also recalls this story, as an example of how the book turned the commonplace in his world into the marvelous: "Tarts are made, according to the recipe of the Vizier's son of Bussorah, who turned pastry-cook after he was set down in his drawers at the gate of Damascus."

22 *"There's the Parrot!"* This episode comes from Daniel Defoe's *The Life and Strange Adventures of Robinson Crusoe* (1719). It occurs on the hero's return after his journey around the island in a little boat: "I reached my old bower in the evening, where I found every thing standing as I left it. . . . I got over the fence, and laid me down in the shade, to rest my limbs, for I was very weary, and fell asleep; but . . . what a surprise I must be in, when I was waked out of my sleep by a voice calling me by my name several times, 'Robin, Robin, Robin Crusoe; poor Robin Crusoe! . . . Where are you? Where have you been?'

"I was so dead asleep at first, being fatigued . . . I did not wake thoroughly; but . dozing between sleeping and waking, thought I dreamed that somebody spoke to me: but as the voice continued to repeat Robin Crusoe, Robin Crusoe, at last I began to wake more perfectly, and was at first dreadfully frighted, and started up in the utmost consternation; but no sooner were my eyes open, but I saw my Poll sitting on top of the hedge! and immediately knew it was he that spoke to me; for just in such bemoaning language I used to talk to him, and teach him; and he had learned it so perfectly, that he . . . sat upon my thumb . . . and continued talking to me, Poor Robin Crusoe! and how did I come here? and where had I been? just as if he had been overjoyed to see me again: and so I carried him home along with me."

Especially fond of this story, Dickens often referred to it in his writing. In the essay, "When we Stopped Growing" (*Household Words*, January 1, 1853, p. 361), he again affectionately recalled this episode from the Defoe classic: "We have never grown the thousandth part of an inch out of Robinson Crusoe. He fits us just as well, and in exactly the same way as when we were among the smallest of the small. . . . Never sail we, idle, in a little boat . . . but we know that our boat-growth stopped for ever, when Robinson Crusoe sailed round the Island, and, having been nearly lost, was so affectionately awakened out of his sleep by that immortal parrot."

Woodcut by George Cruikshank, *The Life and Adventures of Robinson Crusoe*, 1831. *Courtesy The Library of Congress*

It was the Parrot, you know. There goes Friday, **23** running for his life to the little creek! Halloa! Hoop! Halloo!"

Then, with a rapidity of transition very foreign to his usual character, he said, in pity for his former self, " Poor boy !" and cried again.

" I wish," Scrooge muttered, putting his hand in his pocket, and looking about him, after drying his eyes with his cuff: " but it's too late now."

" What is the matter?" asked the Spirit.

" Nothing," said Scrooge. " Nothing. There was a boy singing a Christmas Carol at my door last night. I should like to have given him something: that's all."

The Ghost smiled thoughtfully, and waved its hand: saying as it did so, " Let us see another Christmas !"

Scrooge's former self grew larger at the words, and the room became a little darker and more dirty. The **24** pannels shrunk, the windows cracked; fragments of plaster fell out of the ceiling, and the naked laths were shown instead; but how all this was brought about, Scrooge knew no more than you do. He only

23 *Friday, running for his life.* Another episode in *Robinson Crusoe*, the appearance of natives on the beach: "While I was thus looking on them, I perceived . . . two miserable wretches dragged from the boats, where . . . they were laid by, and were now brought out for the slaughter. I perceived one of them immediately fell, being knocked down, . . . and two or three others were at work immediately, cutting him open for their cookery, while the other victim was left standing by himself, till they should be ready for him. In that very moment this poor wretch seeing himself a little at liberty and unbound, nature inspired him with hopes of life, and he started away from them, and ran with incredible swiftness along the sands, directly towards . . . that part of the coast where my habitation was. . . . There was between them and my castle the creek . . . and this I saw he must necessarily swim over, or the poor wretch would be taken there: but when the savage escaping came thither, he made nothing of it . . . but plunging in, swam through in about thirty strokes . . . landed, and ran on with exceeding strength and swiftness."

Dickens again mentioned this episode in "Nurse's Stories" (1860) of *The Uncommercial Traveller*: "No face is ever reflected in the waters of the little creek which Friday swam across when pursued by his two brother cannibals with sharpened stomachs"; and in jest, in a speech given at a dinner of the Printer's Pension Society, April 6, 1864, Dickens explained that "from the savages enjoying their feast upon the beach, I believe I might trace my first impression of a public dinner!" (*Speeches*, Clarendon Press, p. 324).

24 *The pannels shrunk, the windows cracked.* This acceleration of aging as the spirit and Scrooge move forward in his childhood is reminiscent of a similar phenomenon in H. G. Wells' *The Time Machine* (1895) when the Time Traveller describes the passing of years as he moves into the future: "I am afraid I cannot convey the peculiar sensations of time travelling. . . . As I put on pace, night followed day like the flapping of a black wing. The dim suggestion of the laboratory seemed presently to fall away from me, and I saw the sun hopping swiftly across the sky, leaping it every minute, and every minute marking a day. I supposed the laboratory had been destroyed and I had come into the open air. I had a dim impression of scaffolding, but I was already going too fast to be conscious of any moving things. . . . I saw trees growing and changing like puffs of vapour, now brown, now green; they grew, spread, shivered, and passed away. I saw huge buildings rise up faint and fair, and pass like dreams. The whole surface of the earth seemed changed—melting and flowing under my eyes." (See also Henry E. Vittum's comparison of *A Christmas Carol* to *The Time Machine* in the 1966 Bantam edition of the Dickens classic).

25 *there he was, alone again, when all the other boys had gone home for the jolly holidays.* How dear Dickens thought the coming of these holidays were to such schoolchildren and how heartbreaking it must have been to be left behind is indicated in the following from "A Christmas Tree": "And I *do* come home at Christmas. We all do, or we all should. We all come home, or ought to come home, for a short holiday—the longer, the better—from the great boarding-school, where we are forever working at our arithmetical slates, to take, and give a rest."

26 *Fan.* Fanny was the name of Dickens' favorite (but elder) sister; like Fred's mother (as revealed in Stave 4), she too was gifted in music, both as a musician and singer.

27 *the schoolmaster.* One of many unsympathetic educators in Dickens' work (Squeers of *Nicholas Nickleby*; Doctor Blimber of *Dombey and Son*; Mr. Creakle of *David Copperfield*; Bradley Headstone of *Our Mutual Friend*; Thomas Gradgrind of *Hard Times*), drawn from the novelist's experience, fancy, and reading. In the introduction to *Nicholas Nickleby* (1839), Dickens described schoolmasters as "ignorant, sordid, brutal men, to whom few considerate persons would have entrusted the board and lodging of a horse or dog...."

Dickens' attitude toward such insensitive instructors was influenced further by his discovery of Mr. Barlow, "childhood's experience of a bore," the schoolmaster of the popular children's book *The History of Sandford and Merton* (1783–1789), by Thomas Day. "He knew everything," explained Dickens in *The Uncommercial Traveller* (1861), "and didactically improved all sorts of occasions, from the consumption of a plate of cherries to the contemplation of a starlight night.... What right had he to bore his way into my Arabian Nights?... He was always hinting doubts of the veracity of Sinbad the Sailor. If he could have got hold of the Wonderful Lamp, I knew he would have trimmed it and lighted it, and delivered a lecture over it on the qualities of sperm oil, with a glance at the whale fisheries.... I took refuge in the caves of ignorance, wherein I have resided ever since, and which are still my private address." Mr. Barlow was the fictionalized version of such nineteenth-century educators as Sarah Trimmer (satirized by Dickens as "Miss Grimmer" in *A Holiday Romance*, 1868), who in her *Guardian of Education* (1802–1806) saw fairy and other fanciful tales as "only fit to fill the heads of children with confused notions of wonderful and supernatural events, brought about by the agency of imaginary beings." Her influence persisted throughout the nineteenth century and still has not completely died out in education. The man in Dickens' actual childhood who embodied these attitudes of the fictional Mr. Barlow was William James of the Wellington House Academy, "by far the most ignorant man I have ever had the pleasure to know ... one of the worst-tempered men perhaps

knew that it was quite correct; that everything **25** had happened so; that there he was, alone again, when all the other boys had gone home for the jolly holidays.

He was not reading now, but walking up and down despairingly. Scrooge looked at the Ghost, and with a mournful shaking of his head, glanced anxiously towards the door.

It opened; and a little girl, much younger than the boy, came darting in, and putting her arms about his neck, and often kissing him, addressed him as her "Dear, dear brother."

"I have come to bring you home, dear brother!" said the child, clapping her tiny hands, and bending down to laugh. "To bring you home, home, home!"

26 "Home, little Fan?" returned the boy.

"Yes!" said the child, brimful of glee. "Home, for good and all. Home, for ever and ever. Father is so much kinder than he used to be, that home's like Heaven! He spoke so gently to me one dear night when I was going to bed, that I was not afraid to ask him once more if you might come home; and he said Yes, you should; and sent me in a coach to bring you. And you're to be a man!" said the child, opening her eyes, "and are never to come back here; but first, we're to be together all the Christmas long, and have the merriest time in all the world."

"You are quite a woman, little Fan!" exclaimed the boy.

She clapped her hands and laughed, and tried to touch his head; but being too little, laughed again, and stood on tiptoe to embrace him. Then she began to drag him, in her childish eagerness, towards the door; and he, nothing loth to go, accompanied her.

A terrible voice in the hall cried, "Bring down Master Scrooge's box, there!" and in the hall ap-
27 peared the schoolmaster himself, who glared on

Master Scrooge with a ferocious condescension, and threw him into a dreadful state of mind by shaking hands with him. He then conveyed him and his sister into the veriest old well of a shivering best-parlour that ever was seen, where the maps upon the wall, and the celestial and terrestrial globes in the windows, were waxy with cold. Here he produced a decanter of curiously light wine, and a block **28** of curiously heavy cake, and administered instalments of those dainties to the young people: at the same time, sending out a meagre servant to offer a glass of "something" to the postboy, who **29** answered that he thanked the gentleman, but if it was the same tap as he had tasted before, he had rather not. Master Scrooge's trunk being by this time tied on to the top of the chaise, the children **30** bade the schoolmaster good-bye right willingly; and getting into it, drove gaily down the garden- **31** sweep: the quick wheels dashing the hoar-frost and snow from off the dark leaves of the evergreens like spray.

"Always a delicate creature, whom a breath might have withered," said the Ghost. "But she had a large heart!"

"So she had," cried Scrooge. "You're right. I'll not gainsay it, Spirit. God forbid!"

"She died a woman," said the Ghost, "and had, as I think, children."

"One child," Scrooge returned.

"True," said the Ghost. "Your nephew!"

Scrooge seemed uneasy in his mind; and answered briefly, "Yes."

Although they had but that moment left the school behind them, they were now in the busy thoroughfares of a city, where shadowy passengers passed and repassed; where shadowy carts and coaches battled for the way, and all the strife and tumult of a real city were. It was made plain enough, by the dressing of the shops, that here

that ever lived" (in an address given at the Warehousemen and Clerks' Schools, November 5, 1857. *Speeches*, Clarendon Press, p. 240).

Mr. James was the prototype for Mr. Creakle of *David Copperfield*, but perhaps the most horrifying of these ogres of the English academies was "Thomas Gradgrind, sir. A man of realities. A man of facts and calculations." In *Hard Times* (1854, Chapter 1), he offers his theory of education: "Now, what I want is Facts. Teach these boys and girls nothing but Facts. Facts alone are wanted in life. Plant nothing else, and root out everything else. You can only form the mind of reasoning animals upon Facts; nothing else will ever be of any service to them." Characteristically Dickens found these institutions "a pernicious and abominable humbug altogether."

28 *a decanter of curiously light wine, and a block of curiously heavy cake.* As disclosed in *Punch's Snap-Dragons for Christmas* (1845), it was customary at English boarding schools for the masters to offer "half-baked cake and home-made wine" to their departing charges.

29 *the postboy.* The driver of the vehicle.

30 *the chaise.* According to Dr. Johnson's dictionary, "a carriage of pleasure drawn by one horse."

31 *garden-sweep.* The curve of the driveway through the grounds.

32   *Welch wig.* A woolen or worsted cap, originally made chiefly in Montgomery, Wales. In the Charles Dickens Edition of 1868, Dickens changed this spelling to the more common "Welsh wig."

33   *the hour of seven.* Fezziwig has chosen to close the shop early; the usual hour of closing a place of business was nine o'clock.

34   *his capacious waistcoat.* Compare Fezziwig's figure to that of the Ghost of Christmas Present, Stave 3, Note 15. Dickens' jolly characters have particular trouble in covering their generous emotion.

35   *his organ of benevolence.* According to phrenology, the area above the forehead. This pseudoscience popular in the nineteenth century argued that moral and intellectual character was determined by the shape of the skull, which phrenologists divided into about forty sections, or "organs," each corresponding to a moral or mental faculty.

"A 'Page' of Phrenology" by John Leech, *The Illuminated Magazine,* November 1844. *Courtesy The Library of Congress*

too it was Christmas time again; but it was evening, and the streets were lighted up.

The Ghost stopped at a certain warehouse door, and asked Scrooge if he knew it.

"Know it!" said Scrooge. "Was I apprenticed here?"

They went in. At sight of an old gentleman in **32** a Welch wig, sitting behind such a high desk, that if he had been two inches taller he must have knocked his head against the ceiling, Scrooge cried in great excitement:

"Why, it's old Fezziwig! Bless his heart; it's Fezziwig alive again!"

Old Fezziwig laid down his pen, and looked up **33** at the clock, which pointed to the hour of seven. **34** He rubbed his hands; adjusted his capacious waistcoat; laughed all over himself, from his shoes to **35** his organ of benevolence; and called out in a comfortable, oily, rich, fat, jovial voice:

"Yo ho, there! Ebenezer! Dick!"

Scrooge's former self, now grown a young man, came briskly in, accompanied by his fellow-'prentice.

"Dick Wilkins, to be sure!" said Scrooge to the Ghost. "Bless me, yes. There he is. He was very much attached to me, was Dick. Poor Dick! Dear, dear!"

"Yo ho, my boys!" said Fezziwig. "No more work to-night. Christmas Eve, Dick. Christmas, Ebenezer! Let's have the shutters up," cried old **36** Fezziwig, with a sharp clap of his hands, "before a man can say, Jack Robinson!"

You wouldn't believe how those two fellows went at it! They charged into the street with the shutters—one, two, three—had 'em up in their places—four, five, six—barred 'em and pinned 'em—seven, eight, nine—and came back before you could have got to twelve, panting like race-horses.

"Hilli-ho!" cried old Fezziwig, skipping down from the high desk, with wonderful agility. "Clear away, my lads, and let's have lots of room here!

Hilli-ho, Dick !   Chirrup, Ebenezer !"

Clear away !   There was nothing they wouldn't have cleared away, or couldn't have cleared away, with old Fezziwig looking on.   It was done in a minute.   Every movable was packed off, as if it were dismissed from public life for evermore ; the floor was swept and watered, the lamps were trimmed, fuel was heaped upon the fire ; and the warehouse was as snug, and warm, and dry, and bright a ball-room, as you would desire to see upon a winter's night.

In came a fiddler with a music-book, and went up to the lofty desk, and made an orchestra of it, and tuned like fifty stomach-aches.   In came Mrs. Fezziwig, one vast substantial smile.   In came the three Miss Fezziwigs, beaming and loveable.   In came the six young followers whose hearts they broke.   In came all the young men and women employed in the business.   In came the housemaid, with her cousin, the baker.   In came the cook, with her brother's particular friend, the milkman.   In came the boy from over the way, who was suspected of not having board enough from his master ; trying to hide himself behind the girl from next door but one, who was proved to have had her ears pulled by her Mistress.   In they all came, one after another ; some shyly, some boldly, some gracefully, some awkwardly, some pushing, some pulling ; in they all came, anyhow and everyhow.   Away they all went, twenty couple at once, hands half round and back again the other way ; down the middle and up again ; round and round in various stages of affectionate grouping ; old top couple always turning up in the wrong place ; new top couple starting off again, as soon as they got there ; all top couples at last, and not a bottom one to help them.   When this result was brought about, old Fezziwig, clapping his hands to stop the dance, cried out, " Well done !" and the fiddler plunged his hot face into a pot of porter, **37** especially provided for that purpose.   But scorning

36 *"before a man can say, Jack Robinson!"* "The words of this very popular saying [current in the late seventeenth century]," explained Albert F. Blaisdell in his 1899 edition of *A Christmas Carol*, "originated from a famous comic song. The last line is 'And he was off before he could say Jack Robinson.' The words were sung to the tune of the 'Sailor's Hornpipe.' " Robinson was an old man who reputedly had the habit of calling on his friends and leaving unexpectedly before his name was even announced. Jack Robinson eventually was included among Twelfth Night characters (see Stave 3, Note 10).

37 *porter.* Porter's beer, or porter's ale, a cheap popular drink, dark brown and bitter.

38 *forfeits.* Any one of many popular parlor games played at Christmas in which a fixed penalty is demanded of the player who misses his turn. According to the chapbook *Round about our Coal-Fire* (1740), forfeits were "generally fixed at some certain Price, as a Shilling, Half a Crown, etc., so everyone knowing what to do if they be too stubborn to submit, making themselves easy at discretion"; by the early nineteenth century, payment in coin was universally replaced with that of a kiss. By the time *A Christmas Carol* was written, the playing of such games had fallen out of favor. "The Game of Forfeits is now, we believe, very rare in London," reported an anonymous author in *Holiday Book of Christmas and New Year* (1852); "it is too romping and noisy an amusement for the chilling atmosphere and somewhat too stately decorum of our modern drawing rooms." The games remained popular in the country, and neither Dickens nor Scrooge's nephew thought them too boisterous for their London revels. Several of the more popular forms of forfeits are played by Fred and his Christmas guests in Stave 3.

39 *negus.* A drink made of wine (usually port or sherry), hot water, sugar, nutmeg, and lemon juice; so named after its inventor Colonel Francis Negus (d. 1732). *Punch's Snap-Dragons for Christmas* (1845) noted that the particular flavor of this punch derived from an orange stuck with cloves being plunged rapidly into the hot mixture; and that it may have its origins in the pagan Saturnalia cults. Dickens was particularly fond of this drink; he mentions it frequently in his work (*The Pickwick Papers*, Chapter 45; *Dombey and Son*, Chapter 49; *Our Mutual Friend*, Part I, Chapter 6).

40 *mince-pies.* A staple of the medieval English Christmas table, which has survived to the present. The Protestants had objected to the Christmas pie as a superstitious symbol of the Roman Church; the ingredients (as late as the eighteenth century, being "Neat's tongues, chicken, eggs, sugar, currants, lemon, and orange peel with various spices") were said to correspond to the gifts of the Magi, and the pies were generally oblong in imitation of the crèche. Fortunately they were preserved among the Christmas customs in Cornwall; an ancient Cornish recipe was included in Sandys' introduction to his book of carols, and perhaps Dickens was familiar with such a mince pie: "A pound of beef-suet chopped fine; a pound of raisins do. stoned. A pound of currants cleaned dry. A pound of apples chopped fine. Two or three eggs. Allspice beat very fine; and sugar to your taste. A little salt, and as much brandy and wine as you like."

Sandys suggested that it was best to use little or no meat, as the pie would be lighter and stay fresher longer; he also advised that a piece of citron would be an improvement on these ingredients. Perhaps the tradition flourished longer in Cornwall because of a Cornish superstition: "in as many houses as you can eat mince-pies during Christmas, many happy months will you have in the ensuing year."

rest upon his reappearance, he instantly began again, though there were no dancers yet, as if the other fiddler had been carried home, exhausted, on a shutter; and he were a bran-new man resolved to beat him out of sight, or perish.

38   There were more dances, and there were forfeits, and more dances, and there was cake, and there **39** was negus, and there was a great piece of Cold Roast, and there was a great piece of Cold Boiled, **40** and there were mince-pies, and plenty of beer. But the great effect of the evening came after the Roast and Boiled, when the fiddler (an artful dog, mind! The sort of man who knew his business better than you or I could have told it him!) struck

Preliminary pencil and wash drawing by John Leech for "Mr. Fezziwig's Ball." *Courtesy The Houghton Library, Harvard University*

Frontispiece by John Leech, *Christmas Books*, "Cheap Edition of the Works of Charles Dickens," 1852. *Courtesy The Library of Congress*

up "Sir Roger de Coverley." Then old Fezziwig **41** stood out to dance with Mrs. Fezziwig. Top couple too; with a good stiff piece of work cut out for them; three or four and twenty pair of partners, people who were not to be trifled with; people who *would* dance, and had no notion of walking.

But if they had been twice as many: ah, four times: old Fezziwig would have been a match for them, and so would Mrs. Fezziwig. As to *her*, she was worthy to be his partner in every sense of the term. If that's not high praise, tell me higher, and I'll use it. A positive light appeared to issue from Fezziwig's calves. They shone in every part of the dance like moons. You couldn't have predicted, at any given time, what would become of 'em next. And when old Fezziwig and Mrs. Fezziwig had gone all through the dance; advance and retire,

41 "*Sir Roger de Coverley*." Also known as the "slip or Sir Roger." According to popular tradition, this dance was named in honor of the Baronet of Coverley, a member of the fictitious club of Joseph Addison's *The Spectator* (1711); it was supposedly invented by Sir Roger's great-grandfather, Roger of Cowley, near Oxford. Actually it is a much older dance, having been brought over to England with the Normans. This dance, similar to the Virginia reel, is a "country-dance" (a corruption of the French *contredanse*), in which the partners are arranged opposite each other in two lines. It appears as early as 1696, in John Playford's *Dancing Master*, in which it is explained: the first man goes below the second woman, then round her, and so below second man in his own place; then the first woman goes below the second man, then round him, and so below the second woman into her own place; then the first couple cross over below the second couple, and take hands and turn round twice, then lead up through and cast off into the second couple's place. Dickens' description is more complicated, with additional movements from other dances. The "Sir Roger de Coverley" was the most universally known country-dance in nineteenth-century England, and it was generally the last dance of an evening of merrymaking.

Although not notably accomplished in this art, Dickens himself greatly enjoyed such holiday cavorting. "His dancing was at its best, I think," wrote his daughter Mamie in *My Father As I Recall Him* (1896), "in the 'Sir Roger de Coverley'—and in what are known as country-dances. In the former, while the end couples are dancing, and the side couples are supposed to be still, my father would insist upon the sides keeping up a kind of jig step, and clapping his hands to add to the fun, and dancing at the backs of those whose enthusiasm he thought needed rousing, was himself never still for a moment until the dance was over."

42 *hold hands with.* Dickens apparently felt uncomfortable with this phrase. Technically, it is a dance movement in which the dancers join inside hands. This seems not to have been Dickens' meaning; in the Berg prompt copy, he changed it to "seize," but this too bothered him, so in the Ticknor and Fields public reading edition, it became merely "turn" which agrees with Playford's description in his *Dancing Master.*

43 *corkscrew.* A movement from a Swedish dance, in which all join hands outstretched, face to face. The lead couple threads their way in and out of the other couples, the ladies backing, taking the lead, and then the gentlemen. All hands are raised when they reach the bottom, and passing under the archway, they go to the end of the line, ready for the next and new top couple.

44 *thread-the-needle.* With the partner's hands joined, the lady passes under the man's arm. This dance term comes from the old English game "thread the taylor's needle," described in Strutt's *The Sports and Past-Times of the People of England:* "In this sport the youth of both sexes frequently join. As many as choose to play lay hold of hands, and the last in the row runs to the top, where passing under the arms of the two first, the rest follow: the first then becoming the last, repeats the operation, and so on alternately as long as the game continues."

45 *"cut."* A fancy dance step, in which the dancer, on springing in the air, quickly alternates his feet, one in front of the other, before touching the ground again.

42 hold hands with your partner; bow and curtsey;
43,44 corkscrew; thread-the-needle, and back again to
45 your place; Fezziwig "*cut*"—cut so deftly, that he appeared to wink with his legs, and came upon his feet again without a stagger.

When the clock struck eleven, this domestic ball broke up. Mr. and Mrs. Fezziwig took their stations, one on either side the door, and shaking hands with every person individually as he or she went out, wished him or her a Merry Christmas. When everybody had retired but the two 'prentices, they did the same to them; and thus the cheerful voices died away, and the lads were left to their beds; which were under a counter in the back-shop.

During the whole of this time, Scrooge had acted like a man out of his wits. His heart and soul were in the scene, and with his former self. He corroborated everything, remembered everything, enjoyed everything, and underwent the strangest agitation. It was not until now, when the bright faces of his former self and Dick were turned from them, that he remembered the Ghost, and became conscious that it was looking full upon him, while the light upon its head burnt very clear.

"A small matter," said the Ghost, "to make these silly folks so full of gratitude."

"Small!" echoed Scrooge.

The Spirit signed to him to listen to the two apprentices, who were pouring out their hearts in praise of Fezziwig: and when he had done so, said,

"Why! Is it not? He has spent but a few pounds of your mortal money: three or four, perhaps. Is that so much that he deserves this praise?"

"It isn't that," said Scrooge, heated by the remark, and speaking unconsciously like his former, not his latter, self. "It isn't that, Spirit. He has the power to render us happy or unhappy; to make our service light or burdensome; a pleasure or a toil. Say that his power lies in words and looks; in things so slight and insignificant that it is impossible to add and count 'em up: what then? The happiness he gives, is quite as great as if it cost a fortune."

He felt the Spirit's glance, and stopped.

" What is the matter?" asked the Ghost.

" Nothing particular," said Scrooge.

" Something, I think?" the Ghost insisted.

" No," said Scrooge, " No. I should like to be able to say a word or two to my clerk just now! That 's all."

His former self turned down the lamps as he gave utterance to the wish; and Scrooge and the Ghost again stood side by side in the open air.

" My time grows short," observed the Spirit. " Quick!"

This was not addressed to Scrooge, or to any one whom he could see, but it produced an immediate effect. For again Scrooge saw himself. He was older now; a man in the prime of life. His face had not the harsh and rigid lines of later years; but it had begun to wear the signs of care and avarice. There was an eager, greedy, restless motion in the eye, which showed the passion that had taken root, and where the shadow of the growing tree would fall.

He was not alone, but sat by the side of a fair young girl in a mourning-dress: in whose eyes there were tears, which sparkled in the light that shone out of the Ghost of Christmas Past.

" It matters little," she said, softly. " To you, very little. Another idol has displaced me; and if it can cheer and comfort you in time to come, as I would have tried to do, I have no just cause to grieve."

" What Idol has displaced you?" he rejoined.

" A golden one." **46**

" This is the even-handed dealing of the world!"

46 *A golden one.* The woman is playing with the Biblical story of the Golden Calf (Exod. 32:1–35): While Moses was on Mount Sinai receiving the holy covenant, the Israelites melted down their gold and made an idol in the shape of a calf; it was forbidden by holy law to make false gods. Dickens here suggests that Scrooge has changed his love from the sacred to the profane.

47 *release?* Dickens added in the Ticknor and Fields public reading edition "from our engagement" to specify exactly what the contract concerned.

"The Stolen Shoulders" by John Leech, *The Illuminated Magazine*, October 1843. *Courtesy The Library of Congress*

he said. " There is nothing on which it is so hard as poverty ; and there is nothing it professes to condemn with such severity as the pursuit of wealth !"

" You fear the world too much," she answered, gently. " All your other hopes have merged into the hope of being beyond the chance of its sordid reproach. I have seen your nobler aspirations fall off one by one, until the master-passion, Gain, engrosses you. Have I not ?"

" What then ?" he retorted. " Even if I have grown so much wiser, what then ? I am not changed towards you."

She shook her head.

" Am I ?"

" Our contract is an old one. It was made when we were both poor and content to be so, until, in good season, we could improve our worldly fortune by our patient industry. You *are* changed. When it was made, you were another man."

" I was a boy," he said impatiently.

" Your own feeling tells you that you were not what you are," she returned. " I am. That which promised happiness when we were one in heart, is fraught with misery now that we are two. How often and how keenly I have thought of this, I will not say. It is enough that I *have* thought of it, and can release you."

47   " Have I ever sought release ?"

" In words. No. Never."

" In what, then ?"

" In a changed nature ; in an altered spirit ; in another atmosphere of life ; another Hope as its great end. In everything that made my love of any worth or value in your sight. If this had never been between us," said the girl, looking mildly, but with steadiness, upon him ; " tell me, would you seek me out and try to win me now ? Ah, no !"

He seemed to yield to the justice of this supposition, in spite of himself. But he said, with a struggle, " You think not."

" I would gladly think otherwise if I could," she answered, " Heaven knows ! When *I* have learned a Truth like this, I know how strong and irresistible it must be. But if you were free to-day, to-morrow, yesterday, can even I believe that you would choose a dowerless girl—you who, in your very **48** confidence with her, weigh everything by Gain : or, choosing her, if for a moment you were false enough to your one guiding principle to do so, do I not know that your repentance and regret would surely follow ? I do ; and I release you. With a full heart, for the love of him you once were."

He was about to speak ; but with her head turned from him, she resumed.

" You may—the memory of what is past half makes me hope you will—have pain in this. A very, very brief time, and you will dismiss the recollection of it, gladly, as an unprofitable dream, from which it happened well that you awoke. May you be happy in the life you have chosen !"

She left him ; and they parted.

" Spirit !" said Scrooge, " show me no more ! Conduct me home. Why do you delight to torture me ?"

" One shadow more !" exclaimed the Ghost.

" No more !" cried Scrooge. " No more. I don't wish to see it. Show me no more !"

But the relentless Ghost pinioned him in both his arms, and forced him to observe what happened next.

They were in another scene and place : a room, not very large or handsome, but full of comfort. Near to the winter fire sat a beautiful young girl, so like the last that Scrooge believed it was the same, until he saw *her*, now a comely matron, sitting opposite her daughter. The noise in this room was perfectly tumultuous, for there were more children there, than Scrooge in his agitated state of mind could count ; and, unlike the celebrated herd in the **49** poem, they were not forty children conducting themselves like one, but every child was conducting itself

48 *a dowerless girl.* Dickens deleted the word "orphan" from this description in the galley stage ; apparently the woman is in mourning due to the death of one or both of her parents who have left her nothing.

49 *the poem.* William Wordsworth's "Written in March" (1802) :

> The oldest and the youngest
> Are at work with the strongest ;
> The cattle are grazing,
> Their heads never raising ;
> There are forty feeding like one!

50 *time to greet the father, who.* In the galley stage, Dickens wisely deleted a lengthy, arbitrary passage "in observance of a custom annually maintained on Christmas Eve" from what is already an extraordinary run-on sentence.

"Christmas Presents" by Robert Seymour, *The Book of Christmas*, 1836. *Courtesy The Library of Congress*

like forty. The consequences were uproarious beyond belief ; but no one seemed to care ; on the contrary, the mother and daughter laughed heartily, and enjoyed it very much ; and the latter, soon beginning to mingle in the sports, got pillaged by the young brigands most ruthlessly. What would I not have given to be one of them ! Though I never could have been so rude, no, no ! I would n't for the wealth of all the world have crushed that braided hair, and torn it down ; and for the precious little shoe, I would n't have plucked it off, God bless my soul ! to save my life. As to measuring her waist in sport, as they did, bold young brood, I could n't have done it ; I should have expected my arm to have grown round it for a punishment, and never come straight again. And yet I should have dearly liked, I own, to have touched her lips ; to have questioned her, that she might have opened them ; to have looked upon the lashes of her downcast eyes, and never raised a blush ; to have let loose waves of hair, an inch of which would be a keepsake beyond price : in short, I should have liked, I do confess, to have had the lightest licence of a child, and yet been man enough to know its value.

But now a knocking at the door was heard, and such a rush immediately ensued that she with laughing face and plundered dress was borne towards it the centre of a flushed and boisterous group, just in **50** time to greet the father, who, came home attended by a man laden with Christmas toys and presents. Then the shouting and the struggling, and the onslaught that was made on the defenceless porter ! The scaling him, with chairs for ladders, to dive into his pockets, despoil him of brown-paper parcels, hold on tight by his cravat, hug him round the neck, pommel his back, and kick his legs in irrepressible affection ! The shouts of wonder and delight with which the development of every package was received ! The terrible announcement that the baby had been taken in the act of putting a doll's frying-pan into his mouth, and was more than suspected of having swallowed a fictitious turkey, glued on a wooden platter ! The immense relief of finding this a false alarm ! The joy, and gratitude, and ecstacy ! They are all indescribable alike. It is enough that by degrees the children and their emotions got out of the parlour and by one stair at a time, up to the top of the house; where they went to bed, and so subsided.

And now Scrooge looked on more attentively than ever, when the master of the house, having his daughter leaning fondly on him, sat down with her and her mother at his own fireside; and when he thought that such another creature, quite as graceful and as full of promise, might have called him father, and been a spring-time in the haggard winter of his life, his sight grew very dim indeed.

"Belle," said the husband, turning to his wife **51** with a smile, "I saw an old friend of yours this afternoon."

"Who was it ? "

"Guess !"

"How can I ? Tut, don't I know," she added in the same breath, laughing as he laughed. "Mr. Scrooge."

"Mr. Scrooge it was. I passed his office window; and as it was not shut up, and he had a candle inside, I could scarcely help seeing him. His partner lies upon the point of death, I hear; and there he sat alone. Quite alone in the world, I do believe."

"Spirit !" said Scrooge in a broken voice, "remove me from this place."

"I told you these were shadows of the things that have been," said the Ghost. "That they are what they are, do not blame me !"

"Remove me !" Scrooge exclaimed. "I cannot bear it !"

He turned upon the Ghost, and seeing that it

51 *Belle*. Could this name be an abbreviation of "Maria Beadnell," the woman young Dickens loved and lost to what he believed were economic necessities? Scrooge's sentiments toward Belle, David Copperfield's toward Dora, are the same as Dickens' for his Maria; as he wrote Forster in January 1855, "Why is it, that as with poor David [Copperfield], a sense comes always crushing on me now, when I fall into low spirits, as of one happiness I have missed in life, and one friend and companion I have never made?"

The picture of domestic bliss in Belle's household was complete fancy for Dickens (as it was for Scrooge who never experienced it); Dickens did not meet Maria again until both were in middle age, and was so disappointed by what he thought she had become that he caricatured the now Mrs. Maria Winter (could this name have some significance to Scrooge's Christmas vision?) as the pitiful Flora Finching of *Little Dorrit* (1857).

52 *though Scrooge pressed it down with all his force, he could not hide the light.* Dickens seems to say that the light of memory cannot completely be snuffed out; Scrooge, despite his struggles, cannot forget the lesson the spirit has taught him.

looked upon him with a face, in which in some strange way there were fragments of all the faces it had shown him, wrestled with it.

"Leave me! Take me back. Haunt me no longer!"

In the struggle, if that can be called a struggle in which the Ghost with no visible resistance on its own part was undisturbed by any effort of its adversary, Scrooge observed that its light was burning high and bright; and dimly connecting that with its influence over him, he seized the extinguisher-cap, and by a sudden action pressed it down upon its head.

52 The Spirit dropped beneath it, so that the extinguisher covered its whole form; but though Scrooge pressed it down with all his force, he could not hide the light: which streamed from under it, in an unbroken flood upon the ground.

He was conscious of being exhausted, and overcome by an irresistible drowsiness; and, further, of being in his own bedroom. He gave the cap a parting squeeze, in which his hand relaxed; and had barely time to reel to bed, before he sank into a heavy sleep.

Preliminary pencil and wash drawing by John Leech for "The End of the First Spirit." *Courtesy The Houghton Library, Harvard University*

STAVE THREE.

———•———

THE SECOND OF THE THREE SPIRITS.

AWAKING in the middle of a prodigiously tough snore, and sitting up in bed to get his thoughts together, Scrooge had no occasion to be told that the bell was again upon the stroke of One. He felt that he was restored to consciousness in the right nick of time, for the especial purpose of holding a conference with the second messenger despatched to him through Jacob Marley's intervention. But finding that he turned uncomfortably cold when he began to wonder which of his curtains this new spectre would draw back, he put them every one aside with his own hands; and lying down again, established a sharp look-out all round the bed. For he wished to challenge the Spirit on the moment

1 *Gentlemen of the free-and-easy sort.* Sporting types; a "free-and-easy" was a gathering place, catering to smoking, drinking, singing, and gambling.

2 *who plume themselves.* Who pride themselves, generally over an insignificant point, to which they have no just claim.

3 *acquainted with a move or two.* Worldly.

4 *equal to the time-of-day.* Ready for whatever might happen.

5 *pitch-and-toss.* A form of "heads-or-tails," or, as Ahn explained in his notes to the 1871 edition of *A Christmas Carol,* "a street gambling game in which pence are pitched, or thrown, at a certain mark, and then tossed in the air, the player who pitches his coin nearest the mark having the privilege of tossing up the remaining pence and of claiming all with their faces up."

6 *spontaneous combustion.* A popular medical myth of the early nineteenth century, which argued that a person's body chemicals could be so "inborn, inbred, engendered in the corrupted humours of the vicious body itself" that the individual could be destroyed suddenly in a self-generated conflagration.
Dickens was widely criticized for killing his character Mr. Krook of *Bleak House* (1853) by spontaneous combustion. A critic, G. H. Lewes, protested in *The Leader* (December 11, 1852) that evidence for such a phenomenon was lacking; in the next number of the journal, Dickens responded with heavy irony by attacking those "men of science" who believed that "the deceased had no business to die in the alleged manner." The two then exchanged letters; Lewes who found Dickens' reply "humourous, but not convincing" finally published two open letters to the novelist in *The Leader* (February 5 and 12, 1853) in which he concluded that "the evidence in favour of the notion is worthless; that the theories in explanation are absurd; and, that, according to all known chemical and physiological laws, Spontaneous Combustion is an *impossibility.*" (See Gordon S. Haight, "Dickens and Lewes on Spontaneous Combustion," *Nineteenth Century Fiction,* X (1955), pp. 53–63.)
Dickens was still not convinced and presented his final defense of Mr. Krook's demise in his preface to the Charles Dickens Edition of *Bleak House* (1868): "I have no need to observe that I do not willfully or negligently mislead my readers, and that, before I wrote that description I took pains to investigate the subject. There are about thirty cases on record, of which the most famous, that of the Countess Cornelia di Baudi Cesenate, was minutely investigated and described by Giuseppe Bianchini ... of Verona, otherwise distinguished in letters, who published an account of it ... in 1731. ... I do not think it necessary to add to these notable facts ... the recorded opinions and experiences of distinguished medical professors

of its appearance, and did not wish to be taken by surprise and made nervous.

1,2 Gentlemen of the free-and-easy sort, who plume **3** themselves on being acquainted with a move or two, **4** and being usually equal to the time-of-day, express the wide range of their capacity for adventure by observing that they are good for anything from **5** pitch-and-toss to manslaughter; between which opposite extremes, no doubt, there lies a tolerably wide and comprehensive range of subjects. Without venturing for Scrooge quite as hardily as this, I don't mind calling on you to believe that he was ready for a good broad field of strange appearances, and that nothing between a baby and a rhinoceros would have astonished him very much.

Now, being prepared for almost anything, he was not by any means prepared for nothing; and, consequently, when the Bell struck One, and no shape appeared, he was taken with a violent fit of trembling. Five minutes, ten minutes, a quarter of an hour went by, yet nothing came. All this time, he lay upon his bed, the very core and centre of a blaze of ruddy light, which streamed upon it when the clock proclaimed the hour; and which being only light, was more alarming than a dozen ghosts, as he was powerless to make out what it meant, or would be at; and was sometimes apprehensive that he might be at that very moment an **6** interesting case of spontaneous combustion, without having the consolation of knowing it. At last, however, he began to think—as you or I would have thought at first; for it is always the person not in the predicament who knows what ought to have been done in it, and would unquestionably have done it too—at last, I say, he began to think that the source and secret of this ghostly light might be in the adjoining room: from whence, on further tracing it, it seemed to shine. This idea taking full possession of his mind, he got up softly and shuffled in his slippers to the door.

"The Appointed Time" by H. K. Browne, *Bleak House*, 1853. *Courtesy General Research and Humanities Division, The New York Public Library, Astor, Lenox and Tilden Foundations*

The moment Scrooge's hand was on the lock, a strange voice called him by his name, and bade him enter. He obeyed.

It was his own room. There was no doubt about that. But it had undergone a surprising transformation. The walls and ceiling were so hung with living green, that it looked a perfect grove, from **7** every part of which, bright gleaming berries glistened. The crisp leaves of holly, mistletoe, and ivy reflected back the light, as if so many little mirrors had been scattered there ; and such a mighty blaze went roaring up the chimney, as that dull petrifaction of a hearth had never known in Scrooge's time, or Marley's, or for many and many a winter season gone. Heaped up upon the floor, to form a kind of throne, were turkeys, geese, game, poultry, brawn, **8** great joints of meat, sucking-pigs, long wreaths of **9** sausages, mince-pies, plum-puddings, barrels of oysters, red-hot chesnuts, cherry-cheeked apples, juicy oranges, luscious pears, immense twelfth-cakes, **10** and seething bowls of punch, that made the chamber **11** dim with their delicious steam. In easy state upon

...in more modern days; contenting myself with observing, that I shall not abandon the facts until there shall have been a considerable Spontaneous Combustion of the testimony on which human occurrences are usually received."

The press was amused by Dickens' persistence and chose to jibe him, as in parodies of Phiz's alarming drawing of Mr. Krook's disaster, "The Appointed Time."

7 *living green*. Evergreens.

8 *brawn*. Dr. Johnson in his dictionary identified this traditional Christmas dish as "the flesh of a boar." Sandys in the introduction to his collection of carols noted that it was "of great antiquity, and may be found in most of the old bills of fare, for coronation, and other great feasts."

9 *sucking-pigs*. Young (generally not older than four weeks), milk-fed pigs, often roasted whole.

10 *twelfth-cakes*. Also known as twelfth-night, or twelfth-tide, cakes; a large pastry (generally made of flour, honey, ginger, and pepper), frosted and highly decorated, that is served on Twelfth Night, the last official celebration of the English Christmas, and falling on the eve of Epiphany, January 6. A bean or coin is baked inside and whoever receives the slice with the prize becomes "king" or "queen" of the feast. The custom dates from the thirteenth century. Other items were often baked in the cake to determine other Twelfth Night characters: pea for the "queen," forked stick for the "cuckold," rag for the "slut." By the early nineteenth century, these types (originally representing the court but, later, comic figures) were printed and cut out and placed in a bowl to be drawn by the various members of the party. Certainly the most celebrated Twelfth Night party in literary history was that celebrated by William Thackeray and his children during a stay in Rome; as there were no ready-made Twelfth Night characters from the English papers available for him to cut out, Thackeray drew his own assortment for his children, and from the tales he elaborated for his comic cast, he wrote the charming fairy tale *The Rose and the Ring* (1855), perhaps the most famous Christmas book after *A Christmas Carol*. (See also Note 74.)

11 *bowls of punch*. Although Dickens refers to numerous kinds of holiday punch (the names seem to have been interchangeable with him: in Chapter 48 of *The Pickwick Papers*, a "bowl of bishop" is brought in, but what is ladled out is "negus"), the drink mentioned here must be the Wassail Bowl, or Lamb's Wool, the traditional spirits of Father Christmas. Irving in *The Sketch Book* described this nut-brown beverage as "composed of the richest and

Preliminary pencil and wash drawing by John Leech for "Scrooge's Third Visitor." *Courtesy The Beinecke Rare Book and Manuscript Library, Yale University*

raciest wines, highly spiced and sweetened, with roasted apples bobbing about the surface ... sometimes composed of ale instead of wine, with nutmeg, sugar, toast, ginger, and roasted crabs." The term "Wassail" (or "Wassel") is said to have come from the early fifth century: Rowena, daughter of the Saxon Hengist, on presenting a bowl of punch to the English king Vortigern, greeted him with "Louerd king, wass-heil," "be of good health" (see *A Child's History of England*, Chapter 2). The term "wasseling" (as in *Hamlet*, Act I, Scene 4) is also synonymous with carousing or revelry. "Lamb's Wool" is a corruption of "La Mas Ubhal" (pronounced "Lamasool"), an ancient pagan harvest celebration venerating the apple.

12 *a jolly Giant.* Father Christmas, the ancient patriarch of the English holiday, traditionally a pagan giant dressed in a fur-lined green robe and a crown of holly, carrying mistletoe, the yule log, and a bowl of Christmas punch. The legendary Santa Claus, immortalized by Clement C. Moore in *A Visit from Saint Nicholas* (1823), was in part derived from both this giant and the gift-giving Saint Nicholas; the Ghost of Christmas Present has often been incorrectly identified as the American elf, who would have been unfamiliar to Scrooge. Father Christmas' origins derive from the Roman Saturnalia cults, from Saturn himself; whereas this god devoured his children, Dickens' giant protects the demon girl and boy, Want and Ignorance.

13 *a glowing torch.* Similar to the Ghost of Christmas Past who wore on his crown "a bright clear jet of light." Contrast these two spirits with the Ghost of Christmas Yet To Come, "draped and hooded, coming, like a mist along the ground."

14 *Plenty's horn.* An obvious allusion to the pagan sources of this spirit; the cornucopia (filled with fruits and flowers) often appears in the left hand of the Roman goddess Ceres, in whose honor the Saturnalia rites were celebrated.

15 *its capacious breast.* The breast is traditionally the center of emotion; the spirit is overflowing with generous good feeling.

12 this couch, there sat a jolly Giant, glorious to see;
13 who bore a glowing torch, in shape not unlike
14 Plenty's horn, and held it up, high up, to shed its light on Scrooge, as he came peeping round the door.

" Come in !" exclaimed the Ghost. " Come in ! and know me better, man !"

Scrooge entered timidly, and hung his head before this Spirit. He was not the dogged Scrooge he had been; and though its eyes were clear and kind, he did not like to meet them.

" I am the Ghost of Christmas Present," said the Spirit. " Look upon me !"

Scrooge reverently did so. It was clothed in one simple deep green robe, or mantle, bordered with white fur. This garment hung so loosely on the
15 figure, that its capacious breast was bare, as if disdaining to be warded or concealed by any artifice. Its feet, observable beneath the ample folds of the

Scrooge's third Visitor.

"Old Christmas" by Robert Seymour, *The Book of Christmas*, 1836. *Courtesy The Library of Congress*

16 *no sword was in it, and the ancient sheath was eaten up with rust.* According to an anonymous author in *Holiday Book of Christmas and New Year* (1852), Father Christmas, in reference to an Anglo-Norman tradition from the thirteenth century, has often been pictured in helmet, surcoat, and shield of the period, the insignia of physical triumph, encircled with holly and evergreens, the emblems of "the victory gained over the powers of darkness by the coming of Christ." Dickens suggests the conquest of military tyranny at the coming of Christ through the civilizing of the warlords by Christian good fellowship.

17 *More than eighteen hundred.* Eighteen hundred and forty-two, to be exact.

18 *The Ghost of Christmas Present rose.* The original manuscript has a paragraph deleted apparently in the galleys: "and as it did so Scrooge observed that at its skirts it seemed to have some object which it sought to hide. He fancied that he saw either the claw of a great bird or a foot much smaller than the Spirit's own protruding for a moment from its robes; and being curious in everything concerning these unearthly visitors, he asked the Spirit what it meant. "'They are not so many as they might be,' replied the Ghost, 'who care to know or ask. No matter what it is, just now. Are you ready to go forth with me?'" Dickens is foreshadowing the appearance of the demon children Want and Ignorance; he wisely dropped this passage which is merely a tease and weakens the sudden appearance of the boy and girl at the climax of this stave. See Note 75.

19 *the people made a ... kind of music.* Notice how carefully Dickens has employed all five senses in constructing his description of the city at Christmastime.

garment, were also bare; and on its head it wore no other covering than a holly wreath set here and there with shining icicles. Its dark brown curls were long and free: free as its genial face, its sparkling eye, its open hand, its cheery voice, its unconstrained demeanour, and its joyful air. Girded round its **16** middle was an antique scabbard; but no sword was in it, and the ancient sheath was eaten up with rust.

"You have never seen the like of me before!" exclaimed the Spirit.

"Never," Scrooge made answer to it.

"Have never walked forth with the younger members of my family; meaning (for I am very young) my elder brothers born in these later years?" pursued the Phantom.

"I don't think I have," said Scrooge. "I am afraid I have not. Have you had many brothers, Spirit?"

17   "More than eighteen hundred," said the Ghost.

"A tremendous family to provide for!" muttered Scrooge.

18   The Ghost of Christmas Present rose.

"Spirit," said Scrooge submissively, "conduct me where you will. I went forth last night on compulsion, and I learnt a lesson which is working now. To-night, if you have aught to teach me, let me profit by it."

"Touch my robe!"

Scrooge did as he was told, and held it fast.

Holly, mistletoe, red berries, ivy, turkeys, geese, game, poultry, brawn, meat, pigs, sausages, oysters, pies, puddings, fruit, and punch, all vanished instantly. So did the room, the fire, the ruddy glow, the hour of night, and they stood in the city streets on Christmas morning, where (for the weather was **19** severe) the people made a rough, but brisk and not unpleasant kind of music, in scraping the snow from the pavement in front of their dwellings, and from the tops of their houses: whence it was mad delight to the boys to see it come plumping down into the

road below, and splitting into artificial little snow-storms.

The house fronts looked black enough, and the windows blacker, contrasting with the smooth white sheet of snow upon the roofs, and with the dirtier snow upon the ground ; which last deposit had been ploughed up in deep furrows by the heavy wheels of carts and waggons ; furrows that crossed and re-crossed each other hundreds of times where the great streets branched off, and made intricate channels, hard to trace, in the thick yellow mud and icy water. The sky was gloomy, and the shortest streets were choked up with a dingy mist, half thawed half frozen, whose heavier particles de-scended in a shower of sooty atoms, as if all the chimneys in Great Britain had, by one consent, caught fire, and were blazing away to their dear hearts' content. There was nothing very cheerful in the climate or the town, and yet was there an air of cheerfulness abroad that the clearest summer air

"The Boys in the Snow" by John Leech, *The Illustrated London News*, December 22, 1855. *Courtesy General Research and Humanities Division, The New York Public Library, Astor, Lenox and Tilden Foundations*

20 *glanced demurely at the hung-up mistletoe.* "The mistletoe is still hung up in farmhouses and kitchens at Christmas," wrote Irving in *The Sketch Book;* "and the young men have the privilege of kissing the girls under it, plucking each time a berry from the bush. When the berries are all plucked, the privilege ceases." A highlight of the Christmas celebration at Dingley Dell was the hanging of the mistletoe.

"The Funny Young Gentleman" by Phiz, *Sketches of Young Gentlemen*, 1838. *Courtesy The Library of Congress*

21 *Norfolk Biffins.* A variety of cooking apple, grown particularly in Norfolk, a county in eastern England; the name comes from "beefing," the deep red-rust color of the fruit. They are baked slowly in a coal oven and crushed between two iron plates into round, flat cakes, and packed in straw. Dickens was fond of the fruit and mentioned it again in Chapter 50 of *Dombey and Son* (1848).

22 *gold and silver fish.* Members of the carp family, commonly sold in glass bowls on London streets. These natives of China were introduced in England as house pets from Portugal about 1690. Eventually they were both imported and native-grown, and according to Henry Mayhew's *London Labour and London Poor* (1851), there were at the time of the story at least seventy sellers of gold and silver fish in London alone.

and brightest summer sun might have endeavoured to diffuse in vain.

For the people who were shovelling away on the house-tops were jovial and full of glee; calling out to one another from the parapets, and now and then exchanging a facetious snowball — better-natured missile far than many a wordy jest — laughing heartily if it went right, and not less heartily if it went wrong. The poulterers' shops were still half open, and the fruiterers' were radiant in their glory. There were great, round, pot-bellied baskets of chesnuts, shaped like the waistcoats of jolly old gentlemen, lolling at the doors, and tumbling out into the street in their apoplectic opulence. There were ruddy, brown-faced, broad-girthed Spanish Onions, shining in the fatness of their growth like Spanish Friars; and winking from their shelves in wanton slyness at the girls as they went by, and **20** glanced demurely at the hung-up mistletoe. There were pears and apples, clustered high in blooming pyramids; there were bunches of grapes, made, in the shopkeepers' benevolence, to dangle from conspicuous hooks, that people's mouths might water gratis as they passed; there were piles of filberts, mossy and brown, recalling, in their fragrance, ancient walks among the woods, and pleasant shufflings ankle deep through withered leaves; there were **21** Norfolk Biffins, squab and swarthy, setting off the yellow of the oranges and lemons, and, in the great compactness of their juicy persons, urgently entreating and beseeching to be carried home in paper bags and **22** eaten after dinner. The very gold and silver fish, set forth among these choice fruits in a bowl, though members of a dull and stagnant-blooded race, appeared to know that there was something going on; and, to a fish, went gasping round and round their little world in slow and passionless excitement.

The Grocers'! oh the Grocers'! nearly closed, with

"Market—Christmas Eve" by Robert Seymour, *The Book of Christmas*, 1836. *Courtesy The Library of Congress*

perhaps two shutters down, or one; but through those gaps such glimpses! It was not alone that the scales descending on the counter made a merry sound, or that the twine and roller parted company so briskly, or that the canisters were rattled up and down like juggling tricks, or even that the blended scents of tea and coffee were so grateful to the nose, or even that the raisins were so plentiful and rare, the almonds so extremely white, the sticks of cinnamon so long and straight, the other spices so delicious, the candied fruits so caked and spotted with molten sugar as to make the coldest lookers-on feel faint and subsequently bilious.   Nor was it that the figs were moist and pulpy, or that the French plums **23** blushed in modest tartness from their highly-decorated boxes, or that everything was good to eat and in its Christmas dress: but the customers were all so hurried and so eager in the hopeful promise of the day, that they tumbled up against each other at the door, clashing their wicker baskets wildly, and left their purchases upon the counter, and came running

23 *French plums.* These fruits, grown in the Loire Valley and imported to the marketplace as prunes, were a highly prized delicacy of the Christmas season. They were often crystallized and packaged in fancy boxes decorated with bright French prints.

"The Goose Club" by Phiz, *The Illustrated London News*, December 24, 1853. *Courtesy The Library of Congress*

24 *the polished hearts...worn...for Christmas daws to peck at.* Ahn, in his notes to the 1871 edition, identified this phrase as a common figurative expression, meaning "for folks to find fault with"; Dickens likely knew it from *Othello* (Act I, Scene 1, lines 60–64):

From when my outward action doth demonstrate
The native act and figure of my heart
In compliment extern, 'tis not long after
But I will wear my heart upon my sleeve
For daws to peck at.

In the Middle Ages, ladies having accepted the favors of their suitors would have such an emblem of their affection sewn on their sleeves. Iago, the speaker in *Othello*, has the opposite purpose from Dickens: the external symbol is a deceptive mask of his true character.

25 *carrying their dinners to the bakers' shops.* On Sundays and on Christmas Day, when bakers were legally forbidden to bake, the poor took their dinners to the bakeshops to cook so that they would have at least one hot meal a week.

26 *incense.* One of the gifts of the Magi, offered as a blessing to the Christ child, born in poverty, and given in the same way here.

back to fetch them, and committed hundreds of the like mistakes in the best humour possible; while the Grocer and his people were so frank and fresh **24** that the polished hearts with which they fastened their aprons behind might have been their own, worn outside for general inspection, and for Christmas daws to peck at if they chose.

But soon the steeples called good people all, to church and chapel, and away they came, flocking through the streets in their best clothes, and with their gayest faces. And at the same time there emerged from scores of bye streets, lanes, and name- **25** less turnings, innumerable people, carrying their dinners to the bakers' shops. The sight of these poor revellers appeared to interest the Spirit very much, for he stood with Scrooge beside him in a baker's doorway, and taking off the covers as their **26** bearers passed, sprinkled incense on their dinners from his torch. And it was a very uncommon kind of torch, for once or twice when there were angry words between some dinner-carriers who had jostled

with each other, he shed a few drops of water on them from it, and their good humour was restored directly. For they said, it was a shame to quarrel upon Christmas Day. And so it was! God love it, so it was!

In time the bells ceased, and the bakers' were shut up; and yet there was a genial shadowing forth of all these dinners and the progress of their cooking, in the thawed blotch of wet above each baker's oven; where the pavement smoked as if its stones were cooking too.

"Is there a peculiar flavour in what you sprinkle from your torch?" asked Scrooge.

"There is. My own."

"Would it apply to any kind of dinner on this day?" asked Scrooge.

"To any kindly given. To a poor one most."

"Fetching Home the Christmas Dinner" by John Leech, *The Illustrated London News*, Christmas Supplement, 1848. *Courtesy The Library of Congress*

27 *"to close these places on the Seventh Day?"* In the name of the church, a Sunday Observance Bill was introduced in the House of Commons by Sir Andrew Agnew several times between 1832 and 1837; it was designed not only to close the bakeries but also to limit the other "innocent enjoyments" of the poor, while not affecting the pleasures of the more leisured classes. Under the pseudonym "Timothy Sparks," Dickens angrily attacked this proposed bill with his *Sunday under Three Heads* (June 1836), in which he noted that a working man emerging from a bakery on Sunday "with the reeking dish, in which a diminutive joint of mutton simmers above a vast heap of half-browned potatoes. . . . would fill Sir Andrew Agnew with astonishment; as well it might, seeing that Baronets, generally speaking, eat pretty comfortable dinners all the week through, and cannot be expected to understand what people feel, who only have a meat dinner on one day out of every seven." The Ghost of Christmas Present likewise attacks such falsely pious people as Sir Andrew Agnew.

" Why to a poor one most ? " asked Scrooge.

" Because it needs it most."

" Spirit," said Scrooge, after a moment's thought, " I wonder you, of all the beings in the many worlds about us, should desire to cramp these people's opportunities of innocent enjoyment."

" I ! " cried the Spirit.

" You would deprive them of their means of dining every seventh day, often the only day on which they can be said to dine at all," said Scrooge. " Wouldn't you ? "

" I ! " cried the Spirit.

27 " You seek to close these places on the Seventh Day ? " said Scrooge. " And it comes to the same thing."

" *I* seek ! " exclaimed the Spirit.

" Forgive me if I am wrong. It has been done in your name, or at least in that of your family," said Scrooge.

"There are some upon this earth of yours," returned the Spirit, " who lay claim to know us, and who do their deeds of passion, pride, ill-will, hatred, envy, bigotry, and selfishness in our name ; who are as strange to us and all our kith and kin, as if they had never lived. Remember that, and charge their doings on themselves, not us."

Scrooge promised that he would ; and they went on, invisible, as they had been before, into the suburbs of the town. It was a remarkable quality of the Ghost (which Scrooge had observed at the baker's) that notwithstanding his gigantic size, he could accommodate himself to any place with ease ; and that he stood beneath a low roof quite as gracefully and like a supernatural creature, as it was possible he could have done in any lofty hall.

And perhaps it was the pleasure the good Spirit had in showing off this power of his, or else it was his own kind, generous, hearty nature, and his sympathy with all poor men, that led him straight

16 Bayham Street, Camden Town, London. *Courtesy The Victoria and Albert Museum*

to Scrooge's clerk's; for there he went, and took Scrooge with him, holding to his robe; and on the threshold of the door the Spirit smiled, and stopped to bless Bob Cratchit's dwelling with the sprinklings **28** of his torch. Think of that! Bob had but fifteen **29** "Bob" a-week himself; he pocketed on Saturdays but fifteen copies of his Christian name; and yet the Ghost of Christmas Present blessed his four-roomed **30** house!

Then up rose Mrs. Cratchit, Cratchit's wife, dressed **31** out but poorly in a twice-turned gown, but brave in ribbons, which are cheap and make a goodly show for sixpence; and she laid the cloth, assisted by Belinda Cratchit, second of her daughters, also brave in ribbons; while Master Peter Cratchit plunged a fork into the saucepan of potatoes, and getting the corners of his monstrous shirt-collar

28 *Cratchit's.* Likely from *cratch,* an archaic English word for crêche, the manger where the infant Jesus was laid. Christmas pies were often cratch-shaped. His name also suggests the scratching of the clerk's pen.

29 *fifteen "Bob" a-week.* A *bob* is the Cockney word for shilling (worth twelve pence), from baubee, a debased copper coin of Scotland, worth an English halfpenny, issued during the reign of James VI of Scotland.

As revealed by C. Z. Barnett in his play *A Christmas Carol; or The Miser's Warning!* (1844), it cost Bob Cratchit nearly a full week's wages to buy the ingredients for the Christmas feast: seven shillings for the goose, five for the pudding, and three for the onions, sage, and oranges.

30 *his four-roomed house.* Willoughby Matchett in "Dickens in Bayham Street" (*The Dickensian,* July 1909) argued that the home of the Cratchits (like that of the Micawbers of *David Copperfield*) was also that of the Dickenses when they lived at 16 Bayham Street, Camden Town, when Charles was a boy. There were six Dickens children then who correspond to the six Cratchits: Fanny is the eldest Cratchit, Martha; Charles is Peter; Letitia is Belinda; Frederick and Harriet are the unnamed Cratchits, also a boy and a girl; and the youngest, Alfred, is Tiny Tim.

31 *Then up rose Mrs. Cratchit....* This scene of domestic bliss in a poor home has its origin in a similar picture in "The Story of the Goblins Who Stole a Sexton" in which the family eagerly awaits the coming of the father and on his arrival the children crowd around him as the Cratchits do around Bob, where "all seemed happiness and comfort." And like that of the Cratchits, the future for this gathering turns to tragedy. See Stave 4, Note 23.

32 *Tiny Tim*. As Johnson explained in "About 'A Christmas Carol'" (cited in Stave 1, Note 37), a glance at the original manuscript discloses that an early name for Tiny Tim was "Little Fred"; in age, he would be the same as Dickens' brother Alfred, but he may also refer to another sibling, Frederick, who like Tiny Tim in Stave 4 died in childhood. Although he had toyed with the idea of creating a sympathetic crippled character in an earlier novel, Dickens found his inspiration for Tiny Tim during his historic visit to Manchester in October 1843, when he visited his sister Fanny and her invalid son Harry Burnett. Several years later, when his nephew did die, Dickens immortalized him as the lost boy Paul Dombey.

(Bob's private property, conferred upon his son and heir in honour of the day) into his mouth, rejoiced to find himself so gallantly attired, and yearned to show his linen in the fashionable Parks. And now two smaller Cratchits, boy and girl, came tearing in, screaming that outside the baker's they had smelt the goose, and known it for their own; and basking in luxurious thoughts of sage-and-onion, these young Cratchits danced about the table, and exalted Master Peter Cratchit to the skies, while he (not proud, although his collars nearly choked him) blew the fire, until the slow potatoes bubbling up, knocked loudly at the saucepan-lid to be let out and peeled.

"What has ever got your precious father then,"

32 said Mrs. Cratchit. "And your brother, Tiny Tim; and Martha warn't as late last Christmas Day by half-an-hour!"

"Here's Martha, mother!" said a girl, appearing as she spoke.

"Here's Martha, mother!" cried the two young Cratchits. "Hurrah! There's *such* a goose, Martha!"

"Why, bless your heart alive, my dear, how late you are!" said Mrs. Cratchit, kissing her a dozen times, and taking off her shawl and bonnet for her, with officious zeal.

"We'd a deal of work to finish up last night," replied the girl, "and had to clear away this morning, mother!"

"Well! Never mind so long as you are come," said Mrs. Cratchit. "Sit ye down before the fire, my dear, and have a warm, Lord bless ye!"

"No no! There's father coming," cried the two young Cratchits, who were everywhere at once. "Hide Martha, hide!"

So Martha hid herself, and in came little Bob, the father, with at least three feet of comforter exclusive of the fringe, hanging down before him; and his thread-bare clothes darned up and brushed, to look seasonable; and Tiny Tim upon his shoulder. Alas for Tiny Tim, he bore a little crutch, and had his limbs supported by an iron frame!

"Why, where's our Martha?" cried Bob Cratchit looking round.

"Not coming," said Mrs. Cratchit.

"Not coming!" said Bob, with a sudden declension in his high spirits; for he had been Tim's blood horse all the way from church, and had come home rampant. "Not coming upon Christmas Day!" **33**

Martha didn't like to see him disappointed, if it were only in joke; so she came out prematurely from behind the closet door, and ran into his arms, while the two young Cratchits hustled Tiny Tim, and bore him off into the wash-house, that he might hear the pudding singing in the copper. **34**

"And how did little Tim behave?" asked Mrs. Cratchit, when she had rallied Bob on his credulity and Bob had hugged his daughter to his heart's content.

"As good as gold," said Bob, "and better. Somehow he gets thoughtful sitting by himself so much, and thinks the strangest things you ever heard. He told me, coming home, that he hoped the people saw him in the church, because he was a **35** cripple, and it might be pleasant to them to remember upon Christmas Day, who made lame beggars **36** walk and blind men see." **37**

Bob's voice was tremulous when he told them this, and trembled more when he said that Tiny Tim **38** was growing strong and hearty.

His active little crutch was heard upon the floor, and back came Tiny Tim before another word was spoken, escorted by his brother and sister to his stool beside the fire; and while Bob, turning up his cuffs—as if, poor fellow, they were capable of being made more shabby—compounded some hot mixture in a jug with gin and lemons, and stirred it round

33 *blood horse.* A thoroughbred, particularly a race-horse.

34 *the copper.* A boiler; it is kept in the washhouse, because the rest of the year it is used to boil Mrs. Cratchit's laundry.

"The Christmas Pudding" by Robert Seymour, *The Book of Christmas*, 1836. *Courtesy The Prints Division, The New York Public Library, Astor, Lenox and Tilden Foundations*

35 *the church.* Matchett in "Dickens in Bayham Street" (cited in Note 30) identified this place as St. Stephen's Church in Camden Town, not far from the Dickens home on Bayham Street.

36 *lame beggers walk.* Cf. John 5:1–10.

37 *blind men see.* Cf. Mark 8:22–26.

38 *Tiny Tim was growing strong and hearty.* Dickens had originally written the following passage: "'Is that so, Spirit?' Scrooge demanded, with an interest he never felt before. 'I hope it is?'
"'I see a vacant seat beside the chimney corner,' said the Ghost. 'The child will die!'"
He wisely deleted this exchange when he found a more effective use for it toward the end of the visit to the Cratchit house.

39 *black swan.* Browne in his notes to a 1907 edition of *A Christmas Carol* identified this as a line from the Latin poet Juvenal, freely translated "a rare bird upon this earth, and exceedingly like a black swan." Such a reference in Dickens' work is almost as rare as a "black swan"; he was not particularly well versed in the Greek and Roman classics.

and round and put it on the hob to simmer; Master Peter and the two ubiquitous young Cratchits went to fetch the goose, with which they soon returned in high procession.

Such a bustle ensued that you might have thought a goose the rarest of all birds; a feathered phenome-**39** non, to which a black swan was a matter of course: and in truth it was something very like it in that house. Mrs. Cratchit made the gravy (ready beforehand in a little saucepan) hissing hot; Master Peter mashed the potatoes with incredible vigour; Miss Belinda sweetened up the apple-sauce; Martha dusted the hot plates; Bob took Tiny Tim beside him in a tiny corner at the table; the two young Cratchits set chairs for everybody, not forgetting themselves, and mounting guard upon their posts, crammed spoons into their mouths, lest they should shriek for goose before their turn came to be helped. At last the dishes were set on, and grace was said. It was succeeded by a breathless pause, as Mrs. Cratchit, looking slowly all along the carving-knife, prepared to plunge it in the breast; but when she did, and when the long expected gush of stuffing issued forth, one murmur of delight arose all round the board, and even Tiny Tim, excited by the two young Cratchits, beat on the table with the handle of his knife, and feebly cried Hurrah!

There never was such a goose. Bob said he didn't believe there ever was such a goose cooked. Its tenderness and flavour, size and cheapness, were the themes of universal admiration. Eked out by the apple-sauce and mashed potatoes, it was a sufficient dinner for the whole family; indeed, as Mrs. Cratchit said with great delight (surveying one small atom of a bone upon the dish), they hadn't ate it all at last! Yet every one had had enough, and the youngest Cratchits in particular, were steeped in sage and onion to the eyebrows! But now, the plates being changed by Miss Belinda, Mrs. Cratchit left the room alone—too nervous to bear witnesses—to take the pudding up, and bring it in.

Suppose it should not be done enough! Suppose it should break in turning out! Suppose somebody **40** should have got over the wall of the back-yard, and stolen it, while they were merry with the goose: a supposition at which the two young Cratchits became livid! All sorts of horrors were supposed.

Hallo! A great deal of steam! The pudding was out of the copper. A smell like a washing-day! **41** That was the cloth. A smell like an eating-house, and a pastry cook's next door to each other, with a laundress's next door to that! That was the pudding. In half a minute Mrs. Cratchit entered: flushed, but smiling proudly: with the pudding, like a speckled cannon-ball, so hard and firm, blazing in half of half-a-quartern of ignited brandy, and **42** bedight with Christmas holly stuck into the top. **43**

Oh, a wonderful pudding! Bob Cratchit said, and calmly too, that he regarded it as the greatest success achieved by Mrs. Cratchit since their marriage. Mrs. Cratchit said that now the weight was off her mind, she would confess she had had her doubts about the quantity of flour. Everybody had something to say about it, but nobody said or thought it was at all a small pudding for a large family. It would have been flat heresy to do so. Any Cratchit would have blushed to hint at such a thing.

At last the dinner was all done, the cloth was cleared, the hearth swept, and the fire made up. The compound in the jug being tasted and considered perfect, apples and oranges were put upon the table, and a shovel-full of chesnuts on the fire. Then all the Cratchit family drew round the hearth, in what Bob Cratchit called a circle, meaning half a one; and at Bob Cratchit's elbow stood the family display of glass; two tumblers, and a custard-cup without a handle.

40 *Suppose somebody should have got over the wall of the back-yard, and stolen it.* This suspicion is not as farfetched as it sounds. As Matchett reported in "Dickens in Bayham Street" (cited in Note 30), "robbery from outhouses and back premises was the peculiar trouble of this otherwise quiet district . . . the mere fact that the Dickens back-yard or garden gave on to a secluded public passage would make the likelihood of being robbed double that of ordinary houses."

41 *A smell like a washing-day! That was the cloth.* Plum pudding was cooked in a cloth, here in a boiler generally used for wash.

42 *half of half-a-quartern.* A tiny amount of spirits as a quartern is only a gill, or one-fourth of a pint.

43 *bedight.* Adorned, dressed; according to Dr. Johnson's dictionary, "an old word, now only used in humorous writings."

44 *"God bless us every one!"* Certainly the most quoted line in the story, this phrase may have been borrowed from a carol in Sandys' collection, the "Holy Well":

> The meanest of them all
> Was but a maiden's son,
>   born in an oxen stall.
> He said God bless you every one
> Your bodies Christ save and see.

These words are given by the Christ child, who, born in poverty, is rebuked by the children of the nobility; appropriately the poor boy Tiny Tim, who will act as Scrooge's salvation, borrows his blessing from the young Jesus.

45 *If these shadows remain unaltered by the Future.* This phrase, here and in lines 11–12, was an afterthought; it does not appear in either place in the original manuscript. Apparently when reading the galleys, Dickens saw the necessity of giving the reader some hope that Tiny Tim would live. See also Stave 5, Note 13.

These held the hot stuff from the jug, however, as well as golden goblets would have done; and Bob served it out with beaming looks, while the chesnuts on the fire sputtered and crackled noisily. Then Bob proposed:

"A Merry Christmas to us all, my dears. God bless us!"

Which all the family re-echoed.

44 "God bless us every one!" said Tiny Tim, the last of all.

He sat very close to his father's side, upon his little stool. Bob held his withered little hand in his, as if he loved the child, and wished to keep him by his side, and dreaded that he might be taken from him.

"Spirit," said Scrooge, with an interest he had never felt before, "tell me if Tiny Tim will live."

"I see a vacant seat," replied the Ghost, "in the poor chimney corner, and a crutch without an **45** owner, carefully preserved. If these shadows remain unaltered by the Future, the child will die."

"No, no," said Scrooge. "Oh no, kind Spirit! say he will be spared."

"If these shadows remain unaltered by the Future, none other of my race," returned the Ghost, "will find him here. What then? If he be like to die, he had better do it, and decrease the surplus population."

Scrooge hung his head to hear his own words quoted by the Spirit, and was overcome with penitence and grief.

"Man," said the Ghost, "if man you be in heart, not adamant, forbear that wicked cant until you have discovered What the surplus is, and Where it is. Will you decide what men shall live, what men shall die? It may be, that in the sight of Heaven, you are more worthless and less fit to live than millions like this poor man's child. Oh God! to hear the Insect on the leaf pronouncing on the too much life among his hungry brothers in the dust!"

Scrooge bent before the Ghost's rebuke, and trembling cast his eyes upon the ground. But he raised them speedily, on hearing his own name.

"Mr. Scrooge!" said Bob; "I'll give you Mr. Scrooge, the Founder of the Feast!"

"The Founder of the Feast indeed!" cried Mrs. Cratchit, reddening. "I wish I had him here. I'd give him a piece of my mind to feast upon, and I hope he'd have a good appetite for it."

"My dear," said Bob, "the children; Christmas Day."

"It should be Christmas Day, I am sure," said she, "on which one drinks the health of such an odious, stingy, hard, unfeeling man as Mr. Scrooge. You know he is, Robert! Nobody knows it better than you do, poor fellow!"

"My dear," was Bob's mild answer, "Christmas Day."

"I'll drink his health for your sake and the Day's," said Mrs. Cratchit, "not for his. Long life to him! A merry Christmas and a happy new year!—he'll be very merry and very happy, I have no doubt!"

The children drank the toast after her. It was the first of their proceedings which had no heartiness in it. Tiny Tim drank it last of all, but he didn't care twopence for it. Scrooge was the Ogre of the family. The mention of his name cast a dark shadow on the party, which was not dispelled for full five minutes.

After it had passed away, they were ten times merrier than before, from the mere relief of Scrooge the Baleful being done with. Bob Cratchit told them how he had a situation in his eye for Master **46** Peter, which would bring in, if obtained, full five-and-sixpence weekly. The two young Cratchits laughed tremendously at the idea of Peter's being a man of business; and Peter himself looked thoughtfully at the fire from between his collars, as if he were deliberating what particular investments he

46 *a situation...for Master Peter.* If Peter Cratchit is the boy Charles Dickens, the mention of such employment at so festive a time is bitterly ironic; it may be a private joke at the author's own expense. The situation young Charles received was at Robert Warren's blacking factory, pasting labels on bottles for six shillings a week. Dickens described this, the most horrid experience of his childhood, in an autobiographical fragment (later adapted in *David Copperfield*, Chapter 11), quoted by Forster in his biography: "No words can express the secret agony in my soul as I sunk into this companionship; compared these everyday associates with those of my happier childhood; and felt my early hopes of growing up to be a learned and distinguished man, crushed in my breast. The deep remembrance of the sense I had of being utterly neglected and hopeless; of the shame I felt in my position; of the misery it was to my young heart to believe that, day by day, what I had learned, and thought and delighted in, and raised my fancy and emulation up by, was passing away from me, never to be brought back any more; cannot be written. My whole nature was so penetrated with the grief and humiliation of such considerations, that even now, famous and caressed and happy I often forget in my dreams...that I am a man; and wander desolately back to that time in my life."

In this passage lies the neglected, hopeless boy who grew into the novelist who defended the children Want and Ignorance. No details are given of Peter Cratchit's specific work. Perhaps Dickens' memories of his own employment were then too painful, but in *David Copperfield* he was finally able to describe "at ten years old, a little labouring hind" who, as the character David Copperfield, drudges in the Murdstone and Grinby warehouse.

47 *a song, about a lost child travelling in the snow.*
Apparently Dickens had no specific carol in mind;
no such song has been found in Sandys' or any other
collection. G. K. Chesterton apparently realized this
omission; in his *Poems* (1926) he included a verse, "A
Child of the Snows," which might stand for Tiny
Tim's song until another might be found.

48 *Peter might have known . . . the inside of a pawn-*
broker's. As Forster has written, when the Dickenses
needed to sell or pawn their belongings (which was
often), it was the child Charles who was "the prin-
cipal agent in these sorrowful transactions." "At the
pawnbroker's shop," Dickens admitted in *David Cop-*
perfield, "I began to be very well known."

should favour when he came into the receipt of
that bewildering income. Martha, who was a poor
apprentice at a milliner's, then told them what kind
of work she had to do, and how many hours she
worked at a stretch, and how she meant to lie a-bed
to-morrow morning for a good long rest; to-morrow
being a holiday she passed at home. Also how she
had seen a countess and a lord some days before, and
how the lord "was much about as tall as Peter;"
at which Peter pulled up his collars so high that
you couldn't have seen his head if you had been
there. All this time the chesnuts and the jug went
47 round and round; and bye and bye they had a song,
about a lost child travelling in the snow, from Tiny
Tim; who had a plaintive little voice, and sang it
very well indeed.

There was nothing of high mark in this. They
were not a handsome family; they were not well
dressed; their shoes were far from being water-
48 proof; their clothes were scanty; and Peter might
have known, and very likely did, the inside of a
pawnbroker's. But they were happy, grateful,
pleased with one another, and contented with the
time; and when they faded, and looked happier
yet in the bright sprinklings of the Spirit's torch
at parting, Scrooge had his eye upon them, and
especially on Tiny Tim, until the last.

By this time it was getting dark, and snowing
pretty heavily; and as Scrooge and the Spirit went
along the streets, the brightness of the roaring fires
in kitchens, parlours, and all sorts of rooms, was
wonderful. Here, the flickering of the blaze showed
preparations for a cosy dinner, with hot plates baking
through and through before the fire, and deep red
curtains, ready to be drawn, to shut out cold and
darkness. There, all the children of the house were
running out into the snow to meet their married
sisters, brothers, cousins, uncles, aunts, and be the
first to greet them. Here, again, were shadows on
the window-blind of guests assembling; and there a

"Going to the Pantomime" by John Leech, *The Illustrated London News*, December 24, 1853. *Courtesy The Library of Congress*

group of handsome girls, all hooded and fur-booted, and all chattering at once, tripped lightly off to some near neighbour's house; where, wo upon the single **49** man who saw them enter—artful witches: well they knew it—in a glow!

But if you had judged from the numbers of people on their way to friendly gatherings, you might have thought that no one was at home to give them welcome when they got there, instead of every house expecting company, and piling up its fires half-chimney high. Blessings on it, how the Ghost exulted! How it bared its breadth of breast, and opened its capacious palm, and floated on, outpouring, with a generous hand, its bright and harmless mirth on everything within its reach! The very lamplighter, who ran on before dotting the dusky street with specks of light, and who was dressed to spend the evening somewhere, laughed out loudly as the Spirit passed: though little kenned the lamp- **50** lighter that he had any company but Christmas!

49 *wo.* Colloquial spelling for *woe.*

50 *kenned.* Knew.

51 *a bleak and desert moor.* In Cornwall, where Dickens, Forster, Daniel Maclise, and Clarkson Stanfield spent about ten days in late October and early November 1842. "I think of opening my new book [*Martin Chuzzlewit*] on the Coast of Cornwall, in some terrible dreary iron-bound spot," Dickens wrote Forster on September 16. The novelist had been touched by the Infant Labour Commission's recent report on child labor in the Cornish mines, and he immediately made plans, as he wrote Dr. Southwood Smith (one of the commissioners of the pamphlet) on October 22, "to see the very dreariest and most desolate portion of the seacoast of Cornwall. . . . Can you tell me of your own knowledge . . . what is the next best bleak and barren part? And can you, furthermore, while I am in those regions, help me down a mine?"

"Blessed star of the morning, such a trip as we had in Cornwall." Dickens recounted the journey to C. C. Felton, December 31, 1842: "If you could have followed us into the earthy old Churches we visited, and into the strange caverns on the gloomy seashore, and down into the depths of the Mines, and up to the tops of the giddying heights where the unspeakably green water was roaring I don't know how many hundred feet below! If you could have seen but one gleam of the bright fires by which we sat in the big rooms of ancient Inns at night, until long after the small hours had come and gone. . . . I never laughed in my life as I did on this journey." He did not open *Martin Chuzzlewit* in Cornwall but rather saved his Cornish experiences for the composition of *A Christmas Carol*, written not only with laughter but also reverence for the lives of the miners.

52 *the burial-place of giants.* An obvious reference to Cornwall, the traditional home of Dickens' boyhood hero Jack the Giant-Killer. The story of Jack and the Cornish Giant was one of the earliest stories to spark the love of reading in the boy. In "A Christmas Tree," he fondly recalled his old storybook: "But, now, the very tree itself . . . becomes a bean-stalk —the marvelous bean-stalk up which Jack climbed to the Giant's house! And now, those dreadfully interesting, double-headed giants, with their clubs over their shoulders, begin to stride along the boughs in a perfect throng, dragging knights and ladies home to dinner by the hair of their heads. And Jack—how noble, with his sword of sharpness, and his shoes of swiftness! Again those old meditations come upon me as I gaze up at him; and I debate within myself whether there was more than one Jack (which I am loath to believe possible), or only one genuine original admirable Jack, who achieved all the recorded exploits."

James Boswell shared a deep affection for these old tales and even considered writing his own versions, but by the nineteenth century the old childhood tales had fallen into disfavor. The popular critic Robert Bloomfield attacked *Jack the Giant-Killer* for its "abominable absurdities." In his autobiography *Recol-*

And now, without a word of warning from the
51 Ghost, they stood upon a bleak and desert moor, where monstrous masses of rude stone were cast
52 about, as though it were the burial-place of giants; and water spread itself wheresoever it listed—or would have done so, but for the frost that held it
53 prisoner; and nothing grew but moss and furze, and
54 coarse, rank grass. Down in the west the setting sun had left a streak of fiery red, which glared upon the desolation for an instant, like a sullen eye, and frowning lower, lower, lower yet, was lost in the thick gloom of darkest night.

"The Logan Rock, Cornwall, climbed by Charles Dickens, John Forster, Daniel Maclise and the Artist" by Clarkson Stanfield, c. 1842. *Courtesy The Victoria and Albert Museum*

Woodcut by John Leech, *Jack the Giant Killer*, 1844. *Courtesy The Library of Congress*

lections of a Lifetime (1856), Samuel Griswold Goodrich (the original "Peter Parley") expressed the common critical opinion of the legends as: "tales of horror, commonly put into the hands of youth, as if for the express purpose of reconciling them to vice and crime. Some children, no doubt have a ready appetite for these monstrosities, but to others they are revolting, until by repetition and familiarity, the taste is sufficiently degraded to relish them. At all events they are shocking to me."

Dickens obviously felt the necessity of defending his innocent childhood reading against such attacks as Goodrich's and those alterations made by *George Cruikshank's Fairy Library*. In his essay "Fraud on the Fairies" (1853), Dickens took exception to Cruikshank's adaptation of the old stories for temperance propaganda; as he wrote a friend on July 27, Dickens' intention in the article was "half playfully, and half seriously . . . to protest most strongly against alteration,—for any purpose,—of the beautiful little stories which are so tenderly and humanly useful to us in

these times when the world is too much with us, early and late."

53 *furze*. Or gorse; Dr. Johnson in his dictionary identified this evergreen plant as "a thick prickly shrub that bears yellow flowers in winter."

54 *the setting sun*. This Cornish sunset was likely the same one described by Forster in his biography: "Land and sea yielded each its marvels to us; but of all the impressions brought away, of which some afterwords took forms as lasting as they could receive from the most delightful art, I doubt if any were the source of such deep emotion to us all as a sunset. . . . I was familiar from boyhood with border and Scottish scenery, and Dickens was fresh from Niagara; but there was something in the sinking of the sun behind the Atlantic that autumn afternoon, as we viewed it together from the top of the rock projecting farthest into the sea, which each in turn declared to have no parallel in memory."

"Botallack Mine, Cornwall..." by Clarkson Stanfield, *Stanfield's Coast Scenery*, 1836. *Courtesy The British Library Board*

55 *"A place where Miners live."* Land's End, Cornwall, likely the Botallick Mine. "The most celebrated tin mines in Cornwall are ... close to the sea," Dickens wrote in *A Child's History of England* (1851, Chapter 1). "One of them, which I have seen, is so close to it that it is hollowed out underneath the ocean; and the miners say, that, in stormy weather, when they are at work down in the deep place, they can hear the noise of the waves, thundering above their heads."

" What place is this ?" asked Scrooge.

55 " A place where Miners live, who labour in the bowels of the earth," returned the Spirit. " But they know me. See !"

A light shone from the window of a hut, and swiftly they advanced towards it. Passing through the wall of mud and stone, they found a cheerful company assembled round a glowing fire. An old, old man and woman, with their children and their children's children, and another generation beyond

"Land's End, Cornwall" by Clarkson Stanfield, *Stanfield's Coast Scenery*, 1836. *Courtesy The British Library Board*

that, all decked out gaily in their holiday attire. The old man, in a voice that seldom rose above the howling of the wind upon the barren waste, was singing them a Christmas song; it had been a very old song when **56** he was a boy; and from time to time they all joined in the chorus. So surely as they raised their voices, the old man got quite blithe and loud; and so surely as they stopped, his vigour sank again.

The Spirit did not tarry here, but bade Scrooge hold his robe, and passing on above the moor, sped whither? Not to sea? To sea. To Scrooge's horror, looking back, he saw the last of the land, a frightful range of rocks, behind them; and his ears were deafened by the thundering of water, as it rolled, and roared, and raged among the dreadful caverns it had worn, and fiercely tried to undermine the earth.

Built upon a dismal reef of sunken rocks, some league or so from shore, on which the waters chafed and dashed, the wild year through, there stood a **57** solitary lighthouse. Great heaps of sea-weed clung to its base, and storm-birds—born of the wind one might suppose, as sea-weed of the water—rose and fell about it, like the waves they skimmed.

56 *a Christmas song.* As noted by Sandys in *Christmastide* (1860), Cornwall was well known for its Christmas songs, several of which were said to be over three hundred years old. Those also sung in church usually had the refrain "Nowell, nowell, good news, good news of the gospel."

57 *a solitary lighthouse.* Likely the Longships. While reading about Cornwall before his trip, Dickens wrote Forster in early August 1842: "I have some notion of opening the new book in the lantern of a lighthouse!" The next book was *Martin Chuzzlewit,* which begins not in a Cornish lighthouse but in a Wiltshire village.

"The Lighthouse" by Clarkson Stanfield, *The Dickensian,* April 1909. *Courtesy General Research and Humanities Division, The New York Public Library, Astor, Lenox and Tilden Foundations*

58 *grog.* A mixture of spirits (originally rum) and water, from "Old Grog," the nickname of Admiral Vernon (1745), known for his coat of grogram (a coarse fabric of silk, wool, and mohair) and a fondness for the drink; it was generally given to sailors as a substitute for straight rum.

59 *It was a much greater surprise to Scrooge to recognise it as his own nephew's.* Compare Fred's startling appearance to his introduction in Stave 1; Scrooge breaks this pattern of being shaken by each arrival of his nephew by himself bursting in on Fred and his party on Christmas Day in Stave 5.

But even here, two men who watched the light had made a fire, that through the loophole in the thick stone wall shed out a ray of brightness on the awful sea. Joining their horny hands over the rough table at which they sat, they wished each other **58** Merry Christmas in their can of grog; and one of them: the elder, too, with his face all damaged and scarred with hard weather, as the figure-head of an old ship might be: struck up a sturdy song that was like a Gale in itself.

Again the Ghost sped on, above the black and heaving sea—on, on—until, being far away, as he told Scrooge, from any shore, they lighted on a ship. They stood beside the helmsman at the wheel, the look-out in the bow, the officers who had the watch; dark, ghostly figures in their several stations; but every man among them hummed a Christmas tune, or had a Christmas thought, or spoke below his breath to his companion of some bygone Christmas Day, with homeward hopes belonging to it. And every man on board, waking or sleeping, good or bad, had had a kinder word for another on that day than on any day in the year; and had shared to some extent in its festivities; and had remembered those he cared for at a distance, and had known that they delighted to remember him.

It was a great surprise to Scrooge, while listening to the moaning of the wind, and thinking what a solemn thing it was to move on through the lonely darkness over an unknown abyss, whose depths were secrets as profound as Death: it was a great surprise to Scrooge, while thus engaged, to hear a hearty **59** laugh. It was a much greater surprise to Scrooge to recognise it as his own nephew's, and to find himself in a bright, dry, gleaming room, with the Spirit standing smiling by his side, and looking at that same nephew with approving affability!

"Ha, ha!" laughed Scrooge's nephew. "Ha, ha, ha!"

If you should happen, by any unlikely chance, to know a man more blest in a laugh than Scrooge's nephew, all I can say is, I should like to know him too. Introduce him to me, and I 'll cultivate his acquaintance.

It is a fair, even-handed, noble adjustment of things, that while there is infection in disease and sorrow, there is nothing in the world so irresistibly contagious as laughter and good-humour. When Scrooge's nephew laughed in this way: holding his sides, rolling his head, and twisting his face into the most extravagant contortions: Scrooge's niece, by marriage, laughed as heartily as he. And their assembled friends being not a bit behindhand, roared out, lustily. **60**

"Ha, ha! Ha, ha, ha, ha!"

"He said that Christmas was a humbug, as I live!" cried Scrooge's nephew. "He believed it too!"

"More shame for him, Fred!" said Scrooge's niece, indignantly. Bless those women; they never do anything by halves. They are always in earnest.

She was very pretty: exceedingly pretty. With a dimpled, surprised-looking, capital face; a ripe little mouth, that seemed made to be kissed—as no doubt it was; all kinds of good little dots about her chin, that melted into one another when she laughed; and the sunniest pair of eyes you ever saw in any little creature's head. Altogether she was what you would have called provoking, you know; but satisfactory, too. Oh, perfectly satisfactory!

"He's a comical old fellow," said Scrooge's nephew, "that's the truth; and not so pleasant as he might be. However, his offences carry their own punishment, and I have nothing to say against him."

"I'm sure he is very rich, Fred," hinted Scrooge's niece. "At least you always tell *me* so."

"What of that, my dear!" said Scrooge's nephew.

60 *behindhand.* Tardy.

61 *He don't. . . . He don't.* Cockney dialect (as in "the major don't know," *Dombey and Son*, Chapter 31). Dickens was obviously uncomfortable using this awkward phrasing: in the original manuscript, he first wrote "doesn't" and then replaced it with "don't"; in the Berg prompt copy, he altered it to "does no" and then crossed out the alteration. Some reprints of the story replace "don't" with "doesn't."

Slater explained in the 1971 Penguin edition of *A Christmas Carol* that Dickens attempted in the 1840s "a style more colloquial than which Dickens usually adopted in his big novels." This experiment explains some of the odd spellings and Cockney slang throughout the text and results in a more "rhetorical" use of punctuation "based on speech rhythms rather than on grammatical sense. This involved especially the lavish use of dashes, colons and semicolons." Apparently Dickens was not completely sure of his intentions; many of the superficial changes made from edition to edition are in punctuations and contractions. It was such experimentations which so offended Samuel Rogers (as cited in note 31 to the Introduction) that he "said there was no wit in putting bad grammar into the mouths of all his characters, and showing their vulgar pronunciation by spelling 'are' 'air,' a horse without an h: none of our best writers do that."

62 *tucker.* A piece of lace or other delicate material, worn in the neckline of a woman's dress and covering part of the bosom.

63 *aromatic vinegar.* A solution of acetic acid, strongly perfumed, used as a specific against headaches. T. W. Hill in his notes to *Little Dorrit* (*The Dickensian*, Spring Number 1946) described its preparation: "A mixture of 1 oz of camphor, 15 grs of oil of cloves, 10 grs of oil of cinnamon, 6 grs of oil of English lavender, half a pint of acetic acid. It is usually poured over small pieces of sponge and kept in a tight-stoppered bottle."

61 "His wealth is of no use to him. He don't do any good with it. He don't make himself comfortable with it. He has n't the satisfaction of thinking—ha, ha, ha!—that he is ever going to benefit Us with it."

"I have no patience with him," observed Scrooge's niece. Scrooge's niece's sisters, and all the other ladies, expressed the same opinion.

"Oh, I have!" said Scrooge's nephew. "I am sorry for him; I could n't be angry with him if I tried. Who suffers by his ill whims? Himself, always. Here, he takes it into his head to dislike us, and he won't come and dine with us. What 's the consequence? He don't lose much of a dinner."

"Indeed, I think he loses a very good dinner," interrupted Scrooge's niece. Everybody else said the same, and they must be allowed to have been competent judges, because they had just had dinner; and, with the dessert upon the table, were clustered round the fire, by lamplight.

"Well! I am very glad to hear it," said Scrooge's nephew, "because I have n't any great faith in these young housekeepers. What do *you* say, Topper?"

Topper had clearly got his eye upon one of Scrooge's niece's sisters, for he answered that a bachelor was a wretched outcast, who had no right to express an opinion on the subject. Whereat Scrooge's niece's sister—the plump one with the

62 lace tucker: not the one with the roses—blushed.

"Do go on, Fred," said Scrooge's niece, clapping her hands. "He never finishes what he begins to say! He is such a ridiculous fellow!"

Scrooge's nephew revelled in another laugh, and as it was impossible to keep the infection off; though

63 the plump sister tried hard to do it with aromatic vinegar; his example was unanimously followed.

"I was only going to say," said Scrooge's nephew,

" that the consequence of his taking a dislike to us, and not making merry with us, is, as I think, that he loses some pleasant moments, which could do him no harm. I am sure he loses pleasanter companions than he can find in his own thoughts, either in his mouldy old office, or his dusty chambers. I mean to give him the same chance every year, whether he likes it or not, for I pity him. He may rail at Christmas till he dies, but he can't help thinking better of it—I defy him—if he finds me going there, in good temper, year after year, and saying Uncle Scrooge, how are you? If it only puts him in the vein to leave his poor clerk fifty pounds, *that's* something; and I think I shook him, yesterday."

It was their turn to laugh now, at the notion of his shaking Scrooge. But being thoroughly good-natured, and not much caring what they laughed at, so that they laughed at any rate, he encouraged them in their merriment, and passed the bottle, joyously.

After tea, they had some music. For they were a musical family, and knew what they were about, when they sung a Glee or Catch, I can assure you: **64, 65** especially Topper, who could growl away in the bass like a good one, and never swell the large veins in his forehead, or get red in the face over it. Scrooge's niece played well upon the harp; and played among other tunes a simple little air (a mere nothing: you might learn to whistle it in two minutes), which had been familiar to the child who fetched Scrooge from the boarding-school, as he had been reminded by the Ghost of Christmas Past. When this strain of music sounded, all the things that Ghost had shown him, came upon his mind; he softened more and more; and thought that if he could have listened to it often, years ago, he might have cultivated the kindnesses of life for his own happiness with his own hands, without

64 *Glee.* A musical composition for three or more voices with distinct parts for each to form a series of interwoven melodies, usually of a light or secular nature.

65 *Catch.* A comic canon or round for three or more voices, in which, after the first singer has finished a line, the second begins or "catches" the words, and is followed by the third and so on, so that each is singing a different line at the same time.

66 *blindman's buff.* Compare Topper's performance to that of an equally riotous blindman in Irving's *Sketch Book:* "Master Simon...was blinded in the midst of the hall. The little beings were as busy around him as the mock fairies about Falstaff; pinching him, plucking at the skirts of his coat, and tickling him with straws. One fine blue-eyed girl of about thirteen, with her flaxen hair all in beautiful confusion, her frolic face in a glow, her frock half torn off her shoulders, a complete picture of a romp, was the chief tormentor; and, from the slyness with which Master Simon avoided the smaller game, and hemmed this wild little nymph in corners, and obliged her to jump shrieking over chairs, I suspected the rogue of being not a whit more blinded than was convenient."

67 *another blindman.* Dickens suggests not only another player in the actual game but also Cupid, the blinded god of Love.

"A Christmas Canticle" by John Leech, *The Illuminated Magazine,* December 1843. *Courtesy The Library of Congress*

resorting to the sexton's spade that buried Jacob Marley.

But they did n't devote the whole evening to music. After a while they played at forfeits; for it is good to be children sometimes, and never better than at Christmas, when its mighty Founder was a child himself. Stop! There was first a game at **66** blindman's buff. Of course there was. And I no more believe Topper was really blind than I believe he had eyes in his boots. My opinion is, that it was a done thing between him and Scrooge's nephew; and that the Ghost of Christmas Present knew it. The way he went after that plump sister in the lace tucker, was an outrage on the credulity of human nature. Knocking down the fire-irons, tumbling over the chairs, bumping up against the piano, smothering himself among the curtains, wherever she went, there went he. He always knew where the plump sister was. He would n't catch anybody else. If you had fallen up against him, as some of them did, and stood there; he would have made a feint of endeavouring to seize you, which would have been an affront to your understanding; and would instantly have sidled off in the direction of the plump sister. She often cried out that it was n't fair; and it really was not. But when at last, he caught her; when, in spite of all her silken rustlings, and her rapid flutterings past him, he got her into a corner whence there was no escape; then his conduct was the most execrable. For his pretending not to know her; his pretending that it was necessary to touch her head-dress, and further to assure himself of her identity by pressing a certain ring upon her finger, and a certain chain about her neck; was vile, monstrous! No doubt **67** she told him her opinion of it, when, another blindman being in office, they were so very confidential together, behind the curtains.

Scrooge's niece was not one of the blind-man's

buff party, but was made comfortable with a large chair and a footstool, in a snug corner, where the Ghost and Scrooge were close behind her. But she joined in the forfeits, and loved her love to **68** admiration with all the letters of the alphabet.

Likewise at the game of How, When, and Where, **69** she was very great, and to the secret joy of Scrooge's nephew, beat her sisters hollow : though they were sharp girls too, as Topper could have told you. There might have been twenty people there, young and old, but they all played, and so did Scrooge ; for, wholly forgetting in the interest he had in what was going on, that his voice made no sound in their ears, he sometimes came out with his guess quite loud, and very often guessed right, too ; for the sharpest needle, best Whitechapel, warranted not to **70** cut in the eye, was not sharper than Scrooge : blunt as he took it in his head to be.

The Ghost was greatly pleased to find him in this mood, and looked upon him with such favour that he begged like a boy to be allowed to stay until the guests departed. But this the Spirit said could not be done.

" Here's a new game," said Scrooge. " One half hour, Spirit, only one ! "

It was a Game called Yes and No, where **71** Scrooge's nephew had to think of something, and the rest must find out what ; he only answering to their questions yes or no as the case was. The brisk fire of questioning to which he was exposed, elicited from him that he was thinking of an animal, a live animal, rather a disagreeable animal, a savage animal, an animal that growled and grunted sometimes, and talked sometimes, and lived in London, and walked about the streets, and wasn't made a show of, and wasn't led by anybody, and didn't live in a menagerie, and was never killed in a market, and was not a horse, or an ass, or a cow, or a bull, or a tiger, or a dog, or a pig, or a cat, or

68 *loved her love to admiration with all the letters of the alphabet.* The old parlor game "I love my love with an A," popular in both Great Britain and the United States; it was also used by mothers to teach the alphabet. Each player must complete a series of sentences using the next letter of the alphabet in each blank. The pattern is given in *Our Mutual Friend* (Book II, Chapter 1): Jenny Wren addresses her visitors, "I'll give you a clue to my trade, in a game of forfeits. I love my love with a B because she's Beautiful; I hate my love with a B because she is Brazen; I took her to the sign of the Blue Boar, and I treated her with Bonnets; her name's Bouncer, and she lives in Bedlam.—Now, what do I make with my straw?" (The answer is "ladies' bonnets"; she is the Doll's Dressmaker.) Lewis Carroll similarly plays with the old parlor game in *Through the Looking-Glass* (1872, Chapter 7): Alice however must in loving her love begin with an "H," because her companions in Looking-Glass Land aspirate their A's.

69 *How, When, and Where.* Another game of forfeits, in which each player in turn must ask, "How do you like it?" "When do you like it?" and "Where do you like it?"

The author's son, Sir Henry F. Dickens, recalled in *Memories of My Father* (1928) another parlor game similar to the one at Fred's Christmas party but called "The Memory Game": "One of the party started by giving a name, such as, for instance, Napoleon. The next person had to repeat this and add something of his own, such as Napoleon, Blackbeetle, and so on, until the string of names began to get long and difficult to remember. My father, after many turns, had successfully gone through the long string of words, and finished up with his own contribution, 'Warren's Blacking, 30, Strand.' He gave this with an odd twinkle in his eye and a strange inflection in his voice which at once forcibly arrested my attention and left a vivid impression on my mind for some time afterwards. Why, I could not, for the life of me, understand. When, however, his tragic history appeared in Forster's Life, this game at Christmas, 1869, flashed across my mind with extraordinary force, and the mystery was explained."

70 *Whitechapel.* A district in East London, the location of large needle factories, and which gave its name to a particular make of needle.

71 *Yes and No.* "In this particular game," explained Percy Fitzgerald in *The Life of Charles Dickens* (1905, p. 214), "Boz himself excelled...however, he would reverse the process, going out of the room while we fixed on some subject. Then he came back and plied us with a shower of enquiries until he actually *forced* his way to the solution...."

a bear. At every fresh question that was put to him, this nephew burst into a fresh roar of laughter; and was so inexpressibly tickled, that he was obliged to get up off the sofa and stamp. At last the plump sister, falling into a similar state, cried out :

"I have found it out! I know what it is, Fred! I know what it is!"

"What is it?" cried Fred.

"It's your Uncle Scro-o-o-o-oge!"

Which it certainly was. Admiration was the universal sentiment, though some objected that the reply to "Is it a bear?" ought to have been "Yes;" inasmuch as an answer in the negative was sufficient to have diverted their thoughts from Mr. Scrooge, supposing they had ever had any tendency that way.

"He has given us plenty of merriment, I am sure," said Fred, "and it would be ungrateful not to drink his health. Here is a glass of mulled wine ready to our hand at the moment; and I say 'Uncle Scrooge!'"

"Well! Uncle Scrooge!" they cried.

"A Merry Christmas and a happy New Year to the old man, whatever he is!" said Scrooge's nephew. "He wouldn't take it from me, but may he have it, nevertheless. Uncle Scrooge!"

Uncle Scrooge had imperceptibly become so gay and light of heart, that he would have pledged the unconscious company in return, and thanked them in an inaudible speech, if the Ghost had given him time. But the whole scene passed off in the breath of the last word spoken by his nephew; and he and the Spirit were again upon their travels.

Much they saw, and far they went, and many homes they visited, but always with a happy end. The Spirit stood beside sick beds, and they were cheerful; on foreign lands, and they were close at home; by struggling men, and they were patient in their greater hope; by poverty, and it was rich. In almshouse, hospital, and jail, in misery's every refuge, where vain man in his little brief authority **72** had not made fast the door, and barred the Spirit out, he left his blessing, and taught Scrooge his precepts.

It was a long night, if it were only a night; but Scrooge had his doubts of this, because the Christmas **73** Holidays appeared to be condensed into the space of time they passed together. It was strange, too, that while Scrooge remained unaltered in his outward form, the Ghost grew older, clearly older. Scrooge had observed this change, but never spoke of it, until they left a children's Twelfth Night party, **74** when, looking at the Spirit as they stood together in an open place, he noticed that its hair was gray.

"Are spirits' lives so short?" asked Scrooge.

"My life upon this globe, is very brief," replied the Ghost. "It ends to-night."

"Twelfth Night in London Streets" by Robert Seymour, *The Book of Christmas*, 1836. *Courtesy The Library of Congress*

72 *vain man in his little brief authority*. In his notes to the 1971 Penguin edition, Slater identified this phrase as referring to *Measure for Measure*, Act II, Scene 2, lines 116–21:

> ...but man, proud man!
> Dress'd in a little brief authority,—
> Most ignorant of what he's most assured,
> His glassy essence,—like an angry ape,
> Plays such fantastic tricks before high heaven
> As make the angels weep....

73 *the Christmas Holidays*. In Dickens' day, the holiday season ran for twelve days, from Christmas Day until Epiphany, January 6. See Note 76.

74 *a children's Twelfth Night party*. The Twelfth Night festivities were particularly energetic in the Dickens household because they also celebrated his son Charles Boz Dickens' birthday. For these parties the novelist often invited "some children of a larger growth" from his wide circle of literary friends. In a letter to a friend, C. C. Felton, December 31, 1842, Dickens announced his plans for one of these entertainments: "The actuary of the National Debt couldn't calculate the number of children who are coming here on Twelfth Night, in honor of Charley's birthday, for which occasion I have provided a Magic Lantern and divers other tremendous engines of that nature. But best of it is that Forster and I have purchased between us the entire stock in trade of a conjuror.... And ... if you could see me conjuring the company's watches into impossible tea caddies, and causing pieces of money to fly, and burning pocket handkerchiefs without hurting 'em ... you would never forget it as long as you live."

"Twelfth Night" by Robert Seymour, *The Book of Christmas*, 1836. *Courtesy The Library of Congress*

This "entire stock of a conjuror" was pulled out for several Twelfth Nights to come. "One of these conjuring tricks," recalled his daughter Mamie in *My Father As I Recall Him* (1896), "comprised the disappearance and reappearance of a tiny doll, which would announce most unexpected news and messages to the different children in the audience; this doll was a particular favourite, and its arrival equally awaited and welcomed." Dickens himself reveled in these demonstrations and he proudly wrote his friend William Macready (then in America) of the marvelous entertainment on Twelfth Night of 1844: "Forster and I conjured bravely; that a plum-pudding was produced from an empty saucepan, held over a blazing fire kindled in Stanfield's hat without damage to the lining; that a box of bran was changed into a live guinea-pig, which ran between my godchild's feet . . . and you might have heard it (and I daresay did) in America; that three half-crowns being taken . . . and put into a tumbler-glass . . . did then and there give jingling answers to the questions asked of them by me . . . to the unspeakable admiration of the whole assembly."

Dickens did not have to exaggerate this response; Mrs. Thomas Carlyle, one of the guests at this particular party, admitted that Dickens was the greatest conjuror she had ever seen.

The entire evening was not limited to magic tricks; there was also dancing. Mamie Dickens recalled another party for which her father had insisted she and her sister Katie teach John Leech and himself the polka: "My Father was as much in earnest about learning to take that wonderful step correctly, as though there were nothing of greater importance in the world. . . . No one can imagine our excitement and nervousness when the evening came on which we were to dance with our pupils. Katie, who was a very little girl was to have Mr. Leech, who was over six feet tall, for her partner, while my father was to be mine. My heart beat so fast I could scarcely breathe. . . . But my fears were groundless, and we were greeted at the finish of our dance with hearty applause, which was more than compensation for the work which had been expended upon its learning."

" To-night !" cried Scrooge.

" To-night at midnight. Hark! The time is drawing near."

The chimes were ringing the three quarters past eleven at that moment.

" Forgive me if I am not justified in what I ask," said Scrooge, looking intently at the Spirit's robe, " but I see something strange, and not belonging to yourself, protruding from your skirts. Is it a foot or a claw !"

" It might be a claw, for the flesh there is upon it," was the Spirit's sorrowful reply. " Look here."

From the foldings of its robe, it brought two children; wretched, abject, frightful, hideous, miserable. They knelt down at its feet, and clung upon the outside of its garment.

" Oh, Man ! look here. Look, look, down here!" exclaimed the Ghost.

They were a boy and girl. Yellow, meagre, ragged, scowling, wolfish; but prostrate, too, in their humility. Where graceful youth should have filled their features out, and touched them with its freshest tints, a stale and shrivelled hand, like that of age, had pinched, and twisted them, and pulled them into shreds. Where angels might have sat enthroned, devils lurked, and glared out menacing. No change, no degradation, no perversion of humanity, in any grade, through all the mysteries of wonderful creation, has monsters half so horrible and dread.

Scrooge started back, appalled. Having them shown to him in this way, he tried to say they were fine children, but the words choked themselves, rather than be parties to a lie of such enormous magnitude.

" Spirit ! are they yours ?" Scrooge could say no more.

" They are Man's," said the Spirit, looking down upon them. " And they cling to me, appealing from their fathers. This boy is Ignorance. This girl is **75**

75 *This boy is Ignorance. This girl is Want.* Through these two children, Dickens expresses metaphorically his strongest plea in the story for an active concern for the children of the poor. The novelist knew through his own childhood how little it might have taken to alter his own condition. "I know I do not exaggerate, unconsciously and intentionally, the scantiness of my resources and the difficulties of my life," he wrote in the autobiographical fragment quoted by Forster in his biography. "I know that if a shilling or so were given me by any one, I spent it in a dinner or tea. I know that I worked from morning to night, with common men and boys, a shabby child.... I know that I have lounged about the streets, insufficiently and unsatisfactorily fed. I know that, but for the mercy of God, I might have been, for any care that was taken of me, a little robber or a little vagabond." During part of his childhood, Dickens was a companion to these children protected by the Ghost of Christmas Present.

Dickens found his inspiration for this boy and girl during a visit to the Ragged Schools of Field Lane, Holborn, free institutions for poor children, located in the dismal part of London where Fagin lived. As he wrote Miss Burnett Coutts, September 16, 1843, Dickens expressed his concern for these students "who know nothing of affection, care, love, or kindness of any sort": "I have very seldom seen, in all the strange and dreadful things I have seen in London and elsewhere, anything so shocking as the dire neglect of soul and body exhibited in these children. And ... I know ... that in the prodigious misery and ignorance of the swarming masses of mankind in England, the seeds of its certain ruin are sown, I never saw the Truth so staring out in hopeless characters, as it does from the walls of this place. The children in the Jails are almost as common sights to me as my own; but these are worse, for they have not arrived there yet, but are as plainly and certainly travelling there, as they are to their Graves." (*Letters*, Clarendon Press, Vol. 3, p. 562).

Soon after *A Christmas Carol* was published, in a speech delivered at the Polytechnic Institute in Birmingham, February 28, 1844, Dickens repeated his warning: "Now there is a spirit of great power, the Spirit of Ignorance, long shut up in a vessel of Obstinate Neglect, with a great deal of lead in its composition, and sealed with the seal of many, many Solomons, and which is exactly in the same position. Release it in time, and it will bless, restore, and reanimate society; but let it lie under rolling waves of years, and its blind revenge at last will be destruction." (*Speeches*, Clarendon Press, p. 61).

Dickens did not easily forget the boy Ignorance and the girl Want. In his last Christmas book, *The Haunted Man* (1848), he returned to their theme in the child with no name: "a baby savage, a young monster, a child who had never been a child, a creature who might live to take the outward form of man, but who, within, would live and perish a mere beast."

76 *twelve.* This hour, of course, corresponds to the twelfth or last Christmas holiday when the Ghost of Christmas Present must depart; note also that while the first two spirits came at the stroke of one or the beginning of the day, the Ghost of Christmas Yet To Come in its black shroud appears at the stroke of twelve, the traditional bewitching hour, being the final hour of the day.

Want. Beware them both, and all of their degree, but most of all beware this boy, for on his brow I see that written which is Doom, unless the writing be erased. Deny it!" cried the Spirit, stretching out its hand towards the city. "Slander those who tell it ye! Admit it for your factious purposes, and make it worse! And bide the end!"

"Have they no refuge or resource?" cried Scrooge.

"Are there no prisons?" said the Spirit, turning on him for the last time with his own words. "Are there no workhouses?"

76 The bell struck twelve.

Scrooge looked about him for the Ghost, and saw it not. As the last stroke ceased to vibrate, he remembered the prediction of old Jacob Marley, and lifting up his eyes, beheld a solemn Phantom, draped and hooded, coming, like a mist along the ground, towards him.

Preliminary pencil and wash drawing by John Leech for "Ignorance and Want." *Courtesy The Houghton Library, Harvard University*

STAVE FOUR.

◆

THE LAST OF THE SPIRITS.

THE Phantom slowly, gravely, silently, ap- **1**
proached. When it came near him, Scrooge bent
down upon his knee; for in the very air through
which this Spirit moved it seemed to scatter gloom
and mystery.

It was shrouded in a deep black garment, which
concealed its head, its face, its form, and left nothing
of it visible save one outstretched hand. But for
this it would have been difficult to detach its figure
from the night, and separate it from the darkness by
which it was surrounded.

He felt that it was tall and stately when it came
beside him, and that its mysterious presence filled
him with a solemn dread. He knew no more, for
the Spirit neither spoke nor moved.

1 *The Phantom.* The Ghost of Christmas Yet To
Come, wearing a "dusky shroud" and protecting
Scrooge in the "shadow of its dress," is of course
Death, "cold, cold, rigid, dreadful Death." This Spirit
may seem an odd choice for a Christmas ghost, but
during the holidays Dickens often reflected on the
death of loved ones.

Not even with all the bright activity of the Christmas season can he remove from his fireside "the shadow
that darkens the whole globe... the shadow of
the City of the Dead." "Of all the days in the year,"
he explained in "What Christmas Is, As We Grow
Older" (*Household Words*, Christmas Number, 1851),
"we will turn our faces towards that City upon
Christmas Day, and from its silent hosts bring those
we loved, among us. City of the Dead, in the blessed
name wherein we are gathered together at this time,
and in the Presence that is here among us according
to the promise, we will receive, and not dismiss, thy
people who are dear to us!"

Dickens' most devastating depiction of this holiday
specter is in "A December Vision" (*Household
Words*, December 14, 1850). In its slow, steady, un-

moving persistence; in its ability to enter any place at will; in its shaded face and its ghostly eyes, this image of death is the same spirit as the Ghost of Christmas Yet To Come. Dickens' coupling Death with Christmas is not difficult to justify. The holidays come at the end of the year, a time of recollection and resolution. The Birth of Christ has often been used as a reminder of the Crucifixion. The Christmas song "I Wonder As I Wander" laments "how Jesus the Savior was born for to die."

2 *downward.* A printer's error; in the second edition, Dickens corrected this word to "onward."

"I am in the presence of the Ghost of Christmas Yet To Come?" said Scrooge.

2   The Spirit answered not, but pointed downward with its hand.

"You are about to show me shadows of the things that have not happened, but will happen in the time before us," Scrooge pursued. "Is that so, Spirit?"

The upper portion of the garment was contracted for an instant in its folds, as if the Spirit had inclined its head. That was the only answer he received.

Although well used to ghostly company by this time, Scrooge feared the silent shape so much that his legs trembled beneath him, and he found that he could hardly stand when he prepared to follow it. The Spirit paused a moment, as observing his condition, and giving him time to recover.

But Scrooge was all the worse for this. It thrilled him with a vague uncertain horror, to know that behind the dusky shroud there were ghostly eyes intently fixed upon him, while he, though he stretched his own to the utmost, could see nothing but a spectral hand and one great heap of black.

"Ghost of the Future!" he exclaimed, "I fear you more than any Spectre I have seen. But, as I know your purpose is to do me good, and as I hope to live to be another man from what I was, I am prepared to bear you company, and do it with a thankful heart. Will you not speak to me?"

It gave him no reply. The hand was pointed straight before them.

"Lead on!" said Scrooge. "Lead on! The night is waning fast, and it is precious time to me, I know. Lead on, Spirit!"

The Phantom moved away as it had come towards him. Scrooge followed in the shadow of its dress, which bore him up, he thought, and carried him along.

They scarcely seemed to enter the city; for the city rather seemed to spring up about them, and encompass them of its own act. But there they were, in the heart of it; on 'Change, amongst the **3** merchants; who hurried up and down, and chinked the money in their pockets, and conversed in groups, and looked at their watches, and trifled thoughtfully with their great gold seals; and so forth, as Scrooge had seen them often.

The Spirit stopped beside one little knot of business men. Observing that the hand was pointed to them, Scrooge advanced to listen to their talk.

"No," said a great fat man with a monstrous chin, "I don't know much about it, either way. I only know he's dead."

"When did he die?" inquired another.

"Last night, I believe."

"Why, what was the matter with him?" asked a third, taking a vast quantity of snuff out of a very large snuff-box. "I thought he'd never die."

"God knows," said the first, with a yawn.

"What has he done with his money?" asked a red-faced gentleman with a pendulous excrescence **4** on the end of his nose, that shook like the gills of a turkey-cock.

"I haven't heard," said the man with the large chin, yawning again. "Left it to his Company, perhaps. He hasn't left it to *me*. That's all [I] know."

This pleasantry was received with a general laugh.

"It's likely to be a very cheap funeral," said the same speaker; "for upon my life I don't know of anybody to go to it. Suppose we make up a party and volunteer?"

"I don't mind going if a lunch is provided," observed the gentleman with the excrescence on his nose. "But I must be fed, if I make one."

Another laugh.

"Well, I am the most disinterested among you,

3 *'Change.* The London Exchange. See Stave 1, Note 5.

4 *a pendulous excrescence.* A hanging wart.

5 *black gloves*. "It is customary at most English funerals," explained Ahn in his 1871 edition, "to present all those who attend as mourners with a pair of black gloves, which of course likewise prove useful on other occasions." As these were given to everyone, one need not have been particularly close to the deceased to wear the gloves. That this gentleman refuses to show even this small respect to the dead is a remarkable insult from one who says he was Scrooge's most particular friend. That he would even refuse a free meal shows how little moved anyone is by the miser's death. By finding no worldly use for that free lunch and pair of gloves, this gentleman, like Scrooge, is the perfect utilitarian.

6 *Old Scratch*. The Devil.

7 *skaiter*. Not until the Charles Dickens Edition of 1868 did the author change this word to the more common spelling "skater."

"Tom-all-alone's" by H. K. Browne, *Bleak House*, 1853. *Courtesy General Research and Humanities Division, The New York Public Library, Astor, Lenox and Tilden Foundations*

after all," said the first speaker, "for I never wear **5** black gloves, and I never eat lunch. But I 'll offer to go, if anybody else will. When I come to think of it, I 'm not at all sure that I wasn't his most particular friend; for we used to stop and speak whenever we met. Bye, bye!"

Speakers and listeners strolled away, and mixed with other groups. Scrooge knew the men, and looked towards the Spirit for an explanation.

The Phantom glided on into a street. Its finger pointed to two persons meeting. Scrooge listened again, thinking that the explanation might lie here.

He knew these men, also, perfectly. They were men of business: very wealthy, and of great importance. He had made a point always of standing well in their esteem: in a business point of view, that is; strictly in a business point of view.

"How are you?" said one.

"How are you?" returned the other.

6 "Well!" said the first. "Old Scratch has got his own at last, hey?"

"So I am told," returned the second. "Cold, isn't it?"

"Seasonable for Christmas time. You're not a **7** skaiter, I suppose?"

"No. No. Something else to think of. Good morning!"

Not another word. That was their meeting, their conversation, and their parting.

Scrooge was at first inclined to be surprised that the Spirit should attach importance to conversations apparently so trivial; but feeling assured that they must have some hidden purpose, he set himself to consider what it was likely to be. They could scarcely be supposed to have any bearing on the death of Jacob, his old partner, for that was Past, and this Ghost's province was the Future. Nor could he think of any one immediately connected with himself, to whom he could apply them. But nothing doubting that to whomsoever they applied they had some latent moral for his own improvement, he resolved to treasure up every word he heard, and everything he saw; and especially to observe the shadow of himself when it appeared. For he had an expectation that the conduct of his future self would give him the clue he missed, and would render the solution of these riddles easy.

He looked about in that very place for his own image; but another man stood in his accustomed corner, and though the clock pointed to his usual time of day for being there, he saw no likeness of himself among the multitudes that poured in through the Porch. It gave him little surprise, however; for he had been revolving in his mind a change of life, and thought and hoped he saw his new-born resolutions carried out in this.

Quiet and dark, beside him stood the Phantom, with its outstretched hand. When he roused himself from his thoughtful quest, he fancied from the turn of the hand, and its situation in reference to himself, that the Unseen Eyes were looking at him keenly. It made him shudder, and feel very cold.

They left the busy scene, and went into an obscure part of the town, where Scrooge had never penetrated before, although he recognised its situation, and its bad repute. The ways were foul and narrow; the shops and houses wretched; the people half-naked, drunken, slipshod, ugly. Alleys and archways, like so many cesspools, disgorged their offences of smell, and dirt, and life, upon the straggling streets; and the whole quarter reeked with crime, with filth, and misery.

Far in this den of infamous resort, there was a low-browed, beetling shop, below a pent-house roof, **8,9,10** where iron, old rags, bottles, bones, and greasy offal, were bought. Upon the floor within, were

8 *beetling.* Projecting, overhanging.

9 *shop.* Commonly called a "rag-and-bottle shop," like Mr. Krook's establishment in *Bleak House* (1853). "The stench in these shops is positively sickening," wrote Henry Mayhew in *London Labour and London Poor* (1851). "Here in a small apartment may be a pile of rags, a sack-full of bones, the many varieties of grease and 'kitchen-stuff,' corrupting an atmosphere which, even without such accompaniments, would be too close. The windows are often crowded with bottles, which exclude the light; while the floor and shelves are thick with grease and dirt. The inmates seem unconscious of this foulness.... The door-posts and windows of the rag-and-bottle-shops are often closely placarded, and the front of the house is sometimes one glaring colour, blue or red; so that the place may be at once recognized, even by the illiterate, as the 'red house,' or the 'blue house.'" These places are not to be confused with the "marine-store shops," which did not deal in "kitchen-stuff." According to Mayhew, these merchants were more obvious at Christmastime when their signs and handbills sported pictures of great plum puddings; they hoped these cuts would encourage the poor to sell them their miscellaneous items to pay for their holiday feasts.

10 *a pent-house roof.* A roof sloping up against a wall.

"The Lord Chancellor copies from memory" by H. K. Browne, *Bleak House*, 1853. *Courtesy General Research and Humanities Division, The New York Public Library, Astor, Lenox and Tilden Foundations*

11 *masses of corrupted fat.* Grease, drippings, and other "kitchen-stuff" were purchased by the rag-and-bottle shops and then resold, the grease to candle-makers and soap-boilers, and the drippings to the poor as a substitute for butter.

12 *charwoman.* A servant hired by the day to do odd housework; she was obviously hired, not by Scrooge, but by whoever was settling the miser's affairs.

13 *"If we haven't all three met here without meaning it!"* These three ghouls are reminiscent of the Three Weird Sisters, in *Macbeth*, who meet at night in "the fog and filthy air" to compare their horrible plunder.

piled up heaps of rusty keys, nails, chains, hinges, files, scales, weights, and refuse iron of all kinds. Secrets that few would like to scrutinise were bred

11 and hidden in mountains of unseemly rags, masses of corrupted fat, and sepulchres of bones. Sitting in among the wares he dealt in, by a charcoal-stove, made of old bricks, was a gray-haired rascal, nearly seventy years of age; who had screened himself from the cold air without, by a frousy curtaining of miscellaneous tatters, hung upon a line; and smoked his pipe in all the luxury of calm retirement.

Scrooge and the Phantom came into the presence of this man, just as a woman with a heavy bundle slunk into the shop. But she had scarcely entered, when another woman, similarly laden, came in too; and she was closely followed by a man in faded black, who was no less startled by the sight of them, than they had been upon the recognition of each other. After a short period of blank astonishment, in which the old man with the pipe had joined them, they all three burst into a laugh.

12 "Let the charwoman alone to be the first!" cried she who had entered first. "Let the laundress alone to be the second; and let the undertaker's man alone to be the third. Look here, old

13 Joe, here's a chance! If we haven't all three met here without meaning it!"

"You couldn't have met in a better place," said old Joe, removing his pipe from his mouth. "Come into the parlour. You were made free of it long ago, you know; and the other two an't strangers. Stop till I shut the door of the shop. Ah! How it skreeks! There an't such a rusty bit of metal in the place as its own hinges, I believe; and I'm sure there's no such old bones here, as mine. Ha, ha! We're all suitable to our calling, we're well matched. Come into the parlour. Come into the parlour."

The parlour was the space behind the screen of rags. The old man raked the fire together with an old stair-rod, and having trimmed his smoky **14** lamp (for it was night), with the stem of his pipe, put it in his mouth again.

While he did this, the woman who had already spoken threw her bundle on the floor and sat down in a flaunting manner on a stool; crossing her elbows on her knees, and looking with a bold defiance at the other two.

"What odds then! What odds, Mrs. Dilber?" **15** said the woman. "Every person has a right to take care of themselves. *He* always did!"

"That's true, indeed!" said the laundress. "No man more so."

"Why, then, don't stand staring as if you was afraid, woman; who's the wiser? We're not going to pick holes in each other's coats, I suppose?" **16**

"No, indeed!" said Mrs. Dilber and the man together. "We should hope not."

"Very well, then!" cried the woman. "That's enough. Who's the worse for the loss of a few things like these? Not a dead man, I suppose."

"No, indeed," said Mrs. Dilber, laughing.

"If he wanted to keep 'em after he was dead, a wicked old screw," pursued the woman, "why wasn't **17** he natural in his lifetime? If he had been, he'd have had somebody to look after him when he was struck with Death, instead of lying gasping out his last there, alone by himself."

"It's the truest word that ever was spoke," said Mrs. Dilber. "It's a judgment on him."

"I wish it was a little heavier one," replied the woman; "and it should have been, you may depend upon it, if I could have laid my hands on anything else. Open that bundle, old Joe, and let me know the value of it. Speak out plain. I'm not afraid to be the first, nor afraid for them to see it. We knew pretty well that we were helping ourselves,

14 *stair-rod.* A brass bar that keeps stair carpets down.

15 *What odds then!* What does it matter.

16 *pick holes in each other's coats.* Have a quarrel.

17 *old screw.* Slang for a miser, apparent in the name "Scrooge."

18 *mounting the breach.* A military phrase meaning "taking the lead": the word "plunder" to describe the man's booty appropriately follows this phrase.

19 *a seal or two, a pencil-case, a pair of sleeve buttons, and a brooch of no great value.* Being the undertaker's man, this gentleman in faded black likely found these items on or in the clothes with which he dressed the body.

before we met here, I believe. It 's no sin. Open the bundle, Joe."

But the gallantry of her friends would not allow of **18** this; and the man in faded black, mounting the breach first, produced *his* plunder. It was not **19** extensive. A seal or two, a pencil-case, a pair of sleeve-buttons, and a brooch of no great value, were all. They were severally examined and appraised by old Joe, who chalked the sums he was disposed to give for each upon the wall, and added them up into a total when he found that there was nothing more to come.

" That 's your account," said Joe, " and I wouldn't give another sixpence, if I was to be boiled for not doing it. Who 's next ?"

Mrs. Dilber was next. Sheets and towels, a little wearing apparel, two old-fashioned silver teaspoons, a pair of sugar-tongs, and a few boots. Her account was stated on the wall in the same manner.

" I always give too much to ladies. It 's a weakness of mine, and that 's the way I ruin myself," said old Joe. " That 's your account. If you asked me for another penny, and made it an open question, I 'd repent of being so liberal, and knock off half-a-crown."

" And now undo *my* bundle, Joe," said the first woman.

Joe went down on his knees for the greater convenience of opening it, and having unfastened a great many knots, dragged out a large and heavy roll of some dark stuff.

" What do you call this ?" said Joe. " Bed-curtains !"

" Ah !" returned the woman, laughing and leaning forward on her crossed arms. " Bed-curtains !"

" You don't mean to say you took 'em down, rings and all, with him lying there ?" said Joe.

" Yes I do," replied the woman. " Why not ?"

" You were born to make your fortune," said Joe, " and you 'll certainly do it."

" I certainly shan't hold my hand, when I can get anything in it by reaching it out, for the sake of such a man as He was, I promise you, Joe," returned the woman coolly. " Don't drop that oil upon the blankets, now."

" His blankets ?" asked Joe.

" Whose else's do you think ?" replied the woman. " He isn't likely to take cold without 'em, I dare say."

" I hope he didn't die of anything catching ? Eh ? " said old Joe, stopping in his work, and looking up.

" Don't you be afraid of that," returned the woman. " I an't so fond of his company that I 'd loiter about him for such things, if he did. Ah ! You may look through that shirt till your eyes ache ; but you won't find a hole in it, nor a thread-bare place. It 's the best he had, and a fine one too. They 'd have wasted it, if it hadn't been for me."

" What do you call wasting of it ?" asked old Joe.

" Putting it on him to be buried in, to be sure," replied the woman with a laugh. " Somebody was fool enough to do it, but I took it off again. If calico an't good enough for such a purpose, it isn't good enough for anything. It 's quite as becoming to the body. He can't look uglier than he did in that one."

Scrooge listened to this dialogue in horror. As they sat grouped about their spoil, in the scanty light afforded by the old man's lamp, he viewed them with a detestation and disgust, which could hardly have been greater, though they had been obscene demons, marketing the corpse itself.

" Ha, ha !" laughed the same woman, when old Joe, producing a flannel bag with money in it, told out their several gains upon the ground. " This is the end of it, you see ! He frightened every one away from him when he was alive, to profit us when he was dead !   Ha, ha, ha !"

" Spirit !" said Scrooge, shuddering from head to foot. " I see, I see.   The case of this unhappy man might be my own.   My life tends that way, now. Merciful Heaven, what is this !"

He recoiled in terror, for the scene had changed, and now he almost touched a bed : a bare, uncurtained bed : on which, beneath a ragged sheet, there lay a something covered up, which, though it was dumb, announced itself in awful language.

The room was very dark, too dark to be observed with any accuracy, though Scrooge glanced round it in obedience to a secret impulse, anxious to know what kind of room it was.   A pale light, rising in the outer air, fell straight upon the bed ; and on it, plundered and bereft, unwatched, unwept, uncared for, was the body of this man.

Scrooge glanced towards the Phantom.   Its steady hand was pointed to the head.   The cover was so carelessly adjusted that the slightest raising of it, the motion of a finger upon Scrooge's part, would have disclosed the face.   He thought of it, felt how easy it would be to do, and longed to do it ; but had no more power to withdraw the veil than to dismiss the spectre at his side.

Oh cold, cold, rigid, dreadful Death, set up thine altar here, and dress it with such terrors as thou hast at thy command : for this is thy dominion ! But of the loved, revered, and honoured head, thou canst not turn one hair to thy dread purposes, or make one feature odious.   It is not that the hand is heavy and will fall down when released ; it is not that the heart and pulse are still ; but that the hand WAS open, generous, and true ; the heart brave, warm, and tender ; and the pulse a man's.   Strike, Shadow, strike !   And see his good deeds springing from the wound, to sow the world with life immortal!

No voice pronounced these words in Scrooge's ears, and yet he heard them when he looked upon the bed. He thought, if this man could be raised up now, what would be his foremost thoughts? Avarice, hard dealing, griping cares? They have brought him to a rich end, truly!

He lay, in the dark empty house, with not a man, **20** a woman, or a child, to say he was kind to me in this or that, and for the memory of one kind word I will be kind to him. A cat was tearing at the door, and there was a sound of gnawing rats beneath the hearth-stone. What *they* wanted in the room of death, and why they were so restless and disturbed, Scrooge did not dare to think.

"Spirit!" he said, "this is a fearful place. In leaving it, I shall not leave its lesson, trust me. Let us go!"

Still the Ghost pointed with an unmoved finger to the head.

"I understand you," Scrooge returned, "and I would do it, if I could. But I have not the power, Spirit. I have not the power."

Again it seemed to look upon him.

"If there is any person in the town, who feels emotion caused by this man's death," said Scrooge quite agonized, "show that person to me, Spirit, I beseech you!"

The phantom spread its dark robe before him for a moment, like a wing; and withdrawing it, revealed a room by daylight, where a mother and her children were.

She was expecting some one, and with anxious eagerness; for she walked up and down the room; started at every sound; looked out from the window; glanced at the clock; tried, but in vain, to work with her needle; and could hardly bear the voices of the children in their play.

20 *He lay ... with not a man, a woman, or a child, to say he was kind to me in this or that, and for the memory of one kind word I will be kind to him.* Compare Scrooge on his deathbed to William the Conquerer on his, as described by Dickens in *A Child's History of England* (1851–1853): "The moment he was dead ... the mercenary servants of the court began to rob and plunder; the body of the king in the indecent strife, was rolled from the bed, and lay alone, for hours, upon the ground. O Conquerer, of whom so many great names are praised now, of whom so many great names thought nothing then, it were better to have conquered one true heart, than England."

21 *boarding.* Here used in an unusual sense, saved for him and put by the fire to be kept warm.

At length the long-expected knock was heard. She hurried to the door, and met her husband; a man whose face was care-worn and depressed, though he was young. There was a remarkable expression in it now; a kind of serious delight of which he felt ashamed, and which he struggled to repress.

21 He sat down to the dinner that had been hoarding for him by the fire; and when she asked him faintly what news (which was not until after a long silence), he appeared embarrassed how to answer.

"Is it good," she said, "or bad?"—to help him.

"Bad," he answered.

"We are quite ruined?"

"No. There is hope yet, Caroline."

"If *he* relents," she said, amazed, "there is! Nothing is past hope, if such a miracle has happened."

"He is past relenting," said her husband. "He is dead."

She was a mild and patient creature if her face spoke truth; but she was thankful in her soul to hear it, and she said so, with clasped hands. She prayed forgiveness the next moment, and was sorry; but the first was the emotion of her heart.

"What the half-drunken woman whom I told you of last night, said to me, when I tried to see him and obtain a week's delay; and what I thought was a mere excuse to avoid me; turns out to have been quite true. He was not only very ill, but dying, then."

"To whom will our debt be transferred?"

"I don't know. But before that time we shall be ready with the money; and even though we were not, it would be bad fortune indeed to find so merciless a creditor in his successor. We may sleep to-night with light hearts, Caroline!"

Yes. Soften it as they would, their hearts were lighter. The children's faces hushed, and clustered round to hear what they so little understood, were brighter; and it was a happier house for this man's death! The only emotion that the Ghost could show him, caused by the event, was one of pleasure.

" Let me see some tenderness connected with a death," said Scrooge; " or that dark chamber, Spirit, which we left just now, will be for ever present to me."

The Ghost conducted him through several streets familiar to his feet; and as they went along, Scrooge looked here and there to find himself, but nowhere was he to be seen. They entered poor Bob Cratchit's **22** house; the dwelling he had visited before; and found the mother and the children seated round the fire.

Quiet. Very quiet. The noisy little Cratchits were as still as statues in one corner, and sat looking up at Peter, who had a book before him. The mother and her daughters were engaged in sewing. But surely they were very quiet!

" ' And He took a child, and set him in the midst **23** of them.' "

Where had Scrooge heard those words? He had not dreamed them. The boy must have read them out, as he and the Spirit crossed the threshold. Why did he not go on?

The mother laid her work upon the table, and put her hand up to her face.

" The colour hurts my eyes," she said.

The colour? Ah, poor Tiny Tim! **24**

" They 're better now again," said Cratchit's wife. " It makes them weak by candle-light; and I wouldn't show weak eyes to your father when he comes home, for the world. It must be near his time."

" Past it rather," Peter answered, shutting up his book. " But I think he 's walked a little slower

22 *They entered poor Bob Cratchit's house.* The prototype for Tiny Tim's death appears in "The Goblins Who Stole a Sexton." Gabriel Grub is shown a poor family's tragic Christmas where "the fairest and youngest child lay dying." Like Scrooge on viewing the Cratchits' day of mourning, the sexton looked upon the boy "with an interest he had never felt or known before." Fortunately Dickens was more restrained in his sentiments in describing the Cratchit family scene; in the earlier version, he portrays the other children gazing on the tranquil corpse with the knowledge "that he was an Angel, looking down upon, and blessing them, from a bright and happy Heaven."

Children's death caused by an indifferent society is a frequent subject in Dickens' work. The most familiar examples of child mortality in his novels are those of Little Nell in *The Old Curiosity Shop* and Paul Dombey of *Dombey and Son.* Dickens revived his quasireligious view of infant death in his sentimental short story, "A Child's Dream of A Star" (in *Reprinted Pieces,* 1868). Dickens well knew the common tragedy of child mortality among the poor; a brother and sister died in infancy.

23 " 'And He took a child, and set him in the *midst of them.' "* One of Dickens' favorite passages from the Bible (Matthew, 18:2; and Mark, 9:36). In *The Life of Our Lord* (1849), which he wrote for his own children, Dickens gave his interpretation of this episode from the Gospels: "The Disciples asked him, 'Master, who is the greatest in the Kingdom of Heaven?' Jesus called a little child to him, and took him in his arms, and stood him among them, and answered, 'a child like this. I say unto you that none but those who are as humble as little children shall enter into Heaven. Whosoever shall receive one such little child in my name receiveth me. But whosoever hurts one of them, it were better for him that he had a millstone tied about his neck, and were drowned in the depths of the sea. The angels are all children.' Our Saviour loved the child, and loved all children. Yes, and all the world. No one ever loved all people, so well and so truly as He did."

Appropriately the young Cratchits are reminded of this story at Christmastime when "its mighty Founder was a child himself."

It has no place in "the gloomy theology of the Murdstones," which "made all children out to be a swarm of vipers (though there *was* a child once set in the midst of the Disciples)" [*David Copperfield,* Chapter 4].

24 *the colour?* Dickens crossed out "Black" in his manuscript; Mrs. Cratchit and the girls are sewing their mourning clothes.

25 *little Bob in his comforter—he had need of it, poor fellow.* A strange place for a pun. Perhaps here, Dickens, like Scrooge earlier, "tried to be smart, as a means of distracting his own attention" from the sadness of this scene.

than he used, these few last evenings, mother."

They were very quiet again. At last she said, and in a steady cheerful voice, that only faultered once :

" I have known him walk with—I have known him walk with Tiny Tim upon his shoulder, very fast indeed."

" And so have I," cried Peter. " Often."

" And so have I !" exclaimed another. So had all.

" But he was very light to carry," she resumed, intent upon her work, " and his father loved him so, that it was no trouble—no trouble. And there is your father at the door ! "

25 She hurried out to meet him ; and little Bob in his comforter—he had need of it, poor fellow—came in. His tea was ready for him on the hob, and they all tried who should help him to it most. Then the two young Cratchits got upon his knees and laid, each child a little cheek, against his face, as if they said, " Don't mind it, father. Don't be grieved ! "

Bob was very cheerful with them, and spoke pleasantly to all the family. He looked at the work upon the table, and praised the industry and speed of Mrs. Cratchit and the girls. They would be done long before Sunday he said.

" Sunday ! You went to-day then, Robert ? " said his wife.

" Yes, my dear," returned Bob. " I wish you could have gone. It would have done you good to see how green a place it is. But you 'll see it often. I promised him that I would walk there on a Sunday. My little, little child ! " cried Bob. " My little child ! "

He broke down all at once. He couldn't help it. If he could have helped it, he and his child would have been farther apart perhaps than they were.

He left the room, and went up stairs into the room above, which was lighted cheerfully, and hung with Christmas. There was a chair set close beside the child, and there were signs of some one having been there, lately. Poor Bob sat down in it, and when he had thought a little and composed himself, he kissed the little face. He was reconciled to what had happened, and went down again quite happy.

They drew about the fire, and talked; the girls and mother working still. Bob told them of the extraordinary kindness of Mr. Scrooge's nephew, whom he had scarcely seen but once, and who, meeting him in the street that day, and seeing that he looked a little—"just a little down you know" said Bob, enquired what had happened to distress him. "On which," said Bob, "for he is the pleasantest-spoken gentleman you ever heard, I told him. 'I am heartily sorry for it, Mr. Cratchit,' he said, 'and heartily sorry for your good wife.' By the bye, how he ever knew *that*, I don't know."

"Knew what, my dear?"

"Why, that you were a good wife," replied Bob.

"Everybody knows that!" said Peter.

"Very well observed, my boy!" cried Bob. "I hope they do. 'Heartily sorry,' he said, 'for your good wife. If I can be of service to you in any way,' he said, giving me his card, 'that's where I live. Pray come to me.' Now, it wasn't," cried Bob, "for the sake of anything he might be able to do for us, so much as for his kind way, that this was quite delightful. It really seemed as if he had known our Tiny Tim, and felt with us."

"I'm sure he's a good soul!" said Mrs. Cratchit.

"You would be surer of it, my dear," returned Bob, "if you saw and spoke to him. I shouldn't be at all surprised, mark what I say, if he got Peter a better situation."

26 *keeping company with some one, and setting up for himself.* He will soon be of marrying age. See Stave 1, Note 27.

"Only hear that, Peter," said Mrs. Cratchit.

"And then," cried one of the girls, "Peter will **26** be keeping company with some one, and setting up for himself."

"Get along with you!" retorted Peter, grinning.

"It's just as likely as not," said Bob, "one of these days; though there's plenty of time for that, my dear. But however and whenever we part from one another, I am sure we shall none of us forget poor Tiny Tim—shall we—or this first parting that there was among us?"

"Never, father!" cried they all.

"And I know," said Bob, "I know, my dears, that when we recollect how patient and how mild he was; although he was a little, little child; we shall not quarrel easily among ourselves, and forget poor Tiny Tim in doing it."

"No, never, father!" they all cried again.

"I am very happy," said little Bob, "I am very happy!"

Mrs. Cratchit kissed him, his daughters kissed him, the two young Cratchits kissed him, and Peter and himself shook hands. Spirit of Tiny Tim, thy childish essence was from God!

"Spectre," said Scrooge, "something informs me that our parting moment is at hand. I know it, but I know not how. Tell me what man that was whom we saw lying dead?"

The Ghost of Christmas Yet To Come conveyed him, as before—though at a different time, he thought: indeed, there seemed no order in these latter visions, save that they were in the Future— into the resorts of business men, but showed him not himself. Indeed, the Spirit did not stay for anything, but went straight on, as to the end just now desired, until besought by Scrooge to tarry for a moment.

"This court," said Scrooge, "through which we hurry now, is where my place of occupation is, and has been for a length of time. I see the house. Let me behold what I shall be, in days to come."

The Spirit stopped; the hand was pointed elsewhere.

"The house is yonder," Scrooge exclaimed. "Why do you point away?"

The inexorable finger underwent no change.

Scrooge hastened to the window of his office, and looked in. It was an office still, but not his. The furniture was not the same, and the figure in the chair was not himself. The Phantom pointed as before.

He joined it once again, and wondering why and whither he had gone, accompanied it until they reached an iron gate. He paused to look round before entering.

A churchyard. Here, then, the wretched man **27** whose name he had now to learn, lay underneath the ground. It was a worthy place. Walled in by houses; overrun by grass and weeds, the growth of vegetation's death, not life; choked up with too **28,29** much burying; fat with repleted appetite. A worthy place!

The Spirit stood among the graves, and pointed down to One. He advanced towards it trembling. The Phantom was exactly as it had been, but he dreaded that he saw new meaning in its solemn shape.

"Before I draw nearer to that stone to which you point," said Scrooge, "answer me one question. Are these the shadows of the things that Will be, or are they shadows of the things that May be, only?"

Still the Ghost pointed downward to the grave by which it stood.

"Men's courses will foreshadow certain ends, to which, if persevered in, they must lead," said Scrooge. "But if the courses be departed from,

27 *A churchyard.* Gwen Major in her article (cited in Stave 1, Note 21) identified this graveyard as that of All Hallows Staining, Star Alley, off Mark Lane, in the Langborn Ward.

28 *vegetation's death.* Weeds and rank grass kill other plants.

29 *choked up with too much burying; fat with repleted appetite.* Dickens is being ironic in describing the graveyard in terms of eating and abundance.

Preliminary pencil and wash drawing by John Leech for "The Last of the Spirits." *Courtesy The Houghton Library, Harvard University*

the ends will change.   Say it is thus with wha [you show me!"

The Spirit was immovable as ever.

Scrooge crept towards it, trembling as he went ; and following the finger, read upon the stone of the neglected grave his own name, EBENEZER SCROOGE.

" Am *I* that man who lay upon the bed ?" he cried, upon his knees.

The finger pointed from the grave to him, and back again.

" No, Spirit !   Oh no, no !"

The finger still was there.

" Spirit !" he cried, tight clutching at its robe, " hear me ! I am not the man I was. I will not be the man I must have been but for this intercourse. Why show me this, if I am past all hope ?"

For the first time the hand appeared to shake.

" Good Spirit," he pursued, as down upon the ground he fell before it : " Your nature intercedes for me, and pities me. Assure me that I yet may change these shadows you have shown me, by an altered life !"

The kind hand trembled.

" I will honour Christmas in my heart, and try to keep it all the year. I will live in the Past, the Present, and the Future. The Spirits of all Three shall strive within me. I will not shut out the lessons that they teach. Oh, tell me I may sponge away the writing on this stone !"

In his agony, he caught the spectral hand. It sought to free itself, but he was strong in his entreaty, and detained it. The Spirit, stronger yet, repulsed him.

Holding up his hands in one last prayer to have his fate reversed, he saw an alteration in the Phantom's hood and dress. It shrunk, collapsed, and dwindled down into a bedpost.

The Last of the Spirits.

STAVE FIVE.

⸺•⸺

THE END OF IT.

Yes! and the bedpost was his own. The bed was his own, the room was his own. Best and happiest of all, the Time before him was his own, to make amends in!

"I will live in the Past, the Present, and the Future!" Scrooge repeated, as he scrambled out of bed. "The Spirits of all Three shall strive within me. Oh Jacob Marley! Heaven, and the Christmas Time be praised for this! I say it on my knees, old Jacob; on my knees!"

He was so fluttered and so glowing with his good intentions, that his broken voice would scarcely answer to his call. He had been sobbing violently in his conflict with the Spirit, and his face was wet with tears.

A sketch of "Old Scrooge" by John Leech, the Albert Schloss autograph album, 1844. *Courtesy The Beinecke Rare Book and Manuscript Library, Yale University*

1 *Laocoön.* The famous Roman statue of the fifth century B.C., found in the baths of Titus in 1506, and now housed in the Vatican. According to Virgil (*The Aeneid*, II, 230), this Trojan priest and his two sons were strangled by serpents, because Laocoön offended the goddess Athena. Scrooge's tangled socks thus reflect this picture of twisted snakes. This fine metaphor was an afterthought; Dickens added it in the galleys.

" They are not torn down," cried Scrooge, folding one of his bed-curtains in his arms, "they are not torn down, rings and all. They are here: I am here: the shadows of the things that would have been, may be dispelled. They will be. I know they will!"

His hands were busy with his garments all this time: turning them inside out, putting them on upside down, tearing them, mislaying them, making them parties to every kind of extravagance.

" I don't know what to do!" cried Scrooge, laughing and crying in the same breath; and making 1 a perfect Laocoön of himself with his stockings. " I am as light as a feather, I am as happy as an angel, I am as merry as a school-boy. I am as giddy as a drunken man. A merry Christmas to everybody! A happy New Year to all the world. Hallo here! Whoop! Hallo!"

He had frisked into the sitting-room, and was now standing there: perfectly winded.

" There's the saucepan that the gruel was in!" cried Scrooge, starting off again, and frisking round the fire-place. " There's the door, by which the Ghost of Jacob Marley entered! There's the corner where the Ghost of Christmas Present, sat! There's the window where I saw the wandering Spirits! It's all right, it's all true, it all happened. Ha ha ha!"

Really, for a man who had been out of practice for so many years, it was a splendid laugh, a most illustrious laugh. The father of a long, long, line of brilliant laughs!

" I don't know what day of the month it is!" said Scrooge. " I don't know how long I've been among the Spirits. I don't know anything. I'm quite a baby. Never mind. I don't care. I'd rather be a baby. Hallo! Whoop! Hallo here!"

He was checked in his transports by the churches ringing out the lustiest peals he had ever heard.

Clash, clang, hammer, ding, dong, bell. Bell, dong, ding, hammer, clang, clash! Oh, glorious, glorious!

Running to the window, he opened it, and put out his head. No fog, no mist; clear, bright, jovial, stirring, cold; cold, piping for the blood to dance to; Golden sunlight; Heavenly sky; sweet fresh air; merry bells. Oh, glorious. Glorious!

"What's to-day?" cried Scrooge, calling downward to a boy in Sunday clothes, who perhaps had loitered in to look about him.

"EH?" returned the boy, with all his might of wonder.

"What's to-day, my fine fellow?" said Scrooge.

"To-day!" replied the boy. "Why, CHRISTMAS DAY."

"It's Christmas Day!" said Scrooge to himself. "I haven't missed it. The Spirits have done it **2** all in one night. They can do anything they like. Of course they can. Of course they can. Hallo, my fine fellow!"

"Hallo!" returned the boy.

"Do you know the Poulterer's, in the next street but one, at the corner?" Scrooge inquired.

"I should hope I did," replied the lad.

"An intelligent boy!" said Scrooge. "A remarkable boy! Do you know whether they've sold the prize Turkey that was hanging up there? Not the little prize Turkey: the big one?"

"What, the one as big as me?" returned the boy.

"What a delightful boy!" said Scrooge. "It's a pleasure to talk to him. Yes, my buck!"

"It's hanging there now," replied the boy.

"Is it?" said Scrooge. "Go and buy it."

"Walk-ER!" exclaimed the boy. **3**

"No, no," said Scrooge, "I am in earnest. Go and buy it, and tell 'em to bring it here, that I may give them the direction where to take it. Come back

2 *The Spirits have done it all in one night.* The duration of time is often altered in dreams. "I sometimes seemed to have lived for seventy or one hundred years in one night," wrote De Quincey in *Confessions of an English Opium-Eater* (1822); "nay, sometimes had feelings representative of a millennium passed at that time, or, however, of a duration far beyond the limits of any human experience." *Chambers' Encyclopedia* (1874) recorded an amusing example of such time distortion in dreaming: "a clergyman falling asleep in his pulpit during the singing of the psalm before the sermon, and awakening with the conviction that he must have slept for at least an hour, and that the congregation must have been waiting for him; but on referring to his psalm-book, he was consoled by finding that his slumber had lasted no longer than during the singing of a single line." In *The Interpretation of Dreams*, Freud argued that the distortion occurs during the recollection of a dream; the progression of events may have been aroused on waking, and the conscious remembrance may not have been actually dreamed.

3 *Walk-ER!* A Cockney expression of surprise or incredulity, often used by Dickens. T. W. Hill in his notes to *The Pickwick Papers* (*The Dickensian*, Summer number, 1948) offered several theories on the origin of this interjection: "a shortened form of [John] 'Hookey Walker,' a London Magistrate with a hooked nose that gave the title of 'beak' to all magistrates; a hook-nosed outdoor clerk in a London business house whose reports were open to doubt or frankly disbelieved; an aquiline-nosed Jew named Walker who lectured on Astronomy and invited his pupils to 'take a sight' at the heavenly bodies; the doubting pupils imitated his actions behind his back in 'taking a sight' at his nose."

Dickens perhaps was familiar with all these explanations. "Dickens as the boy," explained Rowland Hill, a Dickensian who had seen the author read (as quoted by Phillip Collins in his edition of the Berg prompt copy), "put his thumb to his nose, and spread out his fingers, with a jeer, at the syllable ER. This was a common way to call their pals 'Fools' without using the word."

4 *"I'll send it to Bob Cratchit's!"* Not everyone in Dickens' day approved of Scrooge's generosity. As he wrote Forster, Dickens was irritated "that the *Westminster Review* considered Scrooge's presentation of the turkey to Bob Cratchit as grossly incompatible with political economy." A review in the June 1844 issue in referring to *A New Spirit of the Age* objected to the author R. H. Horne's praise of Dickens. ("His influence upon his age is extensive—pleasureable, instructive, healthy, reformatory. If his *Christmas Carol* were printed in letters of gold, there would be no inscriptions which would give a more salutary hint to the gold of a country.") The reviewer took this occasion to attack Dickens' economics: "In the *Christmas Carol* . . . a great part of the enjoyments of life are summed up in eating and drinking at the cost of munificent patrons of the poor; so that we might almost suppose the feudal times were returned. The processes whereby poor men are to be enabled to earn good wages, wherewith to buy turkeys for themselves, does not enter into the account; indeed, it would quite spoil the *dénouement* and all the generosity. Who went without turkey and punch in order that Bob Cratchit might get them—for, unless there were turkey and punch in surplus, some one must go without—is a disagreeable reflection kept wholly out of sight. . . ."

Dickens responded to these remarks by creating Mr. Filer, the political economist of *The Chimes* (1844); this morose man shocks the poor ticket-porter Trotty Veck by suggesting that Trotty has snatched his simple indulgence of tripe "out of the mouths of widows and orphans."

5 *Joe Miller.* A popular but illiterate comic actor (1684–1738) whose purported jokes and sayings were collected by the dramatist John Mottley as *Joe Miller's Jests; or The Wit's Vade Mecum* (1739). The book itself was something of a jest; Miller reportedly never made an especially original or amusing remark. Nonetheless, the book soon became the best-known English collection of witticisms, and almost any stray joke was attributed to this apparently humorless actor. Similarly, Dickens referred to this work in *Dombey and Son* (Chapter 12) when he described a character (with heavy irony) as "a perfect Miller or complete Jest Book."

with the man, and I'll give you a shilling. Come back with him in less than five minutes, and I'll give you half-a-crown!"

The boy was off like a shot. He must have had a steady hand at a trigger who could have got a shot off half so fast.

4 "I'll send it to Bob Cratchit's!" whispered Scrooge, rubbing his hands, and splitting with a laugh. "He sha'n't know who sends it. It's **5** twice the size of Tiny Tim. Joe Miller never made such a joke as sending it to Bob's will be!"

The hand in which he wrote the address was not a steady one, but write it he did, somehow, and went down stairs to open the street door, ready for the coming of the poulterer's man. As he stood there, waiting his arrival, the knocker caught his eye.

"I shall love it, as long as I live!" cried Scrooge, patting it with his hand. "I scarcely ever looked at it before. What an honest expression it has in its face! It's a wonderful knocker!—Here's the Turkey. Hallo! Whoop! How are you! Merry Christmas!"

It *was* a Turkey! He never could have stood upon his legs, that bird. He would have snapped 'em short off in a minute, like sticks of sealing-wax.

"Why, it's impossible to carry that to Camden Town," said Scrooge. "You must have a cab."

The chuckle with which he said this, and the chuckle with which he paid for the Turkey, and the chuckle with which he paid for the cab, and the chuckle with which he recompensed the boy, were only to be exceeded by the chuckle with which he sat down breathless in his chair again, and chuckled till he cried.

Shaving was not an easy task, for his hand continued to shake very much; and shaving requires attention, even when you don't dance while you are at it. But if he had cut the end of his nose off, he would have put a piece of sticking-plaister over it, **6** and been quite satisfied.

He dressed himself "all in his best," and at last got out into the streets. The people were by this time pouring forth, as he had seen them with the Ghost of Christmas Present; and walking with his hands behind him, Scrooge regarded every one with a delighted smile. He looked so irresistibly pleasant, in a word, that three or four good-humoured fellows said, "Good morning, sir! A merry Christmas to you!" And Scrooge said often afterwards, that of all the blithe sounds he had ever heard, those were the blithest in his ears.

He had not gone far, when coming on towards him he beheld the portly gentleman, who had walked into his counting-house the day before and said, "Scrooge and Marley's, I believe?" It sent a pang across his heart to think how this old gentleman would look upon him when they met; but he knew what path lay straight before him, and he took it.

"My dear sir," said Scrooge, quickening his pace, and taking the old gentleman by both his hands. "How do you do? I hope you succeeded yesterday. It was very kind of you. A merry Christmas to you, sir!"

"Mr. Scrooge?"

"Yes," said Scrooge. "That is my name, and I fear it may not be pleasant to you. Allow me to ask your pardon. And will you have the goodness"— here Scrooge whispered in his ear.

"Lord bless me!" cried the gentleman, as if his breath were gone. "My dear Mr. Scrooge, are you serious?"

"If you please," said Scrooge. "Not a farthing **7** less. A great many back-payments are included in it, I assure you. Will you do me that favour?"

"My dear sir," said the other, shaking hands with him. "I don't know what to say to such munifi—"

6 *sticking-plaster*. Or "sticking-plaister," a material (linen, silk, or other textured cloth) spread with an adhesive material, used to close superficial wounds such as shaving cuts.

7 *farthing*. One quarter of a penny.

" 'Merry Christmas to you!' " by Robert Seymour, *The Book of Christmas*, 1836. *Courtesy The Library of Congress*

"Don't say anything, please," retorted Scrooge. "Come and see me. Will you come and see me?"

"I will!" cried the old gentleman. And it was clear he meant to do it.

"Thank 'ee," said Scrooge. "I am much obliged to you. I thank you fifty times. Bless you!"

He went to church, and walked about the streets, and watched the people hurrying to and fro, and patted children on the head, and questioned beggars, and looked down into the kitchens of houses, and up to the windows; and found that everything could yield him pleasure. He had never dreamed that any walk—that anything—could give him so much happiness. In the afternoon, he turned his steps towards his nephew's house.

He passed the door a dozen times, before he had the courage to go up and knock. But he made a dash, and did it:

"Is your master at home, my dear?" said Scrooge to the girl. Nice girl! Very.

"Yes, sir."

"Where is he, my love?" said Scrooge.

"He's in the dining-room, sir, along with mistress. I'll show you up stairs, if you please."

"Christmas Dinner" by Robert Seymour, *The Book of Christmas*, 1836. *Courtesy The British Museum*

"December" by George Cruikshank, *The Comic Almanac*, 1835. *Courtesy The Library of Congress*

" Thank 'ee. He knows me," said Scrooge, with his hand already on the dining-room lock. " I 'll go in here, my dear."

He turned it gently, and sidled his face in, round the door. They were looking at the table (which was spread out in great array) ; for these young housekeepers are always nervous on such points, and like to see that everything is right.

" Fred ! " said Scrooge.

Dear heart alive, how his niece by marriage started ! Scrooge had forgotten, for the moment, about her sitting in the corner with the footstool, or

"Heads of the Family" by Robert Seymour, *The Book of Christmas*, 1836. *Courtesy The Library of Congress*

8 *next morning.* St. Stephen's Day, commonly called Boxing Day, when gratuities (or Christmas boxes) are given to those who have provided services during the year; it did not become a Bank Holiday in England until 1871.

Preliminary pencil and wash drawing by John Leech for "The Christmas Bowl." *Courtesy The Houghton Library, Harvard University*

he wouldn't have done it, on any account.

"Why bless my soul!" cried Fred, " who's that ? "

" It's I. Your uncle Scrooge. I have come to dinner. Will you let me in, Fred ? "

Let him in ! It is a mercy he didn't shake his arm off. He was at home in five minutes. Nothing could be heartier. His niece looked just the same. So did Topper when *he* came. So did the plump sister, when *she* came. So did every one when *they* came. Wonderful party, wonderful games, wonderful unanimity, won-der-ful happiness !

8   But he was early at the office next morning. Oh he was early there. If he could only be there first, and catch Bob Cratchit coming late ! That was the thing he had set his heart upon.

And he did it; yes he did ! The clock struck nine. No Bob. A quarter past. No Bob. He was full eighteen minutes and a half, behind his time. Scrooge sat with his door wide open, that he might see him come into the Tank.

His hat was off, before he opened the door; his comforter too. He was on his stool in a jiffy; driving away with his pen, as if he were trying to overtake nine o'clock.

" Hallo ! " growled Scrooge, in his accustomed voice as near as he could feign it. " What do you mean by coming here at this time of day ?

" I'm very sorry, sir," said Bob. " I *am* behind my time."

" You are ? " repeated Scrooge. " Yes. I think you are. Step this way, if you please."

" It's only once a year, sir," pleaded Bob, appearing from the Tank. " It shall not be repeated. I was making rather merry yesterday, sir."

" Now, I'll tell you what, my friend," said Scrooge, " I am not going to stand this sort of thing any longer. And therefore," he continued, leaping from his stool, and giving Bob such a dig in the waistcoat that he staggered back into the Tank again: "and therefore I am about to raise your salary!"

Bob trembled, and got a little nearer to the ruler. He had a momentary idea of knocking Scrooge down with it; holding him; and calling to the people in the court for help and a strait-waistcoat.   **9**

"A merry Christmas, Bob!" said Scrooge, with an earnestness that could not be mistaken, as he clapped him on the back. "A merrier Christmas, Bob, my good fellow, than I have given you, for many a year! I'll raise your salary, and endeavour to assist your struggling family, and we will discuss your affairs this very afternoon, over a Christmas bowl of smoking bishop, Bob!   **10**
Make up the fires, and buy another coal-scuttle **11** before you dot another i, Bob Cratchit!"

Scrooge was better than his word. He did it **12** all, and infinitely more; and to Tiny Tim, who did **13**

9 *a strait-waistcoat.* A straitjacket.

10 *smoking bishop.* This Christmas punch, called by Coleridge "spicy bishop, drink divine," was a popular tavern drink in the eighteenth century. Dr. Johnson, too, was fond of it and defined it in his dictionary as "a cant word for a mixture of wine, oranges, and sugar." Browne in his notes to the 1907 edition explained that the drink is "made by pouring red wine, either hot or cold, upon ripe bitter oranges. The liquor is heated or 'mulled' in a vessel with a long funnel, which could be pushed far down into the fire. Sugar and spice [chiefly cloves, star anise, and cinnamon] are added according to taste. It is sometime called 'purple wine,' and received the name 'Bishop' from its colour."

11 *another coal-scuttle.* Here, another shovelful of coal.

12 *Scrooge was better than his word.* Dickens hinted at the miser's altered spirit in a letter to a friend, September 16, 1855: "Scrooge is delighted to find that Bob Cratchit is enjoying his holiday in such a delightful situation; and he says (with that warmth of that nature which has distinguished him since his conversion) 'Make the most of it, Bob; make the most of it!'" (*Letters*, Nonesuch Press, Vol. II, p. 688).

13 *and to Tiny Tim, who did NOT die, he was a second father.* This statement was an afterthought; it does not appear in the original manuscript. Dickens obviously realized the need to reassure his readers that the shadow of the vacant seat seen by the Ghost of Christmas Present was removed, and that Scrooge was able to save at least one child from the demons of Want and Ignorance.

14 *the Total Abstinence Principle.* This objective of teetotalism, or the abstinence from alcoholic spirits, is here used as a pun in referring to supernatural spirits. Dickens may also have been playing with the ending of "The Story of The Goblins Who Stole a Sexton"; the converted Gabriel Grub, who had so loved his Hollands, swears off drink after his experiences with the goblins.

Dickens expressed respect for the practical good of Temperance, but he had little patience with those advocates who would deny all liquor, no matter how moderately enjoyed (see "A Plea for Total Abstinence," *The Uncommercial Traveller,* 1860). He did receive criticism for his numerous references to drink in *A Christmas Carol.* He answered one such complaint in a letter of March 25, 1847: "I have no doubt whatever that the warm stuff in the jug at Bob Cratchit's Christmas dinner, had a very pleasant effect on the simple party. I am certain that if I had been at Mr. Fezziwig's ball, I should have taken a little negus —and possibly not a little beer—and been none the worse for it, in heart or head. I am very sure that the working people of this country have not too many household enjoyments, and I could not, in my fancy or in actual deed, deprive them of this one when it is so innocently shared. Neither do I see why I should deny it to myself." (*Letters,* Nonesuch Press, Vol. II, pp. 20–21; see also January 26, 1844, Vol. I, p. 563.)

Dickens "enjoyed all the attendant paraphernalia of Christmas, particularly the jovial drinks which attend the season," wrote Fitzgerald in *The Life of Charles Dickens* (1905, pp. 202–3). "To hear him talking of the steaming bowl of punch, with apples 'bobbing about' merrily, of the Garrick matchless gin-punch particularly, and the anticipating zest and relish with which he compounded these mixtures, one would fancy him quaffing down many a tumbler. But alas! How often had it been noted to the general surprise, that his whole enjoyment was in the romantic association! Never was there a more abstemious bibber."

This observation was supported by James T. Fields in *Yesterdays with Authors* (1872, p. 167): "He liked to dilate in imagination over the brewing of a bowl of punch, but I always noticed that when the punch was ready, he drank less of it than any one who might be present. It was the *sentiment* of the thing, and not the thing itself, that engaged his attention."

NOT die, he was a second father. He became as good a friend, as good a master, and as good a man, as the good old city knew, or any other good old city, town, or borough, in the good old world. Some people laughed to see the alteration in him, but he let them laugh, and little heeded them; for he was wise enough to know that nothing ever happened on this globe, for good, at which some people did not have their fill of laughter in the outset; and knowing that such as these would be blind anyway, he thought it quite as well that they should wrinkle up their eyes in grins, as have the malady in less attractive forms. His own heart laughed: and that was quite enough for him.

He had no further intercourse with Spirits, but

14 lived upon the Total Abstinence Principle, ever afterwards; and it was always said of him, that he knew how to keep Christmas well, if any man alive possessed the knowledge. May that be truly said of us, and all of us! And so, as Tiny Tim observed, God Bless Us, Every One!

THE END.

"And so, as Tiny Tim observed, God Bless us Every One!"

Charles Dickens

Twenty Second January 1844.

Autograph of Charles Dickens, the Albert Schloss autograph album, January 22, 1844.
Courtesy The Rare Book and Manuscript Library, Yale University Beinecke

BIBLIOGRAPHY

By CHARLES DICKENS

Sketches by "Boz". Illustrated by George Cruikshank. London: John Macrone, 1836.

"Timothy Sparks," *Sunday under Three Heads.* Illustrated by H. K. Browne. London: Chapman and Hall, 1836.

The Posthumous Papers of the Pickwick Club. Illustrated by Robert Seymour and Phiz. London: Chapman and Hall, 1837.

Oliver Twist; or, the Parish Boy's Progress. Illustrated by George Cruikshank. London: Richard Bentley, 1838.

The Life And Adventures Of Nicholas Nickleby. Illustrated by Phiz. London: Chapman and Hall, 1839.

Master Humphrey's Clock. Illustrated by George Chattermole and Hablot Browne. London: Chapman and Hall, 1840–1841.

The Old Curiosity Shop. Illustrated by George Chattermole and Hablot Browne. London: Chapman and Hall, 1841.

American Notes for General Circulation. London: Chapman and Hall, 1842.

A Christmas Carol in Prose. Illustrated by John Leech. London: Chapman and Hall, 1843.

The Life and Adventures of Martin Chuzzlewit. Illustrated by Phiz. London: Chapman and Hall, 1844.

The Chimes: A Goblin Story of Some Bells that Rang an Old Year Out and a New Year In. Illustrated by John Leech, Daniel Maclise, Richard Doyle, and Clarkson Stanfield. London: Chapman and Hall, 1845.

   Although published in 1844, this book has the date "1845" on its title page. It was customary for holiday books to be dated according to the New Year.

The Cricket on the Hearth, A Fairy Tale of Home. Illustrated by Daniel Maclise, John Leech, Richard Doyle, Edwin Landseer, and Clarkson Stanfield. London: Bradbury and Evans, 1846.

   Issued in 1845.

The Battle of Life, A Love Story. Illustrated by John Leech, Richard Doyle, Clarkson Stanfield, and Daniel Maclise. London: Bradbury and Evans, 1846.

The Haunted Man and the Ghost's Bargain, A Fancy for Christmas Time. Illustrated by John Leech, Clarkson Stanfield, John Tenniel, and Frank Stone. London: Bradbury and Evans, 1847.

Dealings with the Firm of Dombey and Son, Wholesale, Retail and for Exportation. Illustrated by H. K. Browne. London: Bradbury and Evans, 1848.

"Fine Arts: *The Rising Generation...by John Leech,*" *The Examiner,* December 30, 1848, p. 838.

"A December Vision." *Household Words,* December 14, 1850, pp. 265–67.

"A Christmas Tree." *Household Words,* Christmas Number 1850, pp. 289–95.

The Personal History of David Copperfield. Illustrated by H. K. Browne. London: Bradbury and Evans, 1850.

"What Christmas Is as We Grow Older," *Household Words,* Christmas Number 1851, pp. 1–3.

Christmas Books. Frontispiece by John Leech. London: Chapman and Hall, 1852.

A Child's History of England. Frontispiece by F. W. Topham. London: Bradbury and Evans, 1852–1854.

"Where We Stopped Growing," *Household Words,* January 1, 1853, pp. 361–63.

Bleak House. Illustrated by H. K. Browne. London: Bradbury and Evans, 1853.

"Frauds on the Fairies," *Household Words,* October 1, 1853, pp. 97–100.

Hard Times, for These Times. London: Bradbury and Evans, 1854.

Little Dorrit. Illustrated by H. K. Browne. London: Bradbury and Evans, 1857.

Great Expectations. London: Chapman and Hall, 1861.

The Uncommercial Traveler. London: Chapman and Hall, 1861.

Our Mutual Friend. Illustrated by Marcus Stone. London: Chapman and Hall, 1865.

A Christmas Carol...As condensed by himself for his readings. Frontispiece by Sol Eytinge, Jr. Boston: Ticknor and Fields, 1867.

"A Holiday Romance," *All the Year Round,* January 25 to April 4, 1868.

American Notes and Reprinted Pieces. London: Chapman and Hall, 1868.

   Vol. 18 of "The Charles Dickens Edition" of his collected works.

Works. The Charles Dickens Edition. London: Chapman and Hall, 1867–1875.

The Mystery of Edwin Drood. Illustrated by S. L. Fildes. London: Chapman and Hall, 1870.

The Letters of Charles Dickens. Edited by Georgina Hogarth and Mamie Dickens. London: Chapman and Hall, 1882.

The Christmas Carol. A facsimile reproduction of the author's original manuscript. Introduction by F. G. Kitton. London: Elliot Stock; New York: Brentano's, 1890.

The Letters of Charles Dickens. Edited by Georgina Hogarth and Mamie Dickens. London: Chapman and Hall, 1908.

Vols. 37 and 38 of "The National Edition" of *The Works of Charles Dickens.*

The Life of Our Lord. London: Associated Newspapers, 1934.

The Nonesuch Dickens. Illustrated by George Cruikshank and others. Bloomsbury, London: Nonesuch Press, 1937–1938.

The Letters of Charles Dickens, edited by Walter Dexter, 1938, comprise Vols. 9–11.

The Speeches of Charles Dickens. Edited by K. J. Fielding. Oxford: The Clarendon Press, 1960.

The Pilgrim Edition of the Letters of Charles Dickens. Edited by Madeline Storey and Graham Storey. Oxford: The Clarendon Press, 1965–1974.

NOTABLE EDITIONS OF *A CHRISTMAS CAROL*

It is impossible to determine exactly how many times *A Christmas Carol* has been printed. *The National Union Catalogue* lists over two hundred entries, exclusive of every British reprint and the numerous editions of the collected *Christmas Books.* Many of these are reissues, abridgements, retellings, shorthand editions, cheap paperbacks. Those editions included in this checklist are primarily editions with new illustrations or supplementary material such as introductions and annotations.

A Christmas Carol. In Prose. Being a ghost story of Christmas. Illustrated by John Leech. London: Chapman and Hall, 1843.

> A trial printing of the book originally had green endpapers and the title page printed in green and red; but this design displeased Dickens, so the first commercial printing was altered to include yellow lining papers and the page printed in blue and red.

A Christmas Carol. Frontispiece after Leech. Leipzig: B. Tauchnitz, 1843.

A Christmas Carol. New York: Harper & Brothers, 1844.
> Printed in double columns.

A Christmas Carol. Paris: A. & W. Galignani & Cie, 1844.

A Christmas Carol. Illustrations after John Leech. Philadelphia: Carey & Hart, 1844.

A Christmas Carol. Illustrated by John Leech. London: Printed and published for the author, by Bradbury and Evans, 1846.
> Eleventh edition.

A Christmas Carol. New York: Wiley & Putnam, 1847.

A Christmas Carol. Edited by L. Riechelmann. Leipzig: B. G. Teuber, 1864.
> A German textbook with the English text.

A Christmas Carol. Notes by Wilhelm Sturzen-Becker. Örebro: Abraham Bohlin, 1869.

A Christmas Carol. Edited with an introduction and notes by A. J. Demarest. Boston: Houghton, Mifflin and Company, 1871.
> A textbook.

A Christmas Carol. Edited with an introduction and notes by F. H. Ahn. Mentz: Florian Kupferberg, 1871.

A Christmas Carol. Annotations by F. Weeg. Münster: E. C. Brunn, 1872.

A Christmas Carol. Introduction and notes by Immanuel Schmidt. Freienwalde a.d. Oder: Ferdinand Draeseke, 1876.

A Christmas Carol. Edited with introduction and notes by Albert F. Blaisdell. New York: Clark & Maynard, 1882.
> An abridged textbook.

A Christmas Carol. Illustrated by I. M. Gaugengigl and T. V. Chominski. Boston: S. E. Cassino, 1887.

A Christmas Carol. Introduction and notes by Jules Guiraud. Paris: Librairie Classique Eugène Belin, 1889.

A Christmas Carol. Paris: Librairie Charles Poussielgue, 1893.
> A textbook.

A Christmas Carol. With an introduction and notes. Boston: Houghton, Mifflin and Company, 1893.

A Christmas Carol. Notes by Oscar Thiergen. Leipzig: Velhagen & Klasing, 1895.

A Christmas Carol. Illustrated by George T. Tobin. New York: Frederick A. Stokes Company, 1899.

A Christmas Carol. Illustrated by Frederick Simpson Coburn. New York and London: G. P. Putnam's Sons, 1900.

A Christmas Carol. Notes by K. ten Bruggencate. Groningen: Wolters, 1901.

A Christmas Carol. Decorations by Samuel Warner. East Aurora, New York: The Roycroft Shop, 1902.

A Christmas Carol. Illustrated by Bertha B. Davidson. New York and Boston: Caldwell, 1902.

A Christmas Carol. Illustrated by C. E. Brock. London: J. M. Dent & Co.; New York: E. P. Dutton & Co., 1905.

A Christmas Carol. Illustrated by Charles Pears. London: Library Press, 1905.

A Christmas Carol, and The Cricket on the Hearth. Illustrated by George Alfred Williams. New York: The Baker & Taylor Company, 1905.

A Christmas Carol and The Cricket on the Hearth. Introduction and notes by James M. Sawin and Ida M. Thomas. New York and London: The Macmillan Company, 1905.

A Christmas Carol. Illustrated by John Leech. Introduction by Hall Caine. London: William Heinemann, 1906.

A Christmas Carol, The Wreck of the Golden Mary, Richard Doubledick, The Cricket on the Hearth. Edited by Edmund Kemper Broadus. Chicago: Scott, Foresman and Company, 1906.

A Christmas Carol. Introduction and notes by E. Gordon Browne. London: Longmans, Green & Co., 1907.

A Christmas Carol. Illustrated by John Leech and Fred Barnard. Introduction by Sir William P. Treloar. London: Chapman and Hall, 1907.
> Lord Mayor Treloar's edition published in aid of his Home for Crippled Children.

A Christmas Carol, and The Chimes. Introduction by Henry Morley. London: Cassell and Co., 1908.

A Christmas Carol. With an introduction and notes. Topeka, Kansas: Crane & Company, 1908.

A Christmas Carol. Frontispiece by C. A. Shepperson. London: Blackie & Son, 1908.

A Christmas Carol. Illustrated by E. H. Stanton. London: Robert Scott, 1911.

A Christmas Carol. Illustrated by A. C. Michael. London: Hodder & Stoughton, 1911.

A Christmas Carol. With an introduction and notes. Chicago: Ainsworth & Company, 1912.

A Christmas Carol. Illustrated by Milo K. Winter. Edited by Katherine Gill West. Chicago and New York: Rand, McNally & Company, 1912.

A Christmas Carol. Introduction and notes by A. J. Demarest. Philadelphia: Christopher Sower Company, 1912.

A Christmas Carol. Illustrated by Carle Michel Boog. Boston: L. C. Page & Company, 1913.

A Christmas Carol. Illustrated by Spencer Baird Nichols. New York: Frederick A. Stokes Co., 1913.

A Christmas Carol. Illustrated by A. I. Keller. Philadelphia: David McKay & Co.; London and Edinburgh: W. & R. Chambers, 1914.

A Christmas Carol. Illustrated by Honor C. Appleton. London: Simpkin, Marshall, Hamilton, Kent & Co., 1914.

A Christmas Carol. Illustrated by Arthur Rackham. London: William Heinemann; Philadelphia: J. B. Lippincott Co., 1915.

A Christmas Carol ... and The King of the Golden River. Notes by O. J. Stevenson. Toronto: Copp, Clark Co., 1915.

A Christmas Carol. Designed by Alan Tabor, with a frontispiece by Monro S. Orr. London: George G. Harrap & Co., 1916.

A Christmas Carol. Illustrated by Gordon Robinson. London: Charles H. Kelly, 1916.

A Christmas Carol. London: Oxford University Press, 1918.
> A textbook with a vocabulary in Serbo-Croatian.

A Christmas Carol. Illustrated by Harold Copping. London: R.T.S., 1920.

A Christmas Carol. Illustrated by John Leech. Introduction by A. Edward Newton. Boston: The Atlantic Monthly Press, 1920.
> A facsimile of an early Chapman and Hall edition.

A Christmas Carol. Warsaw: Książnica Polska Towarzystwa Nauczycieli Sxkól Wyzszych, 1921.
> A Polish textbook with the English text.

A Christmas Carol. Introduction and notes by Carol L. Bernhardt. Chicago: Loyola University Press, 1922.

A Christmas Carol. Illustrated by John Leech. Introduction by G. K. Chesterton, with a preface by B. W. Matz. London: Cecil Palmer, 1922.
> A facsimile of an early Chapman and Hall edition. Reissued in 1924 by C. E. Lauriat of Boston.

A Christmas Carol. Illustrated by Francis D. Bedford. New York: The Macmillan Company, 1923.

A Christmas Carol. Illustrated by Ethel F. Everett. New York: Thomas Y. Crowell Company, 1924.

At Christmas Time; being A Christmas Carol. Illustrated by John Leech. Essays by William C. Edgar. Minneapolis, Minnesota: The Bellman Company, 1925.

A Christmas Carol. Designed by Richard W. Ellis. New York: privately printed by Everett and Elizabeth Currier, 1925.

A Christmas Carol. Illustrated by Helene Nyce, with a cover design by Frances Brundage. Akron, Ohio, and New York: The Saalfield Publishing Company, 1927.

A Christmas Carol, The Cricket on the Hearth. Edited by Eleanor Tourison. Boston and New York: Allyn and Bacon, 1928.

A Christmas Carol. Designed by Frederic Warde. Mount Vernon, New York: privately printed for Junius Fishburn, 1930.

A Christmas Carol. Illustrated by Gilbert Wilkinson. Foreword by Sir John Martin-Harvey. London: Odhams Press, 1930.

A Christmas Carol. Decorations by W. A. Dwiggins. New York: Press of the Woolly Whale, 1930.

A Christmas Carol. Illustrated by Matilda Breuer. Notes by N. Howard Aitch. Chicago: Hall & McCreary Company, 1931.

A Christmas Carol. Illustrated by Louis Koster. New York: Cheshire House, 1932.

A Christmas Carol. Illustrated by Charles Dunn. Washington: Judd and Detweiler, 1933.

A Christmas Carol. Illustrated by Gordon Ross. Introduction by Stephen Leacock. Boston: The Limited Editions Club, 1934.

A Christmas Carol. Abridged by Edward L. Thorndike. Illustrated by Dorothy Bayley. New York: D. Appleton-Century Company, 1936.

A Christmas Carol. New York: Privately printed by the Plantin Press, 1937.

A Christmas Carol. Illustrated by Corydon Bell. Cleveland, Ohio: Privately printed at the Roger Williams Company, 1938.

A Christmas Carol. Illustrated by Everett Shinn. Introduction by Lionel Barrymore. Philadelphia: John C. Winston Co., 1938.

A Christmas Carol. Illustrated by Donald Gregg. Cleveland, Ohio: Privately printed by A. S. Gilman, 1939.

A Christmas Carol. Illustrated by William Mark Young. New York: Grosset & Dunlap, 1939.

A Christmas Carol. Illustrated by Julian Brazelton. New York: Pocket Books, Inc., 1939.

A Christmas Carol. Illustrated by Erwin L. Hess and F. D. Lohman. Racine, Wisconsin: Whitman Publishing Company, 1939.

A Christmas Carol. Illustrated by Philip Reed. New York: Holiday House, 1940.

A Christmas Carol. Illustrated by Fritz Kredel. Mount Vernon, New York: The Peter Pauper Press, 1943.

A Christmas Carol. Illustrated by Hans E. Schwarz. Birmingham, England: City of Birmingham School of Printing, 1944.

A Christmas Carol. Illustrated by Emil Weiss. London: P. R. Gawthorn, 1944.

A Christmas Carol. Illustrated by Ruth McCrea. Mount Vernon, New York: The Peter Pauper Press, 195–.

A Christmas Carol. Illustrated by Robert Ball. New York: The Macmillan Company, 1950.

A Christmas Carol. Philadelphia: Privately printed for Samuel A. Dalton, 1950.

A Christmas Carol. Initials by Malletto Dean. San Francisco: Printed by the Grabhorn Press for Ransohoffs, 1950.

A Christmas Carol. Illustrated with stills from the Renown Picture's film *Scrooge.* London and Melbourne: Ward Lock & Co., 1951.

A Christmas Carol. Illustrated by John Leech. Washington, D.C.: Privately printed for the National Geographic Society, Washington, D.C., 1954.
> A facsimile of a copy of the 1858 Bradbury & Evans edition, with manuscript notations by Alexander Melville Bell and Alexander Graham Bell, as read to their children on Christmas Eve.

A Christmas Carol. Illustrated by Donald McKay. Mount Vernon, New York: The Peter Pauper Press, 1955.
> A slightly abridged version.

A Christmas Carol. Illustrated by John Leech. Introduction and bibliographical note by Edgar Johnson. New York: Columbia University Press, 1956.
> A facsimile of the first edition.

A Christmas Carol. Illustrated by Maraja. London: W. H. Allen; New York: Grosset & Dunlap, 1958.

A Christmas Carol. Illustrated by Ronald Searle. Cleveland: World Publishing Co.; London: Perpetua Books, 1961.

A Christmas Carol. Illustrated by John Groth. Afterword by Clifton Fadiman. London: Collier–Macmillan; New York: The Macmillan Company, 1963.

A Christmas Carol. Illustrated by John Leech. Chicago: J. G. Ferguson Publishing Co., 1965.
> A facsimile of the second edition.

A Christmas Carol, and The Chimes. Introduction by Walter Allen. New York: Harper & Row, 1965.

A Christmas Carol. Edited with special aids by Henry E. Vittum. New York: Bantam Books, 1966.

A Christmas Carol. Illustrated by Charles Mozley. New York: Franklin Watts, 1969.

A Christmas Carol; the public reading version. Introduction and notes by Philip Collins. New York: The New York Public Library, 1971.
> A facsimile of the author's prompt copy, now in the Berg Collection of The New York Public Library.

NOTABLE EDITIONS OF *CHRISTMAS BOOKS*

Christmas Books. Frontispiece by John Leech. London: Chapman and Hall, 1852.
> "Cheap Edition of the Works of Charles Dickens."

Christmas Books. New York: Harper & Brothers, 1852.

Christmas Books. London: Chapman and Hall, 1862.
> "Library Edition" of Dickens' works, with title-page vignette by Phiz.

Christmas Books. Illustrated by F. O. C. Darley and John Gilbert. New York: J. G. Gregory, 1861.

Christmas Books, and Sketches by Boz. Illustrated by Sol Eytinge, Jr. Boston: Ticknor & Fields, 1867.

Christmas Books. Illustrated by Darley, Gilbert, Cruikshank, and others. Cambridge, Massachusetts: The Riverside Press, 1868.
> Limited to one hundred copies sold by subscription.

Christmas Books. London: Chapman and Hall, 1868.
> "The Charles Dickens Edition," revised by the author.

Christmas Books. Introduction by Edwin Percy Whipple. Boston: Hurd and Houghton, 1876.

Christmas Books. Illustrated by Fred Barnard. London: Chapman and Hall, 1881.

Christmas Books. Introduction by Charles Dickens the younger. London and New York: Macmillan and Co., 1892.

Christmas Books. Introduction by Andrew Lang. London: Chapman and Hall; New York: Charles Scribner's Sons, 1897.
> "Gadshill Edition."

Christmas Books. Introduction by Richard Garnett. London: Chapman and Hall, Ltd., 1900.

Christmas Books. Introduction by G. K. Chesterton. London: J. M. Dent & Co.; New York: E. P. Dutton & Co., 1907.

Christmas Books. Illustrated by Harry Furniss. London: The Educational Book Co., 1910.

Pears' Centenary Edition of Charles Dickens' Christmas Books. Illustrated by Charles Green and L. Rossi. Introduction by Clement Shorter. London: A. & F. Pears, 1912.

Christmas Tales. Illustrated by H. M. Brock. London: George G. Harrap & Co., 1932.

Christmas Books. Illustrated by John Leech and others. Bloomsbury, London: The Nonesuch Press, 1937.
　　Vol. 4, "The Nonesuch Dickens," eight hundred and seventy-seven copies printed.

Five Christmas Novels. Illustrated by Reginald Birch. New York: The Heritage Club, 1939.

Christmas Stories. Illustrated by Howard Simon. Introduction by May Lamberton Becker. Cleveland: The World Publishing Co., 1946.

Christmas Books. Introduction by D. N. Brereton. London: Collins, 1954.

Christmas Books. Illustrated by Landseer and others. Introduction by Eleanor Farjeon. London and New York: Oxford University Press, 1954.

The Christmas Books. Introduction and notes by Michael Slater. Harmondsworth, England: Penguin Books, 1971.

TRANSLATIONS OF *A CHRISTMAS CAROL*

Les Apparitions de Noël. Translated into French. *Révue Britannique,* May to June 1844.

Een Kerssprookje. Translated into Dutch. Amsterdam, 1844.

Stedry wecer. Translated into Czechoslovakian by M. Fialky. Prague, 1846.

Les Apparitions de Noël. Translated into French by Amédée Pichot. Paris, 1847.

Weihnachtsmärchen. Translated into German by E. A. Moriarity and Julius Seybt. Leipzig, 1852.

Et Juleqvad i Prosa. Translated into Danish by L. Moltke. Copenhagen, 1854.

Contes de Noël (Le Chant de Noël). Translated into French by P. Lorain. Paris, 1857.

Bozicna psesma. Translated into Serbo–Croatian by N. Pozora Ubecu, 1868.

Tre Julaftonen. Translated into Swedish. Stockholm, 1870.

Canticos de Natal. Translated into Portuguese by Eugenio de Castilho. Lisbon, 1873.

Una Canzone del Natale. Translated into Italian by Eugenio de Benedetti. Milan, 1873.

Ein Weihnachtslied in Prosa. Translated into German. Elberfeld, 1874.

Karácsoni ének prózában. Translated into Hungarian by Belényesi Gábor. Budapest, 1875.

Joulun-aatto. Translated into Finnish by Waldemar Churberg. Helsinki, 1878.

Cántico de Noche-buena. Translated into Spanish by Henry Spicer. Valencia, 1879.

Et Juleæventyr. Translated into Danish by Albert Andresen. Copenhagen, 1879.

El Cántico de Navidad. Translated into Spanish by Don Luis Barthe. Madrid, 1883.

Koleda prikazka. Translated into Bulgarian by Ilia C. Iovchoff. Bulgaria, 1884.

Ein Weihnachtslied in Prosa. Translated into German. Berlin, 1885–1889.

Roshdesfvenskaya skazka. Translated into Russian. Moscow, 1887.

Cantico di Natale. Translated into Italian by Federigo Verdinois. Milan, 1888.

Chant de Noël. Translated into French. Paris, 1888.

Contes de Noël. Translated into French by Mlle. de Saint-Romain and M. de Gay. Paris, 1890.

Joulu-ilta. Translated into Finnish by D. K. Wyyryläinen. Porvoossa, 1893.

Der Weihnachtsabend, und andere Geschichten. Translated into German by Karl Wilding. Berlin, 19—.

A Christmas Carol. Translated into Japanese by S. Kusano. Sendai, 1902.

Duan na Nodlag. Translated into Irish by Patrick Stephen Dinneen. Ireland, 1903.

Carol Nadolig mewn rhyddiaeth, sef Chwedl am ysbryd. Translated into Welsh by Llew Tegid. Caernarvon, 1905.

A Christmas Carol (Kristnaska sonorado). Translated into Esperanto by Martyn Westcott. London: "Review of Reviews" office, 1905.

Een Kerstlied in proza. Translated into Dutch by J. Kuylman. Amsterdam, 1905.

Los Fantasmas de Nochebuena. Translated into Spanish. Barcelona, 1906.

O Noapte de Craciun. Translated into Rumanian by Marius. Bucharest, 1907.

Cantic de Nadal. Translated into Catalan by F. Girbal Jaume. Barcelona, 1910.

Skruji da Marlei. Translated into Georgian by Nino Nakashizisa. Tiflis, 1911.

Conte de Noël. Translated into French by A. Masson. Illustrated by M. Lecoultre. Paris, 1913.

Et Juleaeventyr. Translated into Danish by Paul Læsoe Moller. Illustrated by Arthur Rackham. Copenhagen, 1917.

Der Weihnachtsabend. Translated into German. Illustrated by Arthur Rackham. Zurich, 1918.

Ein Weihnachtsabend. Translated into German by J. E. Wessely. Weisbaden, 1918.

Karacsonyi enek prozában. Translated into Hungarian by Ernö. Budapest, 1919.

Koleda. Vánocní providka s duchy. Translated into Czechoslovakian by Jan Vána. Prague, 192—.

Nashid al-milad. Translated into Arabic by Muhammad al-Saba'i. Cairo, 1920.

Sykstuolis Skrudzas arba Kaledu apaskymas su vaiduokliais. Translated into Lithuanian (from a Russian translation) by J. Mokinio. Kaunas, Vilnius, 1922.

Bozicna pesem v prozi. Translated into Slovene with an introduction by J. Plestenjak. Ljubljani, 1926.

Cuentos de Navidad (Canción de Navidad). Translated into Spanish by M. Vallvé. Barcelona, 1927.

Dznunti yerk. Translated into Turkish by N. G. Kondayian. Constantinople, 1928.

A Christmas Carol. Un Chant de Noël. English text with French translation by R. Gauillard. Paris, 1929.

Le Grillon du foyer, suivi de Cantique de Noël. Translated into French by Charlotte and Marie-Louise Pressoir. Illustrated by Maurice Berty. Paris, 1931.

Una chanzun da Nadal. Translated into Rhaeto-Romanic by Men Gaudenz. Scuol, 1933.

The Christmas Carol. Translated into Tamil by V. A. Venkatachari. Madras, 1936.

Contes de Noël. Translated into French. Illustrated by Henri Faivre. Paris, 1936.

Canción de Navidad. Translated into Spanish by Luis Macaya. Buenos Aires, 1941.

Een Kerstlied in proza. Translated into Dutch by Hendrik van Tichelen. Illustrated by Irène Nagy. Hoogstraten, 1942.

Conte de Noël. Illustrated by A. Pecoud. Paris, 1946.

Weihnachtserzählung. Translated into German by Max Müller. Iserlohn, 1946.

Drie verhale. Translated into Afrikaans by M. C. Botha. Kaapsted, 1950.

Canción de Navidad. Translated into Spanish. Madrid, 1954.

Chant de Noël. Translated into French, with a preface by André Maurois. Paris, 1954.

Der Weihnachtsabend (ein Weihnachtslied in Prosa). Translated into German by Trude Geissler, with an afterword by Richard Mummendey. Stuttgart, 1954.

Karácsonyi történetek. Translated into Hungarian by Benedek Marcell, Sziannai Tirador, and Geréb Béláné. Budapest, 1958.

Racconto di Natale. Translated into Italian by Bruno Patrineri. Illustrated by Marino. Milan, 1958.

Conto de Natal. Translated into Spanish by Barros Ferriera. Illustrated by Percy Lau. San Paulo, 1965.

Livres de Noël. Translated into French by Marcelle Sibon. Paris, 1966.

ABOUT CHARLES DICKENS

Bredsdorff, Elias. *Hans Andersen and Charles Dickens, A Friendship and its Dissolution*. Copenhagen: Rosenkilde and Bogger, 1956.

Chesterton, G. K. *Charles Dickens*. London: Methuen & Co., 1906.

Dickens, Henry F. *Memories of My Father*. London: V. Gollancz Ltd., 1928.

Dickens, Mamie. *My Father as I Recall Him*. London: The Roxburghe Press, 1896.

The Dickensian, London: The Dickens Fellowship, 1905–1976.

Fields, James T. *Yesterdays with Authors*. Boston: J. R. Osgood and Co., 1872.

Fitzgerald, Percy. *The Life of Charles Dickens*. London: Chatto and Windus, 1905.

Forster, John. *The Life of Charles Dickens*. London: Chapman and Hall, 1872–1874.

Haight, Gordon S. "Dickens and Lewes on Spontaneous Combustion," *Nineteenth Century Fiction*, X (1955), pp. 53–63.

Jaques, Edward Tyrrell. *Charles Dickens in Chancery*. London, New York: Longmans, Green & Co., 1914.

Johnson, Edgar. *Charles Dickens: His Tragedy and Triumph*. Boston: Little, Brown, 1952.

Pacey, W. C. Desmond. "Washington Irving and Charles Dickens," *American Literature*, January 1945, pp. 332–39.

ON DICKENS' WORK

Aldington, Richard. "The Underworld of Young Dickens." *Four English Portraits, 1801–1851*. London: Evans Bros., 1948, pp. 147–89.

Butt, John. "Dickens' Christmas Books." *Pope, Dickens,*

and Others. Edinburgh: Edinburgh University Press, 1969, pp. 127–48.

Chesterton, G. K. *Appreciations and Criticisms of the Works of Charles Dickens*. London: J. M. Dent, 1911.

Collins, Philip, ed. *Dickens: The Critical Heritage.* London: Routledge and Kegan Paul, 1971.

Davis, Earle. *The Flint and the Flame: the Artistry of Charles Dickens.* Columbia, Missouri: University of Missouri Press, 1963.

The Dickensian. London: The Dickens Fellowship, 1905–1976.

Field, Kate. *Pen Photographs of Charles Dickens' Readings.* Boston: J. R. Osgood and Company, 1871.

Ford, George H., and others. *Dickens Criticism: Past, Present and Future Directions.* Cambridge, Massachusetts: A Charles Dickens Reference Center Publication, 1962.

Gilbert, Elliot L. "The Ceremony of Innocence: Charles Dickens' *A Christmas Carol.*" *PMLA*, January 1975, pp. 22–31.

Gimbel, Richard. *Charles Dickens'* A Christmas Carol; *Three States of the First Edition.* Princeton, New Jersey: Privately printed, 1956.

———. "The Earliest State of the First Edition of Charles Dickens' *A Christmas Carol.*" *The Princeton University Library Chronicle*, Winter 1958, pp. 82–86.

Gissing, George. *Charles Dickens: A Critical Study.* London: Blackie & Son, Ltd., 1903.

Hood, Tom. "A Christmas Carol. In Prose. by C. Dickens." *Hood's Magazine*, January 1844, pp. 68–75.

Horne, R. H. *A New Spirit of the Age.* New York: J. C. Riker, 1844, pp. 9–52.

Jackson, T. A. *Charles Dickens: The Progress of a Radical.* New York: International Publishers, 1938.

Johnson, Edgar. "The Christmas Carol and the Economic Man." *American Scholar*, Winter 1951, pp. 91–98.

Kent, Charles. *Dickens as a Reader.* London: Chapman and Hall, 1872.

Maurois, André. *Dickens.* Translated by Hamish Miles. London: John Lane, 1934.

Orwell, George. "Charles Dickens." *Critical Essays.* London: Secker and Warburg, 1946, pp. 7–56.

Slater, Michael, ed. *Dickens 1970.* New York: Stein & Day, 1970.

Steig, Michael. "Dickens' Excremental Vision." *Victorian Studies*, March 1970, pp. 339–54.

Swinburne, Algernon. "Charles Dickens." *A Pilgrimage of Pleasure* . . . Boston: Richard D. Badger and the Gorham Press, 1913, pp. 79–109.

Thackeray, William Makepeace. "A Box of Novels." *Fraser's Magazine*, February 1844, pp. 153–69.

Tillotson, Kathleen. "The Middle Years from the *Carol* to *Copperfield.*" *Dickens Memorial Lectures, 1970.* London: The Dickens Fellowship, 1970.

Tomlin, E. W. F., ed. *Charles Dickens 1812–1870, A Centenary Volume.* London: Weidenfeld and Nicolson, 1970.

Wilson, Edmund. "Dickens: The Two Scrooges." *The Wound and the Bow.* New York: Oxford University Press, 1947, pp. 1–104.

ABOUT JOHN LEECH

Browne, Edgar. *Phiz and Dickens as they appeared to Edgar Browne.* London: James Nisbet & Co., 1913, pp. 19–22.

Frith, William Powell. *John Leech: His Life and Work.* London: R. Bentley and Son, 1891.

Dickens, Charles. "Fine Arts: *The Rising Generation* . . . by John Leech," *The Examiner*, December 30, 1848, p. 838.

Ruskin, John. "The Fireside: John Leech and John Tenniel." *The Art of England.* New York: John Wiley & Sons, 1884, pp. 111–34.

INDEX

Numbers in italics refer to pages with illustrations.